# Her Night With the Duke

It was one night in the middle of nowhere. No one need ever know.

"Are we really doing this?"

He nibbled her ear. "I certainly hope so."

"Just tonight," she stipulated, eager to contain the madness engulfing them both, "and then we part ways. We must agree."

She felt his smile against her neck. "Should I feel terribly used that you only want me for my body?"

"Who could blame me?" He had a fine athletic form. She ran her hands over his arms, feeling the firm roundness of his biceps through his linen shirt. "Do we have an agreement?"

"Whatever you like." His lips rose up to close urgently over hers again.

## Also by Diana Quincy

# HER NIGHT WITH THE DUKE

## Diana Quincy

AVONBOOKS

*An Imprint of HarperCollinsPublishers*

HER NIGHT WITH THE DUKE. Copyright © 2020 by Dora Mekouar. All rights reserved. Printed in the United States of America. No part of this book may be used or reproduced in any manner whatsoever without written permission except in the case of brief quotations embodied in critical articles and reviews. For information, address HarperCollins Publishers, 195 Broadway, New York, NY 10007.

First Avon Books mass market printing: October 2020

Print Edition ISBN: 978-0-06-298679-5
Digital Edition ISBN: 978-0-06-298680-1

*Cover design by Patricia Barrow*
*Cover illustrations by Chris Cocozza*

Avon, Avon & logo, and Avon Books & logo are registered trademarks of HarperCollins Publishers in the United States of America and other countries.

HarperCollins is a registered trademark of HarperCollins Publishers in the United States of America and other countries.

FIRST EDITION

20 21 22 23 24   QGM   10 9 8 7 6 5 4 3 2 1

*For my father, a natural-born writer who did the practical thing and became a civil engineer. While you built the actual bridges, here's to building bridges of all kinds.*

# Chapter One

*September 1814*
*Central England*

*E*lliot Townsend, the Duke of Huntington, led such an ordered existence that he failed to recognize disaster.

Until it was far too late to save himself.

Calamity appeared in the form of a rain-soaked female clad in a simple white gown. The thin fabric was plastered to every considerable curve of her womanly form. She surfaced at the same ramshackle inn, from the same punishing rainstorm.

A washed-out section of Watling Road outside the town of Coventry had forced him to seek shelter at the Black Swan Inn. It was a tattered structure with a lopsided overhanging roof. The inside proved even less inviting than the dubious exterior. Mingled odors of unwashed bodies, perspiration and spirits permeated the inn's damp smoky taproom. Now sipping his too-sweet ale, Hunt cursed himself for not delaying his journey at the first sign of inclement weather.

He could be in London right now finding satisfaction between Georgina's delectably plump thighs. He'd certainly prefer to inhale her delicate flowery perfume rather than a mildewy room full of malodorous strangers. He visited his mistress precisely three times a week, appearing at her Half Moon Street address, which he paid for, every Tuesday, Thursday and Saturday. Hunt rarely deviated from the pattern he'd set early on in their arrangement. Or any arrangement really.

Soon he and Georgie would part ways. Hunt intended to marry before Parliament met in early November, at which time the Season would begin in earnest. He was on his way now to pay court to his future wife. Unease moved through him, but he pushed it away. Surely all men experienced a sense of foreboding before binding themselves to one woman for a lifetime.

He had no reason to be apprehensive. His choice was sound. Lady Victoria was a hidden gem, an unpolished diamond that society's foolish young bloods had overlooked. Hunt congratulated himself on recognizing the fine attributes hidden deep beneath the bookish young lady's retiring exterior and decided lack of conversational polish.

She met all of his qualifications for a wife. Her extraordinary shyness in his presence would eventually pass. What truly mattered was that she was agreeable, of good family, and possessed sufficient intelligence so that Hunt wouldn't be bored to death. Most importantly, Lady Victoria's countenance suggested she would never do anything to dishonor the Huntington title. God knows Hunt's rakehell of an older brother had done enough damage to the family name to last this lifetime.

Phillip Townsend, the seventh Duke of Huntington, drowned during a drunken boat outing four years prior. He left behind numerous unpaid debts, broken hearts and ruffled feathers that Hunt had spent the past four years repaying, mending and unruffling.

From his rickety corner table in the crowded taproom, he swallowed his ale, his attention drawn to the latest castaway who'd joined the tavern's motley group. Her back was to him. His gaze followed the single long dark braid that ran down her back almost reaching a curvaceous arse. Hunt's eyes widened when his gaze hit the bottom edge of the lady's gown.

What he glimpsed there was barely visible. He suspected the woman's intention was to keep them hidden, but Hunt could make out what seemed to be the hems of billowing trousers beneath her straight-cut gown.

"I would like a chamber," she informed the innkeeper.

The man's heavy brows almost met in the middle of his considerable forehead. He cast an appraising look at the woman, his interested gaze lingering well below the woman's face far longer than necessary. "Do you now?"

"Yes, and without delay if you please."

The innkeeper's brows lifted. He seemed uncertain of how to respond to a woman who dressed like a costermonger but commanded him like a queen. Before he could respond, the inn door blew open, and the rain ushered in yet another arrival, a brown-skinned man with a lived-in face stooped over a worn leather valise. The woman addressed the newcomer in an unfamiliar tongue.

She spoke so quickly that the words all seemed to run together. The woman's male companion nodded, set the bag down at her side and withdrew, the wind and rain blowing leaves across the stone flagged floor as he made his exit.

"What are you?" The innkeeper flushed as he stared after the man. "A blackamoor?"

"She's Persian," one of the old soldiers cried out. "No, Arabian, that's it."

One of his companions guffawed. "As if you'd know the difference, you old drunk."

"I 'eard that kind of guttural talk in Egypt," the old soldier insisted, "when we fought against the frogs in Alexandria in '01."

"They got camels out there, don't they?" another of their companions inquired.

The innkeeper scowled at the woman. "We do not accommodate heathens."

"I require a chamber. The roads are impossible to travel on." The woman did not cower. To the contrary, Hunt admired the way she seemed to grow taller. She set a small bulging money pouch on the scarred counter. "I will pay handsomely."

A hush came over the taproom. The once-boisterous throng of soldiers and laborers grew silent, their eyes now fixed on the woman. Even a group of miscreants singing vulgar songs stopped their racket.

The innkeeper realized he had an audience. "You need a place to sleep?" He crossed his arms over a high belly. "Perhaps one of these fine men will see to you. I am certain a wench such as yourself is well used to accommodating her betters."

"Maybe she learned some tricks in her master's harem," one man called out amidst guffaws of approval.

Hunt set down his pewter tankard. He did not care for the restless tension that stretched the air. Nor for the fact that the woman was the lone female in a crush of drunken men already agitated about being cooped up at the inn. Even the serving girls had vanished.

"I will take that chamber now," she said firmly, as if she was ordering fripperies in Mayfair. She paid no mind to the leering ruffians edging ever closer.

Hunt slowly rose from his chair, sliding his hand beneath his tailcoat. His fingers brushed the cool barrel of the flintlock pistol he'd removed from his valise and clipped to his trousers.

He never traveled unarmed. Country roads could be treacherous for a man on his own, particularly a duke. His security team blanched whenever he indulged in these occasional solitary sojourns. The outings were much needed reprieves from the strictures of a title he'd never expected to inherit. A bachelor duke under seventy with fifteen thousand pounds a year tended to draw unwanted attention.

"I got a room yer can share, sweet'eart." A man sitting with the old soldier separated from the crowd and sauntered up to the woman. A huge scar ran down the left side of his face, a jagged line dissecting one ruddy cheek. "'Ow about we go up now and yer ride me like yer people ride a camel in the desert?"

"I got a bigger . . . chamber." Another man, this one small and ragged, stood up, gyrating his bony hips indecently. "Come with me and I'll take yer for the ride of yer life."

"Ain't no reason the wench can't screw us both." Scarface grinned amidst the hoots of encouragement and slid a meaty hand down over the woman's bottom.

Hunt vaulted across the room. "Get your hands off of her!" he bellowed.

A sudden burst of activity followed. Hunt barely registered the woman pivoting. Something glimmered in her hand. Before Hunt, or Scarface for that matter, knew what she was about, the woman had Scarface's arm twisted high up behind his back and the gleaming edge of a curved dagger lodged under his chin.

She stared at Bony Hips, who gaped back with wide, shocked eyes. "Would you still care to be next?" The words were mild, but Hunt noted that her breaths came faster and deeper. "I am more than happy to oblige."

"'Twas just a jest." Raising hands, palms facing front in surrender, Bony Hips edged backward. "Be careful, little lady. Yer might injure someone with that."

"Yes," she agreed, "I very well might."

Scarface paled. "Let me go. Yer hurting me."

"Have you managed to learn some manners?"

He spat his disdain, although his spittle had no hopes of reaching her, given her position. "I'll teach yer some manners, yer barbarian bitch." He attempted to wriggle free, but then winced and groaned when her grip on him didn't ease. "Look around. Yer alone. Do yer think one stupid wench can take us all?"

Murmurs of assent sounded from the assembled crowd. "Let's make 'er pay," somebody called out.

Hunt stepped forward, every muscle in his body rigid. "The lady is not alone." He withdrew his pistol, holding it down by his side, but keeping the weapon in clear view. "She is with me. My flintlock and I shall take it quite personally if anyone tries to take what is mine."

The woman released Scarface with a shove. Fury flashing in her eyes, she pivoted toward Hunt, giving him his first good look at her.

He almost dropped the pistol. She was extraordinary. Enormous almond eyes the color of black tea regarded him with unfettered scorn. Golden honey skin drew tight across a proud forehead and razor-cut cheekbones. She was so striking that he almost forgot to notice that her curved blade was now pointed directly at him.

"Why didn't yer say so ta start with, guv?" Scarface backed away. "That's some prime female flesh you got there, but I ain't one ta poach a gent's doxy."

"As if you could," the woman said. She was not a young girl. Hunt judged her to be in her late twenties. A sense of certainty, a womanly maturity, emanated from her.

Around them, the other miscreants threw jibes.

"Be careful she don't use that blade on yer Thomas, guv!"

"Looks like a 'andful that one, but 'is lordship looks man enough ter tame 'er."

Hoots of amusement followed. Tension seeped out of the taproom as quickly as it had ratcheted up just minutes before. The men in the tavern shuffled back to their tables, leaving Hunt facing the woman and the sharp point of her knife.

Despite his mild alarm, Hunt didn't believe she intended to run him through. Unless, of course, he did something to deserve it. "Is this how you thank me for coming to your rescue?"

"I certainly do not mean to show appreciation by accompanying you to your bedchamber." Her smoky voice slid along his nerves like silk. Hunt had never before encountered anyone like her. He admired her fierceness, the way she wielded that strange dagger like a conquering Amazonian warrior.

"Besides," she added. "I did not require assistance. I had the matter well in hand."

"Oh?" She really was magnificent. "Was your plan to stab every man here?"

"You may be certain that if I had intended to kill you, or anyone, with my *janbiya*, you wouldn't have known it until well after my dagger was buried deep inside your chest."

"A bloodthirsty woman. I quite admire that."

"Do you? Is that an invitation for me to draw your blood?"

"I would be much obliged if you did not poke any holes in me. I am quite partial to keeping my blood contained within my body."

He watched her suppress her amusement as she sheathed her dagger. It dawned on him that he very much would like to see what she looked like when she smiled. Although he remained on edge, unconvinced the agitated tavern-goers had lost all interest in the lady, his vigilance did not keep his body from being supremely aware of her proximity.

"Who are you?" She regarded him with open curiosity. "Few people on the business point of a dagger manage to keep their wits about them. Unless, of course, they are very stupid."

"Or very brave. My name is Elliot Townsend. Just a man passing through." If the reprobates surrounding them realized they had a duke in their midst, particularly one traveling alone, Hunt would find himself rolled and left for dead before dawn.

That's why he wore serviceable clothing more suited to his secretary than a duke. His drenched old greatcoat was more than a decade old, and threadbare enough not to attract undue attention. He'd sent his staff and carriage ahead to the house party hosted by Lady Victoria's brother. He needed time alone to sort through the changes in his life that would come with marriage. "I have told you who I am," he said to the woman. "And who are you?"

"The same as you. Just a woman passing through."

"Your private parlor is ready for you, sir." The innkeeper paused on his way to deliver ale to a nearby table. "It is just as well that your wench will be sharing your private parlor since I have no chambers or parlors left."

The woman cut a resentful look at the innkeeper's departing back. She smothered a sigh. Hunt sympathized. She looked cold, wet and so weary that she might just fall asleep on her feet, yet her steel-blade gaze reflected an unwavering awareness of her surroundings.

"You are most welcome to share my parlor," he offered. "I give you my word that I will behave as a gentleman." Which would be a disappointment. He wouldn't mind seeing what that tall, supple body looked like stripped of clothing. Hunt imagined bedding her would be anything but boring. She'd be a welcome diversion on this dismal evening.

The woman looked around the taproom. "Perhaps I will just be on my way."

"In this weather? It is unsafe."

"And sharing a chamber with a perfect stranger is not?"

She could hardly remain in the taproom alone. "Surely your chances of enjoying solitude and a quiet meal are much enhanced if you are away from this rabble."

"I shall have a bit of sustenance and then be on my way."

He sighed. "I cannot allow you to go back into that storm. You should take the parlor. It is the only room they have left."

"I could not ask you to give up your parlor."

"You have not asked—I have offered." He did not relish the thought of passing the evening in this noisy smoke pit, but he was a gentleman.

Two delicate lines appeared between her bold dark brows. "But where will you pass the night?"

"I shall find someone to bunk with. A little coin can be most persuasive. Besides," he lied, "I am accustomed to less-than-desirable accommodations while traveling."

She hesitated. "Very well."

"Then it is settled."

"I suppose," she said with obvious reluctance, "that I should invite you to take a meal in the parlor so that you shall not be forced to dine in discomfort."

"I accept," he said with alacrity. Ignoring the disappointment in her face, he reached for her valise. "It is this way. Shall we?"

# Chapter Two

Delilah Chambers tightened her hand on the hilt of her dagger.

Keenly aware of the stranger's presence at her side, she fought to regulate her breathing. She was fidgety. Her muscles twitched, still poised for the fight, as though unaware that the danger had passed. At least for now.

*Ala'ana.* She cursed silently to herself. Damnation. The last place she cared to be was trapped overnight at an inn full of hostile men. If only her blasted carriage hadn't thrown a wheel. She and her man, Hashem, had ridden three hours in the storm to reach this miserable place. She'd hoped to at least reach Coventry, a largish town where they could seek decent accommodation without drawing undue attention. But the road proved impassable.

They had no choice now but to wait until morning to continue their journey to Lambert Hall. The Tudor-style manor had once been her home, but the estate now belonged to Edgar, her stepson, a man who detested her. He'd never forgiven Leela for marrying his father.

She would happily steer clear of both Edgar and Lambert Hall if it were not for Tori. Edgar's younger sister had implored Leela to attend the house party at the family estate in Warwickshire. Tenderness suffused Leela at the thought of seeing her stepdaughter again after these two years apart.

She and the motherless nine-year-old girl bonded the moment Leela's late husband, Douglas, had brought his seventeen-year-old bride home to Lambert Hall. Tori's mother, Douglas's first wife, died giving birth to the girl. Nineteen-year-old Edgar hadn't welcomed a stepmother two years his junior. From the start, they bickered like rival siblings—minus any familial affection. The moment Edgar inherited his father's title and lands, he made it clear that Leela was no longer welcome at Lambert Hall.

"Ah, here we are." Coming to a stop, Townsend pushed the door open and stood aside to allow her to enter first. "After you."

Passing directly in front of him, Leela became aware of the man's physicality for the first time. Now that the immediate peril had passed, she noticed how powerfully built he was. Not brawny exactly, but rather solid, and he stood several inches taller than her. Leela was not a petite woman and often stood eye to eye with men. Not so with this man. His outsize presence crowded her.

Her gaze traveled over his weathered buckskins. They were close-fitting, showcasing muscular thighs that required no padding to properly fill them out. The buckskins tucked into muddy, scuffed boots.

The private parlor was less dreary than she'd anticipated, and relatively clean considering their surroundings. The room was sparsely furnished with a lumpy-looking sofa in faded velvet, a scarred chest of drawers and a table with four ladder-back chairs. The scent of the wood burning in the hearth masked a slightly musty odor. Torrents of rain slammed against the window. The space was a welcome reprieve from the taproom.

Leela went straight to the fire. Trepidation crackled throughout her body like tiny icy fireworks going off. Now that the harrowing encounter in the taproom was over, she began to shiver. Her thin dress was soaked through. It felt like the rain's chill had permeated every cell in her body.

Townsend set down her worn bag. "I shall go and see about ordering us some supper." The warm deep tones of his voice soothed her nerves like a balm. "There is a latch on the door. Perhaps you would care to use it until my return."

She secured the door behind him before stripping out of her sodden clothes. To her relief, a porcelain basin atop the chest of drawers contained clean water. Goose bumps rose on her skin as she quickly cleaned and dried her body before changing into a respectable English muslin dress, white with pale stripes, and modest with its long sleeves. But with nothing dry to wear underneath, the cold still seemed embedded in her bones. She pulled the embroidered shawl she'd purchased from Abu Talal's shop in the Al-Bireh souk from her valise and wrapped it around her shoulders.

Restless energy coursing through her body, Leela returned to the fire and pulled her wet hair loose. Kneeling before the hearth's nourishing heat, she reluctantly set down her dagger. Keeping her weapon within easy reach, she worked her hands through the untamed mass of waves. As a girl, she'd often cursed her uncooperative hair, which only grew more outlandish in humid conditions. But during her travels, she'd stopped giving it much thought. Now she simply subdued the willful strands into a braid and forgot about them.

Something moved quietly behind her. The air in the room changed. She was no longer alone. Leela's heartbeat slammed against her breastbone. Snatching up her dagger, she shot to her feet, the shawl slipping from her shoulders. She pivoted to find Townsend staring at her with appreciative eyes.

Surprise lit his handsome face when he registered the weapon in her hand. "You have me at dagger point yet again?" He held out his palms. "I thought we were in agreement that you would not puncture any holes in me."

"How did you get in?" She jerked her *janbiya* higher so that it aligned with his chest, where it could do the most damage.

The darkening of his face suggested he noted her intent. "Through the door."

*Liar.* She brushed a loose curl away from her face. "I latched it."

"I simply pushed the door open," he said stiffly. "It's possible the latch is defective."

"You should have announced your presence." She lowered her dagger and edged away from him.

Forcing a deep breath to calm her restiveness, Leela set her dagger aside. She reached behind her head with both arms to arrange her loose hair into some semblance of order. "Also, it is rude to stare."

"I apologize." He possessed a voice so deep that his words seemed to reverberate through her. "It is just that I have never seen hair quite like yours."

Irritation sidled in alongside her taut nerves. Fate favored most Englishwomen of Leela's acquaintance with smooth docile locks or gentle curls. She didn't care what this stranger thought, but his comments still rankled. Her face growing hot, she opted against braiding her hair and quickly pulled it back into a loose tail at the nape of her neck.

"I did not invite you to share my supper in order to be subjected to your insults," she said sharply. "I have heard quite enough of them for one evening."

"How have I insulted you? It was not my intention."

"I would rather not speak of it any further." She wasn't going to waste her energy on a stranger she'd never see again after tonight.

"I am afraid that is unacceptable." Tension rolled off of him. "If I have caused offense, I should like to know why."

"It is of no importance."

"It is to me. I want to know what I am apologizing for."

"A true gentleman would not mention how . . . impossible . . . my hair is."

"Impossible? If by *impossible* you mean *magnificent*, then I would agree." A slight flush came over his pronounced cheekbones. It drew her eye to the sharp turn of his jaw. His beard had begun to grow in, the bristle far darker than his ruffled wheat-colored hair. "I did not intend to gawk at you but, if I am to be completely honest, I could not help myself because you are . . . ah, your hair is . . . so beautiful."

Despite her chilled state, perspiration trickled down her back. "Beautiful?"

"With your hair loose, those splendid waves make you look like Botticelli's Venus."

Leela drew a sharp breath. The blatant admiration in his eyes prompted a wave of heat to blast through her. She was not an innocent and understood precisely what her body's reaction meant. The strong feminine attraction she felt for this man astonished her.

She hadn't been intimate with anyone since her husband's death. Although she missed being touched by a man in that way, and sometimes pined for the cozy warmth of a man's body in bed beside her, Leela hadn't been seriously tempted during her two years of widowhood. Until now.

"So, Venus, please tell me that I am forgiven." Townsend's tone was light but there was a graveness rooted in those deep blue eyes. "Do not send me away to fend for myself among those ruffians out there."

"I certainly should."

His lips quirked, emphasizing the delicious cut of his mouth, the upper and lower lips of equal fullness. "Surely you would not be so cruel as to send me into the lion's den alone—without you by my side to protect me with that dagger of yours."

"I might still be tempted to use my dagger on you."

"You do not seem like a woman who could be easily tempted by any man."

"You've no idea what I might be tempted into doing." The scene in the taproom had left her jittery. Her body overflowed with excess energy that needed to be expended.

Townsend gave a small, surprised laugh. "I must confess that I have never flirted with a woman who wields a knife so capably."

*Flirted?* Was she flirting? Leela never flirted, had never really known how, nor been interested in perfecting the art. But apparently she *was* flirting . . . If Townsend's reaction was anything to go by.

She watched, fascinated, as his indigo eyes darkened to a shade reminiscent of the Mediterranean Sea on a moonlit evening. "Also," he added, "I have never encountered a woman who can better a man in a physical contest as you just did."

Townsend stepped closer, moving ever so slowly, as if she were a skittish Arabian horse that might scare away at any moment.

Leela's blood hurtled through her veins, but she stood her ground. She'd never been one to frighten easily. "Perhaps you should keep your distance."

"Some men enjoy flirting with danger."

"Are you one of those men?"

"Who enjoys flirting with danger? Not normally,

no." He came closer. Some potent force seemed to push them toward each other. "The truth is I avoid disorderly situations. I abhor chaos and the unexpected. I meticulously plan out my days and my life. I do not like surprises."

His masculine scent, an elixir of leather, rain, horse and warm skin, filled her nostrils. She breathed him in, as if taking the essence of this man into her soul, where it coated her insides with pleasure and desire. "Who is the surprise here? You or me?"

"I've no idea. I cannot seem to think straight at the moment."

The air between them grew tight and airless. It was as though they had both taken the same potion. Leela felt strangely powerful, like she could conquer the world . . . Or this man. The crackle of the fire seemed abnormally noisy as they stared at one another. The rain battered the windows with such vehemence that it was as if the forces of nature were trying to warn them away from a dangerous path.

But she stepped forward to meet Townsend anyway, the frenzy of the taproom and her loneliness pushing her toward this stranger. At the moment, this strong, beautiful man, who somehow did not feel like a stranger, seemed like the only solid real thing she could hold on to in a world of chaos. The intimacy of his gaze made her insides quiver.

"I am thinking of kissing you," he said. It was both a question and a warning.

To her surprise, she wanted him to. Badly. "And

how often do you put your thoughts into action?" She wanted to feel his skin against hers. She wanted to know his taste.

"Not often enough, I think. But I plan to remedy that immediately." He lowered his face to hers and gave a grunt of approval when she lifted her lips to meet his.

The kiss was staggering—hungry, alive and buzzing with energy. It was like lightning, if lightning could also be sweet and tender and wondrous. He deepened the kiss and she opened her mouth to entangle her tongue with his. He tasted of ale and man and promise. And like a salve for her loneliness, if only for an evening.

He kissed a path down her throat with warm ravenous lips. Her arms stole around his shoulders. She pressed herself against him, breathing in the cedar scent of his shaving soap, incredibly aware of the hard planes of his body.

Somewhere deep inside her mind, reason attempted to reassert itself. *Stop. He's a stranger. This could ruin everything you've worked so hard for.* "What are we doing?" she breathed, savoring the feel of his mouth against her sensitive skin. "It is as if I am with fever."

"Whatever it is"—he pulled her closer—"I seem to be afflicted with the same ailment."

The part of her that wanted him, that craved this physical act to cure the strange agitation gripping her body, that was tired of too many evenings spent alone, pushed any negative thoughts away. She was a widow, bound to no man, finally answerable to no one but herself. It was one night in the middle of nowhere. No one need ever know.

"Are we really doing this?"

He nibbled her ear. "I certainly hope so."

"Just tonight," she stipulated, eager to contain the madness engulfing them both, "and then we part ways. We must agree."

She felt his smile against her neck. "Should I feel terribly used that you only want me for my body?"

"Who could blame me?" He had a fine athletic form. She ran her hands over his arms, feeling the firm roundness of his biceps through his linen shirt. "Do we have an agreement?"

"Whatever you like." His lips rose up to close urgently over hers again. Large capable hands gripped her bottom and all thought spilled out of her head. He lifted her, pulling her to him until she cradled his considerable erection between her thighs through her clothes.

"No promises. No expectations." She squirmed against his erection, eliciting a satisfied groan from him. "Tomorrow morning, we forget this ever happened."

"As if any man could forget a woman as remarkable as you." He pressed hot kisses along the length of her neck.

She lifted her chin to allow him better access. "You don't even know me."

"Yet it seems as if I do. It's the damnedest thing." His breath was humid against her neck. "It feels like I've been waiting for you forever."

She didn't understand this strange connection between them either. Yet she understood exactly what he meant. "I must have your word. Just this one night."

"You have it." He halted. "If you are certain. *Please God* tell me you want this as much as I do."

"More." She pushed her breasts against his chest to soothe the aching hardness of her nipples. It was well past time for her to finally do as she pleased. "And I am barren, so we've no worries about . . . consequences."

For once, her inability to bear children was a benediction. For once, it was not a crippling source of inadequacy. This coupling would be the first in her life that wasn't fraught with the hope that she'd finally conceived.

Townsend groaned at the sensation of her soft breasts against his chest. "We have a bargain then."

"Yes." She gripped his face with both hands. His skin was warm, the slight shadow of beard, grown in since his morning shave, was prickly to her touch. "Now stop talking. Unless, of course, talking is what you do best."

Amusement glimmered in his hot gaze. "Oh, I shall be most happy to show you what I do best."

She uttered a sound of surprise when he suddenly swooped her off her feet, his hands cupping her bottom as he lifted her straight up against his body. She'd lived long enough to recognize that the powerful attraction she felt for this man, the intense physical connection that throbbed between them, was precious and rare. She might not find it again. She wasn't going to squander it.

Carrying her across the room, Townsend buried his

face in her breasts, mouthing the tender globes, sucking her nipples feverishly through her dress.

Leela cried out, arching back, reveling in the sensation. "Hurry."

"Such an impatient girl," he teased, clearly delighted by her enthusiasm. He stumbled into the table. Her bottom came down on its surface with a hard, clumsy plop. He sucked the tender skin where her neck met her shoulder. His prickly skin chafed her throat. "I do hope you've put that dagger of yours away."

Impatient, she pulled at the placket of his trousers. "This is the only sword I'm interested in at the moment."

"Damn, woman." A surprised hum of approval came from deep in his throat. "I like a lady who knows what she wants." He pressed himself into her seeking hands. He was hard and bulging, straining against the fabric. He helped her work through the buttons, their fingers entangling as they hurried to free him. His erection sprang out, pointed and eager, and she stroked the long smooth warmth with a kind of reverence that was alien to her.

"Ah, yes." He breathed, undulating his hips into her hand, a pleased grimace on his face. He pulled back and reached for the hem of her dress. She lifted her hips to allow him to draw the thin garment over her head and toss it aside. The cool air prickled Leela's bare skin.

He gently laid her back. But she remained propped back on her elbows so she could watch his mouth trail down her neck and farther still until he reached her breast and took a tip into his mouth. It was a stunning sensation. But she was distracted by his hand sliding to the place between her legs. He paused and she sensed his surprise at the hairless skin he found at the apex of her thighs.

"So smooth," he marveled as he stroked her.

Leela flushed, her entire body hot. In her frenzy, she'd forgotten that he would discover she was different down there. That she'd sugared her private area, never expecting anyone else to discover it. "Among my mother's people, it is common for women to remove all of their body hair."

"How intriguing." His fingers feathered over the smooth folds between her legs.

He would think her a heathen now. English women did not remove their most private hair. Modesty alone would not allow for it. Reality set in. A sick feeling slithered into her stomach. This interlude was indecent. Disgusting even. *What was she doing here?*

Leela awkwardly attempted to sit up. "If you do not care for it—"

Hunger flared in his eyes. "Oh, I most certainly do care for it." Kneeling before her, he pressed a gentle hand flat on her bare belly to keep her in place, and bent his head to brush his lips against her smooth slit. "Allow me to show you how much."

# Chapter Three

*H*unt marveled at the erotic feel of his tongue against the silky hairless folds.

Up until this moment, he'd found nothing more enticing than that small bush between a woman's thighs; the sight of intimate hair always added an element of mystery and allure to any coupling. But now, his prick throbbed with anticipation to delve into this new unexplored territory.

Everything was bare to his gaze, the beautiful pinkish folds blatantly open to him, velvety against his cheek. He tasted her, relishing her earthy essence, flicking his tongue against her most sensitive point, eager to drive her wild. Never before had he been so intent on giving a woman pleasure. She bucked and moaned under his tongue, making his prick swell and throb, greedy to be inside of her.

She hummed deep in her throat and pressed herself against Hunt's tongue. He obliged her, sucking more ardently yet remaining gentle, using his fingers to play with her, to drive her to the edge. It did not take long. Venus tensed, convulsed and cried out. He pressed one last wet kiss against her glistening mons and smiled. Pure animalistic satisfaction pumped through his veins.

Hunt sprang to his feet, desperate to be inside her. Yearning and need twisted through him. He pulled her plump bottom to the edge of the table, where the soft firelight illuminated her bare Junoesque form—a strong silhouette of lush breasts, a curved waist and womanly hips.

There was nothing delicate about her and that enticed him. She was all woman, unapologetically so. Her hair had come loose, the glorious waves framing her face and beautiful breasts like a satiny halo. She stared at him through hazy eyes, her high cheeks flushed, her lips moist and slightly parted.

The sight of her bared body, warm and open to him, drove Hunt to madness. Her skin all over was that same smooth bronze delight, silky and hairless everywhere. Holding her hips up to receive him, he plunged inside of her, wildly and absent of any finesse, stroking furiously. The sensation of her insides caressing his prick was unlike anything he'd experienced with Georgie. Or any other woman.

She moved with him, crying out softly. He used his fingers to coax her to completion. Within him, the pressure built, contractions rocked his groin. He wasn't going to last. When he felt her stiffen, he let himself go, shouting some incoherent utterance of satisfaction as he released into her. Shooting his seed into this woman filled Hunt with a level of relief and pleasure that he hadn't thought possible.

He took a few moments to catch his breath before leaning over to press a kiss against her soft belly, relishing the salty sweet scent of skin and femininity. Her hands caressed his head to pull her to him. As he settled between her breasts, an unexpected rush of tenderness engulfed him.

Hunt rarely allowed himself to be driven by physical impulses. He knew the damage such thoughtlessness could do. His late brother had followed his destructive urges enough for the both of them. But this evening, Hunt lost himself in this alluring woman who'd suddenly appeared in his life like some heavenly gift. As if destiny had brought them together for this one night.

Her skin was satin against his cheek. Unable to distinguish the erratic pounding of her heart from his own, Hunt reconsidered his need for order and distaste of surprises. He feathered his fingers over the tip of her beautiful breast and watched it peak for him.

Embracing the unexpected certainly had its merits.

STRUGGLING TO CATCH her breath, Leela stared up at the wooden nubby ceiling and absorbed what she'd just experienced.

She investigated the heat of his body against hers— the gratifying pulsations between her legs, the noisy rush of blood in her veins, the pounding in her ears. Townsend's rumpled hair felt surprisingly soft against her fingers. She delighted in the sweet press of his weight against her body, not minding in the least the hard surface beneath her head and back and hips. His moist tongue flicked back and forth against her nipple, toying with it. She could feel the impact of his ministrations between her legs.

She'd traveled from Gaza's beaches on the Mediterranean Sea to Jericho in the Jordan Valley, where she'd slept on rocky hillsides under the stars with Bedouin families. But she'd never done anything as outlandish as coupling with a stranger atop a rickety table at a country inn. Leela couldn't make sense of it. She'd never enjoyed herself quite so much.

"You are quiet." She heard the concern in Townsend's voice. "Are you . . . Was it satisfactory?"

It astounded her that he needed to ask. "I'm such a fool." She laughed. "It never occurred to me."

He shifted onto his side, regarding her attentively. "What do you mean?"

"It never occurred to me that a wife could, or even should, be an active participant in the marriage bed."

He pressed his lips to her shoulder. "I would not have it any other way."

"I must have been such a disappointment to Douglas."

"Douglas?"

"My late husband."

"I gather the marriage bed was . . . not satisfactory?"

She studied his beautiful face. "It was nothing like this."

He chuckled, his large hand still toying with her breast. This time she could fully appreciate the sensation of the skin-to-skin contact. "And we still have the entire night."

"There's more?" She had no idea a man could be so randy. But then she remembered this man's youth.

He moved over her and began kissing her again. "So much more."

"That is good. Because I shall definitely require another session before making a credible assessment of your talents."

He chuckled, a low, intimate sound. "You've no idea how happy I shall be to oblige you." She felt the tension in his body relax as he eased himself up off of her. "But perhaps we should try the sofa this time."

He took both of her hands to help her up. She felt shy sitting naked atop the table, open to his interested gaze. But before she could fully consider her disrobed state, he swept her up and carried her over to the sofa.

She couldn't help covering her breasts. She had never shown herself to any man in such a blatant manner. Not even her husband, Douglas, had seen her so.

Townsend took note of her discomfort. "Are you cold?"

"Yes," she lied.

He immediately went to the fire, where he'd hung his cloak to dry, and returned to cover her. "Better?"

"Much." Snuggling into the wool garment, she inhaled the masculine scent that clung to its silk lining, embracing her like a tender lover. She braced for regret to swoop in. To her surprise, it did not. The truth was that she felt no remorse. With the rain hammering away at the windows on this dark night in the middle of nowhere, the inn's cozy little chamber felt quite apart from the world. She'd be obliged to return to reality in the morning.

"May I join you?" Townsend's eyes twinkled as he loomed over her. "Or is your dagger hidden somewhere under there?"

"You might have to search me to find out."

"With pleasure." He grinned, showcasing white, albeit slightly crowded, rows of teeth. "And I will have to be extraordinarily thorough in my exploration."

"I should hope so." Leela resolved to enjoy herself for this one evening. She was unlikely to be with another man in this way for a long time to come. Wedding again would only hamper her ambitious plans for her life. After answering first to her father and then her husband, Leela was finally free to do as she pleased. She could see no place for a man, and certainly not a husband, in her vision of the future.

Her first, anonymously published, travelogue about her time spent in Arab lands was a surprise success. All of London clamored for the next volume of *Travels in Arabia*, scheduled for release several weeks from now. Her publisher eagerly awaited delivery of Leela's third volume, which she was currently writing. Afterward, she intended to continue traveling widely and documenting her adventures for publication.

She didn't care that good society thought such behavior was scandalous for a woman, especially a daughter of the nobility. That's why she needed to become financially independent, so that no one could stop her from pursuing her dream. During her marriage, she'd deferred her childhood ambitions, but she'd never forgotten them. And she would never abandon her aspirations. Certainly not for any man.

Townsend practically tore off his shirt and Leela instantly forgot all about her future goals. She couldn't help staring. His chest was a thing of beauty, a landscape of defined ridges and hard curves. Her hungry gaze followed the dusting of hair that trailed down in a fine line over a hard stomach before disappearing inside the waist of his pantaloons.

She sighed with appreciation. The only other man she'd seen thus was her late husband. She felt guilty about the thoughts now swirling in her mind, but there was truly no comparison between the two men she'd known intimately.

It wasn't that Douglas had been unhandsome. Indeed, in his youth, her late husband had been a much sought-after bachelor and an apparent rake. But the man she wed just after her seventeenth birthday had been well past his physical prime. In his late forties by then, age and debauchery had softened Douglas's body and slackened his muscle tone.

Unlike Townsend. The man wasn't a perfect specimen. He had the rugged look of a pugilist, and his slightly crooked nose suggested it had once been broken, but he also possessed beautiful eyes and a determined jaw. And his body. Well, Townsend was clearly an active man. Perhaps his employment was physical in nature. Maybe he really was a pugilist. That would certainly explain the splendid musculature of his arms and the defined architecture of his stomach.

A sharp rap at the door pierced Leela's reverie.

"Your supper, sir," the innkeeper's muffled voice sounded through the closed door. Remembering that the lock did not work, Leela dived under Townsend's cloak to shield herself. Peeking through a small opening, she watched Townsend bound over to the door just as the man pushed it open.

"I will take that." He used his large frame to shield Leela from the innkeeper's view. "You may go."

The innkeeper craned his neck for a look inside. "I will be happy to bring it in for you, sir."

"No need." Townsend liberated the food tray from the man.

The innkeeper absorbed Townsend's state of undress, the bare chest and partially buttoned trousers. A salacious grin slid across his face. "Interrupting, am I?"

Townsend used his back to shove the door closed. "Get out," he commanded in an icy, patronizing manner that made him sound more like a duke than a mere mister.

Leela sat up, hugging his cloak to her breasts, luxuriating in the intimate feel of the fabric against her bare skin. The garment was well-made, the fabric no doubt expensive. But it was also a bit threadbare. Maybe it had been handed down to Townsend from his employer. Or perhaps he'd picked it up in a second-hand shop on Holywell Street in London, where such establishments abounded.

Townsend set the tray on the table, the movement prompting the muscles in his arms and upper back to contract and slide under ivory skin. "Are you hungry?"

"Famished." Her stomach made an insistent noise. Leela hadn't eaten since morning. She slipped off the sofa, bringing his cloak along to cover herself. She adjusted her hair behind her; it was loose and she had no idea what had happened to the ribbon she'd used to contain it.

She scooped her dress up from the floor. The memory of Townsend tossing it away, the intensity and passion with which he'd made love to her, replayed in her mind. Desire clenched in her stomach. Turning slightly away from him, she struggled to pull her simple gown over her head without losing the coverage of his cloak.

Townsend returned to the door and fiddled with the latch. "There, that should hold. But just in case—" He dragged a chair from the table and wedged it under the iron mechanism. "We wouldn't want any more interruptions this evening."

From the corner of her eye, Leela tracked Townsend as he edged around the table, setting the food out, before crossing to the sofa and reaching for his shirt. Giving Leela his back and, consequently, her privacy, he slipped his white linen shirt over his head.

She felt a rush of gratitude for his consideration, and a pang of regret that he was no longer shirtless.

# Chapter Four

*H*unt sat across from Venus consuming boiled beef and cabbage served with beer.

Ravenous, he cut into his meat and tossed a generous piece into his mouth, chewing appreciatively. The mediocrity of the meal did nothing to curb his appetite.

Swallowing, he reached for his beer. "As it turns out, I'm famished, too."

"You did work up quite the appetite," she allowed with a mischievous smile. She bit enthusiastically into the meat. Her lovely bronze skin was flushed, and that spectacular hair cascaded about her shoulders in glorious untamed waves. He couldn't take his eyes off her.

"I must keep my strength up for our next go at it." Hunt was eager to bed her again. Next time he would pace himself, taking time to explore every part of that nimble body. She was tall for a woman, not at all fragile, and pleasingly curved in all of the places a man hopes to discover when he beds a woman. Her toned arms and legs suggested she regularly engaged in physical activity. "I would not want my performance to disappoint."

Her dark eyes twinkled. "If the first encounter was any indication, you needn't worry."

Completely enchanted, he soaked in the sight of her. She glanced up from her meal and caught him watching her. Her bold brows shifted upward. "Yes?"

"I realize this is somewhat overdue, but do you suppose I could have the honor of knowing your name?"

She laughed, her eyes sparkling. Seeing the effect humor had on that lovely face made Hunt feel like he'd won a prize. "Forgive me. It is just that I cannot fathom that I have lain with a man who does not know my name."

Hunt knew exactly how she felt. Everything about this encounter was out of the ordinary and most certainly out of sequence. He never bedded a woman without both partners having a clear understanding of expectations. And he'd definitely never swived a woman after knowing her less than an hour. He always sated his appetites in an orderly manner. But with this woman, everything felt different. He couldn't think rationally in her presence.

"My name is Leela."

"Leela." He rolled the name over on his tongue, enjoying the sound of it. "I quite like your name." He held out his tankard. "And I am Elliot, as you know."

She clinked her beer against his. "It is a pleasure to meet you, Elliot."

"I assure you that the pleasure is all mine."

"It most definitely was not, but I shan't argue the point."

He'd never met such a forthright woman. He appreciated her candor.

"This is all so unexpected," she continued with a shake of her head, as if she couldn't quite believe they were here together. "You've no reason to believe me, but I do not make a habit of bedding strangers. I've been with no man other than my late husband."

He believed her. He admired the smooth planes of her expressive face, the defined cut of her cheekbones. A woman with her handsome looks would have no trouble finding a suitable second husband. "Will you wed again?"

"No. I have other plans for my future."

"Such as?"

"I intend to chart my own course, and that requires never being beholden to any man again. What of you? Are you married?" She flushed, alarm shadowing her face. "I didn't even think to ask."

"I am not wed," he gently reassured her. "At least not yet."

"But there is a bride on the horizon?"

He nodded. "However, we are not betrothed as of yet." He saw no reason not to be truthful. Leela had made it clear that the last thing she sought was a husband. And she was the one to insist they limit their intimate encounter to this one evening.

"I intend to be faithful once I am wed." He wanted her to know he wasn't a rake who casually bedded women. Despite what had just occurred between them—and would hopefully occur repeatedly before the night was over.

"That is commendable." She studied him. "I wonder what sort of woman would you take to wife?"

"She is a very agreeable girl. Quite shy but clever, I think."

"You *think*?"

"We are not particularly well acquainted." It amazed him how easily the conversation flowed between him and a woman he'd met barely an hour ago. He'd never spoken so candidly to any woman. "I have not spent a great deal of time with the young lady, but I am confident she'll make a suitable wife and mother."

"Your passion for your future bride is not exactly overwhelming."

"It's not as though it's a love match. I respect her, which is far more important. She seems nice enough. And I don't expect we'll be in each other's pockets. Besides, I am not a man given to passion."

"The last thirty minutes would suggest otherwise."

He grinned. "It would, wouldn't it?" He'd never acted so impulsively. Yet he was having the time of his life. "It's quite unusual, I assure you. I am not normally ruled by carnal impulses."

"Should I be flattered that you got carried away this one time?"

"You do drive me mad with lust," he said happily.

"Do you not want a little passion with your wife? Especially considering that you intend to remain faithful to her."

He grimaced and thought of his brother, a man whose entire short life had been driven by impulse. History suggested Phillip's unrestrained nature wasn't entirely his fault. The Townsends were a hotheaded brood. It was in their blood. Fortunately, the defective gene skipped a generation. For almost a century, the decorous generations had saved the dukedom from the destructive urges of the dukes who preceded them.

Phillip's temperament had followed the family tradition. Hunt was determined that his would not. He would never be a wastrel like his brother.

He set his tankard down. "Passion makes people do foolish things. I prefer a more considered approach. This decision will impact the rest of our lives." He sat back, crossing his large arms over his chest. "Enough about me. I am far more interested to learn more about you."

"What would you like to know?"

*Everything.* "Where did you get that knife?"

"It was a gift. It once belonged to my great-grandmother and to her mother before that."

"An heirloom then."

She nodded. "My great-great grandmother's father gave it to her as a wedding gift. He taught her how to use it so she could always protect herself."

"Her poor groom must have felt enormous pressure to perform admirably on his wedding night."

"He seems to have survived the evening intact."

"I'm happy to hear it. Have you had occasion to use the blade? Before this evening I mean."

She shrugged. "No matter where a woman goes, she

will always encounter a man who thinks he has the right to touch her. Whenever that occurs, I disavow them of that notion."

"I'll just bet you do." His pelvis twitched. Instead of scaring Hunt off, the vision of Leela brandishing her strange knife, and knowing how to use it, aroused him. "Who taught you how to use the blade?"

"My cousin Jamal. But Hashem, my dragoman, has helped me hone my skills."

"Dragoman?" A dragoman was a guide and interpreter. Hunt recalled the stooped older servant who'd brought Leela's valise into the taproom. "Have you been traveling?"

"Yes. Extensively."

"And it is just the two of you? Do you always travel without a maid?"

"Hashem's daughter usually goes with us. But Hasna does not travel well here in England. She develops coach sickness." Leela sipped her beer. "We left her at my brother's house in Town."

"Where have you traveled?"

"I spent most of my time visiting my mother's people in a town called Al-Bireh, which is a few miles outside of Jerusalem."

"Jerusalem?" That explained the extraordinary tawny tone of her skin. "Your mother is a Levantine?"

"An Arab, yes. But she came to England at the age of thirteen and was raised in Manchester, which is where I was born. My grandfather was a cotton merchant. My cousins still manage the business. Although I do not know them very well."

Hunt had never visited Manchester, but he knew exports from the Lancashire cotton industry went out into the world market through the port city. "And your father?"

"As blue-blooded an Englishman as they come. And a titled one at that. Their union caused quite a scandal."

Hunt almost spit out his beer. "He *married* her?"

She shot him a look of pure disdain. "You needn't sound so surprised."

"It is just so unusual." Given her Levantine merchant origins, Hunt naturally assumed that Leela's mother was her father's mistress.

"It shocks you that a marquess would wed the foreign-born daughter of a merchant?"

His mouth dropped open. Her father's title was second only to his own. "Your father is a *marquess*?"

"He was," she said coolly. "My brother has since inherited the title."

He could feel her closing off, pulling away from him, which was the last thing he wanted. Hunt was desperate to bed her again. His body, eager and attuned to her proximity, hummed with the need to feel her warmth at least once more. To experience the delicious slide of skin on skin, and the muscles of her *mons* tightening around his prick, inviting him to go deeper.

So he changed the subject, hoping to distract her in order to get back into her good graces. And her bed, of course. "Given your recent travels, I have just read a fascinating travelogue that you might enjoy. It's all the rage in the metropolis at the moment. Perhaps you have heard of it. The first volume is called *Travels in Arabia*."

A strange look came over her face. "Yes, that does sound vaguely familiar. You enjoyed it?"

"Very much. The author's writing is very descriptive. He talks in depth of a significant archeological dig in Gaza. It almost makes me want to take the journey myself."

Her rosy lips curved upward. "Is that so?"

"Yes, indeed." Not that he would ever venture to foreign lands so far afield. His ducal responsibilities prevented him from being able to flit about the world on a whim. That was something his brother would have done without a thought. "How did you come to travel abroad?"

"I was restless after my husband died. Growing up, my mother rarely spoke to us of her homeland. For the most part, she kept that part of who she was, the Arab part, to herself. She was determined to raise my brother and me to be proper English children.

"But on very rare occasions, she would speak wistfully of the country of her birth. Of the sweet clean breezes that swept over the veranda. And the succulent fresh figs they gathered from their orchards. She left Al-Bireh when she was thirteen. I will never forget the yearning in her voice. I was overcome with a desire to know my mother better. To understand where she had come from."

He frowned. "Was it not dangerous to undertake a journey to such a faraway land?"

"No more dangerous than stopping at a shabby inn in the English countryside."

"*Touché.*" He sipped his beer. "I cannot say I am truly surprised that your father was highborn."

"Why do you say so?"

"That much is obvious from your speech and gentlewoman's bearing." He grinned. "Your knife-wielding habit notwithstanding."

She laughed out loud. "I supposed you are wondering how a gentleman as highborn as Papa came to be acquainted with the lowly foreign-born daughter of a merchant?"

He was indeed. In London, the classes rarely mixed. "Where *did* your father meet your mother?"

"In Manchester. Papa and his friend quietly went into business with Mama's father, who exported English cotton to the Levant," she continued. "Papa and his friend were in need of funds. Their estates were no longer as prosperous as they'd once been, so they became business partners with *Cidi* . . . erm . . . my grandfather."

"*See-dee?*" Hunt sounded out the word.

"It means *grandfather* in Arabic. In any case," she continued, "Papa fell desperately in love with my mother, his business partner's daughter, and married her despite almost everyone's objections."

That sounded like a rather messy affair to Hunt. "How did they get on?"

"My parents? They were very devoted to each other. My mother did everything she could to fit into her new role as Papa's marchioness. She never spoke

Arabic again and even shortened her given name from Maryam to Mary."

"How did you learn the language?" He'd heard her speaking to that male servant of hers.

"On my travels."

"Was your parents' union a happy one?"

"Oh yes. They adored each other. I do not think either of them ever regretted their choice."

"That is a surprise. In my experience, venturing too far beyond the bounds of societal expectations rarely ends well."

"Following society's rules can be so boring."

"There is a reason for rules—they keep the necessary order for a society to flourish." He noted that her plate was empty. "Are you finished eating?"

"Yes."

"Good." He came to his feet so suddenly that his chair tipped backward and hit the stone floor with a clatter.

"Why?"

"I should like to search you for that dagger now."

THEY MADE LOVE again just before dawn.

It was slow and sweet, but just as intense as their earlier couplings. With Hunt sitting and Leela facing him, her full breasts bouncing as she took him in and rocked her pelvis against his. Her magnificent hair, a random mix of thick waves and wayward curls, streamed over her shoulders and down her smooth back.

Lovemaking in this way seemed new to her; it had

taken Leela time to catch the rhythm of the movements. Clearly her husband had been as useless as a barrel. Yet, despite an obvious dearth of experience, Leela was an enthusiastic and sensual lover. The best Hunt had ever had.

Which perplexed him. She wasn't the most skilled woman he'd bedded. Nor the most traditionally beautiful. Yet, there was an authenticity between them when they made love, a unique chemistry.

She was in his lap, cuddled against his chest. Sometime during the evening, his cloak had slipped to the floor. She shivered so he rose to retrieve it. She watched him unabashedly, which he did not mind. He even covertly sucked in his stomach and flexed his muscles to improve the view. Yet he couldn't resist teasing her. "You are staring again."

"I cannot help myself. I have never seen an unclothed man before."

He rejoined her, pulling her into his arms and covering them both with his outer garment. "Truly?"

"Douglas was very proper. He never saw me disrobed either."

"I'll never understand how a man could have you in his bed and not take full advantage of the fact."

"I won't hear a word against Douglas," she said firmly. "He was good to me. I couldn't give him children and he never once reproached me for it."

"That suits me very well." He pinched her breast lightly. "Your late husband is the last subject I care to discuss while I have you naked in my arms."

She made a sound of satisfaction. So he pinched the

other as well. He nipples were unlike the rosy-hued breasts of women he'd bedded in the past. These pert tips were a beautiful light caramel. He found the difference intriguing . . . And arousing. He delighted in the sweet taste of hcr nipplcs against his tongue.

But, exhausted after making love thrice over the course of the evening, Hunt settled for touching her—the round breasts that almost filled his hand, the nicely curved waist and plush hips.

A sliver of golden light intruded from behind the curtain. Dawn. His stomach dropped. Soon this interlude would be over. But he wasn't ready to let go of Leela. He stroked a hand down her velvety arm; she had the softest skin of any woman he'd ever touched. Now that their time together was coming to an end, his chest felt hollow. Everything about this chance encounter felt like a missed opportunity.

Hunt smothered those thoughts, shoving the sentimental treacle out of his head. He silently cursed himself for thinking with his prick, just as Phillip had done. His brother had indulged all of his most decadent urges, putting his own selfish interests ahead of duty to their parents or the dukedom. And that had led to disaster. All of his adult life, Hunt had sworn never to be like his brother and he wouldn't begin now.

Leela seemed to sense his altered mood. She shifted in his arms to peer into his face. "Is something amiss?"

He brushed a kiss again her forehead. "No, nothing."

She settled back against his chest. "Elliot?" she said softly. *"Ya umar."*

"What does that mean?"

"*Ya umar?* It is a term of endearment. Literally, it means 'my moon' but the translation would be 'my most beautiful.'"

He was surprised. And moved. His throat hurt. "I should be the one extolling the virtues of your very considerable beauty."

"You deserve a wife who will move your heart. Life is too short to live without love."

Jealousy burned in his belly. "Did you have that kind of love with your husband?"

"No. And I might never find it. But my parents knew what it was to truly love and be loved. My mother left almost everything behind for my father. Papa used to stare at Mama as if he could not quite believe his good fortune. Because of their example, I always knew what my marriage was missing. It saddened me. I do not want you to experience the same sense of loss. You have a choice. I did not."

"Maybe I am not made to love like that."

"Oh, I think you are." She pressed her lips against his chest. "You should wed a woman who looks at you as if you are the moon. Promise me you will at least consider what I have said."

"I promise." Hunt knew he'd never forget this night. He wondered if he'd ever again experience this strangely wonderful feeling with another woman. "I will think about what you've said. You have my word."

"Thank you." She paused. "It's silly. I hardly know you, but I think I shall miss you, Mr. Elliot Townsend."

"And I will miss you, Leela." His voice was hoarse. "More than I can say."

She yawned and snuggled against him. "You have quite tired me out."

"Then rest," he said quietly, tightening his arms around her.

As her breaths deepened, Hunt continued to hold her, relishing the feel of her feminine warmth in his arms. But his thoughts churned. As much as he regretted leaving this remarkable woman, it was time to return to his life as the Duke of Huntington. And to all of the commitments and responsibilities that entailed.

Once Leela was asleep, he slipped away.

# Chapter Five

Delilah? Wake up, Lady Lazy." Tori's laughing voice punctured Leela's deep slumber. "You have been asleep all afternoon."

For a moment, Leela was back at the Black Swan. But then she stretched and yawned, becoming aware of the fine feather mattress cushioning her body. The clean linens snuggled around her smelled of starch and lavender, rather than the tang of warm male skin. Or notes of leather, shaving soap and hard-ridden horses embedded in a well-worn cloak.

Her eyelids fluttered open. Leela squinted up at the Pomona green floral silk canopy overhead. As her soporific fog melted away, her muddled thoughts took on a more distinct shape and the events of the past twenty-four hours—some of which she preferred not to remember—came into focus.

She'd awakened alone at the inn that morning, still wrapped in Elliot's cloak, only to discover that he'd departed without a word of farewell. Disappointment and a sense of loss swept through her. It's not that she'd expected proclamations of undying love from Elliot, but to skulk away without a parting word?

In the light of day, the shabby inn parlor lost all of the previous evening's cozy charm. In reality, it was simply a worn, bare space with tattered furniture. Eager to be gone from the inn, Leela rose despite her exhaustion. Dressing quickly, she summoned Hashem and prepared for a rapid departure. The moment she arrived at Lambert Hall late this morning, she'd retreated to her assigned bedchamber and fallen into a deep sleep.

"I have brought you some tea and rout cakes." Tori came over with the tray as Leela hoisted herself into a seated position. "And if you do not eat them, I will, so you had better get to work or soon I shan't be able to fit into my gowns."

Leela eyed her stepdaughter's sylphlike figure. "As if that could happen." She'd always felt like a giant next to Tori's ethereal presence.

"Now drink," Tori instructed. "I assume you are still partial to tea. I had Cook add mint just as you like."

Leela gratefully accepted the offering. "One can never have enough tea." She took a fortifying sip, the sweet hot liquid soothing her dry throat. "This has the perfect amount of mint."

Her Arab relatives customarily took their tea with either fresh mint or sage. Indulging in deliciously flavored *shay* was one of the few rituals from her past that Mama hadn't discarded once she'd become Lady

Brandon. And her daughter carried on the tradition. One of Leela's first directives as mistress of Lambert Hall was to instruct the gardener to add spearmint and sage to the kitchen herb garden.

"I picked the mint fresh from the garden myself," Tori informed her with a saucy smile, "so naturally that will make the tea even more delicious."

"That explains why it's perfect." Affectionate contentment washed over Leela. Her intense bond with Tori—big sister combined with best friend in the world—remained as intact as ever despite the time they'd spent apart.

Everything was better when Tori was present. She possessed a sunny countenance, practically emitting beams of light whenever she smiled. Leela had been all of seventeen when she'd arrived at Lambert Hall as a young bride. Only eight years separated the two women. She and Tori had practically grown up together.

"You have been sleeping all day when I have been dying to hear all about your journey." Tori shook the linen napkin open and laid it across Leela's lap. "And to make matters worse, you arrived a day late."

"The rainstorm forced me to take shelter at an inn last evening." Leela's face warmed at the memory of Elliot's lips delving into the most intimate parts of her body. "I did not sleep much."

"You poor dear." Tori laid a cool hand against Leela's cheek. "Have you taken ill? You are flushed."

"I am fine. Truly." She reached for a cake, avoiding Tori's seeking gaze. "It's just the heat of the tea."

"I hate that your chamber is so far from mine." Tori went to open the curtains. The sunlight slanted across the young woman's white-gold hair. If angels were real, Leela imagined they must look like Tori, with her gleaming light hair and soft blue gaze. "I am going to insist that Edgar move you back into the family wing where you belong."

Leela surveyed the space she'd been assigned, an overtly feminine room with dainty hand-painted green furniture and complementary floral silks. Two generous sash windows overlooked the gardens at the back of the hall. It was a perfectly respectable accommodation, although not the best guest chamber at Lambert Hall.

"No need. Honestly, this is fine." She knew her husband's heir had deliberately placed her in the guest wing to signal that he no longer considered her family.

Naturally, this was not where she'd slept as Douglas's countess and mistress of Lambert Hall. As the Earl of Devon's wife, Leela had occupied the sizable chamber connected to Douglas's generous rooms in the family wing. But now that her stepson was the earl, she was relegated to a chamber for visitors. "It does not matter where I sleep. As long as you and I can be together, I am content."

"At least you're not staying at the dower house." Tori climbed onto the bed to sit opposite Leela. "That would be entirely too far away."

"Edgar might suffer an apoplexy if I dared to settle at Parkwood." As Douglas's widow, Leela was entitled to live at Parkwood, a cozy home on the estate historically reserved for widows of the estate's previous masters. But after Douglas's death she'd retreated to Highfield, her childhood home, before embarking on her travels. "The very last thing Edgar desires is to have me living full-time on the estate."

"I think you judge my brother too harshly. The last time I rode by Parkwood, workers hired from the village were repairing the roof. Perhaps Edgar is readying the dower house for you."

"I highly doubt it."

"It would be glorious to have you living on the estate permanently. I could walk over every morning and have breakfast with you."

Leela decided to let the topic of Edgar rest. Tori adored her older brother, and as far as Leela could tell, Edgar held his sister deep in his affections and treated her well. He reserved all of his ire for his late father's second wife.

Tori reached for Leela's hand. "I missed you so."

"And I you." Leela squeezed Tori's hand, the girl's fingers looking even paler in contrast to Leela's tawny skin.

"You were gone so long I feared you'd met a handsome Arab man and forsaken me and England."

Elliot's sculpted face flashed in Leela's mind. She'd met a man all right. But he'd slunk away the moment she'd fallen asleep.

"You must tell me about your travels," Tori continued. "Did you meet your mother's relations?"

"Many of them, yes. I became acquainted with cousins I did not even know I possessed." Being surrounded by her mother's family was a novel experience. Lady Brandon's wholehearted embrace of Papa's noble world meant that Leela and her brother, Alexander, saw nothing of Mama's family while they were growing up, except for *Citi*, Lady Brandon's mother, who spent summers with them at Highfield. But *Citi* never joined the guests when Leela's parents entertained.

"Was it strange?" Tori asked. "Could you communicate with them?"

"At first it was quite a challenge. I engaged a dragoman, an interpreter and guide, to translate for me, but after the first year, I was able to communicate in Arabic, at least in a rudimentary way."

Mama would be aghast. Lady Brandon had constantly reminded Leela and Alexander that they were English through and through. Rather than Arabic, she'd insisted they master French, the language of the nobility.

"I want to hear everything." Tori leaned closer. "What was it like? Is it one big desert?"

"Not at all. There are many trees of all kinds. Fig trees with broad leaves and silvery olive trees. Peach, plum and apple trees. And the ground is cultivated with maize, melons, lentils, beans and sesame seeds. I could go on and on."

"So there is grass?"

"I saw a grass that is very tall and strong. It's called broomcorn because they use it to make brooms. And the Arabs make fresh olive oil that is unlike anything

I've ever tasted. Especially when one dips warm bread in the olive oil and then in *za'atar*."

"What is that?"

"Never mind. I promise to tell you all about it, but first you must catch me up on your news." Leela bit into the cake, savoring the sweet buttery taste tinged with notes of rosewater and orange blossom. "Mmm, I have missed rout cakes."

Tori smiled shyly. "I do have news."

"Do not keep me in suspense."

"You have been gone so long that you are unaware that I've been rather unsuccessful on the marriage mart. I've had two fruitless Seasons."

Outrage filled Leela's chest. "Have all of the young men suddenly been struck blind? Or are they simply idiots who fail to recognize a true diamond when they see one?"

"They are neither blind nor stupid." Tori gave her a look. "You know I am not at my best among strangers."

She did know that Tori had never overcome her childhood shyness. "That does not change the fact that you are a lovely girl." It was true. Especially at the moment. Tori's primrose gown flattered the girl's slender form, showing her radiant blue eyes and fine white-blond hair to excellent advantage.

"I know I am passably pretty, but I am terrible at flirting. At balls, when I dance with young gentlemen, I cannot seem to form any coherent thoughts. Artful conversation completely escapes me. I just stumble along like a fool. I'm sure they think I'm touched in the head."

Leela considered the girl's dilemma. Tori preferred the company of those she knew best. Whenever Douglas hosted house parties, the girl would retire to her bedchamber with a book rather than join the guests.

Leela nibbled her cake. "I cannot be much assistance in teaching you the art of flirtation. We shall just have to find the appropriate match for you, a gentleman who is smart enough to appreciate you as you are."

Tori blushed. "I have found him."

"What?" Leela swallowed the last of her cake. "You have?"

Tori's face glowed. "I am to be betrothed to the Duke of Huntington."

"A duke?" Leela had never heard of the man, but she was predisposed to be fond of any person responsible for the glowing expression on her beloved Tori's face. "That's wonderful!"

"Can you believe I am going to be a duchess?"

"I absolutely can." She set her *shay* down on the bedside table. "You have always had a bit of a managing nature."

Tori tossed a pillow at her. "I have not."

Leela caught it and tucked it behind her. "Any man would be fortunate to call you his wife. This duke is getting the better part of the bargain."

"Oh, to be sure." Tori rolled her eyes. "After all, what does Huntington have to offer except for a title, too much money to count and a library collection to die for?" She paused, her expression growing more serious. "It is rather daunting to think of being a duchess, but His Grace says I will be perfect for the role. He prefers my more contained nature and does not care for coquettes."

"His Grace sounds like an insightful man. Do you love him?"

Tori hesitated. "I like him well enough. I know you feel strongly about a love match for me. I imagine that I will grow to love His Grace. At the moment, I feel rather shy around him. I can barely manage to put two words together without stammering like an idiot, but he assures me that will change once we are wed."

"I look forward to meeting the man who is clever enough to know what a gem you are."

"You will not have to wait long." Tori's eyes sparkled with excitement. "He arrived this morning."

"I shall have to make certain he deserves you," Leela declared. "And in the meantime, you must take this time to become better acquainted with the duke to see if he is a man you can fall in love with."

"Well, you will not be able determine whether His Grace *deserves* me, as you put it, if you stay abed all day. We are all meeting on the terrace in an hour when the gentlemen return from hunting."

Leela set her tea down. "I suppose I shall be forced to make myself presentable."

"Excellent. I will meet you there." Tori scooted off the bed. "In the meantime, I will send my maid in to assist you."

Twenty minutes later, Leela was soaking in a hot bath, thinking of Tori's duke and hoping he was worthy. Surely the man was more of a gentleman than Elliot Townsend. What a *hamar* the man was. Only a donkey would behave so rudely. The lout had no manners. Leela had never engaged in a liaison before, but surely the rules of engagement included parting in a respectful, civilized manner. Or writing a note at least.

She sighed long and loud. Closing her eyes, she attempted to push Elliot out of her mind. She tried not to think about his energetic lovemaking, the appealing terrain of his well-formed body, or to imagine him touching her in all of the intimate places where the warm bathwater now lapped against her skin.

Elliot was in the past—a quick, mostly pleasurable interlude that was now over. Between her books and Tori's duke, Leela had far more important matters to attend to.

"YOU ARE UNUSUALLY quiet this afternoon," Thomas Ellis, Viscount Griffin, remarked to Hunt.

The two men picked their way along the muddy edge of the cornfield. The rain had cleared, but the air remained thick with moisture and the ground was a boggy mess. "Are those pre-marital nerves that I detect?"

Before Hunt could answer, the cocker spaniel trotting ahead of them paused, signaling his discovery of a wild pheasant camouflaged in the thick brush. The fowl burst into flight and Griff raised his hunting rifle to take aim.

Hunt wasn't thinking about his impending betrothal, but he *was* thinking about a lady. He couldn't get the memories of glistening waves of sumptuous dark hair draped over smooth, bare honey-colored skin out of this mind.

Lost in thought, he narrowly avoided stepping into a particularly mucky spot and took a moment to stamp his mud-splattered boots on the grass. His black hessians, ringed in brown at the top, were a mess. Before joining Lady Victoria and the other guests on the terrace, he'd need to change into the fine new boots he'd recently acquired from Hoby's at the corner of St. James and Piccadilly.

"Why were you late?" Grimacing, Griff lowered his rifle without taking a shot. Although the viscount rarely complained, Hunt knew his friend was in almost constant pain from an old war injury to his shoulder. "Devon said you were meant to arrive last evening." The Earl of Devon, their host, was the brother of Hunt's soon-to-be betrothed.

The two men started to circle back to the main house. "I was forced to take shelter from the rain," Hunt said. "I stayed at a ramshackle inn."

"That sounds dreadfully uncomfortable."

"You would think so, but it was the most enjoyable evening I can recall in years."

Griff stared at his friend. "And why was that?"

"I had company."

"You?" Griff asked dryly. "Dallying with a woman without first signing a contract?"

"Shocking, I know."

"I cannot believe it." The two men were longtime friends who'd attended Harrow together. That prolonged proximity gave Griff unique insight into the precise manner in which Hunt conducted his life.

"She was remarkable." A hint of melancholy clung to Hunt's words. "And I seem to be unable to get her out of my head."

Griff's icy sapphire gaze settled on Hunt. "Surely, you are not thinking of throwing Lady Victoria over?"

"Of course not. The widow I spent the evening with is not the sort of woman who could fill the role of duchess." He smiled at the memory of Leela wielding her curved dagger, prepared to take on a taproom full of ruffians. "I seriously doubt she would even care to."

"I doubt there's a woman alive who wouldn't jump at the chance to become a duchess."

"I feel certain this one would not. She is a singular woman."

"I suppose that means you've arranged to see her again."

"Not exactly." Remorse filled Hunt at the manner in which he and Leela had parted ways. He'd thought to make a clean break after a delightful interlude. But he now regretted leaving her as though she was a common whore he'd paid for a night of pleasure. If only he'd learned her full name, or at least discovered how to find her.

"I suppose the lovely Georgina's tenure is about to come to an end," Griff commented.

"When I wed, naturally." Hunt had all but forgotten about his mistress. He'd intended to part ways with

Georgie shortly before taking Lady Victoria to wife. But now he contemplated releasing her earlier. He had no desire to visit Georgie again.

"You are obviously taken with this woman you spent the night with," Griff said. "I assumed you planned to make her your mistress."

"Have you forgotten that I am to be wed within a matter of weeks?"

Now that he'd made the decision to take a wife, Hunt saw no reason to delay matters. In a fortnight, Devon would host a ball officially announcing his sister's betrothal to the Duke of Huntington. Exactly one month after that, Hunt would wed Lady Victoria at St. George's Hanover Square. His staff was already deep into planning matrimonial festivities fit for a duke.

"You are not married yet," Griff pointed out as they trudged up the hill toward the main residence, "nor even officially betrothed in the eyes of society. Your tasty piece could fill Georgina's role until you are wed."

The prospect of stealing a few more pleasure-filled nights with Leela prompted Hunt's heart to go a little faster. Just imagining that smoky laugh and silken skin sent a shiver of desire through him. Hope pierced the quiet gloom that had enveloped him since he'd left her.

Griff had the right of it. Until Lady Victoria officially became his duchess, Hunt was technically free to do as he pleased. And nothing delighted him more at the moment than the prospect of locating Leela and enticing her back to his bed.

"I don't even know her full name. Or how to find her."

"You're a duke, man. Why not put all of the vast resources at your disposal to work in order to run your temptress to ground?"

He brightened. "Why not, indeed?" But where to start? He'd send word to his man of affairs in London to immediately begin the search for his mystery lover. Hunt would retain a Bow Street Runner if necessary. Once he found Leela, they could resume their affair long enough for him to get his fill of the way her stunning eyes glowed with satisfaction when he brought her to the peak of pleasure.

By the time he married Lady Victoria, he and Leela would have parted ways and the mesmerizing adventuress would be out of his system for good.

FRESHLY BATHED AND feeling rested, Leela approached the open doors to the terrace, where many of the guests had already gathered.

She ran a light hand over her hair. Tori's maid had done an admirable job corralling Leela's unruly mane into an array of pretty curls atop her head. She shook out her skirts. It had been a long time since she'd worn such a fine dress. There certainly was no need for pink silk gowns with ruffled sleeves while trudging across Wadi Rum in the Jordan Valley.

Leela stepped out onto the stone terrace, which covered the entire back width of the house. It had always been one of her favorite spots at Lambert Hall. When the weather allowed, she and Douglas often

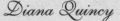

took their morning meal here overlooking the gardens. Leela paused, scanning the crowd for Tori. She smiled when her stepdaughter came into view.

Tori's entire face lit up. "Why, here she is now."

The finely dressed man with dark amber hair standing by Victoria's side turned to greet the new arrival. Leela's gaze traveled from the gentleman's pristine midnight boots over muscular thighs to a trim waist. Wide shoulders were encased in a deep blue tailcoat with gilt buttons. A cream waistcoat, topped with a snowy cravat, covered the broad expanse of his chest.

Her gaze floated upward until Leela locked eyes with the man who somehow felt as familiar to her as an old and dear friend. Her stomach dropped when she met Elliot's horrified expression.

They stared at each other from across the terrace, the rest of the people receding into silent, indistinct shapes as if this were all a dream. Or a nightmare. The only sound Leela could hear was the thick dull throbbing in her ears.

Surely, it was impossible. Someone's idea of a terrible joke. None of this made any sense. Victoria was betrothed to a duke. Elliot was no duke. Although, at the moment, he was certainly dressed like one.

Leela could not tell how long she stood there, as frozen as the statuary in Lambert Hall's extensive gardens, before Tori came over and looped her arm through Leela's, gently tugging her in Elliot's direction. "Come my dearest Delilah. Come and meet the duke."

It was all Leela could do to force her feet to move

alongside Tori, fighting the urge to break away and run as fast and far as she could in the opposite direction. As they drew closer, perspiration trickled down Leela's back. She resisted the urge to blot the perspiration beading on her upper lip.

"Your Grace . . . this is my stepmama . . . Lady Devon." Tori's voice brimmed with buoyant pride as she nervously fumbled through the introduction. "But as you can see . . . she is hardly ancient. She is more like a sister and one's dearest friend . . . in all the world . . . rolled up into one exceptionally beautiful person."

Elliot stood stock-still, glued to his spot. Escape for either of them was impossible. It was like watching a carriage speeding straight toward her and being unable to leap out of the way. All she could do was stand still and brace for disaster.

"Delilah . . . this is the gentleman . . . I told you about," Tori stammered once they came to a stop before him. "Meet His Grace . . . the Duke of Huntington."

Sweat dampened Leela's armpits. She didn't feel well. A gentle gust of wind swept the veranda, threatening to topple her. She watched through a haze of horror as Elliot recovered himself enough to make her a bow.

His deep blue eyes were guarded, his features contorted into passivity. "Lady Devon."

Leela opened her mouth, but no words came out. A violent heave shook her body. Then she bent over and cast her accounts all over the Duke of Huntington's shiny new boots.

# Chapter Six

"Are you feeling better?" The pillow over Leela's head failed to muffle the concern in Tori's voice. "You've been in your chamber since yesterday afternoon."

Leela swallowed, her mouth dry and foul tasting, and forced herself to turn over in the bed to face her stepdaughter. "I'm much improved," she lied, unable to meet the girl's gaze. Her heart raced. It felt like a manic rabbit was bounding around inside her chest. "I must have eaten something on the road that disagreed with me."

Leela was sick to her stomach. Disgust swamped her again. *She'd bedded the man Tori intended to wed.* Searing pain chased after the bunny stomping on her heart.

She fought to draw a full breath. What a catastrophe. Leela didn't even know how to put into words just how abhorrent her current predicament was. *Citi*, her Arab grandmother, would call it a *fatheeha*—a mortifying combination of scandal, disgrace and outrage mixed into one. Sometimes you could find the perfect word in Arabic that did not have an English equivalent. And *Citi* would be right.

Leela couldn't bear to imagine how devastated Tori would be if she ever learned the truth. Yet how could Leela keep it from her? She and Tori were always honest with each other. From the beginning, Leela had vowed to shield the motherless girl from harm. She never imagined she'd be the one to ruin Tori's happiness.

If Leela's dalliance with Elliot was made public, Tori's name would be forever tied to scandal and ridicule. The sweet girl's reputation would be ruined. The undeserved notoriety would be a severe blow to someone with Tori's sensitive nature.

"Darling, please do go and enjoy yourself," Leela implored, while trying to hide the anxiety making her short of breath. "I assure you, all I require is a bit of rest."

"You never stay abed until noon unless you are truly ill." Tori refused to budge. The girl could be as immovable as a stone wall when she set her mind to it. "And you don't seem to be improving. Your breathing is strange and your skin has the most alarming tinge of gray to it."

That was because sleep had eluded her last night. And when Leela did manage to doze off, disjointed images of Elliot, naked and aroused, or with his lips trailing down her belly, drifted in and out of her jagged dreams.

"I am going to ask Devon to call for a doctor," Tori said.

"No, absolutely not." Leela dragged herself upright in bed even though it felt like thick mud was sloshing around inside her head. She gingerly settled back against the pillows and waited for the throbbing in her head to subside. "I'll be better in no time."

Tori carried over the tea tray she'd brought up. She looked divine in an azure riding costume that matched her striking eyes.

"At least try some tea and toast. You haven't eaten anything since you cast your accounts. You must have something." Tori set the tray on the bed and settled her hips next to it to pour the tea. She added a huge quantity of sugar. "Sweet with plenty of mint, just as you prefer."

Leela drank. At least the tea rinsed the terrible taste from her mouth. The *shay's* warmth had a soothing effect on her stomach. She took a tentative nibble of toast.

Tori followed her movements as closely as a mother bird watches her baby. "A little more."

"Someone is Miss Bossy," Leela said dryly. But she did as Tori asked and took another tiny bite.

Tori shifted restlessly on the bed. "Oh, Leela, I cannot wait for you to feel better so that you can become acquainted with Huntington."

Leela coughed, the toast clogging her throat. The very last thing she desired was to spend any time with Elliot. The unwelcome image of the man, naked and splendid, his muscled form glistening in the candlelight, his manhood jutting proudly, flashed in her mind. To Leela's mortification, her entire body felt like it was on fire.

Concern shadowed Tori's eyes. "You're flushed again." She reached over to lay a cool hand against Leela's hot cheek. "We should have known you were taking ill yesterday when you slept for hours after your arrival. You had a fever then, too."

Leela carefully set her cup on the tray. "Have you spent much time with the duke?"

"Not as much as I should like to. We have not been alone, of course." Tori's cheeks were flushed and shiny. "But I suppose there shall be plenty of time for that after we are wed."

Regret and despair swamped Leela anew. If only she hadn't agreed to attend Devon's house party. If she hadn't met Elliot on the road, she'd be properly sharing in Tori's happiness and excitement.

"It is important that you get to know the duke," Leela said carefully, thinking of how easily the man had leaped into bed with a stranger while on his way to visit the woman he intended to wed. "You must make certain that he is honorable and that the two of you suit."

"I thought we would have an opportunity to speak more once he visited us here at Lambert Hall. But His Grace has spent most of his time since arriving in the library with Mr. Foster."

"Who is Mr. Foster?"

"The duke's secretary."

"Huntington brought his secretary to the house party?" Elliot couldn't leave work behind long enough to court Tori as she deserved? Not surprising.

At the Black Swan, Leela felt mild sympathy for his

future bride. But now that she knew who the bride in question was, she wanted to stomp on Elliot's stomach while wearing her heaviest walking boots.

That was one of *Citi*'s favorite utterances. The harshness of some Arabic expressions, learned first from her grandmother during *Citi*'s summers at Highfield, and then more extensively from her Al-Bireh cousins, had taken Leela aback at first. But she'd come to appreciate the colorful Arabic expressions. They might sound extreme, yet the words also had a tongue-in-cheek humor to them. And in the case of Elliot Townsend, the blasted Duke of Huntington, this one seemed particularly apt.

"Yes, his secretary is here," Tori said. "They worked after supper last night and all of this morning. Mr. Foster arrived a day before His Grace. I met him when I went to the library to put away some books. Mr. Foster is a very pleasant man. A bit shy like me as well as an avid reader. It will be nice to see a friendly face once I move into Weston House."

"Weston House?"

"Drink more of your tea," Tori ordered before answering. "Weston House is the ducal residence in Mayfair on St. James Place. Can you imagine me being mistress of such a grand home and having to tell everyone there what to do?"

"You are doing a fine job ordering me around." She inhaled, then exhaled, long and slow. But her mind raced.

*Nice enough.* That's what Elliot had said about Tori. *Very agreeable.* Bitterness rose in Leela's throat when she recalled how dispassionately the duke had referred to his soon-to-be betrothed. Tori wasn't merely *nice enough* and *very agreeable*. She was so much more. Wonderful and beautiful and thoughtful and lively and intelligent and amusing. How could Elliot be so dismissive of a prize like Tori? He didn't deserve her.

"Promise me," she said to Tori, "that you will try to find opportunities to spend time with Huntington. Ask Edgar to facilitate that for you. It's important to see if the two of you suit."

"I certainly cannot hope to do better than a duke!" Tori exclaimed. "All of the other debutantes are envious of me. Any of them would have accepted had the Duke of Huntington offered for them."

"I understand that you are flattered by his attentions," she said gently, "but deciding whom to wed requires very careful consideration. There is no more important decision a woman can make in her life. Your choice of a mate ultimately determines whether you will be happy and content."

"You of all people know I become a bumbling fool when in the presence of strangers, especially handsome young gentlemen. Edgar says it's a miracle that Huntington is interested in me."

"Don't listen to him. Edgar can be a *suttle*."

Tori's eyes twinkled. "Dare I ask what that means?"

"An unfilled bucket. Empty-headed. Someone not exactly known for his intelligence."

Tori laughed. "Edgar is not an empty bucket. I appreciate that he is attempting to be realistic."

"The reality is that you are an amazing person."

"Undoubtedly," Tori teased. Lowering her chin, she fluttered her lashes, purposely exaggerating the affectation. "But how can any young gentleman comprehend the full impact of my wonderfulness when all I do is stammer and blush in his presence like a . . . What did you call it? A *suttle*."

"Stop it. You are anything but empty-headed and you know it. You shouldn't feel that you have to settle."

"How can wedding a *duke* ever be considered settling?" Tori shook her head. "True, it is not a love match, but I do feel Hunt is my destiny. You have always said fate will send the right man to me."

Leela did believe in fate, a concept prevalent among her mother's people. One had free choice, of course, but a person's destiny could not be denied. Her skin prickled. What if Huntington really was Tori's *naseeb*—her fated husband? She couldn't fathom it. Surely *qismat* could not be so cruel.

"His Grace must care for me at least a little," Tori added, "or he would not have offered for me."

Leela reached for the young woman's hand. "Are you trying to convince me or yourself?"

"Maybe both."

"All I ask is that you try to look beyond the title to the man. A title won't keep you company, or hold you, or laugh with you. You belong with a man who can love you deeply and appreciate what a true gem you are." *A man who can think of no woman but you, who would never dally with a stranger.*

"Oh, I do agree! A man would only offer for a young lady he holds in the highest regard, isn't that so?"

"I suppose." Leela could hardly reveal Elliot's ambivalence toward the match, or how he'd demonstrated his irresoluteness by falling into bed with the first available woman outside of London. What sort of man behaved in such a reprehensible manner? Leela wasn't proud of her own actions, but at least she was a widow with no attachments. Unlike Elliot.

"This afternoon, Edgar is taking the guests for a ride down the canal. We shall be out most of the day. Perhaps if you rest today, you'll be well enough to attend the breakfast party tomorrow," Tori said. "I want nothing more than for two of the most important people in the world to me to become acquainted with each other."

Under the blankets, Leela's toes curled. Everything in her wanted to flee, to take her beloved Tori somewhere safe, far away from the Duke of Huntington who, through a horrible chance of fate, had the power to bring their world crashing down around them.

"I will try," she finally said.

"Blast it all!" Edgar burst into Leela's bedchamber later that evening after a cursory knock at her door. "For once in your life, do something for someone other than yourself."

Clad in a faded pink dressing gown worn over her comfortable baggy trousers that tapered at the ankle, Leela suppressed a groan. She'd finally managed to drag herself out of bed to work on the third volume of her book. Not that she'd accomplished much. The inside of her head felt like an ancient rusty church bell was clanging between her ears. She was certainly in no condition to spar with her late husband's heir.

"You might try waiting to enter until you are invited." Seated at a dainty mahogany escritoire inlaid with gold, she casually drew several old letters over her manuscript to conceal it. "As any gentleman should."

"As if I need lessons in decorum from you. Do not forget that this is now my house and I will do as I please."

"How could I forget? You certainly remind me often enough."

Edgar's pale skin drew taut over aristocratic cheekbones. His handsome features, the downward slant of sky-blue eyes, the tight press of his lips, were so reminiscent of his father's that it plucked at Leela's chest. Unfortunately, the similarities between father and son ended there. Douglas had always been kind to her. He had certainly never treated her with cold disdain as his son did now.

"You cannot hide away in this bedchamber forever."

"I am not hiding. You and your guests were out on the canal all afternoon." Edgar enjoyed taking guests for outings on the narrow waterways. Leela had never been.

"Be that as it may, your absence was noted." His gaze lingered on the scattered papers before her. "What the devil are you doing in here anyway?"

She ignored the question. No one knew she'd authored the metropolis's most talked about travel memoir, and she certainly wasn't going to enlighten Edgar. He'd have an apoplexy.

"And what in Hades are you wearing?" He stared

at her *shirwal* in disbelief, his voice rising. "Are my eyes deceiving me? Are those trousers? Are you wearing trousers? Are you determined to disgrace us all by dressing so indecently?"

"By wearing *shirwal* in the privacy of my own bedchamber? Yes," she added in a voice rich with sarcasm, "I am courting scandal and ruin. You have found me out."

"This is no laughing matter. I insist that you make yourself decent and rejoin the house party." Edgar ambled away from her, surveying the chamber. He paused at the chest of drawers at Leela's bedside. "I shall expect to see you at the breakfast party tomorrow afternoon."

She twisted in her chair to track his progress. "I've already promised Tori that I will attend."

He reached for the travelogue by her bed and casually flipped through its pages. "The maids say you spent all afternoon writing letter after letter. To whom could you possibly be writing so many letters?"

"I met many people during my travels." Tension stretched across the back of her shoulders as he leafed through *Travels in Arabia*. She usually kept her book safely tucked out of sight. But she'd needed to look something up that was pertinent to the third volume she was currently working on.

"And yet you haven't sent a single letter. I haven't franked any for you."

"I will send them when I am ready."

"You are, for better or worse, the Countess of Devon and will remain so until I take a wife, which cannot come soon enough. Unfortunately, I have yet to find a suitable bride." To her relief, he set the book down. "The duke has inquired about your health. It is imperative that you give every appearance of respectability at the breakfast party."

Her stomach roiled. "Huntington asked after me?"

"Yes, he expressed concern for your well-being."

*Maleun.* That damned man. The last thing that donkey should do is reveal that he noted her absence.

"Whatever you do, make no mention of your travels." Edgar paused to examine the dressing table littered with Leela's personal effects. His interested gaze took in her combs, hairpins, lotions and perfume. "Try not to draw attention to the fact that you traveled, unchaperoned, in heathen lands."

"I was accompanied by a dragoman."

"A native." His lips twisted. "That is hardly the same as taking an *appropriate* traveling companion."

Naturally, Edgar's idea of a suitable chaperone was a properly pale English matron of a certain age. "Need I remind you that I am a widow? I do not require a chaperone."

"Ah yes, widows are allowed certain liberties." His probing gaze moved over her in a way that caused her scalp to tingle. Leela was accustomed to sparring with Edgar. They'd always squabbled like warring siblings, but what she detected in his gaze now both surprised and unsettled her.

The gleam in his eyes seemed almost . . . Predatory. She clasped the neckline of her voluminous gown more tightly closed at her throat. "If that is all—"

Edgar flushed and averted his gaze. "Victoria has not been a success on the marriage mart. She's too book-mad and people-shy to attract suitors suitable to her rank." He picked up her ornate silver hand mirror, a gift from Douglas, and examined his teeth in its reflection. Edgar had good teeth. "It's a miracle that Huntington wants her."

Leela watched Edgar set her mirror down. "The duke is fortunate to have her."

"On that we might agree. However, society does not concur. And it does not help that Victoria is so in awe of the duke that she can barely string two words together in his presence." He moved to the hand-painted green wardrobe containing her clothing, strolling about like a dog looking to mark its territory. "I intend to host a ball immediately upon our return to London where Victoria's betrothal to the Duke of Huntington will be officially announced."

"Isn't that premature? Tori barely knows the man."

"No, it is not premature." He mimicked her tone. "They shall have plenty of time to become acquainted after they are wed."

The wardrobe door was slightly ajar. Edgar peered at Leela's gowns hanging inside. "In the meantime, you and I must put aside our differences and present a united familial front for Victoria's sake. No one cares to marry into a complicated family, particularly not a man like Huntington, who has family problems of his own to contend with."

"He does?" Leela straightened. "Like what? Tori has a right to know what sort of life she will be agreeing to."

"The previous duke, Huntington's elder brother, was a reckless rake and a gambler. That sort of behavior is known to run in the family. But it appears to skip a generation. The sober, sedate generations clean up the messes created by the wild generations."

"And who currently rules this generation? The rakes or the repentants?"

"History suggests this is the ne'er-do-well generation. However, Huntington is anything but impulsive or irresponsible. He is a model of decorum, civility and discretion. His name has never been touched by scandal."

"He sounds like a complete bore." And nothing like the man she'd spent the night with.

"How fortunate it is for all of us that you are not the one marrying him."

"Tori should be loved and adored by her husband."

"I don't know what heathen ideas you picked up in the desert, nor do I care to know, but kindly do not taint Victoria with these ridiculous notions."

"Yes, only savages believe in love matches."

"Are you suggesting that your marriage to my father, a man thirty years your senior, was a love match?"

"That is different."

"How so? You married a title. Victoria is doing the same."

"I married my father's oldest friend to ease Papa's worries for my future as he lay dying." It had been a horrible time. Doctors could not pinpoint the cause but Leela suspected a broken heart. The stomach ailment that slowly drained the life out of Lord Brandon materialized less than a year after Mama succumbed to influenza.

As he lay dying, Papa had fretted over Leela's future. It would not be easy for a young woman of common foreign blood to marry well, even if she was the daughter of a marquess. "Papa worried that unsavory fortune hunters would take advantage of me. He pleaded with Douglas to give me the protection of his name."

"And you agreed. What a dutiful daughter you are," Edgar said. "How fortunate for you that Father happened to be an earl. Being a countess elevated you."

"My father was a marquess," she shot back.

"Ah, yes." He grimaced. "The Mad Marquess. Everyone thought Brandon was a bedlamite for wedding the granddaughter of a common foreign merchant. My sister is far cleverer than you. She will wed a young and vigorous duke, not a former rake who is ready to be put out to pasture."

Her initial reaction was to tell Edgar to go soak himself in a pile of excrement for a thousand years. Another of the colorfully apt insults she'd learned, this time from her Arab cousins in Al-Bireh. Naturally, they'd found it amusing to teach her all of the indecent words and sayings first, before she'd learned to converse in Arabic. "How can you speak of your father with such a lack of respect?"

Edgar pushed the wardrobe door open wider to inspect its contents. "My father had my respect until he brought you home to fill my mother's place. Imagine, making a girl of your . . . associations . . . the Countess of Devon. I was certain he'd lost his mind."

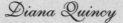

Leela rose and strode over to slam her wardrobe door shut. "Stay out of my things. And leave my chamber. This conversation is over."

"That is not for you to decide. This is my house. You are here at my forbearance."

"I am also here to put on a respectable display for your ducal guest," Leela said. "However, I am seconds away from walking out that door in these trousers for all of your guests to see, particularly your exalted duke."

Alarm lit his eyes. "You wouldn't dare."

"Do you really care to test me?" She started for the door.

"Fine," he snapped, rushing to block her exit. "Just remember to dress and comport yourself in a respectable manner. The guests depart on Monday. Surely, you can keep up appearances for three days."

She shrugged. "We shall see. Just stay out of my way." She practically pushed him out the door. "Otherwise, there's no telling what I might be tempted to do."

# *Chapter Seven*

*M*ake certain you give him a good brushing down," Hunt instructed one of Devon's grooms as he dismounted. Perspiration trickled down his spine after a vigorous early morning run. The air was moist against his skin, the morning dew had yet to burn off. "I worked him hard today."

"You did indeed." Griff eased slowly off his mount, taking care not to jar his left shoulder. "I certainly couldn't keep up. It's as if the hounds of hell were after you."

Hunt might choose hellhounds. No matter how fast or far he'd ridden, he couldn't outrun reality. Leela was the Countess of Devon.

Of all of the women in England, he'd bedded Lady Victoria's stepmama. He had the devil's own luck. And to make matters worse, he couldn't get Leela out of his mind. As hard as he tried to eviscerate all memories of her, images of their extraordinary night together kept infiltrating his consciousness. Running his tongue along the sweet-salty taste of her gleaming skin. Her *mons* gloriously bare and open to his gaze.

Glistening for him. Hunt wasn't promiscuous, but he had swived a decent number of women over the years. None of those experiences had been as profoundly carnal, nor as intimate, as making love with Leela.

"What's got you in such a state?" Griff's voice cut into his thoughts once they were out of earshot of the stable. "If I were to guess, I'd say it involves a certain mysterious widow that you've been unable to run to ground."

"Wrong," he snapped. If only Leela's identity had remained a mystery. "Please keep your conjectures to yourself."

"And you're irritable as well." Griff's sardonic tone grated on Hunt. "It's almost as though you are frustrated."

"Stop prattling on. You're giving me a megrim."

"Wait." Griff's cool gaze sharpened. "I'm wrong about what? About you finding your mysterious enchantress?"

"Yes, and it was all a mistake." Hunt cut a path toward the side garden. "I'd be obliged if you did not mention her again."

"Ouch. Sounds like the subject is a sore one. Where are you going?" Griff gestured toward the main entrance. "Breakfast is this way. Most of the guests will have likely already gathered."

"I've much work to do. Devon has been kind enough to allow Foster and me to set up in his library."

"Is that why you've been noticeably absent for the past three days?" Griff asked. "Why the devil did you bring your secretary with you?"

"Foster always accompanies me when I travel for more than a day or two." Their boots crunched along the gravel path lined with rich blue flowers mixed with red-and-gold autumn-hued leaves. The flowers were so cloyingly cheerful that Hunt had to resist the urge to stomp the ebullience right out of them. "Running a duchy as vast and diversified as Huntington requires my constant attention and oversight."

Irritation flashed in Griff's face. "You should have considered that before dragging me along to this house party."

"I didn't force you to come."

"You are the sole reason I accepted Devon's invitation. I certainly didn't expect you to vanish on me. Of all people, you know I don't relish spending time with relative strangers."

"No one here thinks you killed your parents. Maybe you should stop spending your life hiding out and acting as if you *are* guilty."

Griff's jaw tightened. Hunt immediately regretted his careless words. By silent mutual agreement, they never discussed the tragedy. Even though the murder of Griff's parents hung over their surviving son like Atlas bearing the burden of the world.

Hunt softened his tone. "Nobody listens to those old rumors anymore."

"You mean the ones suggesting that I did away with my own parents? I *was* the only other person there that night. Is it truly possible that I *slept* through my parents' killings?" Bitterness laced Griff's words. "Why *would* the killers spare the fifteen-year-old heir?"

Hunt winced, recalling those dark days at Harrow after the murders. When students whispered that Griff had indeed had the most to gain from his parents' gruesome demise. Sure, a few trinkets were stolen, but the boy inherited his father's title and considerable fortune.

As boys, it was a shared burden of society's unkind scrutiny that initially bonded Hunt and Griff. It was as if the ton held its collective breath waiting for each man's baser nature to emerge.

"My apologies," Hunt said. "I spoke out of turn. I'm not myself."

"Perhaps you should take a break from your duties." Griff's tone lightened. "As they say, 'All work and no play makes Hunt a dull boy.'"

Hunt scoffed. "My late brother adhered to that philosophy, and we both know where that got him."

Besides, Hunt couldn't relax. Everything in his normally ordered world was suddenly off-kilter. For the first time in his life, he found himself in an undesirable situation that couldn't be sorted out by wielding his considerable wealth, influence or carefully honed diplomatic skills.

Crying off from a betrothal to Lady Victoria—official or not—at this late juncture would be a catastrophe. As a duke—and a man—he would emerge relatively unscathed, but the consequences would be dire for Lady Victoria. Being jilted would do immeasurable damage to the young lady's reputation and future marital prospects. None of which she deserved.

Lady Victoria was blameless. As was Leela. The same could not be said for him. As a gentleman who was practically betrothed, Hunt should have been the one to behave more honorably.

"Think of how disappointed Devon's guests are that the ever-reclusive Duke of Huntington has closeted himself away yet again," Griff remarked.

Hunt kicked some pebbles along the path. "You are the recluse. Not me. I simply don't enjoy society functions."

"This isn't just any house party. It's practically being given in your honor."

"I've been at supper." It was torture, the pretense akin to being stretched on the rack. It took everything in Hunt to act as if his world hadn't contorted into something he no longer recognized. He felt like a fake, a fraud. He might as well be Keane treading the boards at Drury Lane.

Pity he couldn't just vanish as Leela had done. She'd stayed out of sight since their unfortunate encounter on the terrace. Devon and Lady Victoria both claimed she was ill. But Hunt knew better.

"It is almost as though you are hiding out," Griff observed.

"Whatever would I be hiding from?" Hunt forced a bland tone.

"That's an excellent question." Griff peeled away from Hunt, heading toward the manor's front entrance. "While you play hide-and-seek, I'm off to my bedchamber."

"What about your breakfast?"

"You are not the only man here who prefers to take his meals in private."

Hunt rolled out his neck as he headed for the Venetian door leading directly into the library. For the first time in his life he felt adrift. He'd stepped outside of the precise parameters he'd built around his life. A man walked the line, made sound decisions, or risked losing his way and ending up dead at the bottom of a lake like his brother. With Leela, Hunt had deviated from his self-imposed rules of conduct only to find he had no idea how to repair the damage he'd done.

A flash of blue silk through the open library door caught his attention. Lady Victoria. He grimaced, chagrined that he'd avoided the lady, when he should be taking this opportunity to become better acquainted with her.

Shadow partially obscured her face. Devon's library was a dark space lined with stepped walnut bookcases. Hundreds of books, bound in morocco and tooled in gold, filled the shelves. Limited light streamed through the Venetian windows flanking the door. Hunt paused there to observe his future bride.

She chatted animatedly with the normally taciturn Foster, whose flushed pockmarked face was alight with interest. They spoke across the library table at the center of the room that Hunt had commandeered to serve as his desk. Made of a walnut wood that matched the shelves, the table contained drawers, cupboards and kneeholes to accommodate Hunt's long legs.

"Remember the author's description of picnicking

in the orchards under the fig trees? And the beautiful fruit gardens laden with oranges and lemons and olives?" she asked.

"And the pomegranate trees with clusters of scarlet flowers," he added. "The author wrote so vividly that I could well envision the abundant cultivated gardens."

"Indeed," she agreed. "I felt as if I could almost taste the figs."

"I always imagined the Levant as one big desert with camels roaming freely," Foster remarked, "which makes me feel quite foolish now."

"That is what I adore about reading. You can learn so much about the world."

"That is very true."

Hunt had never seen this side of Lady Victoria. This cheerful engaging person was miles away from the young lady who mostly blushed, stuttered and stared at the ground whenever Hunt came within twenty feet of her.

"It would be most enchanting to see the ancient city of Petra in person," Lady Victoria said.

"Ah, 'tis but a dream for a man of my limited means. I have no hope of ever making such a journey." Foster gave a rueful grin. "I shall have to content myself with looking at the sketches in the book."

As Hunt's eyes adjusted to the reduced lighting, he registered how Lady Victoria's expression fell at the reminder of Foster's reduced circumstances. But the secretary quickly continued in a bright voice. "Thank you for the loan. I cannot remember the last time I enjoyed a travel memoir quite so much."

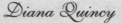

"You are most welcome. I understand the second volume will be published soon." She leaned forward, propping her elbows on the library table's flat broad surface. "I would be happy to loan that to you as well, once I have finished reading it. We could discuss our impressions afterward."

"I would like that," Foster said. "That is very kind of you."

And generous as well. Books were expensive. For someone like Foster, a workingman on a limited income, they were a luxury he could ill afford.

"Good morning," Hunt called out, focusing primarily on the young lady. "You are up early."

Lady Victoria immediately straightened. "Good morning, Your Grace." Her face shuttered when she registered his presence. Hunt watched her reserve click politely, but firmly, into place. "I make a habit of rising early to . . . erm . . . ride."

She smoothed the front bodice of her riding costume, a nervous gesture that drew his attention to a trim form that gave every appearance of curving in all of the desirable places. But her proximity had zero physical effect on him. Unlike Leela. A mere look from the woman had brought him to a point more than once during their short time together at the Black Swan.

Mortified by the direction of his thoughts, Hunt forced himself to say, "Lady Victoria, perhaps you would do me the honor of allowing me to escort you on your morning ride tomorrow."

Surprise flickered across her face. "I should . . . like that"—she blushed furiously—"very . . . much."

"Excellent." A sharp pain spasmed in his chest. God, how had he not seen how young she was before now? "I shall look forward to it."

The moment stretched. An awkward silence lingered among the three of them—Foster maintaining a re-spectful silence, Lady Victoria staring down at her feet and Hunt wondering if he was having a heart attack.

The secretary cleared his throat. "Excuse me, Your Grace, my lady, but I must return to work." He set a book on the library table. "Thank you again for shar-ing this with me."

Hunt recognized the title, *Travels in Arabia*, the in-triguing travelogue he'd recently read.

"It was my pleasure." She smiled brightly, finding her tongue again while reaching for the book. "I am so pleased . . . you enjoyed it." Her smile showcased plush lips and straight teeth so white they put new-fallen snow to shame. Yet the sight stirred nothing in him.

"When did you have time to read a book?" Hunt asked his secretary. The man retreated behind a small oak desk in the corner by the door that had been brought in for him at Hunt's request.

"Lady Victoria was kind enough to loan it to me when I first arrived, Your Grace. I was so engrossed that I read it in two days."

Hunt nodded. "I must admit that I found it riveting."

Lady Victoria's blue eyes rounded. "You . . . you . . . have read . . . *Travels in Arabia*?"

"I have." Hunt forced warmth into his voice, hoping to set her at ease. "I am also looking forward to the next volume."

Interest filled her gaze. "I did . . . not realize," she stammered, "that you enjoy reading . . . for pleasure." All of her easy amiability of just a few minutes ago, from before Hunt joined them in the library, had vanished.

"I do enjoy reading," he said encouragingly, "but you are correct that work keeps me from enjoying as many books as I might like." He saw the hope in her eyes that here, at last, might be something they had in common.

"I shall . . . have to recommend . . . this book . . . erm . . . *Travels in Arabia* . . . I mean to say . . . to Lady Devon." Lady Victoria's cheeks were as colorful as the autumn flowers he'd resisted stomping in the garden. Pallor everywhere but for those hot spots. "She has just . . . returned from traveling in the . . . region."

Hunt jumped at the opening. "I trust the countess is well?" He felt an urgent need to speak with Leela, to settle this indelicate matter between them, to fix it so that the two of them could manage to be in the same room without Leela casting her accounts.

"Delilah is . . . better . . . much improved," the girl responded haltingly. He noted she pronounced it *Daleela*. "So much so, in fact, that my stepmama . . . has promised to . . . join us at the Venetian breakfast party . . . this afternoon."

To hear Lady Victoria refer to Leela as *stepmama* provoked a visceral reaction in Hunt, He felt even more wretched. "Breakfast party?"

"Surely you recall . . . not that I am suggesting . . .

erm . . . that you are forgetful . . . I know you are quite busy—"

Hunt tamped down his irritation and forced a gentle tone. "Recall what?" He wished she would just come out with it. Attempting to have even the most basic conversation with the girl proved excruciating. Surely he wasn't so terrifying that Lady Victoria couldn't bear to look him in the eye.

And then he recalled that she was eighteen, a full dozen years younger than him. Perhaps this was how all eighteen-year-olds behaved? The unbidden memory of how easily the conversation, and everything else, had flowed between him and Leela at the Black Swan assailed him. Making him even more miserable, ornery and guilt-ridden.

"Lord Devon is hosting . . . the entertainment." Lady Victoria finally managed to string the words together. "The neighbors and local gentry . . . have been invited."

"Yes, of course." He'd been so preoccupied with Leela that he'd forgotten about the Venetian breakfast, an afternoon party that would last for hours, going well into the night.

"It is fortunate the weather . . . is so fine." She tilted her dainty chin upward to gaze out the window. Bathed in the soft morning light, her profile was a study in perfection—with a lovely nose and high cheekbones. Yet any instinctual male attraction on his part remained absent. He might as well be a eunuch. "They've already . . . begun to set up the . . . erm . . . tents on the lawn."

She looked over at Foster, who was seated at his desk writing. "I hope you will join us, Mr. Foster." Again, Hunt noted how easily words came to Lady Victoria when she spoke to anyone who wasn't him.

"Thank you, my lady. But I do not think that would be appropriate."

"It's fine," Hunt interjected. Servants were not normally included on such occasions but as the duke's secretary, Foster was not exactly a servant. He was actually of somewhat decent birth, very distantly related to a baron. "You may attend."

"I wouldn't know anyone there, Your Grace."

"I shall ask Devon's steward to introduce you around," Lady Victoria interjected with a warm smile. As before, she didn't stutter when speaking with Foster.

Hunt realized something else that made him feel even worse. If that were possible. Lady Victoria was truly kind. Despite her own obvious discomfort in Hunt's presence, she managed to be generous in her dealings with Foster, a plain-faced man far beneath her in society's eyes, when she had absolutely nothing to gain from it. It spoke well of the young woman that she remained gracious to her inferiors even as she prepared for her future role as a duchess.

A rush of warmth prompted Hunt to do what was expected of a gentleman courting a young lady. "I hope you will save a dance for me, my lady."

"Oh! Of . . . course." She blushed and cast her eyes downward. "I shall be . . . pleased . . . errr . . . very pleased indeed . . . yes."

# Chapter Eight

"What a striking couple!" Aunt Helene admired Tori and Elliot as they glided across the dance floor. "They truly match. They're even wearing similar colors."

Leela sat beside Douglas's spinster aunt, among the matrons perched on stuffed furniture the servants had dragged out to the lawn for the breakfast party. The bright notes of the violin wafted over her as Leela watched the pair dip and swirl among other couples on the wide wooden platform set out on the lawn for dancing. They moved in step to the lively country dance medley performed by the five-piece orchestra set up on the lawn.

"The duke moves with such grace," gushed Mrs. Paget, a neighbor whose estate bordered Devon's. She was a small round woman in her forties attired in swathes of bright yellow flounces that threatened to swallow her up.

Leela's heart beat hard against her ribs. Elliot stood tall, his bearing proud in a muted Mazarine blue tail-coat, tan waistcoat and black pantaloons tucked into gleaming boots. The sun's shadows cut across a strong nose, sharply angled cheeks and an inscrutable expression. Uncommonly graceful for a man of his size, the duke's long, solid legs moved through the steps with skill and ease.

He danced the way he'd made love to her at the Black Swan. Bright energy tempered by a certain languor, his warm body sliding against hers with effortless control. But here on the dance floor, his movements lacked the passion, and the possibility of complete sensual abandon, that had so taken Leela's breath away.

The remembered sensation of Elliot moving inside of her, the sublimity of being intimately joined with him, rolled through her body. Heat suffused her as if she'd been dropped into a pot of scalding water. Mortified, Leela forced her eyes away from the duke.

She focused on Tori instead. Attired in a periwinkle gown that enhanced her singular eyes, the girl was more than a match for the duke. This afternoon, she was a vision of gracious beauty, light on her feet, effortlessly keeping in step to music. Tori had always excelled at her dance lessons.

"It is like they are gold and silver, with her light hair and his dark golden curls," proclaimed Aunt Helene, a steely woman, tall and bony, with a helmet of white hair. "Such beautiful English coloring. I do hope Victoria protects her lovely pale complexion against the sun once they have finished dancing."

As if to punctuate her point, Aunt Helene propped the parasol shielding her higher above her head. Not that it was necessary. All of the ladies, including Leela and Aunt Helene, were wearing wide-rimmed bonnets.

Guests streamed across Lambert Hall's velvety green lawn. Well-dressed gentlemen escorted ladies wearing vibrant afternoon dresses in various shades of pink, peach, blue and yellow. Some visitors settled in cozy seats in the shade of the majestic oak trees, where they could take in the excellent view of splendid land-scaped gardens.

"Who is that imposing-looking gentleman with the scowl on his face?" asked Baroness Wallace, a woman of advanced years who was Aunt Helene's constant companion. An elaborate arrangement of feathers on her bonnet quivered when she spoke. "Do you see who I mean? The dark-haired gentleman over there by himself."

The stranger in question dressed severely in black and possessed a long, elegant face punctuated by a sharp nose. He was attractive, despite his harsh fea-tures. Standing in the shade of an old oak, the man had positioned himself quite apart from the other guests.

"*That* is Viscount Griffin," Aunt Helene said. "He is a particular friend of the duke's."

"Viscount Griffin?" Mrs. Paget stared at the man. "Not the young man they say killed his parents?"

"Nothing was ever proven," Aunt Helene responded in a high-handed manner. "As a friend of the Duke of Huntington, he is most welcome here."

Leela suppressed a snort. The older lady would hap-pily entertain the Ratcliffe Highway murderer—who'd killed seven people in Wapping a few years back—in order to land a duke for Tori.

"I believe Griffin has yet to wed," one of the other matrons remarked, "despite his title and fortune."

"Who would dare?" asked another guest. "Falling asleep in his presence could be detrimental to one's health." Some of the older ladies tittered.

Baroness Wallace's attention returned to the swirling couples. "I do believe this is Huntington and Lady Victoria's second dance. Do you suppose the duke will ask her for a third?"

"I would not be surprised," said Aunt Helene. "His Grace has all but declared his intentions."

Anxiety coiled in Leela's stomach. A third dance with Tori would be tantamount to Elliot publicly confirming his betrothal.

Mrs. Paget's eyes gleamed. "I have heard that perhaps the Earl of Devon will announce his sister's betrothal before everyone returns to London on Monday."

"Now, now." Aunt Helene looked very smug. "We will all just have to wait and see."

The old lady must know a betrothal was all but certain. Unless Tori changed her mind. Which might happen if the young woman spent enough time with Elliot. Would she decide the two of them did not suit? Leela's stomach dipped. What if they did suit?

Whatever happened, Leela wasn't going to allow idle gossip to force Tori into a loveless marriage. The girl had a good head on her shoulders. She just needed time to come to the correct decision.

*You're just jealous.* Was she? Leela had had a full day to ponder that possibility. But she dismissed it.

Obviously, she was physically attracted to Elliot. Their night at the Black Swan, and her body's involuntary reaction to the man just now, conclusively proved that. But there were no emotions involved. She wasn't even certain she liked the man. She'd probably forget all about him the moment she took another lover. Which she would do, if necessary.

Tori's happiness was her goal. If the young woman truly came to love the duke, and if Elliot could return her feelings, Leela would simply resume traveling the world. And when she was in London, she'd visit with Tori, just the two of them, when the duke was absent. But first, Tori must be given every opportunity to make the choice that was right for her.

"Surely all of this talk of a betrothal is premature," Leela said.

Aunt Helene glared at her. "No, it is not." She, like Edgar, had never quite forgiven her brother for making Leela his countess. "You have been away in foreign lands for so long. Naturally you would not be caught up on the happenings this Season."

"Foreign lands?" Mrs. Paget inquired. "Where did you go?"

"I spent most of my time in a town just a few miles outside of Jerusalem." Leela shifted in her chair. Calling attention to her background while in formal company made her uneasy. Mama had spent her married life avoiding all mention of her Arab roots, and would be appalled to hear her daughter speak of them now. "I was acquainting myself with my mother's side of the family."

Mrs. Paget's eyes widened. "Jerusalem? You traveled to the Levant?"

"Ah, yes," Baroness Wallace put in. "I do remember hearing that your mother was . . . erm . . . not English."

"She was not," Leela acknowledged. Papa had been eager to make his marchioness a British subject, which required a private act of parliament. But Mama absolutely refused to participate in the process. Lady Brandon felt pursuing the matter would embarrass Papa by calling attention to his marchioness's foreign blood. Besides, Mama was English in every way that mattered, from her dress and manners, to her perfect polished command of the King's English.

"Do your mother's people live in tents?" Mrs. Paget inquired.

"No, they live in houses made of stone." Leela was accustomed to these sorts of inquiries. They were polite on the surface, but the underlying intent was to point out that Leela was different. "Some are built around a shared central courtyard that all of the rooms open up to."

The Bedouins, pastoralists who never stayed in any one place for long, did live in tents made of goat's hair or sheep's wool. However, in towns and villages like Al-Bireh, where her uncles, aunts and cousins lived, people resided in solid structures. Mama's relations lived in houses made of limestone, but the less prosperous, such as her dragoman, constructed homes with bricks made of mud and straw.

"In many ways, the accommodations are not terribly unlike what we are used to here, although they are certainly not as grand as Lambert Hall," Leela added.

"Naturally." Aunt Helene made a skeptical sound. "I am sure *your* people live in homes that are nothing like ours."

Leela's cheeks warmed. She ignored the older lady's jab. She'd heard it all before. The constant reminders that she didn't belong, even if her father had been a marquess. She might hold the title of countess, but Leela's merchant connections and warm skin tone guaranteed she'd never completely blend in.

She returned to the subject weighing on her mind. "I do hope Lady Victoria will take her time and not be rushed into an unconsidered decision."

The other women gaped at her as if she'd suddenly grown two heads. Baroness Wallace blinked. "Perhaps Lady Devon is unaware that the Duke of Huntington is *the* catch of the Season. He can have any girl he desires. It would be the honor of Lady Victoria's life to be singled out by His Grace."

Leela lifted her chin. "I am inclined to think my stepdaughter is the prize of the Season and any gentleman would be most fortunate to be accepted by her."

"How kind of you to say." Aunt Helene's icy words could freeze the Jordan River. "But now that Lady Victoria's dear papa has met his demise, her *blood* family will see to the girl's best interests."

Biting back a retort, Leela returned her attention to the dancing couples only to discover the duke had quitted the dance floor. Tori had a new partner, a slender fellow who was only slightly taller than the girl. He moved awkwardly, a stark contrast to the assured grace of Tori's previous partner.

"Who is that dancing with Lady Victoria?" she inquired.

"He's a nobody," Aunt Helene answered irritably. "One of the duke's employees. His secretary, I believe. Now that Victoria is likely to become a duchess, she really must be more selective in her associations."

Leela had had enough of Aunt Helene. "Excuse me. I'm feeling rather parched. I shall go and get some lemonade." She wandered away, relieved to escape Aunt Helene and her cronies. She treaded over thick carpets the servants had rolled out to keep the ladies' hems and shoes clean.

The refreshments were laid out in a white tent set up for the occasion. Long tables covered by white cloths offered an abundant feast, silver platters piled with breads, biscuits, cakes, sandwiches and pyramids of stacked fruit including peaches and apricots. Leela bypassed the coffee, tea and claret. She considered indulging in an ice. Deciding against the icy treat, she reached to pour herself a glass of lemonade.

"Allow me."

Leela immediately recognized the deep masculine voice. Chills sprinkled down her back as Elliot came up from behind her and reached for the carafe to pour her drink. She had a fleeting sense of body heat and the remembered scent of warm male skin before he took care to put distance between them. "I can manage," she said stiffly.

"I am sure you can. After all, I have seen how well you handle a knife." He held the lemonade out to her, taking great care to ensure that their fingers did not touch. His serious gaze met hers. "We cannot avoid each other forever, Leela."

She tried to breathe through the sensation that wild horses were stampeding on her heart. "Perhaps not. But we can, and must, maintain our distance from each other."

Up close, the navy-gray of his tailcoat brought out the deep blue in his eyes. It was her first good look at the man since she'd discovered his true identity. All at once he felt both familiar and like a stranger. The same, yet entirely different.

At the inn, he'd worn an easy smile, carelessly tousled hair and time-worn clothing. The man before her was anything but relaxed. He stood impossibly upright. Everything about him spoke of containment— the slickly tamed hair, tight lips and formfitting expensive clothing exquisitely tailored to his masculine frame.

"And don't call me Leela," she added in a sharp whisper. "What if someone hears you? You must take care to refer to me as Lady Devon."

"Lady Devon." He spoke her name with quiet gentleness. "I accept all blame for what has occurred."

"As if that makes any difference," she said softly, stealing a glance at the two footmen attending to the refreshments. She paused, waiting until they filled a tray with glasses of lemonade. The two servants departed with the drinks, leaving Leela and Huntington alone in the tent. "Our behavior was abominable."

"We didn't know. Otherwise . . ."

"You were on your way to visit the woman you hope

to marry." Regret panged through her. "If only you'd remained true to Victoria."

He reddened. "I was not yet betrothed. I am still not."

"It is my fault as much as yours."

"I understand why you might be feeling guilty about what happened between us—"

"Is that so? Why? Because I am a woman? A strumpet?"

"Certainly not." His eyes were warm, the words low and intimate. "I could never think of you in that way."

An answering heat flooded her body before quickly giving way to panic. She could not allow him to summon these sensations in her. There could be nothing between her and Elliot. No softness, no murmured conversations or stolen glances. Any private words, understandings or gestures were a betrayal of Tori.

"Well, that is a relief." She hardened her tone, resolved to drive a necessary wedge between them. "After all, I am not the one who behaved dishonorably."

Surprise lit his eyes. "I understand you are overset."

"The truth is the truth."

"If a man insulted me so, he would find himself facing the business end of a pistol at dawn."

She forced the words out. "That's certainly an effective way to make sure you don't have to take responsibility."

His face clouded. She'd provoked him. Good.

"I am not a married man. I am not even officially betrothed," he hissed in a low voice. "It is perfectly acceptable for a gentleman to take a woman to bed under those circumstances. Do not blame me if you are having misgivings about your part in this. As I recall, you were no innocent miss that evening."

She gasped. "Why you—" His words hurt her to her core, enveloping her like a giant wave throwing her off her feet and knocking the words out of her. She understood all too well what he left unsaid. That his behavior was perfectly acceptable for a man, while Leela had played the part of a lightskirt. Were those his true feelings?

"There you are!" Tori's delighted voice floated between them. "Delilah, I see you've found the duke."

Leela struggled to keep her voice even. "I certainly have."

Tori's gaze bounced from Leela to the duke and back again. "I do . . . hope . . . you are becoming better acquainted."

"Indeed." Elliot's cool eyes were on Leela. "I am beginning to know your dear stepmama so much better."

"Are you well, Leela?" Tori asked. "You are flushed. I do hope you are not with fever again."

She avoided Elliot's gaze. "Actually, I do feel a bit nauseous."

"Oh no!" Tori exclaimed. "I had so hoped you were feeling better. Was it something you ate?"

Leela nodded. "I have consumed something terribly foul."

"Have you now?" There was an edge to Elliot's voice.

"Indeed." She smiled, closemouthed and insincere. "I cannot tell you how much I regret it. There are times something looks particularly appealing, but when you indulge you realize it is not at all what you expected."

He returned a chilly smile. "I know that feeling of regret and distaste very, very well."

Tori's perplexed gaze skittered from the duke to Leela. "Perhaps you should lie down for a bit."

There was nothing Leela wanted more than to escape. But there was Edgar to consider. She'd promised to attend the breakfast party. "I don't think I should, dear. Devon was quite insistent that I attend."

Tori took Leela's hand. "The party will go on for several hours yet. Surely Edgar won't mind if you return to your bedchamber to rest for a half hour or so. He won't even know you're missing."

Leela squeezed the younger woman's hand, grateful for the opportunity to escape. "You are right. I shall go and rest." She forced a disdainful look at Elliot. "Hopefully, the duke won't ask after me and call attention to my absence as he has done previously."

"I do see now how grave a mistake I have made." He gave a stilted bow. "You may rest assured, Lady Devon"—he pointedly emphasized her formal title—"that I most certainly will not ask after you."

"That is kind of you . . . Your Grace," Tori stammered. "If you will . . . excuse us, I shall escort Leela . . . inside."

Leela linked arms with Tori as they left Elliot in the tent staring after them.

"Well," Tori asked once they were away from the duke, "what do you think?"

A knot twisted hard in Leela's chest. She'd deliberately acted quarrelsome and unreasonable. Now surely Elliot would turn his focus to Tori. "Oh, I don't know. I have only just met the man. Besides, it is *your* opinion that matters."

"I have been thinking about what you have said about fate and marrying your true love."

Leela brightened. "Have you?"

"Perhaps Huntington is not my fated mate."

Leela instantly felt lighter. It was like a thousand weightless angels waltzed joyfully inside of her. "Truly?"

"It would be pleasant to have a husband who I enjoy talking to. A gentleman of quality who shares my interests."

The angels inside of Leela's chest pirouetted in unison. "Absolutely."

"But I am not entirely certain."

The dancing halted. "You're not?"

"No, that is why you must spend more time in the duke's presence."

"*Me?* Spend more time in that man's company?" She tried to keep the surprise out of her voice. "Why would I do that?"

"Who better than you to help me decide whether he is the man for me?"

She'd rather have five teeth pulled all at once. "Oh, darling, I cannot make that decision for you."

"You are my dearest friend and the big sister I never had. If I cannot depend upon you to help me with the most important choice I will make in my lifetime, who can I rely on?"

Leela's lungs deflated. "Well, if you have need of me, how can I refuse?"

"Exactly," Tori said happily.

# Chapter Nine

"Why are we up so early?"

Leela struggled to keep up with Tori as they walked across Lambert Hall's wide verdant landscape. She yawned, adjusting her bonnet. After the previous day's encounter with the duke, sleep had eluded Leela yet again. To make matters worse, Tori had dragged her out of bed just before eight o'clock that morning.

"We are going golfing," Tori announced.

"When you say *we*—" she was almost afraid to ask "—who exactly are you referring to?"

"You, me and the Duke of Huntington," Tori chirped, a smile wreathing her face.

Leela resisted a groan. How had she managed to corner herself into spending large amounts of time in the duke's company? At least the house party was almost over. Just two more days. Surely she could last that long. "Who else is going to be there?"

"It's just the three of us. Oh, and perhaps Mr. Foster. He carries His Grace's clubs."

"Is there a reason we have to do this at such an ungodly hour?" Leela lifted her skirts, annoyed to find her hem damp from the morning dew. "And why in the world are we playing golf?"

"Because, Miss Grumpy, Devon learned that His Grace is a golf enthusiast. So he arranged everything."

Leela resisted the urge to roll her eyes. God knows Edgar would happily race naked around Newcastle's horse tracks if it meant securing a ducal alliance for the family. "Doesn't golf require certain essentials? Such as holes in the ground to drop the balls into?"

"Yes, Devon saw to everything."

Leela examined the girl's sparkling eyes, rosy cheeks and easy smile. "Why are you so cheerful this early in the morning?"

Usually Tori preferred to stay in bed reading until it was time for breakfast, which they would very inconveniently miss this morning since they had to play golf with Elliot at this ridiculous hour.

A thought occurred to Leela as Tori's smile deepened. What if she'd misjudged the depth of Tori's feelings for the duke? The girl actually seemed eager for the outing. "Are you growing more attached to His Grace?"

"Oh no," Tori assured her. "I still think he's fearsome."

"Then why all the smiles?"

She looped her arm through Leela's. "Because you're here. Which means I do not have to be alone with him." They rounded a copse of trees, which opened up to a vast expanse of flat wide lawn punctuated with gentle rolling hills.

"Wait a moment." Leela halted. Withdrawing her

arm from Tori's, she stared at the wide swath of short-cut grass stretched out before them. "Surely, this isn't where the meadow used to be? The one with the beautiful wildflowers?"

Tori adjusted her kid leather gloves. "It does look completely different with the grass cut down, doesn't it."

Leela stared in disbelief. "Surely it cannot be."

This had once been one of her favorite places at Lambert Hall, and one of the views she missed most during her travels. The flora was nothing short of breathtaking. Vibrant yellow rattles used to be scattered through the fields as if someone had casually tossed them there. The yellow blooms intermixed with white oxeye daisies and untamed purple gnatweed made for a spectacular view. Then there were the orchids. Her favorites. Just looking at the green-winged orchids in shades of lilac-pink made her happy. But now—

"Yes, silly, it's the same place," Tori said impatiently. "I told you that Edgar took care of everything. He had five holes specially dug so that the duke could indulge in his favorite pastime during his visit. The workers spent weeks cutting the grass down with scythes."

Leela couldn't believe her eyes. Her beautiful meadow was gone. It was like someone painting over a Rembrandt for no good reason. "But how . . . when?"

"Several weeks ago. When the duke first expressed an interest in courting me. Devon immediately started planning the house party. He wants the duke to enjoy his stay."

All of those beautiful flowers and grasses destroyed.

For what? Just so Elliot could hit useless little balls into holes?

"Good morning, ladies." Looking fit and refreshed, Elliot approached carrying a wooden club in his hand. He wore long trousers and a tweed morning coat tailored to his athletic form. An artfully wrought cravat adorned his neck. His secretary, the young man who'd danced with Tori at the breakfast, trailed behind, carrying the rest of the duke's clubs.

Elliot's forehead wrinkled when he spotted Leela. "Lady Devon, what a pleasant surprise," he said smoothly. "Lady Victoria. I do hope I haven't brought you two out too early."

"Not at all." Tori dipped a curtsy. "Good morning, Your Grace."

Leela put her chin up. "Good morning, Duke." She deliberately spit out the word *duke* the way one might utter an expletive. The more rancor she could manufacture between her and Elliot, the better for all concerned.

He narrowed his eyes. She registered the glint of irritation in them. *Good.*

"Are you . . . enjoying the course, Your Grace?" Tori stammered through her question.

"Yes, most certainly. It is delightful." His reassuring words seemed calibrated to put the young lady at ease. "The easy hills and wide expanses make this parkland a pleasure to play on."

"That's just great," Leela mumbled loud enough to be heard.

"I beg your pardon, Lady Devon?" His polite words held a sharp edge.

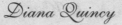

"I said that is just great," she responded in a perfectly polite manner.

He considered her momentarily, before turning his attention to Tori. "Are you ready to attempt your hand at golf?"

"I am afraid Lady Devon . . . and I . . . know . . . very little about golf," Tori managed to say.

"Feel free to go on without us," Leela put in. "We wouldn't want to slow you down."

"Lady Devon is so thoughtful. But you needn't worry about me." Elliot tossed a horsehide-wrapped golf ball into the air. "Foster and I were up quite early. We've already played ten holes."

"Oh dear." Red suffused Tori's face. "I thought . . . we were . . . to meet at half-eight."

"We were," he reassured her. "Ladies do not play the entire course. I thought we would start with some putting."

"Why don't ladies play the entire course?" Leela asked.

"It just isn't done." He shrugged. "I hadn't given it much thought as to why. Primarily, I suppose, because trying to swing the club would be difficult, given your clothing restrictions."

Leela couldn't argue with that. Confining clothes were the reason she donned *shirwal* under her gown when she'd traveled on horseback. The baggy trousers, which tied at the waist with a cord and tapered at the ankle, allowed her to ride without exposing her legs.

"Who would like to go first?" he inquired.

Leela gently nudged Tori forward. "Lady Victoria should."

Tori advanced, her chin tucked in a shy manner. "I shall try my best."

"That is all I can ask." He offered his arm to lead her to the first hole. Leela reluctantly followed with Foster trailing.

"Ah, here we are." Elliot stopped a few feet away from a gentle hill near some woods. He held a hand out behind him. "The putter, Foster."

The secretary stepped forward to take the existing hand-carved club from the duke and replace it with another, this one with a low flat face. Curious, Leela inched forward to take a look at the four-inch hole that had been cut into the ground.

"It isn't very deep," she observed.

"No, just about four inches down." Turning, he walked about eight steps from the hole and halted. He directed Tori to join him, offering instructions on how to hit the ball into the hole.

"To control the ball, you want to roll it more than hit it." He demonstrated as he spoke, his long arms expertly arranged on the club. The jacket he wore emphasized the breadth of his shoulders, his trousers the length of strong legs. "Lean forward, like so."

He gently hit the ball with the face of the putter. "Once you make the stroke, don't lift the head of the club. Keep it low." Even the ball seemed to be unable to resist the duke's will. It dutifully rolled straight into the hole.

Tori nervously took the club. Elliot was patient with her, advising her on her stance. Her first time, she completely missed the ball. But then she improved. Sometimes hitting the ball too short. But before long she was successfully hitting the ball in the hole in three strokes.

Leela couldn't help noting Elliot's patient and encouraging manner with Tori throughout the lesson. He was gentle with her and kind, too. Perhaps he was growing fond of the girl.

To Leela's dismay, jealousy flared in her belly. She ignored the unpleasant sensation. Tamped it down. Obviously she wasn't thinking clearly. There was no other explanation. Unless she was just a terrible, terrible person. Only a bad person would feel an attraction for her stepdaughter's suitor. It was disgusting. Despicable.

"Can I try . . . hitting it very hard . . . just this once?" Tori asked the duke.

He smiled at her enthusiasm. "As you wish."

He showed her how to swing the club. Even though her restrictive gown prohibited Tori from executing the full range of motion required for a proper hit, she still managed to give the ball a good whack. It sailed about five feet off the ground before bounce-hopping across the lawn, momentum propelling the ball into the woods.

"Oh no!" Tori covered her mouth. "I've made a hash of it."

"Not at all," Elliot said. "Foster will retrieve the ball."

The secretary was already trotting toward the woods before the duke finished the sentence.

"Our woods can be confounding." Tori appeared distressed. "He might not see the immense hole near the big oak. It's a bit of a drop. He could fall in. He might get lost."

"That particular wood is easy to get lost in," Leela told the duke. She'd learned that firsthand when, shortly after her marriage, she'd decided to explore her new home. When she hadn't turned up for lunch, Douglas sent everyone in the household, except Aunt Helene, to look for her. Unfortunately, Edgar was the one to find her in the woods. He'd taunted her mercilessly, making frightening animal sounds, before revealing himself and leading her home.

"I shall go and make certain Mr. Foster doesn't get lost." Tori handed the club to Elliot.

Leela watched Tori hurry toward the trees. It struck her that the girl hadn't stammered during her last two exchanges with the duke.

Elliot frowned after her. "Surely it isn't necessary for Lady Victoria to lead Foster out. As a gentleman, I should be the one to do it if a rescue is required."

"Think of how embarrassing it will be if you get lost and Victoria has to save you as well."

"That's absurd. Surely they can't be that bad."

Leela merely shrugged.

Elliot searched her face. "Have you gotten lost in those woods before?"

"What does that have to do with anything?"

His eyes twinkled. "You have, haven't you?"

"Why do you find that so amusing?"

"Because you've traveled the world on your own but somehow you managed to get lost on your own estate."

"I was seventeen years old. Just a girl. And I got a bit turned around is all."

He surveyed the wood. There was no sign of either Tori or Mr. Foster. He held up the putter. "Would you like to give it a try while we wait?"

Leela wanted to say no. The less contact and engagement she had with the man the better. But curiosity triumphed over her caution.

He handed her the putter. "Now, stand with your legs slightly parted."

She adjusted her feet. "Like this?"

"Well, I cannot see your feet but I am sure it's fine." He bent over her showing her how to hold the club. "Hold the shaft like this." He adjusted her fingers. She fought the shiver that coursed through her at his touch. Even though she wore gloves. "Hold the shaft gently, with both hands," he murmured.

He smelled of exertion and male skin. The warmth of his body mingled with hers. She wanted to lay her head against his chest. To close her eyes and savor the sensation of being so close to him.

Unnerved, she smacked the ball, a jerky and inaccurate hit, and dropped the club before practically leaping away from him. "There—I tried it."

His expression dubious, he watched the ball putter only about two feet away. "That wasn't a very good hit. Would you like to try again?"

"No," Leela responded almost before he finished his question. She needed to stay as far away from the man as possible. "Golf really isn't that interesting to me."

"I see." He paused. "I was surprised to see you this morning. I expected Lady Victoria to come alone. With her lady's maid as a chaperone, of course."

"Believe me when I tell you it was not my idea to attend. Victoria seems to think I should become better acquainted with you to help her decide whether to accept your proposal."

His brows shot down, hooding over his gaze. "Is there a possibility that she might not consent to wed me?"

"Are you such a braggart that you assume all women will just fall at your feet at the snap of your fingers?"

His eyes twinkled. "Well, there was one woman, a very discriminating woman as it turns out, who recently told me that I am as beautiful as the moon."

Her heart skipped a beat. "Don't do that."

"Do what?"

"Talk like that," she hissed, her eyes darting to the wood to make certain they were still alone. "What happened at the inn is sordid enough without you constantly referencing it."

"Denying your feelings won't will them out of existence."

"Feelings?" Leela's hands tingled. "Who said anything about feelings?" A single carnal night together was one thing. The possibility of true tenderness between them was quite another. That would truly be a *fatheeha*.

"Let us be very clear with each other," she said.

"The strongest emotion I was overcome with that evening was loneliness. After two years of traveling, you made me feel less alone."

Elliot's serious gaze searched hers. "We both wish our situation were that simple, but it's not."

"It certainly is. Any man would have served the purpose you served that evening."

"It looks like we're just in time for breakfast!" Tori's breathless voice cut between them. She and Mr. Foster emerged from the woods red-faced and out of breath. "I'm famished."

"Darling, I do not think we'll make it back to the house in time for the morning meal," Leela said.

"We won't have to," Tori said. "It looks like breakfast . . . came to us."

The duke looked over Leela's shoulder. "Your timing is indeed perfect, Lady Victoria." He gestured to someone behind Leela. "Set up over there if you will."

She turned to find a team of servants rolling up with wheelbarrows full of everything needed for an alfresco meal. The dozen or so servants quickly set up a table, adding linens, silver and crystal. Breads, sweet buns, cheeses, fruits and jams followed.

"How wonderful!" Tori clapped her hands together. "Did you . . . arrange this, Your Grace?"

"Yes, I thought you might enjoy taking breakfast here on the green." His gaze moved to his secretary. "Did you get lost in the woods, Foster?"

The young man gave his master a sheepish look. "I hate to admit it, Your Grace, but it was a near thing. I am much obliged to her ladyship."

Tori giggled. "It is good that I went after him."

"Indeed." The duke looked at Foster. "You may return to the house."

"Yes, Your Grace." The young man went to gather the duke's clubs.

"I should go as well," Leela put in quickly. She would send Tori's lady's maid back to serve as chaperone. She needed to escape, to gain some control over herself.

"Oh no!" Tori protested. "You must join us for breakfast."

"The staff is here to serve you." Leela didn't look in Huntington's direction. "I'll send your lady's maid."

"Oh, please do say you'll stay," Tori implored. "Shouldn't she join us, Your Grace?"

"I think we have inconvenienced Lady Devon quite enough." He did not spare Leela another glance. He plucked a grape from the food-laden table. "And I, for one, will not complain about having the opportunity to spend some time with you, Lady Victoria."

Tori flushed and Leela registered the panic in her eyes. But this was one time that Leela could not come to the young woman's rescue.

"Enjoy your meal." As she strode across the cut fields where her precious wildflowers once grew, Leela vowed never to be alone with Huntington again. That is how she must always think of him, as the Duke of Huntington, and not as Elliot Townsend, the man she'd been intimate with at the Black Swan. The *hamar* still believed he and Leela had unfinished business between them. She wasn't interested in Huntington's feelings.

Nor her own. Neither of them could afford to become hampered by emotion of any kind.

At least he'd be gone soon. The house party ended the day after tomorrow. Once the guests departed, Devon, Aunt Helene and Victoria planned to stay at Lambert Hall for a fortnight before returning to London for the betrothal ball. Leela intended to remain with them.

As long as she stayed far from London, there'd be no chance encounters with Huntington. No intimate conversations or exploration of feelings. If ever a situation called for a stiff upper lip, this was it.

# Chapter Ten

"Perhaps we should discuss the marriage settlements once the rest of the guests have departed," the Earl of Devon said quietly to Hunt.

"I instructed my solicitor to draw the papers up before I departed London." Hunt sipped his port, his eyes on the salon entrance. "Upon our return to London, I shall make certain everything is in order. The papers will be delivered to you in Town."

Devon's face gleamed with satisfaction. "Excellent."

They were gathered in the salon for drinks before supper. It was a high-ceilinged chamber with damask silk walls of the palest green. Matching upholstered gilt-trimmed chairs and sofas lined the walls and flanked the immense carved white stone fireplace.

Hunt studied Leela's stepson. He didn't hold a strong opinion of Devon. The man was courteous, hospitable and maintained a decent reputation. His estate appeared to be thriving and his finances sound. In other words, there was no hint of scandal or impropriety, an important consideration when it came to aligning his name with that of another noble family.

The houseguests clustered in small groups around the salon, except for Foster, who stood off in a corner in an ill-fitting dinner jacket. Devon's aunt had pressed Hunt's secretary into service after Griff's sudden departure. The viscount had unexpectedly left for London that morning. Lady Helene needed to ensure that an even number of men and women sat to supper.

Hunt and Devon stood apart from the others by a wide bay window that looked out upon the extensive immaculate manicured gardens. Most everyone took care to arrive before the duke, in deference to his rank. However, Leela and Lady Victoria had yet to make an entrance.

He had not seen Leela since yesterday morning's golfing outing. Last night, Devon had arranged a card tournament for the men. They'd supped on their own, the footmen serving in the cards room during a break in the play.

He couldn't stop thinking about Leela. She was deliberately behaving in a contrary manner. He played her words over and over again in his head. She claimed the night at the Black Swan had meant nothing to her. That he'd served as a physical consolation to ease her loneliness. It would be easier if that were true. Hunt knew it was not.

He couldn't quite classify what they meant to each other, but he knew it didn't fit into any of the neat little categories of which he was so fond. He also knew he didn't deserve Leela's ire. He certainly hadn't forced himself on her.

The butler approached and murmured in Devon's ear before stepping away.

"They are ready to serve," Devon informed Hunt. "Unfortunately, my late father's wife has yet to appear."

Devon neglected to mention that his sister was also missing. As if on cue, the mahogany double doors opened, and Leela and Lady Victoria came through them.

As much as he wanted to look away from Leela, he could not. His stomach dropped. He recognized the sensation. It was the same irresistible pull he'd felt when he'd first laid eyes on her at the Black Swan. In desperation, Hunt had half convinced himself that the magnetism between them was an anomaly, a onetime sensation after a tumultuous evening.

But, as infuriating as Leela had been yesterday, and the day before that, Hunt still wanted her. Badly. His body yearned for her. It was like a force of nature he had no control over. Not only did his need of Leela remain as intact as ever, it perhaps even burned brighter now. What a disaster.

Her shimmering silk violet gown made her smooth bronze skin glow. Her eyes, large and dark, made him ache to discover the secrets locked away in those impenetrable depths. He wanted to know her, to cleave only unto her, as he had with no woman before her. And with a desperation that took his breath away. He'd never wanted anything so much.

"Ah, you are here." Devon went to Lady Victoria and proudly took both of her hands into his. "You look lovely, my dear."

Hunt followed, barely able to pull his eyes from Leela. "I agree," he said gallantly. "Lady Victoria is a vision this evening." She wore a white gown that showcased her slender neck and trim figure. However, next to Leela's ample womanly form, Lady Victoria looked like what she was—a young girl.

Leela looked everywhere but at Hunt. Unfortunately, courtesy required that he address her. "Lady Devon is also in excellent looks."

She pretended to look at him, but her gaze fixed on his brows rather than his eyes. "Your Grace is too kind."

They were saved from further conversation when Devon turned to call the assembled guests into dinner.

"Shall we?" As he had on the previous evenings, Devon offered his arm to Baroness Wallace.

Hunt paused. Protocol called for the host to escort the highest-ranked lady into supper. Yet Devon hadn't taken Leela in. That would mean that, as the Countess of Devon, she was acting as hostess. Hunt felt the blood drain from his face. As the gentleman of rank in the room, the duty fell to him to escort his hostess into dinner.

He stared momentarily at Leela. She raised her eyebrows in return, seeming unaware of, or at least unconcerned, with his dilemma. He braced himself. There was nothing to be done for it. He offered his arm. "Lady Devon."

Leela's eyes rounded. He saw her resist a natural inclination to step back, to put distance between them. She didn't move. Hunt felt like an arse with his elbow extended. Did she dare refuse him? A murmur rippled through the guests, making Hunt's blood run cold. Surely, she would not cause a scene.

Tales of the Countess of Devon refusing his escort would no doubt reach London. And the gossips would gleefully speculate about what the Duke of Huntington had done to deserve the public censure.

*He's like his brother after all*, they would say. Hunt had spent the last four years trying to undo the damage Phillip had done. He'd been a model of decorum, his behavior above reproach. He'd worked hard to pay off his brother's numerous debts and to refill the drained ducal coffers. All of that effort to show society that he wasn't his brother—nor any of the reprobate Townsend dukes who had come before him—would be all for naught if Leela publicly rebuffed him.

Somewhere in the sea of faces, Hunt met Lady Helene's shocked gaze. But then a light touch skimmed on his arm.

"Your Grace." Leela stood by his side, her steady gaze finally meeting his shaky one. She settled beringed fingers in the crook of his elbow. "Shall we?"

"Yes." Relief weakened his legs. "This way."

Guests fell into line behind them as they made their way. The dining room was a generous spacc, long and narrow, with pale lilac walls, flowing white plasterwork and ribband-back chairs in solid mahogany.

Hunt registered Devon's surprise as soon as he entered with Leela on his arm. The earl stood at one end of the lavishly set table. Lady Helene followed, escorted by Mr. Paget.

Hunt led Leela to the head of the table opposite Devon. He felt pressure on his arm. He looked askance at Leela. Her jaw was set, but she said nothing. He seated her in the hostess's chair, noting the high color on her cheeks. The other guests quickly took their seats except for Lady Helene, who surveyed the table with a perturbed expression on her face before finally electing to sit close to her great-nephew at the far end of the table.

Hunt reluctantly seated himself to Leela's right. His rank dictated that his place was at the hostess's side. It was going to be a trying evening. It did not help that both Devon and the old lady kept shooting furtive looks their way.

"What the devil are they looking at?" he inquired in a low tone.

"You," Leela answered under her breath. With a serene smile, she nodded as Mr. Paget took the seat to her left. "And me."

His heart thumped. "Why? Surely they don't suspect—"

"How are you, dear sir?" she inquired of Mr. Paget. "It has been quite a long time."

"Eh?" Paget said loudly.

"I trust you are in good health?"

"You will have to speak up, my lady." Paget gestured to his ear. "Infection. Last spring. Can't hear a thing in my right ear." Which was the ear closest to Leela.

"Oh." Her smile slipped. "I am sorry to hear that."

Paget smiled blankly and nodded, clearly having trouble making out her words, and turned to speak to the lady on his other side, where his good ear was.

Leela looked down the table as the guests took their seats. She motioned for Lady Victoria to join them at their end of the table. The girl started for them until she noticed Foster standing by looking completely lost. A kind expression on her face, Lady Victoria directed Foster to a seat at the middle of the table. She hesitated momentarily before seating herself beside the young man.

Leela practically groaned. "What is she doing? Surely she is not going to leave us alone."

If Hunt wasn't so irritated by Leela's desperate attempts to avoid speaking to him, he might actually be amused. "We are hardly alone," he said impatiently. "Why do Devon and his aunt keep staring at us?"

Footmen in burgundy-and-gold livery brought in the first course, fish and soup. Leela summoned one of the footmen with a slight movement of her hand and murmured in his ear.

Hunt's gaze caught on her hand. She wore rings on three of her tapered fingers, cut gold with intricate designs that sparkled when she gestured. Those fingers had touched him intimately. He closed his eyes, remembering the sensation of Leela stroking his prick. And of her fingers digging into his back as she climaxed. Then feathering across his chest as he held her, sweet and warm, in his arms. A shiver ran over the expanse of his skin.

"Wine for Mrs. Paget," Leela directed the footman. "However, Mr. Paget prefers port."

Hunt forced himself to focus. "How do you know that?"

"I was mistress here for some years," she said coolly, still avoiding looking directly at him. "Mr. and Mrs. Paget were frequent guests."

"How many years?" He hadn't asked her before. "How long were you married?"

"Seven years." She gave a footman standing by the sideboard a speaking glance. He immediately stepped forward to refresh some of the guests' drinks.

"It looks like you ran a tight ship."

"My mother taught me how to manage a noble household." She picked up her spoon and dipped it into the white cream soup before her. "I wanted Douglas and his guests to be comfortable."

"Would you care to inform me why Devon keeps staring at us?" Hunt resisted the urge to loosen his cravat. "And I can practically see the daggers in Lady Helene's eyes."

"It is because I am seated in the hostess's seat."

"And?"

"Really." She set down her spoon. "Must I spell it all out?"

"Apparently, yes, you must."

"Who did you seat in this chair when I was absent from supper?"

"I escorted Lady Helene into the dining room." He picked up his fork and cut into the turbot in his plate. "She acted as hostess."

"Exactly." She maintained a serene look, despite the fact that Baroness Wallace, the old aunt's particular friend, was frowning in their direction.

"I don't follow."

"Aunt Helene is Devon's hostess."

"Then why the devil didn't Devon escort you in?" he demanded to know. "You are the highest-ranked lady here."

She smoothed her napkin. "You have so much to learn."

He took a bite of fish. The white lobster sauce was particularly delicious. "Perhaps you should educate me."

"I doubt that's possible."

"Please do try." The woman was as vexing as she was irresistible. "If it is not too taxing on you."

"Very well." She released an annoyed breath. "After my late husband's first wife died, Aunt Helene served as hostess at Lambert Hall for many years. And then I arrived, a seventeen-year-old nobody—"

"The daughter of a marquess is hardly a nobody."

"My father was no ordinary nobleman. He rarely mixed in polite society and was deemed mad for marrying my mother, a woman of low associations."

He could not imagine anyone considering a woman as remarkable as Leela to be beneath their notice. "Go on."

"Lady Helene was not happy to find herself usurped by the daughter of the Mad Marquess and his foreign merchant wife. As soon as Douglas died, Edgar restored Helene to what they both saw as her rightful place as mistress of Lambert Hall."

"I say, what kind of soup is this?" Paget interrupted loudly.

As Leela turned to answer the older man, Hunt reached for his wine. Leela's use of the word *mad* had jogged his memory. He faintly recalled his father speaking about the infamous "Mad Marquess" who'd wed a foreign woman of low origins.

*He should have bedded her, not wedded her*, Father had said. *Some wenches are meant solely for amusement. You cannot make a duchess out of a shopgirl. Remember that, son. Remember your duty.*

Father didn't bother to add, "unlike your brother." He didn't need to. Even as a young boy, Hunt vowed never to be like Phillip.

There were two stillborn babes, both boys, in the decade between the births of the duke's heir and Hunt, his youngest son. Hunt's earliest childhood memories included his parents' unending arguments over Phillip's worsening debauchery. *Perhaps it cannot be helped*, his mother had said with tears in her eyes. *What if the Townsend curse is real and this generation is truly lost?*

Resolved not to wallow in unpleasant memories, Hunt pushed the past aside and reached for his wineglass. As he drank his gaze floated over to where Foster and Lady Victoria were quietly engaged in conversation.

"They're no doubt talking about books," Leela said.

"I beg your pardon?" He saw that he had finally regained Leela's attention. "Are you talking to me?"

"Who else would I be addressing?"

He shrugged. "How should I know? You seem awfully determined to speak to everyone but me."

She closed her eyes. It was possible he heard her counting under her breath. Her lids blinked open. "As I was saying, Victoria told me that your young Mr. Foster is an avid reader, much like herself."

"I caught them discussing that travel book I mentioned to you."

"Which book?" She regarded him with actual interest for the first time all evening. *"Travels in Arabia?"*

"That's the one." He finished off the last bite of his fish.

Leela paused. "And what did Victoria think of it?"

"She raved. As did Foster." Hunt didn't care that they were having one of those politely boring conversations he normally abhorred. At least Leela was acknowledging his presence. "Lady Victoria mentioned looking forward to the next volume, which is due next month."

"The month after next," she corrected.

"Is that so?" He looked at her. "I see that you too are an admirer."

She examined her soupspoon. "I am familiar."

The footmen came to clear away the table. Briskly and efficiently, they removed the white tablecloth and replaced it with a clean one before bringing in the next course. The footmen laid out an assortment of meats, including larded quails, game pies and beef smothered in a rich cream sauce. The footmen circled the table, serving vegetables while the guests helped themselves to the meats.

Hunt was about to tell Leela how Lady Victoria had kindly offered to loan Foster her copy of the book, but she turned to engage Mr. Paget. Hunt marveled at the fact that she'd rather talk to a man who could not hear her than to him.

Turning away, he spent the next hour dancing attendance on the lady seated next to him. The wine flowed freely, lubricating the guests' chatter. Bursts of laughter erupted from the opposite end of the table. One of Devon's friends diverted most of the guests, regaling them with amusing stories about his latest travels. The courses came and went until finally it was time for dessert, and Leela returned her attention to Hunt.

She nibbled on a hothouse strawberry, drawing his attention to her mouth. Her plump lower lip was stained red from the fruit. He resisted the urge to swipe the juice with the pad of his thumb. Or with his own tongue. Her pink tongue darted out to lick her lip. That mouth had kissed him hungrily, had sucked the sensitive skin at the side of his throat, making him crazy with need. His skin warmed. His prick stirred, growing heavy.

"Perhaps if you bothered to spend more time with Lady Victoria," Leela said to him, "she would share her interests with you, rather than your secretary."

"What?" He attempted to concentrate on not coming to a point right there at the supper table.

"Lady Victoria?" She said the words slowly and distinctly. As if he were a simpleton. "You should make an effort."

Hunt reached his limit. He was going to jump out of his skin. Silence was not an option. Turning to Leela, he said, "It is difficult."

"What is?" She leaned closer to hear him. Her scent, warm, feminine and fleeting, reached him, teasing his senses. He inhaled, eager to take that sweet warmth into his lungs.

"If you intend to wed the girl," she said impatiently, "you should trouble yourself to take the time to become acquainted with her. And now you've run out of time."

"I have?" He frowned. "Why?"

"The house party ends tomorrow. All of the guests will be departing."

"The guests, perhaps, but not me."

She stared at him. "I beg your pardon?"

"I'm staying on. It has long been the plan for me to remain at Lambert Hall until we all return to London together for the ball."

She jerked as if she'd been hit. "Surely you jest."

How had no one informed her of the plans? "I am not a man given to joking."

"You are to remain here at the Hall for the entire fortnight?"

"You needn't sound as though someone just condemned you to transportation."

She mumbled something that sounded suspiciously like, "Getting shipped out to Australia would be preferable."

"These next weeks are meant to give Lady Victoria and me time to become better acquainted." Guilt bore down on his chest. "But it feels wrong."

"What does?"

"Contemplating wedding Lady Victoria when all I

can think of is you," he murmured so that only she could hear.

She stiffened, her hands flat on either side of her plate. *"Wallah,"* she said under her breath, "you are a *hamar.*"

The way she said the foreign words did not sound like a compliment. "What does that mean?"

"It means you are a donkey," she whispered back.

Hunt couldn't believe what he was hearing. "Are you calling me a jackass to my face?"

Her eyes blazed. "I cannot think of a more accurate description."

"Someone has to behave like an adult in this situation, and it is very clearly not going to be you." He spoke very softly, keeping an impartial expression plastered to his face for the sake of the other guests. "I am trying to speak honestly and face our dilemma head-on. Unlike you."

"Are you? Really? Right now? Right here?" She smiled graciously when she met the eye of a guest seated several seats away. "Do you think this is an opportune time?" she asked from behind a clenched smile.

"You avoid me at every turn," he whispered furiously. "And even if you didn't, is there ever going to be a good time to discuss how I cannot stop thinking about making love to you when I am supposed to be courting your stepdaughter?"

"That's it!" she burst out, jumping to her feet.

The noisy conversation halted. Guests wearing puzzled faces turned in unison to gawk at Leela. Even the attending footmen paused momentarily to stare before quickly returning to their duties

"Excuse me, Lady Devon?" the earl asked in very deliberate tones from his end of the table.

"That's it for the ladies." Leela collected herself enough to speak in a measured manner. "It is time for us to withdraw. Ladies, let us leave the gentlemen to their port and conversation."

The ladies looked slightly stunned. Baroness Wallace exchanged a questioning look with Lady Helene, who raised her eyebrows in return. The men came politely to their feet despite the fact that the fruit and nuts had just been laid out. They'd barely had time to fill their plates, much less empty them. Hunt caught Mrs. Paget discreetly grabbing a handful of nuts before hiding the contraband in her clenched fist somewhere among her skirts.

"Shall we?" Without waiting for an answer, Leela marched out through the double doors, leading the procession of ladies into the drawing room.

Hunt watched her run away. Which was becoming her specialty. But no matter how far and fast she went, she couldn't outrun the truth.

Neither of them could.

# Chapter Eleven

*Shoo had?"* Hashem asked.

"It's called Parkwood." Leela stared up at the dower house's tranquil ivy-covered brick exterior. The century-old structure seemed completely at ease with itself; in the way of an elderly person who's lived so long they've stopped caring what people think about them. "We're moving in."

*"Han?"* Hashem scratched his head as he scanned the gravelly path that widened into a circular drive before the house. "We do not go to London?" he asked in heavily accented English.

As an interpreter for travelers to Arab lands, the older man spoke a little bit of just about every language. But his command of the King's English had improved considerably after spending two years in Leela's company.

Leela pushed the paneled front door open. "We'll be here for at least two weeks." She certainly wasn't going to spend the next fortnight residing in the same place as Huntington. Moving into the dower house allowed her to distance herself from the man without actually running away.

This way, she wouldn't be forced to share every meal with the duke. Or constantly risk bumping into him in the corridors or gardens. She'd even given up walks in the garden for fear of encountering Huntington. Here at Parkwood, she'd finally be able to regain her equilibrium.

She wandered into the dower house, home to widows of the Earls of Devon since the first earl built Parkwood for his mother more than one hundred years ago. She'd never been inside before now. Douglas's mother passed years before Leela married him so she'd always assumed the house was closed up.

The cozy high-ceilinged entryway led to a generous reception room with pale yellow walls, white plasterwork and wide, soaring windows. Leela released a breath. "It's perfect."

*"Mumtaz."* Hashem nodded his approval. *"Bait hiloo."*

"It is a pretty house." She surveyed the assortment of chairs, sofas and tables of all styles crammed into the room. "But first we must clear some of this furniture. And then we'll move a desk in here. This chamber will be an excellent place to write."

They roamed through the three-story dwelling. The furnishings were exposed even though the place remained uninhabited. No one had covered the chairs, tables and sofas to protect them from dust. Not that it was necessary. The floors and surfaces sparkled. The cleaning duties of the Lambert Hall staff clearly extended to the dower house.

Leela's excitement grew as they explored the rest of Parkwood. She'd expected to spend the day preparing the house for occupancy, and had even worn one of her faded old travel dresses to accomplish the task. But the house was ready for her to move in immediately. Parkwood possessed all of the modern conveniences needed for daily living, including a small but functional kitchen, sunny dining room and comfortable bedchambers abovestairs.

She and Hashem got to work, putting linens on the four-poster bed in the main bedchamber, where Leela would sleep. Moving downstairs, they shifted the chairs and sofas into more inviting arrangements. They stored some of the pieces in the small formal salon across the hall until Leela could hire workers from the village to carry the furniture to the attic. Or perhaps to the storerooms at Lambert Hall. She'd have to consult with Edgar about what to do with the extra furniture. Technically, everything on the estate, including Parkwood and all its contents, belonged to the Earl of Devon.

In a small study at the back of the house, they discovered a Chippendale writing table with two small drawers on each side that would be ideal for writing. Leela searched for rags to put under each intricately carved ebony leg in order to slide the desk into the large front reception room where she envisioned spending most of her time.

As she and Hashem maneuvered the table through the front hall, someone came in the front door.

"Oh, I do beg your pardon," the man said. "We were under the impression Parkwood is not occupied." The man, in his late thirties, wore a brown suit and matching top hat. A woman in a burgundy day dress and matching pelisse accompanied him.

"Not as of yet." Leela swiped a tendril of hair away from her face. She must look a mess, perspiring from exertion with her hair falling down. "But it shall be soon."

"Indeed it shall," the man said. "I know it is premature, as occupancy does not officially begin until the first of the month, but I thought to show Parkwood to Mrs. William today. She is keen to view the furnishings."

The woman wandered past Leela and Hashem and into the reception room. She circled the room. "This will do." Her attention went to the writing table that they'd pushed halfway into the large chamber. "Oh no. I do not want that in here," she said to Leela, making a shooing motion with her hand. "Please take it away."

"I am sorry," Leela said, "but who exactly are you?"

The woman's gray eyes widened. "Aren't you an impudent one? Asking questions of me is not your place."

Mr. William lifted his chin. "Is your master present?"

Leela straightened, understanding dawning. "I have no master."

"All servants have masters," he said irritably. "Now

go and fetch yours unless you want to be turned out of this house without reference."

*"Ya kalb,"* Hashem said pleasantly as he cursed the man. *"Kol khara."*

Mrs. William stared at the servant as if a snake had slipped out of his mouth. "What did he say?"

"That is none of your concern," Leela said. "And I am afraid the only person who is going to be turned out of this house is you."

Mrs. William's pale cheeks reddened. "How dare you! I do not know who you think you are—"

"Allow me to introduce myself," Leela cut in, using her frostiest manner. "I am the Countess of Devon. You may address me as 'My lady' or refer to me as 'Her ladyship.'"

Confusion filled the man's face. "Now see here—"

"You are Lady Devon?" The woman's questioning gaze took in Leela's disheveled appearance. "That cannot . . . How is that . . . What are you playing at?"

Leela understood their confusion. She'd encountered it before, especially when she wasn't dressed to play the part of a noblewoman. She remained quiet while Mr. and Mrs. William grappled with the idea that the untidy olive-skinned woman before them in a faded old dress could truly be a countess.

Mr. William finally ventured to speak. "I have reached an agreement with Lord Devon to lease this property."

Leela frowned. "Lease?" Edgar had rented out the dower house without consulting her?

"Yes." His manner grew more tentative. "We are to move in on the first of the month."

"Devon has no standing to lease this property to you, Mr. William. This is the dower house and it is my right as the widow of the last Earl of Devon to make my home here."

*"Tozz feek,"* Hashem added in a mild voice for good measure.

"What did you say?" Mrs. William asked suspiciously.

"Sorry." Hashem held out his hands, palms up. "No English."

Leela suppressed a smile. "He hopes you haven't been too inconvenienced."

She decided against informing them that her manservant had not only called them dogs, but also suggested they partake of excrement and go fornicate themselves.

After all, Mrs. William appeared affronted enough as it was. "My husband will take this up with Lord Devon. I want this house." Leela couldn't blame the lady for being disappointed. Parkwood was lovely.

"As you like," she said in her most Countess of Devon voice. "Now, if you would kindly see yourselves out. I am not at home to callers." She dismissed the interlopers by giving them her back, pointedly ignoring the indignant huff of Mrs. William's breath as Mr. William ushered his wife out the door.

Then she and Hashem slid the writing table to the exact spot where Leela wanted it, into the beautiful reception room of the lovely house that would make a perfect little hideaway for the next few weeks—until the Duke of Huntington was gone for good.

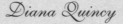

EDGAR STORMED INTO Parkwood several hours later. "What the devil do you think you are doing?"

"Hello, Edgar." Leela, already hard at work at the writing table, was not surprised to see him. "What took you so long?"

"What are you doing here?"

"At the moment?" She adjusted some papers on the writing table to conceal her manuscript. "I'm writing some letters."

"Do not jest with me. You know what I am asking. I do not know what you think you're up to, but I will not have it."

"I am merely asserting my privilege, as the widow of the late Earl of Devon, to stay at Parkwood."

His mouth twitched. "The hades you are. You will pack your things and vacate the premises posthaste."

She shifted in her seat to face him, placing her arm over the back of the tufted tapestry chair. "And why would I do that?"

"Because I have leased this property to Mr. William for the next two years."

"You've leased the dower house without consulting me?"

"Your place now is to live with your brother at his home." Edgar rolled his eyes. "If the man truly exists. One never sees Brandon about in society."

"My brother prefers the country. He has no interest in London or the ton."

"All the more reason for you to go and live with him. He'd no doubt appreciate the company."

"You would like that, wouldn't you?" Leela replied. "However, as a widowed Countess of Devon, I have certain rights. And that includes staying in the dower house for a few weeks if I so choose."

"The hell it is. You've never shown the slightest interest in Parkwood."

"But I am showing one now." She certainly had no intention of returning to the main house with Huntington there.

"You have had your fun playing house," Edgar said. "But it is time to stop this nonsense. The tenants are moving in at the beginning of the month."

"Surely there's another property you can offer them. Because I'm certainly not leaving by the end of the month."

"You little upstart." His eyes snapped with anger. "Who do you think you are?"

Her resolve hardened. Why should she cower before Edgar? "Maybe that is the problem."

"What is?"

"Maybe the problem is that you have never known who I am." She stood up to face him. "I am the daughter of the late Marquess of Brandon, sister of the current holder of that title, and widow of the late Earl of Devon. I am the Countess of Devon. I know my place. It is you who doesn't know yours."

He flushed. "I own this land and everything on it. Including this house." His fists clenched at his sides. "If you do not agree to vacate the premises posthaste, I will physically toss you out myself."

"While we are discussing my rights as your father's widow, I would like to know where my share of the estate income is."

"What?" Edgar spluttered. "Surely you cannot be serious."

"I think it is far past time I assert my dower rights." She was weary of being bullied by Edgar and Helene. "I am no longer the little girl your father brought home as his bride."

"You think you are clever." Fury contorted Edgar's features. "But I assure you this is a fight you will not win."

"We shall see about that." She was done allowing this *tase*, this stupid, stubborn goat, to deny her what was rightfully hers. "You owe me my dower rights. That's one-third of the estate's profits for each of the past two years. And I intend to collect everything I am owed."

## Chapter Twelve

$G$ood day?" Hunt called out, venturing into Park-wood.

Where were the servants? Someone had left the front door ajar. The delicious aroma of fresh-baked bread reached him. He surveyed the dark and narrow front hall. So this was where Leela had run off to. "Lady Devon?"

He heard voices the moment he stepped inside the house. Devon immediately appeared in one of the doorways that opened onto the front hall.

"Huntington?" The earl's forehead wrinkled. "What brings you here? Is Victoria with you?"

"No, she's gone into the village with some of the other guests. But she sent a package to Lady Devon."

Devon's eyes went to the wrapped parcel tucked under Hunt's arm. "Why are you delivering it?"

"I was going out for a walk anyway, so I offered to bring it along. Has Lady Devon truly relocated here?"

Devon shook his head. "No—"

Leela appeared beside the earl. "Yes indeed." Her eyes glittered and her cheeks were flushed. Something leaped in Hunt's chest at the sight of her. "Please come in, Your Grace."

She almost seemed happy to see him. Her manner was extremely cordial. Hunt wondered what she was up to. "Welcome to my home," she added.

He followed her into a spacious sunny room. It was an informal and inviting space decorated with comfortable, slightly faded, furnishings. Papers littered a generous-sized writing desk. "You are living here now?"

"Yes," she said brightly. "This is the dower house and I am the widow of the late Earl of Devon. Isn't that right, Edgar?"

"Indeed," Devon said stiffly. He was flushed as well. There was an undercurrent of something in the room that Hunt couldn't quite interpret.

"I imagine it's rather smaller than you are used to," Hunt said to her.

"Not at all. It is the perfect size for me." She gestured toward his package. "You mentioned having something for me?"

"Yes." He handed her the packet.

"I had forgotten about this." She took it with both hands. It was not exactly light. "It was very thoughtful of Victoria to send it along. Won't you sit? I'll ring for tea."

"That isn't necessary." Edgar ground his jaw. "I'm leaving. Huntington?"

Hunt wanted to stay. Not for tea, but to talk with her. To apologize. It felt like he'd forced her to decamp to the dower house by insisting they speak about unspeakable things. But he stood. "Yes, I'll go out with you."

Leela saw them to the door. She seemed quite cheerful, yet also unsettled. He did not care for the charged silent conversation he detected between her and Devon.

"I trust all is well with Lady Devon," Hunt remarked to Devon as they walked toward the earl's mount.

Devon was clearly rattled. "Yes, you know how women can be," he said lightly. "Most confounding at times."

The earl took the animal's reins into one hand. "I'll walk back with you."

When Hunt saw that Devon intended to proceed on foot in order to accompany him, he waved him on. "Please don't walk on my account. I enjoy the solitude of a stroll."

Devon seemed uncertain. "As you wish," he finally said. After Devon mounted and rode off, Hunt circled back to Leela.

A wizened older man answered the front door. "Yes?"

"I would like to speak with Lady Devon."

"Who is it?" Leela's voice called from somewhere in the bowels of the old house.

The man responded in Arabic. Hunt remembered him then. He was Leela's dragoman. The same man who'd accompanied her to the Black Swan. She replied in the same tongue, and Hunt found himself being escorted into a sunny breakfast room.

Leela was seated at the round table sipping her tea.

Bread and some other strange foods were laid out before her.

"I suppose there's no escaping you," she said by way of greeting. Looking beyond him, she said something to the old dragoman, who nodded and left them alone.

She regarded Hunt over her teacup. "You might as well sit."

It wasn't the most gracious invitation he'd ever received, but he'd take it. He slipped into a carved chair, its seat covered in red Morocco leather. "I came to ensure that you are well."

"Thank you. As you can see, I am fine."

The old man returned with a teacup for Hunt and filled it from the pot on the table. Once he'd withdrawn, Leela asked Hunt, "Are you hungry?"

"The bread certainly smells good." He couldn't quite identify what the other items on the table were. Possibly oil on a plate, and another dark green powder that appeared to have sesame seeds in it.

"This is what Victoria sent with you. That's olive oil from a grove outside of Al-Bireh in Palestine, where my mother's people are from."

"It's very green."

"It's fresh early-harvest olive oil." She tore off a morsel of bread and dipped it into the oil. "Try it."

He took it from her. It was pungent and slightly fruity with a hint of bitterness. "It's delicious."

"I thought you might appreciate it." She dipped a piece of bread in olive oil and then in the dark green powderlike substance before slipping it into her mouth.

He copied her actions and did the same. The aromatic tangy flavor exploded on his tongue. "What is that?"

"It's called *za'atar*."

"What's in it?" He reached for more bread and dabbed the morsel with olive oil before trying the powder again.

"A mixture of herbs and spices, primarily wild thyme and sesame. The tartness you taste comes from the crushed seeds of the sumac plant, which is a kind of shrub."

"It's wonderful." He drank from his tea. There were leaves at the bottom of his cup. Mint, he realized, mixed with black tea to flavorful effect.

"Why are you here, Your Grace?" she asked.

"Must you address me so formally? Will you at least consent to call me Hunt?"

"Hunt," she said. "Why are you here?"

"For two reasons. First, I owe you an apology."

"For what?"

"For the way I left you at the inn. I shouldn't have departed while you were sleeping, without properly taking my leave of you. You deserved better."

"Yes, I did," she said mildly. "Why did you leave like that?"

"Because I wanted so badly to stay with you. I worried about losing my heart to you."

Her eyes softened. "Apology accepted. It really doesn't matter now anyway. And your second reason for coming?"

"I wanted to assure myself that you are well."

"As you can see, I am perfectly fine."

"I feel as though I have forced you from your home."

"No one forced anything upon me. I made the choice to remove myself. Besides, Lambert Hall is not my home. It never was."

"You were once mistress here." Although she acted more like a guest.

"It's Edgar's home now. And he thinks there's no place for me in it."

"Why?"

"Because I am the spawn of the social-climbing daughter of a foreign merchant."

"You're also the daughter of a marquess."

"The Mad Marquess." She held up her porcelain cup in mock salute. "Let us not forget."

"They treat you abominably. Devon and that old aunt of his."

"I don't wish to reside at Lambert Hall. My only attachment was to Douglas, who was kind to me. And, of course, Victoria." She had a faraway look in her eyes. "I've loved her since the moment I first dropped to my hands and knees to coax her out from under the dining room table."

That sounded like Lady Victoria. "When was that?"

"When I first arrived, she was so bashful." She smiled softly at the memory. "But I joined her under the table and we had a tea party."

"Right there on the floor? An imaginary one?"

"Not at all. Douglas ordered tea for us, with apple tarts and apricot cakes. And once we emerged from our party under the table, we were bonded for life."

His chest felt as if a heavy brick with sharp edges was lodged inside of it. "You love her very much."

"Except for my brother, there is no living person who is as dear to me. I could never do anything to hurt her."

If Hunt hadn't comprehended how hopeless matters were between him and Leela, he did now. He could feel her love for Lady Victoria. It was a palpable thing. As was the undertone of emotion that ran between her and the earl. "What about Devon?"

"What about him?"

"What was he doing here?" Devon might detest Leela, but Hunt detected something more troubling about the man's interactions with his stepmother—a masculine hunger edged all of that contempt. Hunt understood that desire all too well. "Why was he alone with you?"

One of her dark brows shot up. "What concern is that of yours?"

"He seemed upset. As did you."

"It was a personal matter."

Jealousy lightninged through him. "How personal?" Devon might be Leela's stepson, but the man was likely older than her. And not unhandsome.

She narrowed her eyes at him. "What are you asking, and why?"

He dipped his bread in the *za'atar*. "Because it matters to me. Even though it should not." He noted the sharp intake of her breath.

"You think I am bedding my stepson."

"I do not." He stared down at the floating leaves of mint in his cup.

There was a sharp edge to her voice. "Perhaps you think a woman who would bed her stepdaughter's betrothed is capable of anything."

"I don't think that." Hunt reached for her hand and held it. He couldn't help himself. To his surprise, she allowed it. "I am preoccupied with thoughts of you when I know I should not be."

"Please," she begged him. "Please stop talking. I cannot speak of it."

"I know you are afraid. But so am I." He stroked the delicate skin at the back of her hand. "I fear losing control of my emotions. I fear I am willing to risk everything, to welcome disaster, to be with you. I fear becoming my brother."

"Your brother?" she echoed.

"Every day I strive to be nothing like him. Phillip was a wastrel. He gambled, he drank, he took liberties with women that he should not have. He was inconsiderate, reckless. He thought of no one but himself and his own selfish needs."

"Devon told me," she said softly. "He also said that family lore suggests the profligate gene skips a generation in your family."

"That's just it. Phillip and I are of the same generation," he said grimly. "Because of that, society waits for me to falter. There are some who believe it is inevitable that I will succumb to the pull of history."

"But Devon says you have a sterling reputation. You've done nothing to suggest you are destined for a life of debauchery."

"What if this capacity for self-ruination is in my

blood? They wait for me to become a prodigal son, to leave a trail of scandals in my wake."

"That's ghastly."

"There is even a wager on the books at White's gentlemen's club. Bets that suggest it is only a matter of time before my so-called 'true nature' emerges."

"You don't believe any of that, do you?" Her fingers curled around his and squeezed. "You are your own man. Only you can determine your destiny."

"I have always thought that. But then I met you." Emotion obstructed his throat. "And for the first time in my life I am tempted to risk everything—scandal, outrage, societal scorn—everything I have feared and fought against for my entire life, for a woman. For you."

Her eyes glistened. "Then perhaps you should leave." She gently withdrew her hand, upending her cup. Neither of them paid attention to the brown liquid bleeding over the white linen tablecloth. "We must agree to never again be alone together." She rose. "You should see yourself out."

And then she walked away from him yet again.

LEELA WENT UP to her bedchamber.

She closed and locked the door before stripping out of her wet dress. When she saw that the liquid had bled through to her chemise, she drew that off as well. The slight breeze from the open window drifted over her bare skin.

She paused, replaying Elliot's words in her mind. The vulnerability in his eyes had taken her aback. He had shared his deepest fears with her. He'd honored her with his deepest truths.

She opened the wardrobe to retrieve a new dress, then paused, before reaching for the garment hidden deep within the closet. The one she'd tried to forget about but couldn't.

Bringing Elliot's cloak to her nose, she inhaled deeply. It still smelled faintly of him, of exertion and leather and masculinity.

On impulse, she wrapped it around her bare body, breathing his fading scent into her lungs. The feel of the wool and silk against her skin made her body flush. Her nipples hardened. She floated the silk over them and moaned at the sensation; the tips of her breasts were unbearably sensitive.

Falling back on the bed, she felt moisture between her thighs. She contracted into a fetal position, trying to contain the intensity of the sensations coursing through her body. She stroked the place between her legs, felt herself tighten. Her body rode the sensations. She felt needy and desperate.

She flipped over on her belly, her leg over a pillow. The glancing sensation of the pillow brushing against her private area was like an electric zing. She ground into it, rocking into the pillow, feeling a perfect friction against the place between her legs where all sensation seemed focused. Adjusting the pillow, she moved her hips against it in slow circular motions until she found the perfect spot to answer her need. It felt sensational.

Her breaths came faster as she rhythmically moved against the pillow. Involuntary moans escaped her throat. Her heart raced. She moved faster and faster, enveloped in Elliot's scent, remembering the taste of him, the feel of him inside of her. The muscles in her lower back convulsed, her muscles spasmed and then released. She rode the sublime sensation, wringing every bit of pleasure out of it, calling out Elliot's name over and over again until she was spent, her body replete, the place between her legs pulsating.

Euphoria physically flooded her. She lay still for several minutes, absorbing the sensations coursing through her body. As her muscles relaxed, her breathing became more even. She stretched, feeling deliciously languorous. Her body felt alive and deeply sensitive.

There was no denying the truth any longer. She felt more than just a physical attraction for the Duke of Huntington. Elliot was the lingering ache in her heart. He was every happy thing she could imagine. The intense connection they'd discovered at the Black Swan had never gone away. It was possible that it never would. Leela gathered Elliot's cloak closer, snuggling into it, a commotion of feeling rioting through her, from the tips of her fingers, to deep in her belly and down to her toes.

She was in terrible, terrible trouble.

## Chapter Thirteen

One day after his fellow guests departed, Hunt accompanied Leela and Lady Victoria to the nearby village.

He'd suggested the outing in order to become better acquainted with Lady Victoria. She, in turn, enlisted Leela to serve as chaperone. The day was cool and overcast, a harbinger of the damp and wintry days that lay ahead. A medieval stone church came into view, its spirelet towering over the surrounding thatched roof cottages and timber-framed buildings.

Leela remained quiet, walking on the opposite side of Victoria, out of Hunt's line of sight, yet he remained profoundly aware of her presence. Lady Victoria was almost chatty, stammering only occasionally, as she conversed with him about books and places she longed to visit. Hunt hadn't thought to take a marriage trip, but perhaps he should consider it as a gift to his future bride.

His conversation with Leela had clarified that there was only one path forward. A dull but intense pain lacerated his chest. There could be no future for him and Leela. An affair or liaison was completely out of the question. And obviously beyond the pale.

Hunt had no choice but to go forward with his initial intention to wed Lady Victoria. Crying off now would create a scandal. He'd made a vow to himself to focus all of his energy on his future wife. His consuming passion for Leela would fade with time. It had to.

Along the way to the village, Lady Victoria asked him thoughtful and intelligent questions about Eaton Park, his country seat in Oxfordshire. Pleased that the young woman appeared more at ease in his company, Hunt took his time telling her all about her future home.

"My estate is not so far from here," he said. "It is about a ten-hour ride in the carriage. If I care to, I could make the trip in just one day as long as I only stopped to change horses along the way."

"Oh!" She appeared delighted. "That is not so far away."

They went past grazing cattle on the village green. Ahead, a stir of excitement caught their attention. People hurried past them toward a young bull on his way to market.

"What is the fuss?" Lady Victoria asked. "May we stop and see?"

"As you like," he said.

They paused to watch. The animal was attached to a post that was level to the ground. The metal chain that tethered the bull to the post was a few yards long. The animal immediately dashed about trying to free itself. The crowd rushed to get out of the way, bumping into each other while laughing, shouting and jeering at the animal. Some spectators toppled to the ground.

"Oh my," Lady Victoria said as she deftly stepped out of the way of one tumbling body.

Leela was not as quick. Some cretin bumped into her and she almost went over. Hunt's arm darted out to grab her before she fell. His fingers burned the moment he touched Leela's wrist, a current sizzling through his arm like rapturous lightning.

"Oh!" Leela made a sound of surprise before reflexively seizing his forearm to steady herself. Heat flashed through Hunt's body the moment her fingers closed around his arm, squeezing hard.

"I've got you," he said. "I won't let you fall."

Their eyes met. A conflagration of heat and desire arced between them. They both immediately dropped their arms and leaped apart. Her cheeks flushed, Leela looked away.

"Leela!" Lady Victoria cried out. "Are you hurt?"

"No. I am well. His Grace kept me from ending up in the mud."

Lady Victoria's grateful gaze fixed on Hunt. "Thank you."

"Of course." He cleared his throat. "I couldn't very well allow Lady Devon to fall over. Pity she did not have her knife in hand to keep interlopers at bay."

Lady Victoria tipped her head to the side. "Her knife?" She frowned. "Have you seen Leela's knife?"

"Erm—" Hunt wasn't certain how to respond.

"His Grace saw my *janbiya* when he came to Parkwood to deliver your package," Leela interjected. "You remember you sent the olive oil and the *za'atar*."

Lady Victoria's brow cleared. "I do remember." She looked to Hunt. "It is quite extraordinary, is it not?"

*Not nearly as extraordinary as the woman who wielded it.* Fortunately, a roar from the assembled crowd drew Lady Victoria's attention away from Hunt and the subject of Leela's knife.

"A lane! A lane!" someone called out. The crush moved in a mass, forming a narrow path leading up to the bull.

Hunt stiffened the moment he realized what was about to occur. "We should go. This is not a spectacle for ladies."

"Why ever not?" Curiosity lit Lady Victoria's face. "What are they doing?"

Her attention went to a young thin man with ginger hair and threadbare clothing. He restrained a restless, barking bulldog between his legs. Short brown fur covered the canine's compact body, except for the patch of white at its chest. Its shortened muzzle was black and wrinkled. The handler abruptly released the dog, which tore down the lane toward the bull, moving with speed and agility.

"What is he doing?" Lady Victoria cried out in alarm. "His dog is going to be hurt." Leela clutched the girl's arm to keep her from dashing after the bulldog.

Eyeing the dog, the bull lowered its head, threateningly moving it from side to side. Hunching its shoulders, the massive beast pawed the ground. He caught the bulldog on his horns and tossed the yelping animal into the air. Leela's expression was grim and pale as the crowd of people closed in to catch the dog.

Lady Victoria cried out in horror. "They've broken the poor dog's neck."

"He is all right," Hunt reassured her. "That's why the crowd catches the dogs."

She stared at him, horrified. "Is this some sort of sport?"

"Unfortunately. They're pinning the bull."

"What does that entail?" Leela asked. "How is any dog supposed to best a bull?"

"The dogs are trained to catch hold of the bull's nose and try to pin the animal down."

Outrage shadowed Lady Victoria's face. "Do you approve of this sort of thing?"

"No, but there are many who enjoy the sport. The dogs are specially bred to participate in pinning the bull." A second bulldog was lined up, its shortened muzzle directed at the bull. The crowd cheered.

"It's despicable." Lady Victoria was almost in tears. "You have to make them stop. Please!"

Eager to spare the young woman any further distress, Hunt stepped forward. "Who owns these two dogs?"

The crowd quieted, staring at the well-dressed man who was clearly out of place in this working-class crowd.

"And who might you be?" asked the young handler, who was barely more than a boy. He held the second dog poised and ready between his knees.

"I am the Duke of Huntington." His voice rang out

through the air. Excited murmurs moved through the crowd.

"They're my animals." The handler's bony chest inflated. "The best bull pinners in the county."

"I'll give you ten shillings for them."

Both Leela and Lady Victoria gasped at the exorbitant number.

The boy gaped, but quickly recovered himself. "Double that and you have a deal."

"Ten shillings and sixpence. That is my final offer." Hunt knew he could easily pay less, but the scrawny boy looked as if he could use the extra coin.

"Sold." The boy grinned. "Pluto and Plunder are yours."

Lady Victoria smiled gratefully at Hunt. "May I go and get your dogs?"

"Certainly, you may." He and Leela watched Lady Victoria make her way through the crowd to take possession of the dogs.

"What are you going to do with them?" Leela asked.

"I have no idea."

"Do you even like dogs?" He heard the smile in her voice.

"Not particularly."

She placed a hand on his forearm. "That was very well done of you. Thank you."

He stared at her gloved hand, warmth spreading through him like wildfire. His body ached for her. He yearned to take her hand in his and raise it to his mouth so that he might press his lips against the tender spot on the inside of her wrist.

"Here we are." Lady Victoria's voice jolted him from his musings. A smile wreathed her face as the two leashed dogs moved restlessly by her side. "What shall we do now?"

"Take them home with us?" Hunt asked dubiously. Both Leela and Lady Victoria laughed as if he'd made a humorous remark.

Leela reached over to take one leash from Lady Victoria. "Now which one is Plunder? What a name."

Lady Victoria pointed to the smaller of the two bulldogs. "That's Plunder and you have Pluto."

Chattering to themselves and cooing to the animals, the two ladies strolled back in the direction of Lambert Hall, barely taking note of Hunt, who dutifully trailed behind them.

THE AFTERNOON AFTER Hunt acquired his new dogs, Leela found herself gliding down the Oxford Canal aboard the narrowest boat she'd ever seen.

While the majority of the houseguests were gone, Mr. and Mrs. Paget, along with Aunt Helene's particular friend, Baroness Wallace, all lived in the neighborhood and had joined the excursion.

"This is the strangest vessel," Leela remarked. "I've never been on one quite like it."

"It must be slender enough to fit in the canal," Tori informed her. "Most narrow boats carry cargo. Others carry mail and parcels. And, at times, passengers."

"You seem very knowledgeable about narrow boats," Baroness Wallace observed.

"I cannot help it," Tori said with a smile. "My

brother is fascinated with canals. He enjoys taking guests for leisurely jaunts down the waterways."

The long wooden boat was about seven feet wide and ten times as long, with a small cabin at the back of the boat. A glimpse inside the boatman's cabin revealed two padded benches, a storage drawer and a stove for warmth and cooking. Four horses tethered to the sides of the tunnel by a long rope walked along the towpath pulling the vessel at a gentle pace.

Mrs. Paget, parasol perched high over her head, peered over the side into the sun-speckled water. "Why look, there's a mallard."

The ladies sat in wooden benches toward the front of the boat. The duke was at the rear of the boat with Edgar and Mr. Paget, learning how the steering mechanism, the hand rudder, worked.

Leela stared at the passing scenery—greenery and the occasional charming stone cottage—and tried not to think of Hunt. Tori slid closer to her.

"I have something to tell you," she whispered urgently.

"What is it?"

"Lady Devon," the baroness interrupted, "I hear you have seen fit to move into Parkwood."

"Indeed I have." Bracing for criticism, she added, "I am very comfortable there. It is a beautiful house."

"Is it?" Mrs. Paget inquired. "I should like to see the dower house."

"You are most welcome to call at any time."

"Parkwood is a family home and has been for more than a century," Aunt Helene said pointedly. "My mother, my grandmother and all of the mothers of the earls of Devon throughout history have resided there."

"And as the widow of the late Earl of Devon, I am following that tradition," Leela said evenly.

Hunt rejoined them, slipping onto the built-in bench next to Tori on one side of the boat. He'd discarded his tailcoat, and looked entirely too dashing in a cream silk waistcoat worn over a white linen shirt, and buff leather breeches tucked into tan-topped leather boots.

Edgar and Mr. Paget followed closely behind the duke. Aunt Helene, who sat in a forward-facing bench, did not take note of their reappearance.

"But you are hardly mother to the next duke." False sympathy filled the older woman's voice. "Sadly, you are not even a mother."

"Neither are you," Leela reminded the spinster. She spoke in a pleasant tone, like one might when commenting on the weather, even though anger stirred deep in her belly. She would never grant Helene the satisfaction of knowing she'd scored a direct hit. The barb stung not because Leela had a burning desire to have a baby, but because Douglas had wanted another child and Leela had failed to give him one.

Aunt Helene stiffened. "I might not have children, but I do have blood ties to Lambert Hall. You do not."

"But she has ties of the heart," Hunt interjected. "Lady Victoria is most fond of Lady Devon."

Aunt Helene's head jerked in Hunt's direction, taking note of his presence for the first time. "Your Grace, how lovely that you have rejoined us."

"Lady Victoria is pleased that Lady Devon is staying at the dower house," he said to the older woman.

"Oh yes, indeed." Tori reached for Leela's hand. "Nothing could make me happier."

"There you have it," Hunt said pleasantly. "Surely Lady Victoria's happiness is paramount."

Edgar beamed. "Huntington would hate for his future duchess to be unhappy."

Leela's heart lurched. *Future duchess?* Hunt had made it official? Audible gasps sounded around her.

"Are you saying what I believe you are saying?" the baroness inquired.

"Is that an announcement?" Mr. Paget asked a bit too loudly.

Edgar smiled. "Of a sort."

"What?" Aunt Helene asked.

Hunt darted a look at Leela before blinking away and taking Tori's hand into his own. The girl's face turned a deep rosy shade as she stared down at their clasped fingers.

"Lady Victoria has agreed to make me the happiest man in all of England," Hunt said carefully, as if willing the words to leave his mouth. "She has done me the great honor of agreeing to be my wife."

"When did this happen?" Aunt Helene asked. "Why wasn't I informed?"

"We're informing you now." Edgar vibrated with satisfaction. "His Grace asked for Lady Victoria's hand yesterday afternoon. And she has consented."

Yesterday afternoon. Shortly after they'd returned

from the village. Hunt must have gone directly to ask Edgar for Tori's hand. Despair carved itself into Leela's chest. It was done. Tori couldn't cry off now. The betrothal was official.

Mr. Paget reached out to shake Hunt's hand. "Allow me to be the first to congratulate you," he said heartily.

"Oh happy day!" Baroness Wallace went to hug Tori. "You will make a wonderful duchess."

Tori returned the baroness's embrace but her worried gaze met Leela's. Forcing a smile, Leela stood to hug Tori. "I wish you every happiness."

Tori hugged her back hard. "Thank you. It all happened so fast. I tried to tell you." She was pulled away to embrace Aunt Helene. Around her, everyone chattered happily. Leela heard none of it. She smiled and laughed when the others did, but had no idea why.

"Tunnel ahead!" one of the boatmen called, cutting into the congratulatory chatter. Leela stared blindly ahead and saw that they were coming up to a long narrow covered passage.

"Now we untether the horses," Edgar informed them.

"How do we get through the tunnel?" Mr. Paget asked, turning so that his good ear faced Edgar.

"Two of the boatmen will leg it," the earl answered. "It should take about fifteen minutes to get through to the other side."

Everyone except for Leela proceeded to the back of the boat to watch the boatmen lie on their backs atop the cabin. They propped their legs up against the tunnel walls at a forty-five-degree angle, walking their feet along the wall. The strength of their legs powered the narrow boat through the dark passage.

Relieved that the others were distracted, Leela sank onto the bench. Her heart raced. Her head pounded. Soon the entire boat was inside the tunnel, pitching her into complete blackness. Her surroundings were cool and cave-like, the damp air pressing against her clammy skin. Sounds of water dripping from the moist tunnel walls echoed around her. Pulling off her gloves, Leela laid a hand against her cool forehead.

Behind her, the boatmen began to sing, stomping their feet against the sides of the tunnel in rhythm, in tune with the shanty.

Oh, blow the man down, bullies, blow the man down!
To me way-aye, blow the man down.

Leela closed her eyes and tried to breathe through the torment in her chest. It was done. Tori would wed Hunt. She would bear his children. Leela had never cared about having children. She'd hoped to get pregnant solely because Douglas wanted another son, not due to any deep desire on her part. But now, the idea of someone else bearing Hunt's children felt like there'd been a death in the family.

Oh, blow the man down, bullies, blow him right down!
Give me some time to blow the man down!

Something warm settled next to her. Even in the darkness, she immediately knew who it was. She knew his masculine scent. She knew *him*. Hunt's hand brushed against hers. Their fingers interlocked as if it were the most natural thing in the world. They sat there silently for a minute or so, intimately connected, drawing strength and comfort from each other.

His lips were at her ear, his breath sweetly humid. "I did it for you."

Her heart twisted. "I know."

"I was afraid that if I waited any longer, I would lose my nerve."

She nodded, even though he could not see her.

His voice was strained. "I swear I will do everything in my power to ensure that Victoria never regrets her choice."

The emotion clogging Leela's throat made words impossible. Instead, she just clung to his hand and let the tears flow.

When the narrow boat emerged from the tunnel several minutes later, Leela had composed herself.

And she was alone again.

## Chapter Fourteen

$\mathcal{T}$he next morning, Leela was at breakfast attempting to review her manuscript and not think of Hunt, when Tori rushed in.

"You aren't angry with me, are you?" The girl was out of breath, her cheeks flushed. "Please tell me you're not disappointed in me."

"Why would I be upset with you?" Leela set her tea down. "Why are you breathing so hard?"

"I ran all the way here. It was my first opportunity to sneak away."

"Sit down." Leela poured the girl a drink of water from the floral porcelain pitcher on the table. "And drink."

Tori collapsed into the chair across from Leela and gulped down half the glass. "I was worried you'd be put out because I accepted the duke's proposal so quickly."

"Darling, this is your life." The ever-present knot in Leela's stomach—the one related to all things Hunt—twisted a little tighter. "All I can do is give you advice. But, in the end, you must do as you please."

"I had hoped to spend more time with Hunt—he said

I should call him Hunt now that we're betrothed—but he was most ardent in his proposal."

Leela's heart fluttered. "Was he?"

"Yes, he seemed so determined to make me his wife that it was difficult to say no."

"Did you want to turn him down?"

"No, not really." She swallowed more water. "He was so wonderful when we visited the village. The way he saved Pluto and Plunder was quite heroic."

Leela had to agree. "Where are the dogs now?"

"Out in the stable. Hunt intends to make them stable hounds at his country estate."

Leela smiled. "It was very kind of His Grace to save the animals."

"You must call him Hunt now that he is to be family."

*Family.* "Very well. It was very kind of Hunt."

"I agree. His gallantry greatly influenced my decision to accept his offer of marriage. And I took Mr. Foster's opinion to heart as well."

"The duke's secretary? He voiced an opinion on whether or not you should wed the duke?"

"No, of course not. Mr. Foster would never be so bold." She finished her water. "I asked him if he enjoyed working for Hunt, and Mr. Foster responded that he could not ask for a more worthy employer. He says His Grace is honorable, generous and fair."

"You must remember that the duke is his employer. Mr. Foster would be foolish to speak against him. He risks losing his position."

"I realize that. But Mr. Foster worked for the last duke as well."

Leela reached for the water pitcher to refill Tori's glass. "Mr. Foster was employed by His Grace's brother?"

"Yes. He assisted the late duke's secretary. When Hunt assumed the title, he elevated Mr. Foster by making him his secretary. Mr. Foster says there never were two brothers more different than those two."

Leela's curiosity piqued. "What did he say about the last duke?"

"Nothing directly. Mr. Foster would never be so indiscreet. But it is obvious from the way he speaks about the current duke that he respects him a great deal. He even seems a little fond of Hunt."

It did not surprise Leela that Hunt was well regarded by the people he employed. He'd proven himself to be a worthy man. "I do believe His Grace will do everything in his power to make you happy." Hunt had told Leela as much. And she believed him.

"Do you?" Delight washed over Tori's face. "Oh, I am so pleased. Your good opinion of him means everything to me."

Leela could not bear to discuss Hunt any longer. It hurt too much. "Are you hungry?"

"No, I've already eaten." Tori paused, sniffing the air. "But what is that delicious smell?"

"It's called *manaeesh*." Leela broke off a piece of the round flatbread on her plate. "Try it. It's *za'atar* mixed with olive oil and then spread onto the dough before baking."

"Well, I am partial to your *za'atar*." She bit into the warm bread and chewed slowly, appreciatively. "This tastes as delightful as it smells."

"It's one of my favorites. I'm fortunate that Hashem is an excellent cook."

Tori examined the *za'atar*-topped bread before taking another bite. "I should warn you that you might have guests soon."

"Oh? Who?"

"Mrs. Paget is up at the Hall. I overheard her telling Aunt Helene that she'd like to accept your offer to take tea here at Parkwood House."

Leela stifled a groan. "Hopefully, she will decide against it."

Voices sounded in the front hallway. One particularly imperious tone left no doubt that Aunt Helene was among the visitors.

Tori's brows lifted. "You could always escape out the back door."

Leela rose, resigned to her fate. "I suppose I shall have to go and greet my guests."

THE TANTALIZING SMELL of fresh-baked bread and mint tea reached Hunt the moment Leela's manservant admitted them to Parkwood.

This was the last place he wanted to be. He'd come along reluctantly, at the urging of Devon, the old aunt and Mrs. Paget, who seemed to spend a great deal of time at Lambert Hall. He had no desire to be inside Leela's house so soon after their last encounter. The more distance they kept between them the better. Crossing into Leela's domain stirred up emotions best left dormant.

"Where has all of the furniture gone?" A frowning

Aunt Helene surveyed the gracious reception room with its pale yellow walls and soaring windows. "Where is Mama's chaise?"

Leela joined them, looking fresh and very desirable with her dark hair pulled up. A few waves had escaped their confinement and draped about the smooth column of her neck and down to her shoulders. Her morning dress—white with red pinstripes—hugged her generous breasts before flowing gently over the rest of her sweet curves. The unbidden memory of running his lips down that neck, of tasting her lush breasts, assailed him. Reality slammed into Hunt when Victoria entered the room behind Leela.

"What a delightful surprise," Leela said to her unexpected guests.

Ignoring Leela's greeting, Devon focused on his sister. "So this is where you ran off to without a word."

"Victoria came to visit with me." Leela defended her stepdaughter. "It isn't as if she left the estate grounds."

"All the same." Devon looked to Hunt. "His Grace will no doubt wish to take Victoria in hand once they are wed."

"Lady Victoria hardly needs to be taken in hand." Hunt felt a rush of protectiveness toward the girl, instinctively coming to her defense the way he might for a younger sister. "I see no fault in the lady's behavior."

Victoria flushed and shot him a grateful smile. He returned her smile, realization hitting that he was growing fond of the bright and amiable young woman. Not with the heated desperateness with which he craved Leela, but in a more familial way. He supposed that was a start. He glanced over at Leela. She watched his warm exchange with Victoria. His gut squeezed at the stricken expression that fleetingly crossed her face.

She quickly masked it with a welcoming smile. "I have already rung for tea. Won't you all make yourselves comfortable?"

"Where? There is hardly room to sit." Glacial resentment poured off of Aunt Helene. "What have you done with Mama's chaise? And Grandmama's marble tables?"

"They are in the small salon across the hall for now," Leela informed her, "until Devon decides where he wants them stored, either in the attic here or up at the Hall."

"Why ever did you move them?" Mrs. Paget took a seat next to Aunt Helene on the gold chintz sofa trimmed in dark wood.

Leela sat in a velvet high-backed armchair opposite the older ladies. "I've recently come to realize that I prefer spaces that are less crowded, a bit more simple."

"You've certainly put your stamp on the place," Hunt said.

Leela's manservant entered with the tea, which she proceeded to serve. To Hunt's disappointment, the source of the delicious fresh bread smell did not appear to be among the cakes and sandwiches set out for the guests. There was certainly nothing as interesting as the *za'atar* he'd sampled from her table. He also noted the lack of mint in the tea. Leela, it seemed, served traditional English tea to her guests.

Refreshments in hand, Hunt and Devon settled into

identical French chairs upholstered in the same cream fabric that adorned the windows.

Leela directed her attention to Devon. "What would you like to do with the extra furnishings? I would like to clear the small salon as well."

"Those marble tables are quite valuable," Aunt Helene put in, her manner as stiff as her immobile hair. "They should not be stored away."

"Then by all means, you are welcome to take them up to the Hall," Leela said.

"There is no need for that." Devon drank from his tea. "None of the furnishings in this house are going anywhere. Lady Devon's accommodation here is temporary."

Leela visibly stiffened. Hunt interceded. "Is this not the dower house?" he asked Devon.

"It has traditionally been so," Devon responded. "However, Lady Devon is hardly here. Victoria tells me she intends to continue traveling."

"I see." Hunt's stomach did a little flip. *She was leaving.* "Is that so?"

"Yes." Leela's measured gaze met his. "I think I shall visit North Africa next. Perhaps Morocco."

"Precisely my point," Devon said with a toss of his hand, "it would be a waste to keep Parkwood open and available to Lady Devon when she is so rarely in residence."

Hunt persisted. "Surely Lady Devon needs a home when she is not abroad. As the previous earl's widow, the lady does have certain rights."

"She can stay with us at Eaton Park," Victoria said

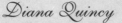

excitedly before catching herself. She blushed and covered her mouth. "That is, if that would be agreeable to you, Your Grace . . . erm . . . Hunt."

He avoided looking in Leela's direction. "Lady Devon would be most welcome."

Of course, he could never turn her away, but Hunt fervently hoped Leela wouldn't come to Eaton Park. If she did, the estate would be ruined for him. Once he knew what it was to have her in his home, among his things, Eaton would always feel empty in her absence.

"I do believe that is Grandpapa's desk." Aunt Helene stared at Leela's writing table. "When we were young, my brother, Devon's grandfather, and I found a secret compartment in it."

"How intriguing!" Victoria clasped her hands together in front of her chest. "Do you think you can still find it, Aunt Helene?"

The old woman pushed to her feet. "Let's have a look, shall we?" Mrs. Paget followed Aunt Helene.

"Is it quite a mess." Leela leaped to her feet and strode over. "Let me clean it off first."

Aunt Helene reached the desk before Leela. Everyone rose and followed the ladies to the writing table.

"Really," Aunt Helene said with disdain. "Why do you have so many papers strewn about your desk like a common clerk?"

Leela hurriedly gathered the documents, stacking them haphazardly and holding them against her chest. A few papers escaped, sailing to the ground. Devon knelt to gather them, but Hunt got there first.

"Allow me." He quickly collected the papers. As he

stacked them, Hunt couldn't help but notice that these were no ordinary letters. In fact, they were not letters at all.

"Here it is!" Aunt Helene exclaimed from her place at the side of the desk. "I just knew I would find it."

Mrs. Paget's eyes widened. "How clever!"

"May I see?" Victoria edged closer.

"Interesting," Devon said, peering over the ladies' shoulders.

Papers in hand, Hunt straightened to find Leela watching him with a question in her eyes. "I'm going to step into the study to put these up."

"I'll accompany you since your hands are full," he said. The others in the room were too busy examining the secret compartment to pay them much mind.

Leela remained silent as she went across the hall. She paused at the front hall table, opening the single small drawer, and withdrew a key. Unlocking the door, she went inside. Hunt followed. Before him was another desk and a long table covered with paper arranged in neat, side-by-side piles. As he came closer, he saw it was a book, sorted and laid out by chapter. She let him look his fill.

"So now you know."

"I suppose I do." He stared down at a chapter entitled, "Journey to the Dead Sea." "You certainly are full of surprises. You wrote *Travels in Arabia*."

She spread linen over the table, concealing her writing. "I hope this will not color your decision to wed Victoria and align yourself with this family."

He frowned. "Why should it?"

"I'm a lady, a countess, who is engaging in trade."

"You are writing under an assumed name."

"Yes, but if anyone learns of this it could cause a terrible scandal."

"All this revelation does is deepen my appreciation. You are a most talented writer." He felt a rush of admiration for her. "The fact that you authored the most acclaimed travelogue in London proves you are even more intriguing and spectacular than I realized."

Pleasure lit her lovely face. His words pleased her. Longing coursed through Hunt's veins. His chest ached for want of her. He couldn't resist stepping closer, near enough to touch her. She didn't move.

He kept his hands fisted by his sides. If he allowed himself to feel the softness of her skin, he'd be lost. Instead, he lightly brushed his lips to the tender place where her neck melted to her shoulder. He buried his face in the nape of her neck, inhaling the scent of soap and warm woman and everything he could not have. She tilted her head, her soft cheek meeting his, embracing him in the only way either of them dared.

"We must stop," she whispered.

"Yes." Sorrow roiling his chest, his need for her unending, Hunt straightened as she stepped away.

The door pushed open. "There you are." Devon appeared in the doorway. His suspicious gaze flitted between the two of them. "What is going on in here?"

"His Grace was kind enough to help me with my letters." Leela busied herself straightening the linen that concealed her manuscript. "Then he asked to see the rest of the house."

A skeptical expression came over Devon's face. "Huntington wants to look around Parkwood?"

"Are you giving a tour?" Victoria's bright face popped up behind Devon. "I should like to come along as well."

"And so you shall," Leela said crisply, deftly ushering everyone out the door. "This way, if you please."

Hunt felt Devon's assessing gaze glued to him as the gentlemen followed the ladies out of the room.

# Chapter Fifteen

*M*y dear Lady Devon, what a lovely surprise. Please do come in."

Mr. Sherman ushered Leela into his dark paneled office on Well Street in Coventry. "I did not realize you've arrived back at Lambert Hall after all of this time. And looking more lovely than ever, I must add."

"Thank you. I returned quite recently." She'd selected one of her finest day dresses to meet with Douglas's solicitor. Lace embellished the high neckline and cuffs of her violet gown. Matching trim adorned her bonnet. She always came away with better results when armored in her countess attire.

"It is certainly our pleasure to have you back among us."

An avuncular, balding man in his fifties, Mr. Sherman balanced round, wire-rimmed spectacles low on the bridge of his nose. Leela was not well acquainted with the solicitor. However, his smile seemed genuine and he'd treated her respectfully in the past, whenever he visited Lambert Hall to meet with her late husband.

"You needn't have troubled yourself to come all

the way to Coventry," he said. "You could have summoned me and I would have called on you as I always did for the late earl."

"I will bear that in mind in the future."

The solicitor hurriedly cleared a stack of books and files from a high-backed red chair opposite his cluttered desk. "Please do take a seat." He set the pile in his arms on a wood-backed chair next to her.

Mr. Sherman's office was small, the shelves littered with haphazardly arranged books. Interspersed among the well-worn tomes were porcelain figurines of dogs and horses in varying sizes. The solicitor settled behind his desk and placed his folded hands atop the papers scattered across the oak surface.

"Now, how may I be of service, Lady Devon?"

"I wish to be enlightened about my dower rights as widow of the late Earl of Devon." She fervently hoped Douglas had left her enough to live independently, so that she could travel and write and have her books published when she pleased, without having to answer to anyone.

"I am happy to be of assistance. However, you should be aware that I no longer serve the current Earl of Devon. Once his father, your late husband, passed, the new earl engaged a new solicitor."

"I see." That worked in the man's favor in Leela's view. "I am here because, as a widow with no expectation of remarrying, it is important for me to secure my future."

Her time at Lambert Hall brought home the precariousness of Leela's financial situation. She could always take shelter with her brother, but she preferred to stand on her own. The widow of an earl had certain rights and she intended to claim them.

There were also the profits from her books to consider. She hadn't collected any money yet, but the first volume had done very well. By her calculation, she was due to collect upward of two hundred pounds from her publisher. Surely, she could manage on her own without having to depend upon anyone else. The idea of fully establishing her independence appealed to her very much.

"I should like to know the full extent of my dower rights."

Mr. Sherman's salt-and-pepper brows drew together. "Your dower rights?"

"Yes, I am entitled, am I not, to one-third of the estate's earnings?"

"Well"—the word was long and drawn out—"I am afraid it is not as simple as that."

"Why ever not?" Unease rippled through her. "Surely my late husband made arrangements to provide for me after his death."

She'd been barely more than a girl when she and Douglas wed. He once told her she would always be looked after, but she never bothered to ask for details. Douglas died suddenly. A heart ailment, the doctor said. What if he hadn't had time to draw up the necessary papers?

Mr. Sherman passed the flat of his hand over his baldpate. "There are times when the dower rights such as you describe are put aside."

"Is that what happened in this case? Did Douglas remove my dower rights?"

Mr. Sherman paused. "I seem to remember that you were not present when the late earl's will was read."

"Yes, I left for my brother's estate, my family home, almost immediately after the funeral."

"Surely the current earl informed you of the terms of his late father's will."

"He did not." Dread filled her. "That is why I am here. Did my husband strip me of my dower rights?"

"He did."

"When?" Her stomach dropped. "Why?"

"The earl summoned me about a year before he died. That was when he changed the terms of the settlement."

"Is that allowed?" Panic edged her words. Why would Douglas disinherit her?

"Yes. Especially if one replaces dower rights with something more valuable."

"I beg your pardon?"

"Lord Devon was concerned that his heir, the current earl, would make it difficult for you to collect estate earnings given . . . erm . . . I understand there were some . . . difficulties . . . between the two of you."

"Yes. Please continue."

"In lieu of one-third of the estate profits, the earl left you a property."

"Which property? Where?"

He rose and shuffled over to a filing cabinet. "I have it here somewhere." After a couple of interminable minutes, Mr. Sherman found what he was looking for.

"Ah, here it is." He squinted as he tried to make out the name. "It's a place called Parkwood."

Her mouth dropped open. "What?"

He regarded Leela over the rim of his spectacles. "Do you know that property?"

"Yes, I do." She tried to digest the unexpected news. "Douglas left me *Parkwood*? Are you certain?"

"Yes, indeed. As well as all of its contents." Mr. Sherman's eyes were on the paper in his hands. "And that's not all."

"I own Parkwood outright?" Delight flooded her. "It's not part of the entail?"

He adjusted his spectacles. "No, that particular property is not entailed."

"And Edgar . . . erm . . . Lord Devon is aware of this?"

"Most certainly. There is more." He scanned the document in his hands. "In addition to the house and all of its contents, the late earl left you four very profitable farms."

"He left me a house and an income?" Leela could hardly believe her good fortune.

"Yes, his lordship was most adamant that you be able to live independently and not have to be at the mercy of his son's largesse."

Tears blurred her vision. Even in death, Douglas continued to look after her. "He understood Edgar very well."

"Apparently." Mr. Sherman gave her a kindly look. "You, young lady, will live very comfortably for the remainder of your life on the income generated by those farms. You will want for nothing. Unless," he added after a pause, "you are an extravagant spender."

"I assure you that I am not."

"There is one more thing. The late earl stipulated that if you ever wish to sell Parkwood, you are required to allow the Earl of Devon the first right of refusal. That is, you must allow his lordship to match any and all offers you receive on the property."

"I see." Leela could hardly believe it. Douglas had left her enough to set up a modest household in London while also funding her travels. Then the other reality hit her. Edgar had tried to rob her of her inheritance.

She rose. "Thank you for your time, Mr. Sherman. You have been most helpful."

He came to his feet as well. "I am pleased to be of service. If there is anything further that I may do for you, please do not hesitate to inquire."

"Actually, there is. I find myself in need of a solicitor."

SHE RETURNED TO Parkwood late that afternoon to find the object of her animosity making himself at home in her front reception room.

"There you are, Delilah." Edgar lounged on her sofa, a glass of brandy dangling from his fingertips. He did not rise, as any gentleman would, when she entered. "I have been waiting for you."

"What are you doing here?" She removed her bonnet. "Where is Hashem?"

"The little foreign man? I sent him on an errand so we could speak privately." Relaxing against the cushions, he spread one arm over the rim of the sofa's curved back and crossed an ankle over the opposite knee. It was not how a gentleman should sit in the presence of a lady.

"What kind of errand did you send Hashem on?"

He took a long, unhurried swallow of brandy. "The sort that will keep him from bothering us for at least a couple of hours."

"I see." The *kalb* was clearly up to something. She was curious to learn what it was before she threw him out of her house.

His gaze roamed over her. "You certainly are in good looks today. Is there a reason you are so dressed up?"

"I had an appointment."

"What sort of appointment."

"A private appointment."

His eyebrows lifted. "Ah. I see."

"I doubt that." She leaned her hips against her writing table, crossed her arms over her chest and waited for him to get to the point.

"I think it is past time you and I came to an understanding." He finished his drink and set the empty glass on the side table with a thunk. "Don't you agree?"

"That depends upon what you have in mind." She did not care for the gleam in his eyes. She'd detected that predatory look once before, when Edgar had visited her bedchamber at Lambert Hall.

"You want this house."

"I do." *And it's mine.*

He rose and sauntered over to her. Coming too close. His breath reeked of alcohol. "I think we can come to an understanding."

"So you've said." She came to her full height. No longer leaning against the desk, she stood almost eye to eye with her stepson. "Are you planning to come to the point anytime soon?"

"You want this house."

"Again stating the obvious. Have you anything new to share?"

He stared at her with glossy eyes. "And I want you."

"What?" It took her a moment to process his words. Edgar had always hated her.

"You are a woman of the world now. You're no longer that innocent girl my father married. Surely you entertained men on your travels."

"I did no such thing." Her muscles stiffened. "I suggest you step away from me."

"It's the perfect solution." He didn't move. "You keep the house and I will visit you from time to time."

"You're foxed."

He shrugged. "I've had a few glasses of brandy, but I know what I want and at the moment it's you."

"You are despicable." He was entirely too close, boxing her in against the desk. To slip past him, her body would have to brush against his. "I have warned you. Step away before I make you regret it."

His gaze lowered to her décolletage. "I've wanted to bed you from the moment Father brought you home. And I think you want it, too."

"You're delusional." Her pulse drummed loudly in her ears. "I want nothing to do with you. Move away."

He studied her face. "May I ask you a question?"

"No."

He leaned closer, his face shiny with perspiration. "You're fucking the duke, aren't you?"

Her lungs deflated. "No."

"I don't believe it. You've swived Huntington. I could tell when I saw you two together the other day. Now you're going to spread your legs for me or I am going to tell Victoria the truth about her stepmother and her future husband."

"You're an idiot. There is nothing going on between me and Huntington—of all people. Now move away." Behind her, Leela felt for the desk drawer. "That is your last warning."

"God, how I've wanted you," he murmured, his lips just inches from hers, his brandy-soaked breath humid against her face. "I'll make it good. I swear it. Much better than Huntington. Or Father. Or any of those Levantine heathens you allowed beneath your skirts."

Behind her, Leela pulled open the drawer and felt around until she found what she was looking for.

"Please say yes." He reached out, placing his hand on her waist.

"Get your hands off me."

His hand slid around her body, brushing her bottom. "You've no idea how much I've wanted to touch you like this. Admit it," he whispered in her ear. "You want it, too."

"You cannot say I didn't warn you." Leela whipped out her *janbiya* and reached up to slash Edgar's cheek in a quick precise motion.

He shrieked and jumped back. "What the devil?" His hand shot up to touch his cheek and came away with the crimson blood staining his fingers. "What have you done?"

"Surely you are smart enough to figure it out."

"You cut me?"

She shrugged. "I did warn you."

"I'm bleeding." Disbelief stamped his face. "How badly did you cut me?"

"Not enough to do any permanent damage, but there will be a scar. Consider it a reminder never to touch a woman who doesn't want to be touched."

"I cannot believe that you took a knife, a *knife*, to my face." He stared at the blade in her hand. "You actually sliced my cheek open."

She reached for a kerchief on her desk to wipe Edgar's blood from her *janbiya*. "Consider yourself fortunate that I didn't slice into something more critical."

He watched her clean her blade. "Where in Hades did you get that? What kind of lady carries a knife?"

"A lady who has to protect herself from men like you." Because Edgar didn't seem inclined to try to stem the bleeding, Leela went to the kitchens and came back with a clean cloth.

She held it out to him. "Here." He blinked, still in some sort of shock and very likely too foxed to think clearly. "I don't want you staining my carpet," she said impatiently. "Hold it against your wound. You might need to have that cut stitched."

Pressing the cloth to his cheek, Edgar stumbled into the front hall to peer at himself in the gilded mirror that hung there. Lifting the bloodstained cloth away, he turned his head and lifted his chin to get a better look at the two-inch gash at the center of his left cheek. "Damnation! It's huge."

"Don't exaggerate. It's not that big."

"If you are so determined to draw my blood, you could have cut my arm or somewhere else. But my *face*? Everyone can see it."

"Exactly."

Edgar followed her back to the reception room. "What am I supposed to tell people about how I got this knife wound?"

"Whatever you like. Tell them the truth."

"Now you've really done it." Edgar slumped into the high-backed velvet chair, still gingerly dabbing the cloth against his cheek. "Don't even think about taking up residence here. You'd better take all of your possessions with you when we return to Town in two days' time."

"And if I don't?"

"I shall personally toss out any personal items you leave behind."

Leela settled on the gold sofa opposite him. "Did you really think I wouldn't find out?"

He examined the bloodstains on the cloth. "What are you talking about?"

"How did you think this would all play out?"

"I thought you would become my mistress—"

"In order to keep the house that I already own?"

"—but clearly that was a mistake . . . Wait," he stammered, his eyes huge. "What . . . I beg your pardon?"

"The appointment I had today was with Mr. Sherman, your late father's solicitor."

Edgar paled. "Why did you meet with Sherman?"

"Why do you think? Because you are determined to deny me what is rightfully mine. I know your father left Parkwood to me. This is my house and has been for two years."

"Oh, very well." He sank back in his chair. "So now you know. Father did leave this pile to you."

"You admit that you've known all along?"

"Of course." He shrugged. "You can hardly blame me for trying to keep Parkwood in the family."

"I certainly can."

"Be reasonable." He winced as he patted his injured cheek with the cloth. "Parkwood has been ours for over a century. You have no ties here. No children who carry Chambers blood. Parkwood must remain in the family."

"I was your father's wife for seven years. He saw me as family. Your thoughts on the matter are irrelevant. I intend to claim what is mine. To that end, I have instructed Mr. Sherman to collect the rents from my farms."

Edgar's jaw tightened. "Those are among our most profitable properties. I need that income. Lambert Hall requires that money to remain prosperous."

"I don't believe you. Douglas loved Lambert Hall. He wouldn't have done anything to jeopardize its future. As to the dower house, you may rent it out to the tenants you have chosen."

He regarded her suspiciously. "Why are you being reasonable about the house now?"

"Because my solicitor will collect the rents for me."

She stood up. "If that is all, I'd like to be left alone in my house now."

Grumbling under his breath, he came to his feet. She followed him into the front hall. Pausing, on the front doorstep, Edgar turned back to face her. "I will send some of the grooms down to remove the extra furniture."

"Do not bother." She was almost amused that he was still trying to cheat her. Almost. "Everything in this house belongs to me. As you well know."

"You don't even want those furnishings." He spoke through clenched teeth. "Just yesterday you couldn't wait to have them hauled away."

"That was before I knew that it all belonged to me. I understand the marble side tables are quite valuable. I may sell them."

He flushed. "Those are family heirlooms that belong with family."

"I agree."

His face brightened. "You do?"

"That is why I shall consider giving you a family discount when I sell them back to you," she said before slamming the door shut in his face.

# Chapter Sixteen

*L*ady Victoria sucked in a breath. "This is the most beautiful place I've ever laid my eyes on."

Hunt couldn't help but smile at the young woman's reaction. One would think he'd presented her with the crown jewels rather than the extensive library at his Mayfair residence. They'd returned to Town three days earlier. Victoria requested this visit to Weston House primarily, Hunt suspected, to examine his book collection.

She stared up at the book-lined walls. "Isn't this the most delightful library you've ever seen, Delilah?"

"Oh yes, indeed." Leela, who'd accompanied Lady Victoria, smiled as she watched the girl wander up and down the rows of books. "This is all very grand."

Hunt's father had seen to that, restoring the historic home after Hunt's debauched grandfather sold away many treasures to finance his gaming habit and numerous mistresses. A serious-minded boy from the start, Hunt's father took to hiding the family treasures before his father could sell them all off. He was aided and abetted by his grandmama, the dowager duchess, who realized her adored son had inherited the disastrously decadent Townsend gene.

Phillip had not yet resorted to selling off family heirlooms before his untimely death. The book collection Lady Victoria now perused remained one of the finest in London. Touring the house, she'd appeared suitably impressed with the stately house's massive mahogany staircase, carved and twisting balusters, generous chambers and fluted walls. But it was the library that truly took her breath away.

Victoria's pale fingers trailed along the book spines as she wandered down the book stacks. "Do you have a travel section?"

Hunt noticed she'd overcome some of her discomfort in his presence. She no longer stuttered and stammered. "Yes, but Foster has just reorganized the books at my request." He shot a discreet look at the attending footman, who silently slipped away. "He will know where to find them."

"Oh, I wouldn't want to disturb Mr. Foster's work."

"Nonsense. His duties are to serve me. And in serving you, Foster serves me." He tried not to look at Leela, even though he felt her presence as keenly as if he were touching her. She'd remained quiet during the tour of his home, although he'd sensed her interest in seeing where he lived. She wore a red spencer over her cream day dress. Red was certainly her color, especially against that dark mane of hers.

"What do you think?" he asked her.

"Victoria will get lost for hours in here."

"But it isn't the library that interested you the most, I believe it was the family sitting room."

Her brows lifted. "What makes you say that?"

"Am I wrong?" He'd noted the way her face lit up when she'd first seen the chamber's silvery oak paneling and full wall of mullion windows.

"Well, it is a lovely room."

"I noticed your appreciation." As he noticed everything else about her. Even though he tried not to. It was just as well that she planned to continue traveling. As much as he could not bear the thought of not seeing her, having Leela around constantly—and knowing he could never have her—was far more agonizing.

Foster arrived in a smart brown tailcoat but still managed to look rumpled all the same. "You summoned, Your Grace?"

"Yes, please show Lady Victoria where you've moved the travel books."

"Certainly, Your Grace."

While his secretary attended to his future bride, Hunt turned to Leela. "I'm pleased you came with Victoria."

"She insisted."

His brows came together. "Still? She seems to have overcome her fear of me."

"I think so as well. But this is all still overwhelming for her."

They watched Foster gesture to the various shelves at the opposite end of the library while Victoria listened carefully, asking questions along the way. "I believe he's giving her a complete rundown of the entire collection," Hunt remarked.

"Do not be surprised if she reads her way through every book in here."

Hunt watched the young woman interact with his secretary in a kind and interested manner. "She'll make a fine duchess."

"You are growing fond of her."

"She possesses a sweet nature and keen intelligence. I feel very protective of her." His gaze met hers. "But it is nothing like—" He didn't finish the sentence. He didn't need to. Understanding leaped in her eyes. An erotic charge of unspoken desire flared between them. She flushed, her eyes darkening. Heat pumped through his blood, shooting through the length of his prick.

"I might have been content with her. Had I not met you." He spoke honestly. They were beyond parsing words.

"Once I am gone, after the wedding, when I resume traveling, you will forget me."

Pressure bore down on his chest. "I won't."

"You must try." Her breath shuddered. "As must I."

"I will do my best." He watched Victoria pull another book from the shelf. "She will never know there is another who owns my heart."

They watched Victoria in heavy silence waiting for the longing to abate to a manageable level where it wasn't quite as excruciating. Oblivious to the emotional current streaming through the chamber, Victoria leafed through a book while Foster left her momentarily only to return with another title.

Finally Hunt spoke. "That's quite a cut Devon has on his cheek. It's certain to leave a scar."

"Is it?"

"He says he ran into a tree branch while riding."

"He really ought to be more careful."

"Branches don't normally cause such a precise wound."

"Don't they?

"That cut looks like it was made by a knife." He looked at her. "Was it you?"

She kept her gaze on Victoria. "Yes."

Fury rose in him. "What did he do?" He'd been correct about the masculine hunger he'd sensed in Devon.

"He attempted to reach an agreement for me to remain in the dower house. Needless to say, I did not care for his terms."

His neck burned. "Did he lay his hands on you?" His lips drew back in a snarl. "I'll kill him."

"I don't need your protection." She finally looked directly at him. "I can take care of myself. Victoria is your concern. I am not."

"You will always be my concern." But Leela was right. It was not his place to come to her defense. He willed himself to calm down. "He took the dower house from you?"

"Not at all." Triumph flared in her face. "It's mine. Douglas left it to me outright."

"You own the house?"

"As well as four surrounding farms and the income they produce. So, you see, I don't need looking after."

"Your late husband left you well looked after." Hunt would welcome the opportunity to take up where her husband left off. To see to Leela's welfare. To her every happiness. To her every need.

"You must put all of your considerable energy into Victoria," she said. "It is the only way forward."

He nodded. "Lady Victoria," he called out, forcing a smile onto his face. "Would you care to see the duchess's rooms now?"

LEELA STARED AT the glass-fronted establishment on Fleet Street. She tucked her finished manuscript under her arm.

Horse-drawn carriages and carts clattered by in the muddy street, the great dome of St. Paul's Cathedral on Ludgate Hill rising up in the near distance. Beyond her own precarious reflection, she could make out the shelves and tables of books within the shop.

She drew a fortifying breath. Beneath her kid leather gloves, her palms were moist. She was about to meet her publisher in person for the first time. For the occasion, she wore a cream muslin gown beneath a full-length forest green pelisse. The lines were simple, the long plain sleeves finished with a narrow trim of lace at the cuffs. She had dressed to be taken seriously. She knew he would be shocked. A lady of quality should not have any business concerns, and if perchance she did, she certainly did not manage her own affairs.

Leela's eye caught on a book at the center of the window showcase at William Edgerton Bookseller. She blinked. Twice. There, on prominent display, stood *Travels in Arabia*. Pride swelled within her, coating her taut nerves with warmth, boosting her confidence.

She'd never before seen her book in a shop. Although Mr. Edgerton had written to her about the great success of *Travels in Arabia*, seeing it for herself now, positioned in a place of pride where all of the passersby could see it, somehow made it more real.

Fizzy with excitement, Leela entered the shop. She momentarily forgot that Mr. Edgerton, her publisher, a man who'd corresponded with author D. L. Chambers for more than a year, had no idea that his bestselling author was a woman.

# Chapter Seventeen

$\mathcal{M}$r. Edgerton had a face like a raw slab of beef.

Marbled red-and-pink splotches adorned not only his cheeks, but also his forehead and chin. Deep crevices bracketed a moist pouting mouth. Despite a pugilistic exterior, Leela's publisher was tidily attired and spoke with an air of refinement.

"Good afternoon," she said to him. "I am Lady Devon."

"The Countess of Devon?" His face lit up. "How fortunate we are to have a noble lady such as yourself visit our humble establishment. How may I be of service, Lady Devon?"

She glanced at the clerk busily stacking books on a nearby shelf. Edgerton was a bookseller as well as a publisher. "Perhaps we can speak more privately?"

When he hesitated, appearing momentarily confused, she continued, "Do you have an office?"

"Certainly. This way, my lady." He led her back through a corridor and into a small but tasteful office full of books and dark woods. He took care to leave the door ajar to avoid any appearance of impropriety.

"Now, what can I do for you, my lady?" Curiosity lit his gaze once he was seated behind his orderly desk. "Do you perhaps have a library to furnish?"

"No, nothing like that." Sitting opposite her publisher, Leela settled her packaged manuscript on her lap with her reticule perched atop it. She smiled at him. She felt as though she knew the man. How would he react once Leela revealed she'd written his bestselling book? "It is good to meet you in person." She enjoyed their correspondence. Mr. Edgerton's letters were businesslike, but also edged with humor and wit.

His exuberant brows drew together. "Have we corresponded?"

"Yes." She summoned her courage. "I am D. L. Chambers."

He stared at her, a polite expression frozen on his meaty face.

She added, "I am the author of *Travels in Arabia*."

"Ludicrous," he exclaimed on a breath of disbelief.

"Nonetheless, it is true."

"You're not a man."

"No indeed."

"You're supposed to be a man."

"You may have assumed me to be a man. But I never said that I was." Although, to be honest, of course she knew Mr. Edgerton assumed her to be a man.

He stared at her, slowly shaking his head from side to side. "I'm afraid I don't understand."

"Really, it's not that complicated, Mr. Edgerton." She withdrew a short stack of letters from her reticule and offered it to him. "Here, this should clarify matters for you. It is your correspondence with D. L. Chambers."

Cynicism etched the lines of his craggy face. "How did you get these?"

"You sent them to me." Exasperated, she held up her package. "This is the finished manuscript for volume three, which is due next week. I completed the book early and thought to deliver it to you in person."

His eyes went to the package, his interest apparent. "Mr. Chambers has completed the third volume?"

"There is no Mr. Chambers," she finally snapped. Really, the man was beyond irritating. "There is me, Delilah Lydia Chambers, the author of *Travels in Arabia*." She rose. "But since you do not believe me, I'm of a mind to go and see whether another publisher might be interested in purchasing volume three."

Mr. Edgerton jumped to his feet. "Now, now, Lady Devon, there is no need to get hysterical." He hurried around his desk. "You just gave me such a surprise is all. It is most unusual for a lady to engage in trade."

"I am a writer, Mr. Edgerton. I write." She'd never referred to herself in that way. As an author. It felt good, empowering. Leela retook her seat. "Now, if we could speak of important matters pertaining to the publication of my books."

"Certainly, certainly. Please do calm down." He settled back behind his desk. "I have eagerly awaited the delivery of volume three. There is great anticipation surrounding the release of volume two next month. And may I laud you on your punctuality? Most . . .

erm . . . members of your sex are not necessarily known for their promptness."

"Is that so?"

He rushed on. "Now if you could just give the fair copy over to me, we'll have the compositor begin the work of typesetting posthaste."

"Of course." Leela made no move to hand over the manuscript. "But first, I'd like to complete the business surrounding volume one."

"And what business might that be?"

"I should like to collect my fee."

"Your fee?"

"Yes, as you know, I have yet to be compensated for volume one. Our agreement stipulates that once the first volume has made a profit in excess of three-hundred pounds, I am to receive seventy-five pounds."

Mr. Edgerton winced.

"Is something amiss?" she asked.

"Not at all. It is just that"—a distasteful expression came over his face—"I have never discussed finances with a lady before. It is, as you know, a bit . . . unseemly. When we negotiated the conditions for the purchase of volumes one and two of *Travels in Arabia*, I naturally assumed you were a gentleman."

The grip on her manuscript tightened. "Are you suggesting that now that you know I am a female, you don't intend to abide by our agreement?" Leela's heart stuttered when he paused. She added, "And that you are no longer interested in volume three?"

"Not at all." He quickly found his tongue. "The

book is a great success and I am not so foolish as to turn away an opportunity that will enrich my business concern. Bookselling is a chance business. Bestselling volumes are not easy to come by."

"Very well then," she said crisply, "shall we proceed?"

He paused. "Is there perchance a male who could act as your representative in these matters? A brother, perhaps?"

"No, Mr. Edgerton, there is not." She could ask Alexander. He was currently away, seeing to what his butler said was an urgent business concern. Leela could certainly reach him if she needed to, but why should her brother handle her business affairs?

Alexander knew nothing about her books, and she had no idea whether his negotiating skills were superior to hers. "I write these books on my own, without any male assistance, and I can certainly steer their journey into the world. Do you have my fee or not?"

"Yes, of course. Please calm yourself. I have already written the check." He reached into his desk drawer and looked through some checks before finding the one he sought. "Considering the success of *Travels in Arabia*, it is with great pleasure that I present this check to you."

Leela gazed at the check, the first money she'd ever earned. Society might consider it unseemly for a woman to do any kind of paying work, but a heady sense of accomplishment rippled through Leela. "Thank you." Folding the check, she placed it inside her reticule. "Now, about volume three."

"Given the success of volume one, I am certain that you can expect to receive your seventy-five pounds for volume two in very short order." He glanced at the package on Leela's lap containing volume three. "I anticipate that volume three will also be much sought after. The lending libraries have already ordered all three volumes of *Travels in Arabia* in advance."

"The lending libraries? Is that good?"

"Very good indeed. Books are costly. Only the very wealthy can afford to buy them. Lending libraries make up the majority of book sales. Now if you'd like to leave the manuscript for volume three with me—"

"I would be happy to. As soon as we negotiate the terms for volume three."

His brows lifted. "You needn't concern yourself with these matters. The terms will be the same as for the first two volumes."

"No, I do not think so."

"I understand if you are perchance confused," he said kindly. "This is why ladies do not generally represent themselves in financial matters. Numeric calculations can be vexing."

"You are very kind, but I believe it is you who is confused."

"I?" He straightened in his chair. "In what way?"

"I fully intend to renegotiate the terms for volume three."

He looked affronted. "That is not generally done, my lady."

"Nevertheless, that is how I should like to proceed." Seeing how much Mr. Edgerton wanted her manuscript boosted Leela's confidence in her position. "Given the success of volume one, and the likely success of volume two when it is released in a few weeks, I should like to come to a different understanding for volume three."

"What sort of deal are we talking about? I assume you'd like a higher fee?"

"Precisely."

He waggled his finger at her. "You are a very canny young lady. Very well, I shall give you a fee of one hundred pounds once I earn three hundred pounds in profit, which you understand, means once I cover all of my expenses."

"I want two hundred pounds."

He gaped at her, his already flushed face turning a more mottled red. "That's outrageous."

"I disagree." She spoke calmly, although her heart beat erratically against her ribs. "We both know you stand to earn hundreds, and possibly well over a thousand pounds on all three volumes of *Travels in Arabia*. I am simply asking to be fairly compensated. In all, I shall only be receiving three-hundred and fifty pounds for all three volumes. Surely that is not too much to ask."

"It certainly is. The answer is no. Absolutely not."

"Is that your final word on the matter?"

"Yes, I'm afraid I must stand firm on this."

"Very well." She came to her feet, tucking her manuscript under her arm. "Good day then."

He shot up. "Where do you think you're going with my manuscript?"

"It is my manuscript and I am going to take it to another publisher who will pay me what it's worth."

"If you leave with that manuscript, do not expect to receive your fee for volume two."

She rounded on him. "We already have an agreement regarding volume two," she said hotly. "My fee is seventy-five pounds."

"Not exactly. You are to receive seventy-five pounds once I have made a profit in excess of three-hundred pounds. My expenses are quite high. There is no telling if I will make such profit."

"You intend to cheat me out of my fee," she fumed, knowing there would be no way for her to prove his deception. It was not as though she had access to his accounts.

"You are the one who is cheating *me*, young lady. We had a gentleman's agreement on all three books. But you've turned out not to be a gentleman. This is what happens when ladies act unnaturally. Writing books and business negotiations are the purviews of men."

"We had no such agreement on volume three. We never discussed a payment fee."

"Now, please settle down and take a seat. Surely, you can attempt to be less emotional."

"No, I don't think that I can." Leela was past tired of being told what to do. She certainly wasn't going to let a man she barely knew order her about. "Our business is concluded, sir. You have openly admitted your intention to cheat me and I do not associate with cheaters."

"You should take care about who you offend, Lady Devon." The words took on an ominous tone. "I understand you are a countess in name only. Your husband is dead. You are of dubious blood, the product of an eccentric father, to put in kindly, and a mother of . . . low associations. I guess it should not surprise me that a woman of your origins would take to traipsing around the world and turning to trade."

She kept her head high. "Given that my associations offend you, Mr. Edgerton, I will assume you have no interest in volume three."

"I could expose you. If you do not give me that manuscript, I might just tell all of London that the author of *Travels in Arabia* is none other than the Mad Marquess's daughter."

"You could, but I doubt you will."

"Why is that?"

"Because you have just as much to lose. With the second volume coming soon, you won't chance losing sales by exposing my true identity." She spoke with far more confidence than she felt.

He studied her. "Are you willing to risk your reputation on that?"

"I am. Because it is most obvious that your love of money exceeds your devotion to societal rules of decorum." She nestled the manuscript more firmly under her arm. "I think I shall hold on to this. Good day, Mr. Edgerton."

LEELA HAD LITTLE time to think about Mr. Edgerton or her publishing frustrations in the days that followed.

The week leading up to Tori's betrothal ball was a whirlwind of shopping, fittings and small dinner parties. Leela and Hunt managed not to be alone together and rarely exchanged more than a few polite words. The duke was attentive to his future bride and Tori seemed more comfortable than ever in Hunt's company.

Not only had the girl completely stopped stammering in his presence, she'd actually blossomed. Tori had never looked lovelier. She had a certain glow, the spark of a young woman in the throes of a burgeoning romance. Leela often caught Tori and Hunt engaged in animated chatter punctuated by quiet laughter. Leela tried to ignore the stabbing sensation in her chest when she glimpsed the obvious warmth between them. Tori's happiness was all that mattered.

Their impending betrothal was London's worst-kept secret. The official announcement at the upcoming ball hosted by Edgar was a formality. Word spread quickly that society's most exacting duke had settled on the bookish daughter of an earl who had drawn few other suitors.

Leela's own emotions were confused, her happiness for Tori tempered by her own profound sense of loss. She resolved to hasten plans for her voyage to Morocco. The sooner she removed herself from the situation, the better for all involved. Until then, Leela managed to keep her distance by staying at Peckham House, the family townhome in London that now belonged to her brother, the Marquess of Brandon.

Alexander was still away, attending to business matters. He rarely came to London anyway, preferring

Highfield, his country estate. Few in London would recognize the Marquess of Brandon if he strolled past them on the street.

The day before the betrothal ball, Leela holed up in her mother's old sitting room at Peckham House and attempted to distract herself from the upcoming nuptials by focusing on the details of her upcoming trip. Most of the house was closed up since her brother rarely visited, but he retained a skeletal staff, old servants of their parents, to look after the place. Hashem and his daughter Hasna were temporarily part of the small staff, with Hasna serving as Leela's lady's maid. When Leela traveled to Morocco, they would both accompany her.

Leela was poring over maps and other guides when the butler appeared to tell her she had a visitor. "Who is it?"

Stokes appeared suitably impressed. "The Duke of Huntington, my lady."

"He's here?" Her heartbeat went faster. "Now?"

"Indeed, my lady."

"Is Lady Victoria with him?"

"No, my lady. His Grace says he is here on a most urgent matter."

"Very well." Anticipation welled up in her. Even though it shouldn't. "Please show him in."

Hunt appeared moments later. Leela went to him. "Is something amiss? Is Victoria well?"

"Victoria is fine."

She exhaled, her nerves settling. "Thank goodness." She allowed herself to soak in the sight of him for the last time before he became another woman's husband. When they were in public, Leela normally averted her gaze because it hurt too much to look at him. Yet she couldn't deny herself now. Hunt's masculine appeal remained as potent as ever. His deep green tailcoat settled perfectly over broad shoulders. His midnight blue eyes stared directly into hers. It suddenly seemed very warm. "What is it then? What brings you here?"

"Victoria is well but something is very definitely amiss."

"What?"

He sank into the nearest chair. "I don't think I can go through with it."

"What do you mean?"

"Victoria. We should end this farce now, before the ball."

She shook her head in jerky, frantic motions. He couldn't cry off. "It has already gone too far." She knelt beside his chair and tried to ignore the way the notes of leather and soap—his masculine scent—thrilled her senses. "All of society knows your betrothal will be announced tomorrow. It was already too late when we first met at the inn. We just didn't know it."

"But now we do." He spoke with urgency, looking at her with a plea in his eyes. "Do you not see that the world is a completely different place to me now?"

"But this is not all about you," Leela hissed, alarm bells ringing from every cell in her body. "It is of no account if you view the world in a different light. The fact remains that the world hasn't changed, no matter if we have. I'm still the closest thing Victoria has to a mother or a sister. I will not betray her. There is nothing, *nothing* in this world that is more important to me than her happiness. And she truly seems happy."

"You want her to be happy at our expense." Anguish ravaged his handsome face. "Doesn't she deserve a husband who loves her?"

"You *will* love her."

"Stop saying that," he said, heat radiating off his body. "Repeating it over and over will not make it true. I have only ever truly cared for one woman in my life, and that woman is you."

She wanted to touch him, to take his hand and reassure him, but she did not dare. Instead, she straightened and moved away, putting a safe distance between them. If such a thing were possible. "You are not thinking clearly."

He rose and followed her. "I have never been more clearheaded than I am at this moment." Restless energy poured out of him. "I was thinking clearly when you took me into your body. When I put my tongue to the most intimate part of you. When I tasted you until I brought you off. I wasn't confused when you sat on my lap and rode me like—"

She covered her ears. "Stop it!" she cried, turning away. "You must leave."

"It's too late for that. There's nowhere for me to go." He gripped her arm, turning her to him. "Don't you see? All I want is to be by your side."

His fingers felt like fire on her arm. "That's just your nerves talking. It happens before one marries. I had the same nerves when I wed Douglas."

"I don't want to live without you," he said hoarsely. "And I know you feel the same."

"You are wrong."

He released her arm. "What a liar you are. You are too afraid to live your life honestly." Contempt saturated each word. "What happened to the fearless woman who doesn't allow idle talk to keep her from traveling the world and doing as she pleases?"

"I haven't a care about what people say about my adventures. The only person I have to please is myself."

"And being with me would please you. Don't bother to deny it, because I know it's true. Are you not tired of playing the role of the self-sacrificing damsel? First, you sacrificed your needs to marry the man your father chose. And now you sacrifice your happiness for Victoria. When will you finally take what you want for yourself?"

"And what, exactly, do you think I want? Marriage to you?" She shook her head. "I want nothing more than to escape the ton's judgmental gaze. I am tired of constantly being found lacking by a society that can never look past my foreign blood and merchant connections. I will never fit the ton's expectations of what a duchess should be. Nor do I care to."

"All that matters is that we be together. In whatever form that takes."

"I could never do anything to steal Victoria's happiness from her," Leela said vehemently. "I hate myself whenever I think of what we did. We can never be together. You will never find a bride more decent, lovely and loyal than Victoria."

His shoulders slumped. "This is really it then."

"Yes." Relief and despair mingled in the breath she released. "It is."

"It never seemed completely real until today." And then more quietly he added, "But if the only way you will stop hating yourself is for me to wed Victoria, then I will do as you ask. I would do anything for you."

He stepped toward her but Leela backed away. She could not bear to have him too close without being able to touch him. "Go then. And promise me that you will never again speak to me of love. This is the last intimate conversation we shall ever have."

He stared at her with such tenderness that she battled the urge to burst into tears and throw herself into his arms.

"Goodbye, Delilah," he said quietly. "I will do all that you ask. But no matter where I am or what I am doing, whenever I look at the moon, I shall think of you."

And then he left.

# Chapter Eighteen

Oh no." Tori peered out her bedchamber window. "It's raining."

"*Citi* says rain on your wedding day is good luck," Leela said.

Tori turned away from the glass pane. "Do you think the same applies to betrothal parties?"

"Why not? I think we should assume the best."

Belowstairs, the servants and extra hired help bustled about, setting out lavish floral arrangements and sufficient candles to set the entire city aflame. Meanwhile, in the kitchens, staff prepared enough food to feed the entire city. More than two hundred people were expected to attend the grand event.

Tori examined her reflection in the mirror. She wore a simple white dressing gown but her hair was arranged in an updo with becoming ringlets falling about the nape of her neck and shoulders. "How does my hair look?"

"You look beautiful."

Tori studied the beaded silver ball gown laid out on

her bed. "This truly is the most beautiful gown I have ever seen."

A strange energy emanated from the girl today, excitement certainly, and nerves as well, but it was all tempered with an edge of something Leela could not identify. "Are you well, Tori?"

Tori's eyes were bright. "Yes, why do you ask?"

"You seem a little . . . not exactly out of sorts—" Something about Tori's countenance made her uneasy.

"I am mere hours away from making a monumental change in my life. This evening, I reach the point of no return."

"You make wedding the duke sound like being condemned to a life sentence." Hunt's tortured expression from the previous day flashed in Leela's mind. Thoughts of him were like a tear in her heart, a wound festering in her chest. But she was determined to smile and dance and rejoice with Tori on such a special evening in the young woman's life. The problem was that Tori didn't appear particularly happy at the moment, even though she had seemed so in recent weeks.

"Well, marriage is a life sentence, is it not, no matter who one weds?" Tori paused, a faraway look in her eye. "Leela, do you still believe in destiny when it comes to having a fated mate? What is it that you call it?"

"*Naseeb*. Yes, I suppose I still believe in it." Although after Hunt, Leela wondered whether the person you were fated to marry could be someone other than the love of your life.

"So do I." Tori sighed, a dreamy look on her face. "Now more than ever."

"Does that mean you are in love?"

"Yes." Tori's eyes glistened. "And I should grab that love and hold on to it, should I not?"

"Absolutely." Emotion strained Leela's voice. "Love is a rare and wondrous thing." She gazed at the beautiful young woman and knew with a certainty that her sacrifice, hers and Hunt's, was worth it.

"No matter the risk? I should fight for it, for love?"

Leela stilled. She was confused. "Do you feel you have to fight for your future husband's love?"

"If there are obstacles to my marrying the man I love beyond measure, I should fight to overcome them, should I not?"

"What is this really about?" Tori was making Leela very nervous. Had Edgar revealed his suspicions about Leela and Hunt? "You know you can always speak frankly with me."

"I have heard Hunt keeps a mistress here in the city. A former actress."

Leela exhaled. "Where did you hear that?"

"Servants tend to gossip. Apparently it is not exactly a secret."

"I do not know if the duke has a mistress," Leela said honestly, "but I do believe Hunt is an honorable man who intends to be faithful to you. Has he given you any reason at all to doubt his devotion?"

"Not in his treatment of me. He *is* all that is kind and considerate. But it feels as though there is a part of Hunt's heart that he keeps tucked far away from me."

"Once you are wed and living together, the love between you and Hunt will grow and deepen."

"But what if that piece of his heart that he keeps hidden away already belongs to his mistress?"

Leela swallowed. "Why would you think that?"

"Sometimes, when he thinks I am not paying attention, Hunt looks so very sad. What if he is sad because he truly loves this other woman and cannot be with her?"

"Nonsense. The duke has chosen to marry you." She spoke forcefully, determined to rid Tori of any doubts. It might be a lie, but it was for Tori's own good, for her future. "If he was so enamored of another woman, Hunt would not be rushing to the altar. You must put these misgivings aside and focus on your own happiness."

"I don't think Hunt loves me."

"He is clearly very fond of you. Romantic love on his part will surely follow." It had to.

Tori shrugged and smiled. Her strange mood broken. "Yes, I am sure you are right." She ran a hand over the beaded silk fabric of her gown. "I'll soon be wed. Can you believe it?"

"Babies will soon follow, no doubt, just as you have always wanted. And you'll be married to a worthy man who will always care for and admire you."

"That is my hope." Hers eyes sparkled. "I am so happy to be taking a chance on love."

Tori's maid entered. "It is time to dress, my lady."

Leela got up to leave. "I shall go on down. I cannot wait to see you in that gown."

Tori grabbed Leela's hand as she passed. "You will always stand by me, won't you? No matter what?"

"Always." Leela squeezed the girl's hand, emotion filling her chest. "There is nothing I would not do for you."

HUNT MOUNTED THE stairs to Devon House. There were just five steps, but he might as well be climbing Black Mountain, the highest point in Herefordshire. Only this evening it felt there was also a boulder on his back.

The rain had stopped. A wet autumn chill permeated the air, but the icy dread engulfing Hunt had nothing to do with the weather. Up ahead, the shiny black front door stood ajar. Through it, he glimpsed the assembling guests dressed in their regalia, helping themselves to Devon's expensive champagne. Once Hunt crossed the threshold to join them, there would truly be no turning back. A few hours from now, he'd be as good as wed.

Breathing hard through the tightness in his chest, he gazed up at the brick-fronted edifice facing Berkeley Street. Bright light blazed from every front-facing sash window. Devon had clearly spared no expense when it came to candles.

The line of carriages carrying guests to the ball wound around the corner. Around him people alighted from their carriages. Those already standing on the walkway greeted Hunt politely, deferentially, before stepping aside to make way for him.

Hunt entered to find the house already crowded with

guests. The buzz of dozens of conversations melded with the orchestra music swirling through the chambers. The rooms were already too warm. By evening's end, they would be unbearably tropical.

Devon and Lady Helene stood in the front hall greeting the arriving guests, Devon in black finery and the old lady with her hair piled higher and stiffer than ever, the style a nod to the long-past era of her youth. There were only the two of them in the receiving line. As Countess of Devon, Leela's proper place was beside the earl and his aunt. But she was nowhere to be found.

Hunt paused before the imperious old woman. "My lady."

"Your Grace." Satisfaction glittered in her leathery face. "'Tis destined to be an evening to remember."

"Indeed." He moved on to be greeted by Devon.

"Huntington." The earl's voice bubbled with good cheer. "Ready for our families to be joined?"

"Most certainly." Hunt's eyes flew to the neat line marring Devon's cheek. The wound no longer looked red and angry, but it would leave a scar. Hunt smothered the urge to plant his fist in the middle of the man's smug face. Leela wouldn't have cut Devon if he hadn't deserved it.

Devon paused. "I hope you will be patient with Lady Victoria." The earl's concern for his sister appeared genuine.

"I will see to it that she is safe, protected and cared for. You needn't worry on that score. Where is Lady Victoria?"

"I am assured that she is on her way down. She's been in her chamber most of the day."

Hunt frowned. "Has she taken ill?"

"It is nothing serious."

"If she isn't well—"

"She is fine, I assure you. You know Victoria. Being the center of attention is not easy for her. I just saw my sister. She looks stunning, if I may say. She'll be along momentarily."

"Very well." Hunt resisted the impulse to loosen his cravat. He wore dark new evening clothes commissioned especially for this evening. Now he wished he could strip them—and all they represented—away.

He wandered through the public rooms. Roaming footmen in burgundy-and-black livery bore trays containing refreshment. Vases bursting with fresh-cut flowers scented the air, which vibrated with an excitement that Hunt sensed but did not feel within himself.

He spent the next hour mingling with the guests, stopping at appropriate intervals to exchange meaningless chatter. He danced with a few of the women, all the while scanning the crowds, searching for the cherished face that did not belong to his future bride. His breath stopped momentarily when he finally spotted Leela chatting with Mr. Paget and his wife.

She wore a vibrant scarlet gown that enhanced her warm skin and dark hair. Her upswept curls bared a long regal neck. To Hunt's shame, longing throbbed through him. A decent man would avert his gaze and never look in Leela's direction again. From here on forward, all of Hunt's attention must center on his future wife, a kind and clever girl who deserved his devotion.

"What are you staring at?"

"Griff," Hunt said to his friend. "You made it."

Viscount Griffin peered in the direction where Hunt's attention had been focused. "Ah, the lovely stepmama. I doubt she'll remain a widow for long."

Hunt repressed the urge to pummel something. "It is good to see you, Griff."

"I decided that witnessing your betrothal is worth the effort." Griff's face was pale. Deep grooves bracketed his mouth. Society's unwelcome scrutiny wasn't the sole reason the viscount rarely appeared in public. Chronic pain from his war injuries also kept him confined to his home.

"I'm pleased you found attending worth the inconvenience."

"As if I could miss this evening. The notoriously finicky Duke of Huntington has finally deigned to take a bride."

"It had to be done." Hunt reached for champagne from a passing footman and gulped half of it down.

Griff's brows went up. "Nerves?"

"Something like that." Hunt poured the rest of the glass down his throat.

"Need a little something to bolster you for the matrimonial road ahead?"

Hunt tried to subtly loosen his shoulders. "Getting married is not for the faint of heart."

"From the pallor on your face, I'd say it's more akin to facing the gallows."

"I hope that I am making the correct decision . . . for both me and Lady Victoria."

"I don't think I've ever seen you so keyed up." Concern lined Griff's forehead. "Normally, once you make a decision, you have complete confidence in it."

"The situation is complicated."

"Is Lady Victoria not to your liking? Have you found her to be disagreeable?"

"No, not in the least. I've grown very fond of the young lady and wish only the best for her."

"Then what is the problem?"

He grimaced. "I am not certain that I am what is best for her."

"Is this about the family curse? You are not your brother or any of your other blasted debauched ancestors."

"No, this has nothing at all to do with some ridiculous curse."

"What then?" Griff paused, contemplating. "This isn't about the woman you met at the inn near Coventry?" When Hunt didn't respond, Griff's eyes sharpened. "Oh my God, it is. Do not tell me you are actually in love with this other woman?"

Hunt grabbed another glass of champagne from a passing tray. "It makes no difference now." Gloom weighted every syllable. All of the muscles in his body were fatigued and achy, as if he'd been struck by influenza.

"I've never seen you like this," Griff said. "Who is she?"

"Someone who can never be mine."

"The way you were looking at Lady Devon just now—" Comprehension dawned, followed by a horrified expression. "Good God, man. Not the stepmama?"

"Don't be ridiculous." Hunt drained the champagne in his hand in one go and reached for another.

Griff's worried gaze followed his actions. "Take it easy on the drink. You don't want to be foxed when the announcement is made."

"To the contrary. Being out of my mind might be the only way I'll manage to get through the evening."

"Now *that* sounds just like something Phillip would have said."

Hunt froze. Getting drunk was precisely what his brother would have done. He summoned a nearby footman and handed the full glass of champagne over to him. "You have the right of it," he admitted to Griff. "I need to pull myself together."

It wasn't as though Lady Victoria was a terrible troll. He enjoyed her company. He could make it work. He had no choice. Wallowing in misery for the rest of his life certainly wasn't a viable option. He and Victoria might even find some semblance of contentment as long as Leela stayed an ocean or two away from them.

"Your Grace." Devon appeared. "It is time. Shall we?"

"Yes, indeed." Hunt nodded, feeling more sure of himself than he had in a long time. His course was set. It was time to embrace it. Lady Victoria would make a fine wife and an excellent mother. In time, this madness over Leela would pass. Or at least diminish to a manageable level of pain. "Let's get this done, shall we?"

With a nod to Griff, he followed Devon to the small platform at the end of the large reception chamber where the five-piece orchestra was set up. They stood at the foot of the platform while the musicians finished the piece they were playing.

Hunt scanned the room. "Where is Victoria?"

"There she is." Devon motioned with his chin. "My sister will join us once we make the announcement."

Hunt spotted his future wife in a glittering silver evening gown and upswept hair. She looked elegant, beautiful even. He was a fortunate man. He shouldn't forget that.

She waited in a narrow alcove off the main room, a maid by her side. Victoria appeared to be staring out the double doors leading to the garden. Behind her, Leela was bent over busily adjusting Victoria's skirt, baring bronze smooth shoulders he had once had the pleasure of pressing his lips to, and the long neck that he'd nuzzled. Hunt quickly averted his gaze. But not before agony lanced his chest, the sensation so intense that Leela might as well have plunged that knife of hers directly into his heart.

The musicians stopped playing. A hush came over the room. Anticipation dangled in the air. It was time. Hunt followed Devon onto the landing.

"Good evening and thank you for coming." A beaming Devon addressed the crowd. Guests poured in from the other reception rooms to hear the big announcement.

Devon continued. "As many of you are aware, we are gathered this evening to celebrate a momentous occasion, the joining of two great families." Murmurs of excitement rippled through the crowd.

A sense of calm that had eluded Hunt for weeks settled over him. He finally felt more like himself. His course was set. He would follow it. Effortlessly, he picked up where Devon left off.

"It is with the greatest pleasure that I announce my betrothal to Lady Victoria Chambers, who has done me the great honor of agreeing to become my wife." He stretched one arm toward the alcove, beckoning his future bride to join them on the platform. "My lady?"

He looked in Victoria's direction but she was no longer there. Leela stood alone in the alcove staring back at Hunt with a horrified expression on her face. "Lady Victoria?" he repeated, confused.

"She's gone," Leela whispered.

Hunt stared back at her. "What?"

An ominous silence descended upon the room.

"What the devil do you mean?" Devon whisper-hissed at Leela.

The young maid who'd been standing with Victoria just moments ago rushed in through the alcove's double doors, her face flushed with excitement. "She's gone, my lord," she shrieked to Devon. "She's run away. Lady Victoria says she cannot wed the duke."

The rustling in the crowd began as soon as the enormity of the moment sank in. His Grace's intended bride had run away. The venerable Duke of Huntington, the epitome of decorum and discretion, had just been jilted in the most public and humiliating way possible.

# Chapter Nineteen

"Where the devil did she go?" Devon roared, towering over the young maid. "You will reveal all to me this instant if you value your position in this house."

The servant trembled. "As I told you, my lord, she did not say."

"Stop screaming at her, Devon," Hunt said wearily. "You've got her so frightened she can barely speak."

They'd retired to the library, away from prying eyes. Hunt sank into the brown leather sofa. Leela and the old aunt were in chairs opposite him watching Devon admonish the cowering young lady's maid.

"Please, Miss—" Hunt paused. "What is your name?"

"Martha, sir . . . I mean, Your Grace."

"Martha," Hunt said gently, still numb with shock, "did you see the direction in which she went? If your mistress is out there alone on foot, she is in great danger and we must find her."

"She's not on foot." Fear etched Martha's wide face. "And she ain't alone."

"What do you mean?" Devon demanded.

"A man helped her into a hackney and they raced away," the girl said.

Hunt blinked. Nothing about this evening made any sense. "What man?"

"I can't say," Martha answered. "It was dark and I couldn't see his face. They embraced and then he helped her into the hackney cab and off them went."

"Did they say anything to one another?" Leela asked.

The maid nodded. "The young man asked her if she was sure, and she said aye, that she was, that she loved him and that Lady Devon had convinced her that love was worth fighting for, no matter what."

"What?" Rage contorted Devon's face. He rounded on Leela. "You knew about this?"

"Why am I not surprised?" Aunt Helene fanned herself with a lace kerchief. "This is a disaster. I shall never be able to show my face in society again."

Hunt took in Leela's pale face. "You did this?"

"Did you encourage Victoria to run off?" Devon demanded. "To abandon everything for love?"

"Not exactly, but something like that." Leela licked her dry lips. "I thought she was referring to the duke. I certainly never encouraged her to abandon His Grace."

Devon scoffed. "That's a likely story. She was all but betrothed to Huntington by the time you returned from roaming the world. If only you had stayed gone. Perhaps you had an interest in seeing her jilt the duke."

"That's enough, Devon." Hunt's voice was like ice. He looked at Leela. "Why would Victoria feel she had to fight for my love?"

Her dark gaze held his. "She suspected you might be in love with another woman."

His heart sank. "Why would she think that?"

"She felt you were guarding your heart because it belonged to someone else."

Hunt flushed. "And you advised her to fight for love no matter what the cost."

Her pale cheeks colored. "Yes."

"Interesting."

They were interrupted by a tap on the door. The butler poked his head inside.

"I told you we are not to be disturbed," Devon bellowed at the man.

"Yes, my lord." The butler cleared his throat. "But I thought you'd care to be advised immediately that two notes have just been delivered. They are from Lady Victoria."

"What?" Devon snapped. "What are you waiting for then? Hand them over at once."

The butler did as his master asked. "One is addressed to His Grace. The other to Lady Devon."

Hunt bolted from his position on the sofa. "Give it here."

Devon handed one note to Hunt and proceeded to open the other.

Leela jumped to her feet. "The second note is addressed to me."

Devon barely glanced at her as he unfolded the letter. "Be that as it may, as her guardian, I intend to see for myself if you are responsible for corrupting my sister."

"How dare you!" Leela exclaimed. "That is my private correspondence. You have no right."

Devon glared at her. "I have every right."

"Give her the letter," Hunt said coldly. "Now."

Devon paused before reluctantly handing the missive over to Leela.

Hunt scanned the note addressed to him, absorbing its contents in dazed disbelief. After a minute, he looked up. "It is done."

"What is?" Devon demanded to know. "What did Victoria say?"

"That she intends to wed Foster because she is in love with him."

"Foster?" the old lady asked. "Who in the world is that?"

"My secretary." Hunt folded Victoria's note and slipped it into his pocket. "Rather, my former secretary," he clarified before walking out the door.

LEELA STARED AT Tori's letter for what had to be the fiftieth time. The words were finally sinking in a full week after Devon's disastrous ball.

*My dearest Leela,*

*Please forgive me if you feel I have deceived you.*

*I truly intended to honor my commitment to wed the Duke of Huntington even though my heart led me elsewhere. The time I spent with Mr. Foster at Lambert Hall has been the most meaningful of my life. We did not expect to fall in love and we both tried to fight our feelings. His Grace has been all that is decent and kind to each of us, but I have come to realize that Mr. Foster is indeed my destiny.*

*He appeared in my bedchamber on the evening of the ball and pleaded with me to come away with him. (He came in through the window. Isn't that romantic?) Still, I was determined to honor my pledge to His Grace, but when I saw Mr. Foster waiting for me in the garden, I knew that I must follow my heart, as you have always urged me to do.*

*I shall be in communication soon, if you will still receive me. In the meantime, please do not worry. I am in the very capable and loving hands of my future husband.*

*With love always,*
*Victoria*

Slumping back in her chair, Leela stared out the sitting room window. How had she missed all of the signs that Tori had developed feelings for another man?

Had the young woman seated herself next to Mr. Foster at dinner out of kindness? Or had she felt drawn to the man? And what of Tori's surprising enthusiasm for the early morning golf outing? She'd known Mr. Foster would be present. Even their going into the woods together to search for that lost golf ball now seemed suspect. Tori and Mr. Foster *had* emerged after several minutes looking decidedly flushed. After their return to town, had Tori asked for a tour of Weston House in hopes of seeing Mr. Foster? Clearly, it was Mr. Foster, and not the duke, who was responsible for that recent glow on Tori's face.

Leela and Hunt were so caught up in each other that they hadn't noticed what was occurring right before them. And now they were left to deal with the consequences.

Tori's defection triggered an enormous scandal. Society couldn't get enough of the tale of the shy debutante who jilted the handsome but intimidating Duke of Huntington. Everyone in London seemed invested in Tori's story. The broadsheets screamed with speculation about the runaway bride's current whereabouts. Some maintained Tori's brother locked the unbiddable girl away at Lambert Hall, punishment for shaming her family and humiliating the Duke of Huntington. Another paper reported sighting Lady Victoria on the continent in the company of her Italian lover.

The city's most renowned cartoonists also immortalized the scandal. One caricature depicted Hunt stripped of his dignity, in the form of a tailcoat, left only in his underclothes as a bosomy, wild-haired girl, presumably Tori, danced a jig on his head. Hunt, who purposely lived a decorous life devoid of scandal and gossip, found himself at the center of a firestorm brought on by Tori's dramatic defection.

Leela hadn't heard a word from Hunt since that disastrous evening, but that didn't keep him from occupying her thoughts. The papers reported that the duke was in seclusion. Leela couldn't blame him for trying to disappear.

Her musings were cut short when the butler appeared to announce that the Earl of Devon was waiting to see her. She folded the letter and put it aside, coming eagerly to her feet. Perhaps Edgar had news of Victoria.

"Have you heard from her?" Devon inquired the moment he strode into the sitting room.

"No. Nothing." She sank back into her chair. "I suppose that means you haven't either."

"Not a word. Where can she be?" He planted a fist on his hip while massaging the back of his neck with his other hand. "I assumed they were headed to Gretna Green to wed, but there's been no sign of them along the North Road."

"You sent someone after her?"

"Of course. I am her guardian. It is my duty." He plopped into a comfortable chair near Leela. "Although I have obviously failed miserably. She's ruined herself in such a spectacularly public fashion that her reputation will never recover. She's thrown everything away for a social-climbing fortune hunter."

"We don't know for certain that Mr. Foster is after Tori's money." Once a woman married, everything she owned became the property of her husband. Tori was truly at Mr. Foster's mercy.

"Of course he is," Edgar said bitterly. "Imagine the impoverished relation of a baron having the audacity to reach so high above himself as to marry the daughter of an earl."

"Maybe he truly cares for her."

"Victoria had better hope so, for her sake. Because she has no funds of her own."

"How can she have no money?"

"Father knew I would take care of Victoria and see to her future, her dowry, all of it." He scowled. "Unlike what he did with you, practically leaving you half of the estate. The old man was out of his mind."

"Or in his right mind," she murmured, "and it was nowhere near half of his estate."

"So you see," Edgar continued as if Leela hadn't spoken, "Victoria has truly made a cake of herself. Let's see just how much she enjoys trading her feather bed for a straw mattress."

"I just hope she is safe and well." Leela rubbed the pads of her fingers against her forehead to quell the headache taking form there.

"Meanwhile, the duke has gone completely out of his mind."

She straightened. "How so?"

"He's holed himself up in that house of his on St. James Place. I had a note delivered advising Huntington that I have engaged a pair of runners to locate Victoria."

"And?" she prompted, eager to hear any news of Hunt.

"I received a brief note in reply informing me that His Grace has no interest in Victoria's whereabouts given that any connection between him and Lady Victoria—and, by extension, our entire family—is irretrievably severed."

"He sounds very angry, which is understandable considering the circumstances."

"You don't know the half of it. Huntington also demanded that I cease all future communication as any amity that once existed between our two houses is at an end."

"Perhaps he will calm down a bit after some time has passed."

"I, for one, will not hold my breath. Besides, who could blame the man? He's been brought low, publicly humiliated by a foolish young girl who rejected a duke in favor of a clerk with no fortune or connections to speak of." He rubbed his eyes, his exhaustion apparent. "She has ruined her life."

"How is Aunt Helene faring?"

"She refuses to emerge from her bedchamber. She takes all of her meals in private and is not at home to any of her friends who have called."

Edgar did not look like he planned on leaving anytime soon, so Leela rose to reach for the bellpull. "I'll ring for tea. You look as if you could use it."

"What I could use is something much stronger."

"The only spirit I keep up here is sherry."

"If you please."

She filled two glasses, handed one to Edgar and settled back down with hers. "Where would Tori and Mr. Foster go if not to Gretna Green? Who else would marry them?"

"I've no idea."

"There is a question that has been bothering me all week."

"Just one?" He emptied his glass in two swallows.

"Why didn't Tori leave you a note? She sent one to me and one to Huntington but nothing to you. Why is that?"

"She was angry with me."

"About what?"

"As usual, you were the cause of discord." There was no heat in his words.

"How so?"

"She discovered that I hadn't told you about your inheritance."

Leela smiled for the first time in a week. "That's my girl. You must admit, that was very badly done of you."

"I will admit no such thing. You ran away right after Father's death and didn't bother to stay around for the reading of the will. Besides, I honestly don't believe you deserve Parkwood. It should stay in the family. You've no children to leave it to."

"Which naturally means I'm not worthy." She also spoke without anger. This was probably the most honest conversation she and Edgar had ever had, and possibly their only real adult conversation. They still didn't care for each other, but their mutual love for Tori bonded them. They were the two people in the world who cared the most for the young woman.

"I suppose, however," he said with exaggerated disdain, "that I do owe you an apology for my transgression against you at Parkwood. I overstepped."

"When you tried to make me your whore?"

He winced. "Must you be so indelicate?"

"Is there a more ladylike way to discuss such a base transaction?" she asked, both amused and utterly shocked that Edgar would deign to apologize to her about anything.

"I am trying to say that I am sorry. That was very badly done of me. I was foxed."

"That is no defense. Do you make a habit of forcing yourself on women?"

"Of course not." He looked affronted. "You may ask anyone."

She already had, at least among the servants. Edgar could be petty and high-handed, but he apparently did not abuse his employees or demand sexual favors from them.

"Now," he continued, "don't you think you owe me an apology?"

She looked at him in surprise. "Whatever for?"

"Isn't it obvious?" He gestured toward his cheek. "For scarring me!"

"No indeed," she said cheerfully.

He harrumphed. They were both quiet for a moment. Leela sipping her sherry and Edgar keeping whatever thoughts he had to himself.

After a minute or two, he spoke. "Just so that we are clear. This détente between us does not, in any way, mean that I accept your ownership of Parkwood. If there is any way on earth that I can retake control of the dower house I will do so. By any means necessary."

She swallowed the last of her drink. "I shall consider myself forewarned." She rose. "More sherry?"

He held out his empty glass. "Why not?"

# Chapter Twenty

Leela slammed the door behind her as she exited Smith and Sons Publishers the following week.

Fuming, she marched down Albemarle Street. Yet another publisher had turned her down. When she first reached out to Mr. Smith, the publisher expressed great eagerness to collaborate with the author of *Travels in Arabia*. He'd written that he was very interested in publishing the third volume. Unfortunately, the *hamar*'s enthusiasm faded the instant he met D. L. Chambers in person and realized that *he* was in fact a *she*.

Leela was running out of options. Smith and Sons was her last hope of finding a reputable publishing home for her manuscript. Everyone else had turned her down. Frustration rippled through her. She had a hit book on her hands, but no publisher willing to touch it merely because she was a female demanding a fair share of the profits. *Ufff.* If only she could publish the darn thing herself.

"Lady Devon," a masculine voice called out to her. "I thought that was you."

Leela was so caught up in her thoughts that she almost collided with the man. She looked up into icy blue eyes framed by thick dark brows. It took Leela a moment to place that face.

"Viscount Griffin." She vaguely recalled the man, a guest from Edgar's house party at Lambert Hall. Although she hadn't seen much of him. He spent a great deal of time in his bedchamber and, if memory served, he'd quit the house party early to return to Town.

"Good day, my lady." He tipped his tall black beaver hat. "I hope you are well."

"As well as can be expected." She saw no reason to pretend the disaster with Tori hadn't occurred. As a guest at the ball, Griffin had witnessed the debacle firsthand. "Given the circumstances."

"It is a most unfortunate situation." His harsh face darkened. "For all involved."

She remembered then that Griffin was a particular friend of Hunt's. "I trust His Grace is recovering from the shock."

"I have not seen Huntington since . . . that unfortunate evening."

"But I thought you were a particular friend of his."

He paused. "If I may speak plainly."

"Please do." Her pulse quickened. "Is something amiss with His Grace?"

"Hunt lives a lonely life. His immediate family—his father, mother and brother—are all gone. He has cousins, but they are not close."

"What of you? Aren't you his friend? Should you not have inquired about his well-being after what occurred?"

"After your stepdaughter humiliated the man by jilting him in front of all of society?"

She registered the cold anger in his voice. "I should think His Grace needs a friend by his side now more than ever."

"He isn't receiving callers." Griffin's hand slid gingerly over his shoulder. He grimaced. "The butler says he is not at home to visitors. Hunt is isolating himself. I am concerned for his well-being."

"He shouldn't be alone after what happened."

"On that we agree. Perhaps you will think to call on him. He might be at home to you."

"Why would he see me?"

He did not answer, but that was answer enough. She felt her face heat. "I do not know what His Grace has told you—"

"He has told me nothing."

"Then I do not see—"

Impatience flashed on his face. "Perhaps I am mistaken in my assumptions. If I am, I must beg your pardon."

A knot formed at the back of her throat. "But what if he won't see me?"

His imposing expression softened a bit. "What if he will?"

LEELA DECIDED TO start with a letter. She took care writing it, inquiring after Hunt's health and expressing her deep regret over what had happened with Tori. When she'd finished, she sent for Ivor, one of her brother's footmen, who'd been with the family for many years.

"Please deliver this to Weston House, the Duke of Huntington's residence," she instructed. "His Grace may care to send a reply."

"I'll await His Grace's reply, my lady," Ivor assured her before going off on his errand.

She watched from the window as he went down the street, her thoughts swirling. She was worried about Hunt. Her concern had increased tenfold after her encounter with Viscount Griffin the previous afternoon.

Once Ivor disappeared from view, Leela sat down to work on her Morocco trip. She was behind in both research and planning. She spread maps out over the table and examined them, trying to determine a route. But after a half hour or so, she gave up on trying to concentrate and paced her mother's sitting room.

She paused by the window and stared out, unseeing. What was taking so long? Weston House wasn't so very far away. She couldn't imagine that Hunt's response would be lengthy. She spotted the footman, Ivor, coming down the street.

She waited impatiently for him to come up. There was no guarantee of a reply, her note did not require it, but she fervently hoped Hunt would send some word, even just a sentence or two, to reassure her that he was well. She instructed Ivor to enter almost the second he tapped on her door.

"Well," she asked impatiently when the footman paused, "did you deliver the note?"

"I did, my lady."

"And?" Why was he staring at the floor? "What happened? Did His Grace send a reply?"

"Not exactly, my lady."

She noticed a letter in his hand. "Is that his reply?"

"No, my lady. It is your letter."

"My letter? I thought you said you delivered it?"

"I did, my lady, it's just that His Grace sent the letter back . . . erm . . . unopened."

"He did what?"

"He refused delivery, my lady."

"Are you certain? Did you see him?"

"No, my lady, but the butler informed me that His Grace did not want the letter and instructed him to return it to me to return to you." He blushed. "I beg your pardon, my lady."

"It's not your fault." She all but snatched the letter out of his hands. "You may go."

She resumed pacing the room after he left. This time it wasn't impatience but anger that fueled her private tirade. How dare Hunt return her letter unopened? Surely, he couldn't blame her for Tori's defection. Not when she'd done everything in her power to assure that their match would flourish.

As she began to calm down, Leela decided to re-send the note the following day. Hunt was obviously out of sorts. Surely, he would not send her letter back again tomorrow.

But he did. Not just the following day but the day

after that as well. By the fourth day, when Ivor returned from his delivery errand with a downcast look, Leela had had enough.

"Did he return it again?" she asked, already knowing the answer.

"Yes, my lady." He handed the now-worn letter back to her.

Leela bit her lip. The rejection stung. And it confused her. Why would Hunt take his anger at Tori out on Leela? "Thank you, Ivor." She tossed the letter into the wastebasket. "That will be all."

"Should I return to Weston House again tomorrow?"

"No, that won't be necessary. I'll see to His Grace myself."

THE FOLLOWING DAY, Leela took the carriage to Weston House. Ivor went ahead to use the door knocker. The massive front door opened just as Leela approached it.

"Lady Devon has come to call on His Grace, the Duke of Huntington," Ivor informed the man Leela assumed to be the butler.

"I regret to inform her ladyship that His Grace is not at home to callers."

"He will see me," Leela said. "Please inform him that I am here."

"My apologies, Countess Devon, but I cannot do that."

"Are you the butler?" she asked in her most imperious tone.

"I am Hayes, my lady, His Grace's underbutler."

"If you do not tell Huntington that I am here, I will enter this house and search every chamber until I locate him."

The underbutler looked concerned. "You could do so, of course, my lady, but His Grace is truly not at home."

"Do you mean to say that he is not in this house right at this minute?"

"No, my lady."

Leela entered the house, surprising the underbutler, who immediately stepped back to allow her to pass. "That is fine. I have all afternoon. I will await His Grace's return."

"I am afraid you are wasting your time, Lady Devon."

"I will decide for myself when my time is being put to good use."

"Yes, my lady, it is just that you could be waiting for several days."

She frowned. "He's truly gone then?"

"Yes, my lady. He had his valet pack his bags and His Grace went off on his own."

"He's alone?" Just as he'd been the evening they'd first met. When Leela had mistaken him for a clerk or a laborer.

"Indeed, my lady."

"Where did he go?"

"I'm afraid I cannot say, my lady."

"Please, you must tell me. I am concerned for his well-being."

His stone-faced expression softened a fraction. "I honestly do not know, my lady."

"Where does Huntington normally go when he is . . . in low spirits?"

The underbutler peered over one of his shoulders and then the other. Seeing none of the other staff in the vicinity, he leaned a tad closer, his voice pitched low. "He returns home, my lady, to Eaton Park."

"Thank you," she said gratefully.

"Now, if there is anything else I can do for you—"

"There is not." She left Weston House, hurrying to her waiting carriage.

"Where to now, my lady?" Ivor asked.

"We're going to Oxfordshire."

His eyes bulged. "Now, my lady?"

Leela forced herself to stop and consider her position. It would take a full day's ride to reach Eaton Park. And although she trusted Ivor, the coachman was new to her. And servants gossiped. "I suppose His Grace isn't interested in a family apology," she said. "We should return to Peckham House for now. But first thing in the morning, I think I shall return to Lambert Hall."

"You're going back to the country, my lady?"

"Yes, to Parkwood, the dower house," she lied. "I could use the serenity after the excitement of the last fortnight."

"Very good, my lady." He shut the door and secured it so they could be on their way.

# Chapter Twenty-One

She left early the following morning with Hashem driving the horses.

Her manservant was discreet. The last thing Hunt needed was more gossip. It was preferable that no one know Leela had gone to see him. Along the way, they stopped only to change the horses and for a bite to eat. The late afternoon sun shone down on them by the time they reached Oxfordshire.

A mile-long, tree-lined drive led to Eaton Park's mammoth stone manor. Two imposing Jacobean towers soared from the roof, looming over the rest of the manor like sentries standing guard. Eaton Park was formidably beautiful, not unlike its master. A shiver went through Leela. She could hardly wait to see Hunt again, to make certain for herself that he was well.

Her carriage pulled up to the entrance. The long open-fronted loggia, supported by columns and styled with arches, spanned the house's facade. Double oak doors opened to reveal a surprisingly young butler.

Leela lifted her chin. "I am the Countess of Devon. I wish to see His Grace, the Duke of Huntington."

"I am Hughes, at your service, my lady." The man possessed a head of thick sandy hair and had yet to reach his fortieth year. "I regret to inform you that His Grace is not at home."

"Will he be away from home for long?"

"He should return in an hour's time, Lady Devon."

"Then I shall wait," she said in her loftiest manner, "if you will kindly admit me."

"I am afraid His Grace is not at home to visitors."

"Surely he will see me," she pressed. "I have, after all, come all the way from Town."

Hughes paused. Leela had placed him in the untenable position of potentially facing his master's wrath or turning away a countess who'd been long on the road.

"Surely you don't mean to keep me out here on the doorstep," she pressed. "I am fatigued and would welcome the opportunity to freshen up and perhaps have some tea while I await His Grace's return."

"Of course, Lady Devon." He reluctantly admitted her. She'd given him no choice really. "This way, if you please."

She followed the young butler through the outer hall and into the great hall, a magnificent galleried space with a spectacular dome at its center. He led her to a large reception room off the front hall with peach silk walls and generous-sized windows.

"If you will make yourself comfortable, Lady Devon, I shall ring for tea and refreshment. In the meantime, I will assign a maid to see to your comfort until His Grace returns. She will show you to the ladies' retiring room should you like to refresh your-self."

Once he left her, Leela went to the windows and stared out over swaths of green lawn that went on as far as her eye could see. A female servant appeared.

"I am Abigail, my lady. I am to look after you while you are here at Eaton Park." The girl was young and eager to please. She escorted Leela to the ladies' retir-ing room, where she took care of her bodily needs and washed her face and her hands. She returned to the reception room to find the tea tray waiting for her. She dismissed the young maid and indulged in sandwiches and desserts before settling down to await Hunt's re-turn.

Abigail checked in on her several times over the next few hours. Once night fell, the servant brought in a sup-per tray and then went to close the curtains. Hughes, the butler, reappeared once Leela finished eating. "Lady Devon, His Grace has directed me to assign you to a guest chamber where you can pass the night."

She straightened. "He's back?"

"Not exactly, my lady. His Grace returned only briefly and went out again."

Irritation flashed through Leela. Hunt thought he could avoid her. Well, she would wait him out for as long as it took. "I see. Please take me to my room."

Abigail led Leela to a beautifully appointed pink silk chamber with an enormous four-poster bed and a plush sitting area before the lit hearth. A part of Leela was surprised Hunt hadn't given her one of his worst guest chambers. Anything to get her to leave.

To the contrary, these accommodations were luxurious, comfortable and inviting. Neatly stacked soaps and creams were available on the dressing table. Someone had set a selection of books and pitcher of water on the bedside table. Leela fell asleep almost the instant her head touched the pillow.

She was awakened by Abigail the following morning, after an unexpectedly restful night. The servant arrived with a breakfast tray laden with enticing breakfast foods.

"I had hoped to take breakfast with His Grace," Leela said as the girl set the tray on the bed.

The girl flushed. "I am afraid His Grace is not at home."

"Where is he?"

"I cannot say, my lady."

Frustrated, Leela picked at her breakfast before rising to dress. Then she went to find Hughes. She located him in the butler's pantry inventorying the silver.

He set down the polished platter in his hands. "Good morning, Lady Devon."

"Where is Huntington?"

"He has gone out. His Grace left instructions for staff to see to your every comfort this morning before your noon departure."

Leela's temper flared at Hunt's unsubtle way of kicking her out of his house. But she wasn't going anywhere. "Then he will be back at noon?"

"No, my lady. His Grace was very firm that he will not be entertaining any callers for the foreseeable future."

She flushed. "Where is he? I must see him."

"I am afraid I cannot say."

"Cannot or will not?"

A pained expression crossed Hughes's face. "They are one and the same, Lady Devon, as I am sure you understand. It is my place to serve His Grace and to see to his every wish, command and comfort."

Leela retreated, unwilling to put the nice young butler in the middle of her apparent feud with Hunt. She returned to her bedchamber. Frustrated, she gazed out of the window and contemplated her next moves.

That's when she spotted him.

Off in the distance, Hunt strode across the low-cut grass with a golf club in hand, followed by a groom carting the rest of his clubs.

"I've got you!" she said triumphantly, although there was no one present to hear her. She rushed down the stairs and hurried toward the entrance.

Hughes appeared out of nowhere, keeping pace alongside her. "May I be of service, Lady Devon?"

"No," she said cheerily, coming to an abrupt stop at the door. The attending footman quickly opened the double doors for her. "I think I shall go for a walk. Then I will instruct my man to prepare for our noon departure."

"Very good, my lady," he called out after her.

She stomped in Hunt's direction, keeping her gaze fixed on his tall form. Now that she finally had him in her sights, she wasn't going anywhere until she forced him to talk to her. She could have sworn he spotted her because he froze and stared in her direction for a few moments.

Her heart sped up. She'd missed him. He looked incredibly appealing in fawn breeches that fit his muscular thighs like a second skin. The tweed morning coat emphasized the wide breadth of his athletic form. A burgundy cravat hugged his throat.

She hastened her pace, eager to speak with him. Their gazes caught and held. She smiled, happiness soaring inside of her. She'd missed him.

Hunt frowned. Then turned and started to walk away in the opposite direction. Speeding up, Leela chased after him. She stumbled over something and almost lost her balance. It was one of his infernal golf balls. She snatched it up and raced after him. He had longer legs and moved at a fast clip. And he wasn't burdened by a double layer of skirts. He headed toward a wooded area, where he could lose her quite easily.

She yelled out to him. "What are you going to do? Hide in the woods?" He was getting away. Frustrated, she hurled the golf ball at his retreating form. "Don't you dare run from me, you coward!"

He turned in time to see the golf ball sailing toward him. If she hadn't been so angry, she might have laughed at the way his eyes widened before he jerked out of the way, the ball narrowly missing his head.

"What the devil do you think you're doing?" he snapped.

"I'm trying to knock some sense into that thick head of yours, you *tase*."

"You are no doubt insulting me yet again." Anger glittered in his deep blue eyes. "What is a *tase*?"

"If you must know, it is a stupid stubborn goat," she snapped back when she finally staggered up to him.

"Did you come all this way to insult me?"

"Why are you running away from me?" she gasped, out of air.

"I am not running. I am merely trying to avoid you."

She clamped her fists on her hips. "Why?"

His jaw was taut. "Because the very sight of you infuriates me."

She leaned over, trying to catch her breath. "I know you are angry at Victoria and I don't fault you—"

"You could not be more wrong," he interrupted. "I am not angry with Lady Victoria."

"You're not?" She straightened. "Why not? She jilted you. Humiliated you."

"Yes, thank you." Looking pained, Hunt held up a staying hand. "I don't need a list to remind me of what occurred. I assure you it is entrenched in my memory." He looked to the groom who carried his clubs and handed his putter to the older man. "You may go now." The man bowed and trudged away carrying his burden.

Hunt watched after him for a moment. "Manley is too old to carry my clubs. I'll have to get a new caddie." He spoke through clenched teeth. "Now that Foster is no longer available."

"I know you are angry. Devon told me what happened. That you want nothing further to do with him."

"Quite right. But my desire to stay clear of Devon

has nothing whatsoever to do with his sister's desertion."

"It doesn't?" Her jaw slackened. "Then why are you angry with him?"

"It doesn't matter."

"It does to me."

He released an exasperated breath. "He obviously overstepped so grievously with you that you felt compelled to knife the man."

"Oh." Pleasurable warmth swept through her body. "You're snubbing Devon on my account."

"Don't look so pleased. I also want nothing to do with you."

"Me? Why? What did I do except everything in my power to help you and Victoria reach the altar?"

"That is precisely what you did," he hissed. "You pushed us both toward marriage when it was clear neither of us wanted it. Both Victoria and I almost allowed *you* to force us into a betrothal with disastrous results."

"I cannot believe—" Words failed her. Her body vibrated with indignant fury. "You blame *me* for this disaster."

"You loved Victoria enough to push her to follow her heart. To never settle for less."

"And what is wrong with that?"

His mouth twisted with disdain. "But when it came to me, you insisted that I quash any feelings that I might have. I was supposed to ignore my heart. I wasn't supposed to do what made me happy. And I listened to you because I cared so deeply for you.

I would have done anything for you, even if it was against my better judgment."

She felt light-headed. "Oh." *He cared deeply for her. Still.*

"Because I listened to you, I am the laughingstock of London." He flushed. "Thanks to you, I am the subject of ridicule and humiliation. My name is on the tongue of every gossip in the kingdom. Everything I sought to avoid for my entire adult life is now upon me. And it is all due to your machinations."

"I never intended for you to be hurt or humiliated. I am so sorry."

He did not seem at all moved by her apology. "If you truly regret your actions, go away and don't ever come back." He turned from her. "I never want to see you again."

She trailed after him into the wooded area. "Please don't ask me to do that."

He spun around, fury written all over his face. Dappled sunlight dotted his cheeks. "What is it that you want from me?" he practically shouted. "Haven't you done enough? Why are you even here?"

"I came to make certain that you are well. I am worried about you."

"It's a bit late for your concern." He spread his arms wide, palms up. "But, as you can see, I am fine. Now you can go."

She couldn't bear to leave matters between them in such a terrible state. "Can we just go back to the house and talk calmly?"

"About what? There's nothing left to say."

Leela felt a sense of rising panic. He truly wanted her gone. The idea of never seeing Hunt again, and, worse, knowing he hated her, was unthinkable.

"Can we not be friends?"

"Friends." He laughed without mirth, an ugly, harsh sound. "No, we cannot be friends."

"I miss you." Her voice caught. She took a moment to gather herself. "The thought of leaving here and never setting eyes on you again is unbearable."

He shook his head. "Stop talking like that," he said angrily. "It is too late. I no longer feel the same about you. I have no tenderness left in me. I might hate you."

She stepped closer. "You don't hate me. You're afraid of me."

He reflexively moved back, maintaining a certain distance between them. "Think what you will. Just go and leave me in peace."

"It is too bad that golf ball missed its mark. Maybe it would have knocked some sense into you."

"For God's sake, Leela, what do you want from me?"

"I want you to have the courage to be honest. You could never hate me any more than I could hate you."

His eyes darkened. The air between throbbed with expectation. "I don't want you here."

"Why is that? Is it because you still desire me?" Attraction arced between them. She felt the pull of it. Hunt must sense it as well.

Anger lit his face. "Is that what you want? Do you want me to fuck you right here?"

"Is that what you want?" She would not let him drive her away with crude words.

His face changed. Surprise certainly, but she also registered the desire in his gaze. "Go away, Leela, before we both do something we will regret."

"There is no obstacle between us now. Nothing to stop us." The words spilled out of her before she even knew what she was saying. "We are both adults without any attachments."

"Is that what you think?" He gave a harsh laugh. "Imagine what the broadsheets will say when they discover I've taken up with my runaway bride's stepmama."

"I don't care what they say."

"Why are you doing this?" He stared at her, conflicting emotions warring on his face. "This is madness."

"I cannot help what I feel. Can you?"

With a groan, he practically lunged for her, pressing her back up against the rough surface of the old oak. Cradling her jaw in his large hands, he angled her mouth up toward his before his lips came crashing down on hers, rough, insistent, uncontrolled. His tongue invaded her mouth, giving her no quarter, hungrily tangling with her tongue.

Leela almost sobbed with relief. Tears squeezed from her closed eyes as she soaked up the feel of him, the taste of him, coffee and something minty. His heat flowed over her and mingled with her own.

"Elliot," she murmured as he blazed a trail of kisses and love bites down her neck. Her knees almost buckled when he urgently sucked the tender spot where her neck melded into her shoulder.

He caught her in a ruthless embrace, his unrelenting body pressing into every soft curve in hers, fiercely claiming her. "Are you certain you want this?" he growled.

She reached for the buttons of his breeches, the backs of her fingers brushing the prodigious bulge she found there. "More than I've ever wanted anything."

"So be it." He lifted her skirts and shoved them out of the way. His fingers found the wetness between her thighs. He circled the bud where so much sensation throbbed. "You're ready."

He kissed her hard, plundered her mouth, taking everything that she willingly gave. He laid her onto the thick carpet of leaves and moved over her. She spread her legs to receive him. He positioned himself between her thighs and the feel of him at her entrance was like a bolt of electricity. He pushed into her in one sharp motion, filling her completely. "Is this what you want?"

Her body clutched him, urging him farther inside of her. "Yes." She sighed with relief. She was finally where she was supposed to be. "Hurry."

He began to move inside of her. Quick, urgent motions that were delicious in their pointed deliberation. Not gentle exactly. But he wasn't hurting her. His eyes were on hers as he stroked into her. "Tell me that you like it."

She grabbed his hair with both hands and stared into his blue sea eyes. "I love it." *I love you.* She kissed him hard. Hunt groaned and something inside him released, that cold control gone. He stroked into her with relentless urgency. Her heart slammed, her blood pumping through her veins. Shivers sprinkled down her spine as the exquisite pressure built inside of her, sending her spiraling headlong into a shattering bliss that made her cry out.

He made a guttural sound as he froze deep inside of her, releasing into her, shuddering as the pleasure of the release rocked him. He lay there for a moment with his face in her neck. She embraced him, relishing his warmth and strength.

He pulled away and she immediately felt cold. He came to his feet, buttoning his breeches. Leela followed his movements in a contented daze, the sublime sensations of their coupling still flowing through her like a lazy river. The pulsing between her legs still delivering glorious pleasure.

He looked at her with no expression on his face. "You got what you wanted."

*Oh yes.* She nodded. "I certainly did."

"Good. Now that you got what you came for, you can leave and never come back." He turned and strode away without looking back.

# Chapter Twenty-Two

*I*t was all Hunt could do not to break into a run as he left Leela behind.

If he looked back, he would be lost. The truth was that he was too weak to stay with her and too weak to leave her. He wanted to hate her. In fact, he'd been convinced he hated her until she'd chased him down and demanded to be heard.

She was magnificent. Her eyes flashing. Her bearing proud. Leela was passionate and unafraid. Unlike him. She was right to brand him a coward. Hunt was afraid. He feared the man he became when he was with Leela. In her presence, he would willingly throw everything away just to see her smile, or to experience the way those sultry eyes lit up when she saw him.

The double doors opened immediately as he approached the entrance. Hughes met him at the door.

"Is all well, Your Grace?"

Hunt brushed by the man. "Have a bath prepared for me immediately."

"Yes, Your Grace, right away." He hurried after

Hunt. "I did inform Lady Devon that you weren't receiving visitors."

They'd been in full view of the house out on the green. No doubt the entire staff had witnessed Leela hurling a ball at his head. For the first time in more than a week, Hunt felt the urge to smile. Few people, man or woman, dared to take a duke to task the way she had.

"Don't concern yourself. I know better than most that Lady Devon can be difficult to dissuade once she sets her mind to something." He took the stairs two at a time.

"She did not return with you."

"I'm sure Lady Devon will be along shortly." Remorse twisted in his chest at the way he'd left her. She'd never looked more beautiful with her flushed cheeks and soft curls that had escaped their pins. The warm scent of her skin still clung to him. She'd given herself to him completely. He had not done the same. He'd slaked his lust and left her. "Prepare a bath for Lady Devon as well."

Hughes stopped on the landing. "Very good, Your Grace."

Hunt threw open the door to his bedchamber, startling his valet, who stood by the dressing room folding Hunt's cravats. "They're preparing my bath," Hunt informed the man, eager to be alone with his thoughts and roiling emotions. "Please see to it."

"Yes, Your Grace."

Once Hunt was alone, he stalked over to the window and stared out over the green. There was no sign of Leela. Was she still in the woods? He cursed loudly.

He owed her an apology. And much more. That was certain. Once he bathed and got ahold of himself, he would seek her out and issue his apology before she departed. His gut hollowed at the thought of Leela leaving Eaton Park. In the short time since her arrival, Leela's presence in his house had made the old pile of bricks feel more alive.

Once he'd bathed and dressed, Hunt called for Hughes. "Where is Lady Devon?"

"The countess is preparing for her departure, Your Grace. Her coach just pulled up to the front entrance."

*She was leaving.* "Why wasn't I informed?"

Hughes blinked. "Your Grace? Your instructions were that you did not wish to see her."

"Never mind," Hunt said irritably. He strode down the corridor and trotted down the stairs, eager to speak with Leela, to apologize. He found her manservant waiting by the coach, but no sign of Leela herself.

"Where is Lady Devon?"

The old man shrugged his shoulders. "No English," he said apologetically. Hunt strode back through the entrance. His heart lifted when he spotted Leela coming down the stairs.

She paused to speak with his butler. "Thank you, Hughes. And please express my regards to the rest of the staff for their excellent care of me."

"Certainly, my lady. It has been my pleasure. May I wish you a safe journey home?"

"You may, thank you. Goodbye."

She marched toward the entrance with her head held

high, staring straight ahead as if Hunt wasn't present. He intercepted her before she reached the open door.

"Lady Devon."

She finally met his gaze, her eyes filled with hostility. She was so magnificent that his chest hurt.

"I must apologize—"

"Get out of my way." Her hand swung out to slap him hard across the face, the force of it almost knocking him off-balance. The butler gasped and behind Hunt the footman uttered a sound of surprise.

Hunt held a cool hand against his burning cheek. "I deserved that and much worse."

"Don't I know it. Get out of my way."

"At least give me a moment to apologize."

"No." She moved to go around him.

He followed, getting ahead of her and dropping hard on his knees on the marble floor facing her. "I beg of you. Grant me just three minutes of your time."

"What are you doing?" She flushed, darting a look from Hughes's astonished face to the rounded disbelieving gaze of the footman standing sentry at the entrance.

"What does it look like I'm doing?" Hunt asked. "I am on my knees begging for your forgiveness."

"Don't be a fool," she snapped. "Get up."

Behind her, Hughes, who'd recovered his usual inscrutable expression, motioned for the footman to exit. The front doors clicked shut behind Hunt. The butler turned away from the drama playing out before him, deliberately staring up at the ceiling.

*"Yikhrib baitak,"* she said. "Stop this silliness at once."

Hunt's knees hurt from kneeling on the hard surface. "I'm prostrating myself, embarrassing myself in front of my staff. And you know how much I abhor making a scene."

"Get up," she hissed.

"Only if you agree to hear me out. You don't have to accept my apology, but please at least hear me out."

"Oh, very well." She rolled her eyes. "Just get up."

"Thank God." He stiffly stood, his hands rubbing his sore kneecaps. "This marble floor was killing my knees."

She avoided looking at him. "Kindly speak your piece so that I may leave."

"Perhaps we can go someplace a little more private?" When she did not object, he escorted her to the nearest drawing room.

"I have been a complete idiot," he began, closing the door behind them.

"Wrong," she interrupted. "I'm the fool. Thank goodness Victoria escaped you. Unlike me, she was clever enough to see the real you. But I won't be making that mistake again. I finally see you exactly for who you are."

"I have no excuse for my shabby treatment of you." He tried to explain himself. "It's just that you overwhelm me. I don't know how to handle the intensity of my feelings for you. My brother followed his emotions and—"

"Oh, spare me. I've heard quite enough about this stupid family curse of yours. You are in control of your own life. And of your contemptible actions."

"Intellectually, of course, I realize that."

"This is the second time you've run away after we've made love. You deserted me at the inn and just now in the woods. You make a habit of abandoning me precisely when I am at my most vulnerable. What kind of a woman keeps coming back to a man who treats her so poorly? I'm a fool."

"I'm the fool and we both know it."

She crossed her arms over her chest and rested her hips against the back of the sofa. "That's indisputable."

"It was because I felt so strongly about you that I pursued a betrothal with Victoria, against my own instincts."

She held up a hand. "By all means, castigate me for forcing a poor, powerless man into a betrothal. Do not worry, I shall depart shortly and will never bother you again."

"I was wrong to blame you. I was wrong to leave you at the inn. And I was an absolute bastard to leave you the way I just did."

"On that we both agree."

"You were right back there. I am a coward. When we made love, it was the happiest I'd ever been. And that scared me. I do reckless things when I am around you. I lose control."

"How fortunate that you and your control will be completely safe now that I am leaving for good."

He stepped closer. "I want you to stay. I promise never to treat you so shabbily again. You have no reason to trust me, but if you give me another chance, I promise I shall never disappoint you."

She looked away; a tear slipped down her cheek. "You hurt me."

"I know." His heart squeezed. "I realize I don't deserve your forgiveness, but I am desperate for it."

She finally looked at him. "I am afraid to give you the power to hurt me again."

"You once told me I was like the moon."

"That seems like a long time ago."

"If I am the moon, then you are my sun. The sun can shine on its own, but I cannot shine without you."

Her eyes softened. "That's an old Arabic proverb. It's in my book."

"I know." He stepped closer and reached for her gloved hand. "My life is dull and lusterless without you. I want nothing more than to bask in your sunshine. Please let me."

She gave a reluctant smile. "That sounds rather poetic."

"Does that mean you accept my apology?"

"I don't know," she said stubbornly. "You don't deserve to be forgiven so easily."

"While you are considering the situation, may I demonstrate how sorry I am?"

She narrowed her eyes. "How do you intend to do that?"

"It involves me getting back on my knees."

Her breath caught. "Does it?"

He moved closer and set his hands on the tops of her thighs. "Yes."

"What else does it entail?" she asked breathlessly.

He spread her legs wider with his hands, massaging the tops of her thighs. "Expert use of my tongue."

"Oh." Her cheeks were bright. "I happen to know that you have a very clever tongue. *At times,*" she added.

He leaned forward and angled in to press his mouth to hers. Keeping his lips relaxed, he kissed her long and slow, taking his time, savoring the sweet sensation. She smelled clean and warm from her recent bath. Her breath had the aroma of cloves from her tooth powder.

He nipped her bottom lip and then the top. His tongue brushed between her lips. Then dipped inside the warm smoothness of her mouth. She was reluctant at first, allowing the kiss without actively participating in it. He was in no hurry. He coaxed her gently, sipping delicately from the nectar he found there, moving his tongue in lazy strokes, tempting her until she relented, hesitantly at first, and then more enthusiastically, moving her tongue in tandem with his until they were practically sparring in the most sensual way of his experience. Heat and pleasure built inside of him.

She abruptly broke the kiss and turned her head to the side. "I hate myself for being so weak."

"I don't deserve your forgiveness. I know that." He dropped to his knees. "But please let me worship you as you deserve."

Lifting her skirts, he bared shapely calves in fine white silk stockings. When she did not object, he ran a hand up her leg, caressing her calf. He pushed her skirts higher, revealing the garters that held up her stockings and the smooth bronze skin at the top of her thighs. The weight of her skirts disappeared from his hands. He realized Leela held the crumpled dress high up against her chest, baring her clean, smooth private place to his hungry gaze.

Adrenaline pumped through him. But Hunt forced himself to go slow. To make it good for her after how he'd hurt her. To pay this delicious penance. The scent of her arousal filled his senses as he pressed his lips to the inside of her thigh. Leela moaned and widened her legs, improving his access to the treasure of her most intimate place.

He licked his way up her thigh, sucking at the crease between her thigh and her mons, where her leg met her hips.

She bucked a little, but stifled a groan from deep in her throat.

"Does this feel good?" he murmured as he moved to her other thigh, licking and kissing his way toward the core of her womanhood.

"It is fine, I suppose." She held herself back even as he felt her body responding.

"I shall have to try harder to please you." He relished the challenge. He moved up, skipping the place between her legs, to press his lips against her bare mound atop her sex.

"Elliot," she sighed. "Oh, Elliot. You hurt me."

"I'm sorry, my love, let me show you how sorry." He finally ventured to where she wanted him most, tonguing and kissing her opening. He swirled his tongue around the tiny bud where so much female pleasure was centered. She writhed and moaned, and the beautiful pressure built within him. His balls drew up tight, his prick throbbed.

"Ahhh!" she exclaimed as she lost her balance and suddenly flipped backward over the couch, disappearing from his sight.

"Leela!" He leaped over the furniture to find she'd tumbled over the sofa and onto the floor. When he reached her she was laughing. He kissed her hard and she rolled over on top of him and worked to unbutton the placket of his trousers.

"But I haven't finished pleasuring you yet," he protested. Weakly.

"We'll finish together." She freed his erection, stroking him in firm movements. Her hands on him felt so good that his eyes almost rolled to the back of his head. Then she was lowering herself onto him until he was fully seated in her sublime snug warmth. She began to move over him, her hair now wild and free. Her eyes in a glittery daze.

She controlled the pace and the intensity. He followed her lead, undulating with her, making guttural sounds of pleasure as her insides caressed his prick. Blood rushed to his groin. It was unbearably good. He wasn't going to last. Sensation rushed at him. Warmth surrounded his balls. He felt lighter, freer, braced for the thrill of climax.

"Leela!" he called out as the tension shattered and he released into her.

She froze, threw her head back and arched into her climax. Then collapsed onto Hunt's chest. Hunt wrapped his arms around her and drew her to him.

"Am I forgiven?"

She made a noncommittal sound and snuggled into the warmth of his body.

Hunt pulled her closer and could not remember ever feeling more content. "I'm here and I am staying," he whispered in her ear, his chest tight with emotion. "And I won't leave until you send me away."

HUNT'S FINGERS EXPLORED between Leela's legs.

They were entwined on his massive carved wood bed where they'd spent the night together in his cavernous bedchamber. Again, she marveled at his vigor.

Last night, he'd made love to her again, going slowly, exploring every part of her. Hunt, she discovered, was very thorough once he set his mind to something. It was wondrous to be on the receiving end of so much determined energy, of his ardor and zeal. And his stamina astounded her. Douglas had been much more quick about this business.

"What was that you said to me yesterday when you were determined to leave Eaton Park?"

She yawned. "When?"

"You said something to me in Arabic when you were trying to get me off the floor when I was begging for your apology."

"Oh that. Nothing. It's just something Arabs tend to say when they're angry with someone."

"Say it again."

*"Yikhrib Baitak."*

"What does it mean?"

"Something along the lines of, 'May God destroy your house.'"

"So harsh." He chuckled. "But I suppose I deserved that."

"But I rather like your house now." She pressed a kiss against his lips. "Particularly your bedchamber."

"I'm rather fond of it, too." Elliot's finger traced a path along the intimate slit at the apex of her thighs. "Does it hurt?"

She stretched, her body still humming from the lingering sensations of intensely enjoyable lovemaking. "Does what hurt?"

He feathered his fingers over the smooth folds. "Removing the hair."

"Somewhat." It was difficult to carry on a conversation with his hand down there. "Among the Arab women it is often a communal ritual. My cousins and aunts would come together to make the special sugaring to remove all of the hair from their arms, legs and . . . elsewhere."

His seeking fingers stilled. "You watch each other do this?"

She smiled at his shock. "No, the most private removal is done in privacy behind a curtain. But the rest, our arms and legs, we did while we were together."

All while gossiping, laughing and drinking delicious *shay* flavored with either mint or rosemary.

Leela had balked at first; the concept of removing her body hair was completely alien to her. Ultimately, however, curiosity about the customs and cultural traditions of her mother's people, and a desire to share a sense of belonging, had prompted her to try the ritual.

*Beauty requires courage*, her aunt had said laughingly when Leela had winced at the pain the first time she'd tried sugaring. But once she'd experienced the results of the procedure and reveled in the silky feel of hairless arms and legs, Leela had regularly joined the sessions and had even sugared on her own upon her return to England.

"Does it feel different?" he asked.

"A bit. You have taught me that it heightens my pleasure. I am more sensitive to a man's touch when I am bare down there."

"Is that so?" He dipped under the bed linens.

"What are you doing?" she asked as his lips trailed down her stomach.

"I am keen to find out just how sensitive you are."

# Chapter Twenty-Three

Later, they breakfasted in Hunt's old-fashioned bedchamber.

Sitting in comfortable stuffed chairs pulled up to a round table with carved legs, they feasted on a massive spread of food. Warm buns, kidney pie, beer, coffee, cheeses, breads, plum cake, hard-boiled eggs and a slab of beef.

Contentedly wrapped in Hunt's too-large dressing gown, Leela helped herself to a second helping of steak and kidney pie. "Mmm, this might be what I missed most when I was abroad."

"Kidney pie?" he asked dubiously.

"I suppose a lady can remove herself from England but you cannot remove—"

"England from the lady," he finished for her. "What else did you miss?"

She chewed as she considered the question. "Ratafia cakes. And definitely sponge cake."

"Any nonfood items?" he asked, clearly amused.

"The English countryside. There's really nothing

quite as beautiful." Sipping her coffee, she surveyed the red-and-white furnishings framing the four-poster bed. Her attention went to the tester adorned with ostrich feathers, a row of matching upholstered chairs and the century-old tapestries lining the walls. "Most apartments in Town are smaller than your private rooms," she observed.

He smiled, settling his elbow on the table and cradling his jaw as he openly took in the sight of her. "Eaton Park was built more than one-hundred-and-fifty years ago when the first Dukes of Huntington treated their bedchambers as public reception rooms and received visitors while lying in bed."

"Imagine receiving visitors in your bedchamber."

A naughty spark lit his eyes. "As long as the visitor is the most alluring woman I've ever laid eyes upon, I'm happy to receive her in my bed at any time."

He looked impossibly appealing in his red silk banyon. He wore nothing underneath. The robe was loosely belted, exposing the mouthwatering expanse of male skin all the way to his waist. She tried not to sigh too loudly in appreciation at the sight of his articulate musculature. Amber hair sprinkled his chest and belly and his dark golden hair was still tousled from their bed play.

"Elliot—" She hesitated to give voice to the subject weighing on her mind.

"What is it?" Hunt cut two slices of cheese, keeping one for himself and putting the other on Leela's blue-and-gold patterned porcelain plate.

"I don't want to bring up an uncomfortable topic."

"Clearly you do. So out with it." He bit into a hard-boiled egg. "What is on your mind?"

"Do you think she is safe with Foster?"

He paused. "Are you trying to ruin my appetite? The last person I care to think about is my double-crossing former secretary."

"I am so worried about Victoria. It's been a fort-night and we haven't heard a word from her. I'm des-perate to know what kind of man this Mr. Foster is."

"If you had asked me before all of this occurred whether Foster is an honorable man, I would have said yes."

"What do you say now?"

He shrugged. "He was hardworking, honest and very capable. He fully immersed himself in his work. Honestly, he could probably run the duchy without me there to oversee matters. However, I cannot speak to his intentions toward Victoria. I have no idea what he was thinking when he stole away with her."

"Is he a fortune hunter?"

"I would not have thought so. But I suppose it's possible."

"She has no money. Can he afford to keep her? Devon told me he won't give Victoria anything. Not a shilling."

He refilled their coffee. "Foster seemed responsible enough with his earnings, and I gave him generous bonuses. But he certainly cannot keep her in the com-fort to which an earl's daughter is accustomed."

"I'm sick with worry. If only I knew she was safe."

"If I know anything about Victoria and Foster, it is that they are both smart, enterprising and generally averse to risk. They'll turn up when they are ready to make a reappearance."

"I hope you are right." She exhaled. "Forgive me for raising a sensitive topic?"

"It's already forgotten," he said dismissively. "If the cost of getting you into my bed was public humiliation and ridicule, then it was well worth it. Honestly, I haven't thought about that unpleasant business since you arrived."

Hunt did appear far less perturbed by the calamity that drove him from town now than when Leela first arrived at Eaton Park. "When will you return to London?"

"Next week. I have government business." He gave her a speculative look.

"What is it?" she asked.

"Will you stay here with me until then? Or will your absence draw unwanted attention?"

"The staff at my brother's house thinks I'm at Parkwood, so they won't miss me."

"That's very convenient."

"Isn't it?" She reached for a warm bun. "I could become accustomed to being spoiled so terribly."

He pushed the plate of warm buns closer to her so it was within easy reach. "I've only just begun to spoil you," he said softly. "I have much to make amends for."

Her insides warmed. "Are we having an affair then?"

"I certainly hope so. I am the most fortunate of men to have a mistress as mesmerizing as you."

She balked. "I never said I would be your mistress."

His face fell. "But I thought you agreed to continue our liaison?"

"I have. But I am no man's mistress. That sounds like a kept woman and the only person keeping me is myself."

"So what are you saying?"

She rose and slipped into his lap, wrapping her arms around his neck to wipe that look of concern off his face. "We are having a clandestine affair." She pressed a kiss just below his ear. "We'll be secret lovers for as long as we wish to continue our liaison."

He put his arms around her and pulled her in for a long slow kiss. "You've no interest in becoming a duchess?"

She shook her head. "For the first time in my life, I am finally free of society's disapproving gaze. I intend to continue writing and traveling without worrying about what anyone thinks. Besides, you don't want a half-Arab duchess. The last thing you need is more scandal."

"You are also a countess. And the daughter of a marquess."

"And a foreign merchant's granddaughter," she reminded him. "There are people who will never see beyond my origins, or my dark eyes and skin tone. I witnessed how hard my mother tried. She shed everything from her past, but Mama was never truly accepted."

"You are not your mother. You were born and raised here. Your father was an English lord."

"Nevertheless, to the ton I am forever tainted by

Mama's *inferior* connections." Her chest knotted. "Since the day I wed, I've been judged and found wanting. As good as Douglas was to me, I felt trapped in a society that turned up its nose at me. I never want to be in that situation again. Besides, imagine what the ton will say if they learn you've taken up with your betrothed's stepmama."

"We were never formally betrothed," he corrected. "But I will admit that I would prefer to avoid another scandal at all costs. I do not relish being the subject of gossip. I am still trying to live down my brother's infamy. Not to mention this calamity with Victoria."

"Then we are in accord. No more talk of marriage." She put her forehead to his. "Let us just resolve to enjoy ourselves."

"And our liaison continues once we return to Town?"

"Absolutely, if you wish it." She paused. "Will it be difficult for you to face everyone?"

He thought about it for a minute. "No, not when I have so much to look forward to." Surprise tinged his words, as though he'd just come to the realization. He pressed his lips to her shoulder. "I shall just get on with it. It will not be long before another scandal eclipses this one. As it turns out, Victoria jilting me just might be the best thing that's ever happened to me."

"Her loss is definitely my gain."

"So it is settled." He stood up with his arms around her waist and walked her backward toward the linens they'd rumpled through the night. "Upon our return to Town in five days' time, we shall continue to be lovers, but you are not my mistress."

"Precisely." She glanced behind her. "What are we doing?"

"You are my visitor"—he picked her up and tossed her onto the soft feather mattress—"and I should like to receive you in my bed."

She giggled and reached up to embrace him as he lowered himself on top of her.

"REMEMBER THE POINT of the game is to get the ball in the hole by using the fewest strokes," Hunt said patiently.

"I understand that perfectly." Leela blew a loose tendril of hair away from her face. "But my muscles do not seem to want to cooperate."

Her face was flushed and her marvelous hair slowly escaped its pins. Hunt had to keep himself from staring at Leela. He could hardly believe that she was here with him. That she'd agreed to continue their liaison indefinitely. "The position of your arms is perfect. However, you must allow your hips to support the force of the swing."

"What do my hips have to do with hitting a ball?" Leela grumbled. "And, if you ask me, the ball is entirely too small. It's almost impossible to hit." Her enthusiasm for the game was diminishing rapidly because she couldn't muster enough power for her swing.

They were halfway through the golf course at Eaton Park. Two aides proceeded far out ahead of them, tasked with running down any errant balls. A caddie carrying their clubs tucked under his arm trailed Leela and Hunt at a discreet distance. It was an overcast day, with a slight chill. The air smelled like autumn.

Hunt smiled. "You are rather fetching when you are irritated."

She scowled. "You have an advantage because you play in pantaloons while I have to manage these blasted skirts."

"Come now. Becoming proficient at golf takes some time. You aren't doing too badly for a novice."

Leela gave an inelegant snort. "It took me eight strokes to land my ball anywhere near the target. You managed to very neatly do the same in just three strokes." They strolled across the green grass to where their balls had landed.

"If your skirts are such a bother, I, for one, would not object to your wearing those peculiar trousers of yours."

"Which trousers?"

"The ones you wore under your skirts at the Black Swan, the evening we met."

Her eyes rounded. "You noticed that, did you?"

"I noticed everything about you that evening."

"Hmm. I don't recall what you were wearing." She lowered her voice. "But I clearly recall the spectacular view once you removed your clothing."

Hunt's blood warmed. Contentment washed over him. He hadn't considered that Leela might be such an engaging companion. He savored every minute with her. Beyond the bed sport, which was extraordinary, he enjoyed the simple pleasures of just being with her—the bantering and easy intimacy, the conversation that flowed so easily, the companionable silences. These past few days proved that their first evening together at the Black Swan was no anomaly.

"We're a good fit, you and I," Hunt remarked. "I look forward to a long affair. Until we're both old and gray, I hope."

"Or at least until you are compelled to marry and produce an heir."

His mood darkened. "Don't speak of it."

"We both know our eventual parting is inevitable."

He studied her. "Because you will tire of me?"

"Because you will do your duty. And even if I were not a scandalous choice for your duchess, I am most likely barren and you need an heir."

The reality of his need to fulfill his duty settled like a heavy weight on his shoulders. "I have years before I even need to think of securing the succession."

"Not so long ago you were eager to wed as soon as possible."

"That was before I met you. There are men in my position who do not marry until they are in their late forties."

"That's more than a decade away."

"Precisely." He brightened at the prospect of continuing their affair well into the future. "I'll need at least fifteen or twenty years to get my fill of you."

She said nothing, but he saw that his intention to prolong their affair pleased her. They reached their balls, which were a few feet apart, and within close proximity to the target. Hunt lined up with his club and with a gentle tap, ushered the ball into the hole.

"You make it look so easy." She rolled her eyes and then stepped up to take her turn. The ball fell short of the mark. It took two additional tries for her ball to finally join Hunt's.

Hunt turned to his caddie. "That will be all, Martin." He gestured to the aides stationed farther out along the green. "And tell the others, will you? Lady Devon and I will manage on our own from here. We'll just practice our putting."

"Very good, Your Grace." The caddie went off to join the others.

Hunt bent to retrieve both balls from the hole and lined one up for Leela. "Just tap the ball gently. Don't force it."

She focused and hit the ball. It sputtered to a stop about a foot from the target. Leela shook her head. "I should just give up. I clearly do not possess the necessary skill for this game."

"Nonsense, you're coming along quite nicely. Besides, you do have at least a decade to perfect your golf swing."

That prompted a smile from her. "I rather like the idea of having several years with you. But I should probably just stick to writing." She kicked at the grass. "Although that may not be an option for much longer."

"How can that be?" He lined up and tapped his ball, sending it in a straight line into the hole.

"I cannot find a publisher for the third volume."

He frowned. "Surely, *Travels in Arabia* has been successful enough to merit a third volume."

"One would think. But apparently the objection to

women who not only work, but also demand to be paid their worth is greater than a thirst for money."

"What does that mean?"

"Once my publisher discovered that D. L. Chambers is in fact a woman, he declined to pay me what I think the third volume is worth. He also found it distasteful to be forced into discussing business concerns with a female."

"Why not take your book to another publisher?"

"I tried. But they all turned me away. They are shocked that a gently bred lady wants to publish books that might bring her fame."

"That's ridiculous and bad business. They stand to make a great deal of money off volume three. You've already proven you can sell books. Isn't volume two coming out in a few weeks?"

"Yes, but my publisher purchased the second volume before he discovered my true identity. Once he learned that I am a female, he declined to pay me what I believe volume three is worth."

He felt a surge of pride in her. "You asked for more money."

"Given the success of the first volume of *Travels in Arabia*"—a defensive tone crept into her voice—"I believe I deserve it."

"I agree," he said quickly, wanting to reassure her of his support. "The publishers are foolish. There's almost no risk involved in taking you on, and you were correct to ask for more money."

"There's a risk if anyone discovers that D. L. Chambers is a woman. Apparently, my lack of a male appendage is a problem."

"Not for me." He came over and pulled her close for a lengthy kiss, his tongue lazily, tenderly playing with hers. "I thank God that you are a woman."

"You are just trying to distract me to get me off my game."

His hands dropped down her lower back to squeeze her behind. "Is it working?"

"Most definitely." She nestled in his arms. "I wish there was another way to get volume three published."

"Why not publish by subscription? Surely, enough subscribers would sign up to purchase the book in advance of publication."

"I'd still need someone to actually print the book. All of the reputable publishing houses in London have turned me away." She sighed. "If only I could publish the third volume on my own."

An idea came to him. "Maybe you can."

"How would I manage that?"

He took her hand. "By taking your future into your own hands." He turned and began striding back toward the house with Leela in tow.

She stumbled along after him before righting herself. "Where are we going?"

"You'll see."

"WE CAN PRODUCE up to four tons of paper per week," Mr. Rutledge said loudly, clearly proud of this accomplishment. He had to speak over the noisy machines.

"The installation of cogs and rollers of the Fourdrinier steam powered machine has made us very productive indeed."

Hunt's surprise turned out to be a visit to Mr. Rutledge's paper mill, located in a rural retreat about an hour away from Eaton Park. Fascinated, Leela watched the moving belt receive a mixture of clumpy wood pulp and water.

"It's the latest technology." The paper mill owner addressed Hunt and all but ignored Leela as they stepped away from the machine and into a quieter section of the mill. "Very few paper mills have this machine. The newspapers have been able to expand their production due to this papermaking technique."

As the water was suctioned away, steam-heated rollers evenly distributed the fibers, forming a continuous sheet of paper, which was further smoothed by more rollers. The sheet was then dried by the combined forces of heat, suction and pressure. The machine was enormous and very noisy.

"What about novels?" Leela asked. "I imagine large print runs of books are also possible?"

"Yes indeed." Mr. Rutledge directed his answer to her question at Hunt. "Combining the fourfold method of wetting, pressing, drying and finishing paper into one mechanized format has made printing books far more efficient that the old processes when each of those steps must be painstakingly performed on its own."

"Remarkable," Hunt said.

"Do you print many books?" she asked.

"Yes, ma'am." He finally spared a glance at Leela.

"You will address the Countess of Devon as 'my lady,'" Hunt instructed the man.

"Countess?" An obviously dubious Mr. Rutledge studied Leela more closely. She'd chosen to wear a simple white day dress with a matching pelisse rather than one of her imposing countess gowns. "Forgive me, my lady. As I was saying, we print mostly Bibles and prayer books. As you can imagine, there is great demand for religious texts."

They took their leave of Mr. Rutledge a short time later, crossing over to the local tavern appropriately named the Paper Mill, to get something to eat.

Once they were seated and served, Hunt took a long draught of his beer. "What do you think?"

"Of the paper mill? The Fourdrinier machine is very impressive." She registered the eagerness in his eyes. "You think I should engage Mr. Rutledge to print the third volume of *Travels in Arabia*?"

"Actually no. As it happens Mr. Rutledge is selling the mill."

"Oh." Her mood dimmed. "There is no telling if the new owner will take kindly to dealing with a woman. Mr. Rutledge could barely bring himself to address me."

"I could buy the mill for you."

She shook her head. "No."

"It would be a good investment for me."

"It's a generous offer and really very sweet of you."

"Why does it feel like a 'however' is coming?"

"*However*," she said, "having you buy a paper mill in order to print my books is still giving someone else power over the publication of my writings and it could complicate matters between us."

"Surely you cannot think I would ever cheat you or try to stop you from publishing your books."

"Of course not. But that sort of an arrangement would mean that I still have to be dependent on someone else to get my books out into the world. I prefer to keep our relationship strictly personal."

He sat back in his chair, his disappointment clear. "I thought it was the perfect solution for you."

"I appreciate the offer, truly I do. Besides, your future wife won't take kindly to any arrangement that keeps your former lover in your life. And I would not blame her."

He scowled. "I'm not even wed yet, but this imaginary future duchess is already making a nuisance of herself."

"If I had the funds, I would buy the paper mill myself."

"I could lend you the money, but something tells me you would not accept it from me."

Leela smiled. "You have the right of it." She grew pensive. She could ask her brother for a loan, but Alex was nowhere to be found at the moment. Stokes knew how to reach the marquess in case of an emergency, but securing a loan to purchase the paper mill hardly qualified as an emergency. She reached for her pewter mug. "I'll just have to find another way."

"I would never bet against you once you set your mind to something."

She clicked her mug against Hunt's. "You are a smart man indeed."

# Chapter Twenty-Four

The following week, Leela was back at her brother's London townhome plotting her Morocco trip when Stokes appeared with a surprise visitor.

Seated at the desk in her mother's sitting room, Leela twisted in her chair to speak with the butler. "Who is it?"

A familiar face wrapped in a hooded black cape popped up behind him. "It's me," Tori said warily. "If you will receive me."

"Tori!" Leela bolted from her chair and rushed over to her stepdaughter. She pulled the girl in for a tight hug. Stokes quietly withdrew, closing the door behind him.

"I've been so worried about you." Relief flowed through Leela to have Tori's slight frame safe in her arms, the girl's familiar floral scent swirling around her. "Are you well?"

"I'm perfectly fine." Tori hugged her back hard. "I didn't mean to worry you. I hope you aren't angry with me."

The vulnerability in Tori's voice made Leela's heart

squeeze. She pulled back, her hands firmly on the girl's shoulders. "I am not angry with you. But I do need to understand what happened."

"And I so want to explain." Tori removed her cloak, exposing a simple brown gown with a white fichu tucked into the wide square neck. The hem stopped at Tori's ankles, as was common for women of the working class, revealing sturdy leather shoes.

"Why are you dressed like this?" The rough fabrics were far from the silks and muslins with intricate lace and embroidery that Tori normally wore. "Where are your clothes?"

Tori smiled ruefully. "I left my brother's house with nothing but the gown on my back. And I have sold my betrothal gown to help support Mr. Foster and me."

"Why isn't Mr. Foster working to provide for you? Are you . . . Mrs. Foster yet?"

Tori's eyes sparkled. "Yes, I am an old married lady now."

"Are you content?"

"I have never been more so." The young woman's cheeks were flushed, her eyes sparkled. She was radiant. "Mr. Foster is everything to me."

"And he treats you well?"

"He is all that is good and agreeable. I could not ask for a better husband and life companion."

"I'm so pleased to hear it." Relief loosened the tight muscles across the back of Leela's shoulders after weeks of worry. "Now you must ask Edgar for your clothes."

"I already have. He has declined to give me anything, including my clothing."

"You saw Edgar?"

"Yes, just now, before I called here."

"Why won't he give you your things?" She tucked an errant tendril behind Tori's ear. "He has no use for them. It will cost him nothing to restore your possessions to you."

"He said he would rather burn my things than return them to me after how I embarrassed and humiliated him before all of London."

Leela looked heavenward. "Leave it to Edgar to make your jilting Huntington all about him." She took the girl's hand and guided her to the sofa.

"How is the duke?" Tori's voice was subdued. "I feel terrible about running off like that and leaving Hunt to face the scandal I created. Have you seen him?"

Leela settled beside the girl. "Yes, he was very upset at first, but he isn't angry with you."

Her eyes widened. "He isn't? Why not? I would be if I were in his position. He'd be well within his rights to hate me."

"He understands that you might have felt pressured to wed him. He does not fault you. However, he does feel some animus toward Mr. Foster."

"That explains why no one will hire Mr. Foster. They do not want to incur the duke's wrath."

"Mr. Foster is without employment? How are you surviving?"

"He has some savings, but spent most of it to cover

the costs incurred by our journey to Gretna Green. I sold my betrothal gown for more than one hundred pounds so that has been very helpful."

"But Edgar had the North Road watched. You were not spotted."

"We left the main road as often as possible. And Mr. Foster decided we should travel mostly at night."

"You are accustomed to having every luxury at your disposal. The route you chose will bring you down in the world," Leela warned, even though it was too late to change anything. "You will face hardships you could never have imagined."

"I didn't intend to form an attachment to Mr. Foster. And we both fought it. But it grew more and more evident to me that he is indeed my *naseeb*. I tried to ignore my growing love for Mr. Foster because I thought any formal attachment between us was impossible."

"What changed your mind?"

"I actually proposed to Mr. Foster because I knew he would never presume to ask for my hand. He confessed to loving me but said he would not allow me to ruin my future by wedding him when I was destined to become a duchess."

"When did this happen?"

"When we visited Weston House, Huntington's London home, that first time. You will recall that Mr. Foster was showing me around His Grace's library. It was fortunate that you and the duke were so engrossed in conversation that you barely paid us any attention. Do you recall that afternoon?"

Leela flushed. "Vaguely," she lied. In truth, she

remembered that afternoon most vividly. Hunt had promised to look after Victoria after revealing he would never love his wife as much as he cared for Leela.

"After Mr. Foster declined my offer of marriage, I was determined to do my duty to my family by marrying Huntington. The duke was kind to me but I did not experience the same intensity of feeling that I do for Mr. Foster. I realize that might sound silly."

"It does not. You felt an attraction for Mr. Foster that you did not feel for the duke."

"Exactly! Mr. Foster came to me the night of the betrothal ball. He climbed up that old tree by my bedchamber window. He said he was a selfish fool to compromise my future, but that he loved me and couldn't bear to live his life without me. He begged me to consider marrying him."

"And you accepted."

"Not right then, no. How could I? The guests were all there waiting for the announcement. Hunt and Edgar and you expected me to go forward. And I am not the sort of girl to cause a scandal."

"No, you certainly are not."

"And then you came up to my bedchamber. And I know you naturally assumed I was speaking of the duke when you urged me to fight for love."

"But you were referring to Mr. Foster." Tori's strange mood just before she ran away now made perfect sense.

She nodded. "I thought about our conversation while Edgar and Hunt announced the engagement at the ball. That's when I spotted Mr. Foster watching me through the doors that lead to the garden. Suddenly, my future flashed before me. I could do what was expected and wed the duke. I'd live a life of leisure and luxury as Hunt's duchess, with warmth and fondness, certainly, but absent of true romantic love. With Mr. Foster, I'd have a husband who understood my very soul. And would it have been fair to Hunt for me to wed him when I loved another?"

"No, it would not have." A new wave of remorse swept over her for having pushed Hunt to wed Tori. "What will you do now?"

"We have let apartments on Holborn Street. The money from my gown should see us through for several months if we live modestly."

Leela was familiar with the neighborhood. Holborn was a respectable area, but it was a far cry from the elite West End, where Tori had grown up. "Are you truly prepared to live a modest life?"

"I do not need mansions or castles to be happy. Our house is quite cozy. What makes it a home is that Mr. Foster is there with me." She paused. "There is only one luxury that I shall miss."

"And what is that?"

"Books. Mr. Foster tells me they are very dear and that we shan't be able to afford them just now."

"I have some money. You must take whatever you need."

"No," Tori said, with a firm shake of her head. "I won't take charity. Mr. Foster and I will have to make do. We put ourselves in this situation and we will have to see our way through it."

"Then at least accept a loan of books from our library here."

"Do you think your brother would approve? Society will see me as a pariah and he is a marquess."

"Alexander does not give a wit about what society thinks. I'm certain he would not mind."

"Very well. It would be difficult to live without reading and discussing books with Mr. Foster."

"And you must accept a wedding gift from me."

Tori set her jaw. "I won't take money."

"I am gifting you a subscription to the lending library."

Tori's face brightened. "I would be able to read the latest books. I am so looking forward to volume two of *Travels in Arabia*. As is Mr. Foster."

Leela smiled. One day soon, she would reveal the truth about her book to Tori. But this didn't seem to be the time. They had so much more to talk about at the moment.

She rang for Stokes and met him at the door to the sitting room. After asking for the tea tray, she quietly instructed the butler to prepare a generous food basket for Mrs. Foster to take with her when she departed.

"Tea would be lovely." Pleasure brightened Tori's face. "I would so enjoy a strong cup of tea."

Leela felt a pang of empathy for the girl. Strong tea would now be a treat for someone of Tori's reduced circumstances, especially given the high price of the imported drink.

Her resolve strengthened. She could never allow Tori to fall into poverty. But that's exactly what would happen if all of London declined to employ the young woman's husband for fear of offending the duke. Leela had to find a way to secure Tori's future.

Settling next to her beloved stepdaughter, she took the girl's hand in hers and kissed it. "Now, you must tell me everything—about your wedding, your husband and your new home. Don't leave anything out."

"I THOUGHT YOU'D never come." Hunt met Leela at the door of Weston House and whisked her inside and into his arms. A strong gust of wind came in with her. It had been raining all day. Inhaling her sweet rose-water scent, he said, "I've missed you."

"It's only been two days," she reminded him.

"An eternity. Are you suggesting you haven't had time to miss me?"

She clung to him. "No, I missed you terribly."

Warmth blossomed in his chest. "That's what a man desires to hear."

She wore a velvet burgundy cloak. It was damp. He pushed away the hood that shrouded her face in shadows. "Let me have a good look at that glorious face of yours."

He cradled the back of her head in his hands and brought his lips to hers, nipping and licking. He explored the roof of her mouth, the soft satin of the insides of her cheeks, before hungrily intertwining his tongue with hers. "I want you right here. Right this minute." He relieved her of her cloak and tossed it away.

Her hands were already going to the placket of his

pantaloons. "The servants," she gasped between urgent kisses.

"Are all off for the evening." He bunched up her skirts, his hand reaching between her legs, finding the moist smoothness he was desperate for. "God, you're beautiful."

Her clever hands freed his shaft. "As are you." She bit his lip, the sensation going straight to his prick, which was already thick and long. She stroked him in strong firm motions. The pleasure was almost more than he could stand. He was going to spend before he even got inside her.

He backed her up to the nearest wall and pressed her hard against it. She straddled him with one of her legs. He crouched down and pushed into her. The relief was so intense that his throat ached. Slipping his hands under her bottom, he hoisted her up against him.

Leela wrapped both legs around his waist. She arched her back and sank her fingers into his hair, tugging at it. The rough touch aroused Hunt even more. "Do you like this?" he demanded to know, thrusting into her hard and fast.

"Yes." She rocked her pelvis in rhythm with his movements. "Oh yes." She slid her hands up under his linen shirt and dug her nails into the skin of his back. Their sharp breaths, the thumping sound as he thrust into her, echoed up through the high ceilings of his marbled entryway. Outside, the wind roared.

He increased his pace, sweat pouring down his back. "Is this good? Is this how you want it?" he rasped. He wanted it to be the best for her.

She flattened her palms against his cheeks and stared into his eyes. "Everything with you is good. The best."

His heart felt like it was exploding. A primal sound tore from his throat. "I'm not going to last," he said desperately.

Her only response was to moan as she rocked against his pelvis. Staring into her eyes made him lose control, the building pressure snapped and he poured himself into her, her channel milking everything out of him. Pleasure rushed at him; the world went black.

He heard her cry out, felt her insides throb around him. He buried his face into the side of her neck, holding her close as her intense climax tore through her.

And the world had never seemed so perfect.

# Chapter Twenty-Five

*N*aked, Leela stretched out on the soft blankets Hunt had set out before the enormous hearth in his bedchamber. "This is so cozy I don't ever want to leave."

"That would suit me." Hunt lay on his side next to her with his weight propped on an elbow. The fire provided the only light in the chamber, bathing his bare form in a soft glow. Leela's appreciative gaze slid over the masculine curves and ridges of his body, the firm ripples in his stomach, his male parts soft and relaxed. He disappointed her by sitting up to shift behind her, settling her between his thick thighs with her back against his chest.

She made a sound of protest.

"Are you uncomfortable?"

"No, this is supremely relaxing." She loved the feel of his strong warm body cushioning hers, his arms encircling her, making her feel safe and protected. "But I lost the superior view."

He chuckled, his breath humid in her ear. "What a naughty girl you've turned out to be."

"I've discovered that women who misbehave tend to lead far more interesting lives. If I followed the rules that you find so dear, I wouldn't be here right now. Nor would I have written *Travels in Arabia*."

He kissed her neck. "It's clearly time for me to rethink my views on society's strictures."

"I feel like my life truly began once I started following my heart, rather than the ton's expectations of how a lady should behave." She paused. "Speaking of those who break the rules—"

"Yes?" He nibbled her ear, sending delightful shivers through her.

"I saw Victoria today."

To her regret, he stopped tending to her lobe. "You certainly know how to ruin the mood."

She hugged his arms tighter around her. "Does her defection still bother you?"

"How can it when I have you here in my arms?"

"Victoria deeply regrets how she treated you and sends her most profound apologies."

"Please assure Victoria that I accept her apology and bear her no ill will. I have already told you that I do not hold her responsible. But Foster is another matter. His betrayal is unforgivable."

"Surely, you can find it in your heart—"

"I employed the ungrateful whelp. I brought him up in the world by making him my secretary despite a decided lack of experience. I saw promise in him." He released a long sigh. "Clearly, I was mistaken."

"No one will employ Mr. Foster. They fear offending you."

His body stiffened around her. "Foster's employment prospects, or lack thereof, are none of my concern."

"He and Victoria have no means of support. One word from you could change—"

"You go too far." His voice cooled. "Do not request that I assist them."

Leela was desperate to rectify Tori's current predicament. "I'm not asking that you do anything directly, but perhaps if you let it be known that you hold no ill will toward anyone who might employ Mr. Foster—"

"You ask too much. I will take no action against Foster, but nor will I assist him in any way."

She turned to face him, wrapping her arms tightly around him. "Don't be angry with me." She kissed his forehead and then his cheek.

"Perhaps if Foster had approached me before creating this scandal, things might be different." He shook his head. "I would give you almost anything. But not this."

"Let's not speak of it again."

"Nothing would please me more."

She kissed him thoroughly, silently asking for his forgiveness. He responded, his tongue dancing with hers, but not quite as passionately as she'd become accustomed to. As she pulled back from him, she glimpsed the ormolu clock on his bedside table. It was past time for her to return home before the staff started to gossip about her late nights out.

"It's late." She rose to go.

He watched her, his expression tense. "You are leaving?"

"You know I cannot stay the night."

Hunt followed her movements as she found her chemise and slipped it over her head. The silence between them was heavy with unsaid words. After watching her dress, he said, "If you mean to punish me for not coming to Foster's rescue after the way he humiliated me—"

"That's not it at all. It's well past midnight." She reached behind her head, her fingers separating her hair, working with rapid efficiency to tame the mass of curls into a single braid down her back. "I cannot arrive back to my brother's home too late. The staff will talk."

"As you like." He rose and walked naked to his dressing room. She could not help but admire the view of his firm buttocks and muscular thighs. The breathtaking sight made her want to throw caution to the wind and remain with him through the night just so she could run her hands all over his beautiful form.

He reappeared, still barefoot, but now wearing trousers and an untucked white linen shirt. "I'll walk you down."

She finished braiding her hair and followed him out. They found her cloak strewn across the marble floor in the front hall where Hunt had tossed it during their frantic coupling. Her insides stirred at the memory of Hunt taking her up against the wall.

In silence, Hunt reached for the outer garment and gently set it on Leela's shoulders. She could not bear his coolness. It was as though the sun had stopped shining on her.

She caught his hand and brought it to her lips with both hands. "Please don't be angry. I won't mention Victoria again." She pressed a kiss into his wide palm.

He wrapped his arms around her from behind. "Victoria is important to you. You must always feel at liberty to speak of her in my presence. But Foster is another matter entirely." He pressed his face into the side of her neck, inhaling deeply. "Please do not allow him to come between us."

"Never." She turned in his arms to meet his hungry lips. He kissed her heatedly. She melted against him.

"Stay," he murmured against her lips.

"Stop tempting me," she protested. "You seem to have forgotten that we mean to avoid a new scandal."

"You make me forget everything, except my desperate desire to be with you every hour of every day."

"I'll return tomorrow. I promise."

He reluctantly released her, leaving Leela free to pull the hood of her cloak over her face to conceal her identity.

"Is your man waiting?"

"Yes, I asked Hashem to return for me at midnight. He should be outside."

Hunt opened the door to a blast of icy wind.

"You don't have to come out," she said. "It's cold and you're not properly attired."

"Nonsense. I'll see you to your coach."

He went out with her, barefoot and coatless, a protective arm around her waist holding her close to shield her from the worst of the chill. The streets were empty. Those members of the ton out attending parties had yet to return. Those who'd stayed in, were likely taking shelter in the warmth of their homes.

Another squall blew over them, whisking Leela's hood away from her face. She did not bother to attempt to rectify the situation because they'd already reached her brother's carriage.

"I miss you already." Hunt planted a hard kiss on her lips before handing her up into the conveyance.

"Tomorrow," she said. It was a promise. A vow. A reaffirmation that while they might not have forever, she intended to make the most of every day, every year that they did have together.

As Hashem directed the horses away from Weston House, Leela peered out the window to see Hunt staring after them, straight spine, hands on his narrow hips, seeming oblivious to the cold. She felt a rush of longing. Her chest panged. She immediately understood what the sensation signaled. She loved him. Intensely. Irrevocably. For the first time in her life, she understood what it was to be in the throes of a deep, desperate, wonderful, all-consuming love.

Suddenly, a decade did not seem like nearly enough time.

STILL FRETTING ABOUT Tori's situation, Leela called on Edgar the following day.

"At the very least, give your sister her clothing and other personal effects."

"Absolutely not," he intoned after receiving her in his study. "She gets nothing. Not a shilling, nor a frippery, nor a gown. As a matter of fact, I have already had her entire wardrobe delivered to the secondhand sellers on Hollywell Street."

"You *sold* Tori's things?" she asked incredulously. "I shouldn't be surprised. You can always be counted upon to profit from another's misfortune."

"Do not treat me as if I am the villain here. Victoria chose to run away with a penniless nobody. Now she must live with the consequences of her ill-advised actions."

"I cannot believe you sold her things. At least do the decent thing and give her the proceeds from the sale."

He scowled. "Why would I do that?"

"Oh, I don't know." The words leaked with sarcasm. "Perhaps because she is your sister?"

"I paid for that foolish girl to have two seasons. *Two.* Whatever I earn back after selling her things will pale in comparison to what I lavished upon Victoria to assure her future. Do you know how expensive it is to bring a young lady out? To outfit her for a single Season?"

"Whatever it was, you can well afford it."

"She could have been a duchess. Instead, she chooses someone of zero consequence? No, I will not lift one finger to assist her. She must live with the results of her foolish choices." Edgar crossed his arms over his chest. "Now, the subject of Victoria is closed. Is there anything else you'd like to discuss?"

"No." Thoroughly disgusted, she turned to go. "It was a mistake to come here. I've clearly wasted my time."

"Not so fast, if you please. You've had your say and now I'd like to have mine."

The smug expression on his face made her uneasy. "What are you about?"

"Please have a seat and I will happily tell you."

She reluctantly joined him on a plush leather sofa, settling on the opposite end from Edgar. "Very well. I am seated. Get on with it."

He squared an ankle over his knee, laying his arm along the back of the sofa. "How have you been spending your evenings, my dear Lady Devon?"

"What business is that of yours?"

"It is my concern if you are swiving my sister's former betrothed."

The air left her lungs. "Your language is appalling."

"What is truly appalling is the fact that you pretended to love Victoria while bedding her betrothed. This is why she ran away, is it not? She discovered that you seduced the man she was supposed to marry."

"This is ridiculous." She started to rise.

"I saw you leaving his house last evening."

Leela settled back in her seat with a hard thump.

Edgar continued. "Huntington was in dishabille, barefoot in the street like a pauper. I saw him escort a woman out. There was no doubt as to what the two of them had been up to. The woman was cloaked and hooded so I could not see her face. And then a fortuitous gust of wind pushed her hood away and revealed the identity of the duke's doxy."

"Are you following me?"

"My, but you do like to flatter yourself. No, I was visiting a friend. I spotted you and Huntington just as I was about to depart. Isn't that a happy coincidence?"

"The duke and I are adults. Neither of us is married or otherwise pledged to another."

"He was practically betrothed to your stepdaughter," Edgar said sharply. "Do not pretend there is no scandal here."

"Do what you want with the information." Leela came to her feet. "It is of no consequence to me if you want more gossip to surround the Devon title. After all, I am still Lady Devon."

"Do not remind me." His lip curled. "As soon as this business with Victoria's elopement dies down, I shall take a wife and give the title to a lady who is worthy."

"Then I suggest you concentrate on finding your unfortunate bride. Prolonging the scandal by revealing my association with the duke will not help your cause."

"You are correct," he said behind her, from where he remained seated. "However, there is someone who would abhor another scandal tied to his name—even more than I."

Leela froze. She could not allow Hunt to suffer another scandal. Nor was she prepared to give him up. Not yet. She faced Edgar. "What do you want?"

He smirked. "Can you not guess?"

A chill went through her. "Parkwood."

"Bravo!" He clapped his hands together. "You have the right of it. I do indeed want the dower house. You may be brazen, but you are certainly not a fool."

"You cannot have it."

"Oh, come now. Don't be petulant. I told you I would do whatever is necessary to get the house back.

It is rightfully mine. And one day, a long time from now, my future wife will reside there, which is as it should be."

Her eye caught on the whitening scar on his cheek. The one she'd put there. She regretted the absence of her knife now. She might have gifted him with another mark on the other cheek. Parkwood and the surrounding farms were her only real assets. She might never find someone to publish her future books.

At the same time, an answer to her problems began to take shape in Leela's head. "I'm not giving you my house."

"You might care to reconsider—"

"But I will sell it to you."

His forehead lifted. "After all of your declarations of love for the property, I am surprised you would part with it so easily."

"You leave me no choice," she snapped, injecting a forced anger to mask her rising exhilaration. "But you must pay me its full value. I'll take nothing less."

"Done. We are in agreement. I'll send over my offer and the papers tomorrow." He spoke quickly as if he feared she might change her mind. "We shall finally be truly free of each other. Once I marry and there is a new Lady Devon, you will scarcely be a memory at Lambert Hall."

"That will suit us both admirably."

He grinned, clearly pleased with himself. "Come now, Delilah, don't be a spoilsport just because I have finally outmaneuvered you. After all these years, in the end, without Father to protect you, I emerge the winner."

Leela looked daggers at him. "I shall leave you to celebrate your victory." She turned away, unable to suppress her smile for much longer. She slammed the door behind her to make her angry exit more convincing. But by the time she reached the street, she was laughing.

# Chapter Twenty-Six

The moment Hunt found a plausible reason to call upon Leela in broad daylight, he went directly to Peckham House.

He found her seated at her escritoire engrossed in some papers. He took a moment to admire the view. She wore a violet dress that complemented her tawny skin. Her sumptuous hair, which she'd gathered loosely in a ribbon, streamed down her back. Her beautiful eyes lit up when she turned in her seat and realized who her visitor was. She rose. "What are you doing here?"

He pulled her to him, hungry for her soft warmth. "Is that any way to greet your lover?"

She enthusiastically returned his tender, unhurried kiss, their tongues meeting and mating, as if they were made for this. For each other.

"Much better. Now I am convinced that you are pleased to see me."

"I am always happy to see you. Perhaps too much so."

"There is no such thing."

"I don't know about that." Her eyes clouded. "I think about you entirely too much."

"The obsession is mutual." He produced a pair of kid leather gloves from his pocket.

"What are those?"

"Victoria left them behind at Weston House when she visited. I was ecstatic to find them in the library among the books because it gave me an excuse to call on you now, rather than waiting for you to come to me under the cover of darkness."

She shook her head. "We're quite the pair, you and I." She pulled away. "Would you like a sherry?"

"Yes, that would be lovely."

She crossed the room to fix their drinks. Glass clinked as she poured the sherry. Hunt's gaze latched on to the papers on her desk. He recognized Devon's seal.

"You have dealings with Devon?"

"Yes. Actually, I am about to conclude some business with him."

He peered down at the papers, which included a bill of sale. "What sort of business?"

"I sold Parkwood back to him. He intends to make it part of the entail so that no future hussy countesses can get their hands on it."

"You gave him the dower house?" He turned to stare at her. "Just like that?"

"I sold it to him for an excellent price."

"What aren't you telling me?" Something wasn't right. He studied her. The glitter in her eyes, the flush

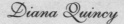

in her cheeks. "You were determined to hold on to that house."

"Well, he did force my hand." She handed him his sherry.

"How did he do that?"

"By threatening to reveal our affair to the world."

His mouth fell open. "Devon knows?"

"Yes, it was rather bad luck. He apparently has a particular friend who lives near you."

"Lady Bellmore."

"Who is she?"

"A widow. She's Devon's paramour."

"Really?" She took her sherry to her stuffed arm-chair and settled in. "Well, it is just our luck that Edgar's mistress lives across the street from you. He saw me leaving Weston House late at night."

"Damnation." Parkwood was an important asset for Leela, and Hunt's failure to be sufficiently discreet had resulted in her loss of it. "I am sorry."

"Don't be." She gestured for him to take the stuffed chair adjacent to hers. She seemed remarkably upbeat for someone who'd just lost a valued property. "It has all worked out beautifully."

"How can you say that?" He sat heavily in the chair. "This is all my fault."

"Stop trying to take credit for my victory."

"How is this a win for you?"

Triumph flashed in her face. "Because I now have the funds to purchase the paper mill."

"But at what cost? You've been forced to surrender Parkwood."

"That house represented security. Tori was all that bonded me to Lambert Hall, and now that Edgar has completely forsaken her, it is well past time that I sever all bonds to the Hall and its occupants."

"You truly don't regret the loss of the house?"

"I admit, I was tempted to send Tori and her Mr. Foster to live there and collect the rents from the farms Douglas left me. Just to spite Devon."

"Do not tell me you've sold the farms as well?" As far as Hunt knew, the farms were her only reliable source of income. Unless her brother, wherever in Hades he was, provided an allowance for her.

"Of course I didn't relinquish the farms. Naturally, Edgar wanted them, but I declined. He gets Parkwood and only Parkwood. Nothing else." She paused. "Besides, Douglas stipulated in his will that if I wanted to sell Parkwood, that Edgar must be allowed to buy it at a fair price."

"And now you get Devon's silence, I take it."

"That was the whole point."

"Can he be trusted?"

"In general? No. However, the last thing Edgar wants is another scandal attached to the Devon title. He's intent on wedding as quickly as possible in order to replace me as Countess of Devon."

"You shall still be the dowager countess."

"True. But I do not intend to go about in society. I disdain the ton as much as it disdains me. I am probably more eager to leave *good society* behind than Edgar is to be rid of me."

"What happens now?"

"I have already sent word to my solicitor, Mr. Sherman in Coventry, to handle the purchase of the factory. Next, I suppose I must learn how to run a paper mill."

"Wrong." He surged to his feet and dropped to his knees before her. "Next, I'm going to have my way with you."

"Now? Here?"

He began lifting the hem of her gown. "Why do you think I invented an excuse to come and see you?"

"That was very clever of you." She watched him bare her stocking-clad knees.

"Indeed." His hand dipped under her skirts. "And now I intend to claim my reward."

"THIS IS VERY kind of you." Tori accepted the food basket from Leela. "But you really must stop giving us things. We are hardly paupers."

Leela drew off her cloak. "I reserve the right to bring gifts to my stepdaughter whenever I feel compelled to do so." Earlier in the week, she'd sent over coal, candles and an assortment of dried goods, including tea and pyramid sugar.

"An occasional gift, perhaps," Tori allowed, "but you've given us far too much. We shall soon run out of space to store it."

"Don't exaggerate." Leela surveyed the room. "I haven't sent that much."

Tori's new home shared a back wall with the home behind it. The modest abode consisted of three small rooms: two unseen chambers upstairs and this snug space that served as a kitchen, eating space and sitting room all in one. A coal stove kept the space warm. The ceilings were low, and the narrow windows on only one wall did not allow much light in. But Tori kept the space tidy and it somehow felt homey despite the Spartan conditions.

"You both are always welcome to come and stay with me at Peckham House," Leela said, not for the first time.

Tori smiled. She wore another of her rough plain gowns that stopped at the ankles, but her eyes were clear and sparkling, and a becoming flush painted her cheeks. "You are that horrified by my reduced circumstances?"

"Not at all. I just want you to be comfortable."

Tori went to the stove to prepare the tea. "I am happy. That is far more important."

Leela settled into one of two faded side chairs with fully upholstered backs, the only seating in the room. The fabric was so timeworn that Leela couldn't discern its original color. She made a mental note to see to the delivery of a sofa so that Tori would have a more comfortable place to sit.

Leela watched Tori pour the tea. "Everything is well?"

Tori's eyes glistened. "Supremely so. Mr. Foster is kind, attentive and very loving." She blushed as she said the last words, which Leela took as a sign that Tori found the marriage bed to be most satisfactory.

She sipped her tea. "And where is your Mr. Foster now?"

"Searching for work." Tori sat in the only other chair in the room. "There are two postings on Bond Street that he is looking into. We have high hopes that he will secure employment soon."

"Are people still turning him away?"

"I am afraid so." Concern lit her eyes. "Have you spoken to Huntington? Is he well?"

"Yes." Leela's cheeks heated at last night's memory of playing golf on the putting green in Hunt's garden. Each time she missed the hole, she'd been required to discard a piece of clothing. Needless to say, Hunt had done everything in his power to keep her warm.

"And?" Tori prompted, jarring Leela away from her reminiscences.

"I have spoken to the duke. He wanted me to assure you that he bears you no ill will and that he accepts your apology unreservedly."

"He is all that is kind." Tori studied her. "Have you been spending time with the duke?"

Leela shifted in her seat. "I do see him on occasion." She wanted to tell Tori about her liaison with Hunt, but it felt like it was too soon. "I suppose you could say that we have become friends."

"Have you? I am so pleased." Tori clasped her hands together before her chest. "Hunt deserves a good friend like you. It makes me feel less guilty to know he is not entirely alone."

"He is doing well. That I can assure you."

"Perhaps he will assist Mr. Foster in securing a position."

"No." Leela spoke firmly. "That he will not do. He is very angry with Mr. Foster for his defection."

"Oh." Tori slumped a little. "I see."

"But I shall help you in any way I can. I hate to see you experience any hardship."

Tori's face shone. "It is no hardship at all to be wed to Mr. Foster. You know I have never cared for silk gowns and glittering balls. Mr. Foster and I do the things I truly enjoy together. We read and discuss books. We go for walks. We understand each other."

The door opened and Mr. Foster came in. "My darling, I am home." He wore a plain brown suit and was neat in appearance. He startled once he spotted Leela. "Oh, I do beg your pardon, Lady Devon. I did not realize we had a guest."

"Welcome home, dearest." Tori went to her husband and slipped her arm through his. Their gazes met and heat arced between them. The tenderness and physical attraction between Tori and her husband was as apparent as writing on a wall.

Leela felt a spasm in her chest. To her surprise, she envied her stepdaughter. Tori had lost life's material pleasures, but she'd gained a husband who loved her, a companion to share her life with.

"Come and say hello." Tori drew her husband closer.

"Mr. Foster," Leela said. "I hope you are well."

"I am. I must thank you for your generous gifts. I hope you are enjoying your visit with . . . my wife." He stood behind Tori's chair, his hand on her shoulder. There was nowhere else in the room for him to sit.

"I am greatly enjoying your wife's company. However, it is you that I have come to see."

"Me?" he asked.

"Him?" Tori said at the same time.

"Yes," Leela affirmed. "I am in the process of acquiring a paper mill that will require an intelligent young man to oversee its operation. I hope you will accept the position. It will require a move to Oxfordshire."

"But I know nothing of running a mill," he protested, although a hopeful expression marked his features. "I would not want to reward your generous offer with incompetence on my part."

"His Grace assures me that you are an intelligent young man. The current manager, Mr. Avery, is staying on. He is a very able man and will train you to work alongside him."

"Is the mill doing well at the moment?" he asked.

Leela nodded. "My solicitor assures me that the paper mill is very profitable under Mr. Avery's direction."

Tori and Mr. Foster stared at each other. Tentative hope bubbled between them. Mr. Foster looked back at Leela and swallowed. "It is a very generous offer."

Tori leaped out of her chair and bounded over to engulf Leela in a hard hug. "You are such a dear. He will not disappoint you."

"Victoria, wait," Mr. Foster said.

Tori regarded her husband expectantly. "Yes?"

"As I was saying, your offer is most generous, Lady Devon, but I cannot accept."

"You can't?" Tori's eyes rounded. "Why not?"

"I am not qualified to run a mill, and I should not

like to impose on Lady Devon's generosity and good-will."

"I am not worried about your abilities," Leela assured him. "His Grace says you are a very competent young man."

"That is good of His Grace to say, but I cannot accept."

"Won't you at least take some time to think about it before rejecting my offer outright?" Leela asked.

"My answer will not change."

Leela exhaled. "I'm sorry to hear that."

His features softened. "I do appreciate your concern for your stepdaughter's welfare," he said politely. "I give you my word that I shall look after Mrs. Foster. But I cannot accept charity. My wife and I must find our own way."

"It is not charity, my love," Tori said gently. "She is offering you a position."

"Lady Devon already has an able manager in her employ. She does not need me. I learned a great deal while working for His Grace. I am confident my experience will serve me well enough to secure a situation on my own merits."

Leela admired the young man's determination to succeed without assistance from his new wife's affluent family. "I am disappointed," she said with a warm smile, "but I also understand your decision."

"Thank you, Lady Devon." Mr. Foster paused. "As to His Grace, I sincerely regret any inconvenience I have caused him, but I cannot regret marrying my wife."

"Perhaps Huntington will eventually come to see that," Leela said, "but it will take time."

Tori frowned, as if something had just occurred to her. "But there's still something that I do not understand."

"What is it?" Leela asked.

"Why did you buy a paper mill, of all things?"

Leela swallowed the last of her tea. "I suppose it is time you both learned who wrote *Travels in Arabia*."

# Chapter Twenty-Seven

"Was that good?" Leela asked while kneeling naked before Hunt on the floor of her bedchamber.

"It was marvelous." Hunt stared down at the goddess on her knees, at her luscious breasts, the bare expanse of smooth, warm-toned skin. "If you did it any better, my head might explode."

His legs still trembled from the force of his release. He'd come hard and fast, the vision of Leela's lips wrapped around his prick proving as erotic as the sensation of being inside her hot, eager mouth. He'd never imagined a well-bred lady could enjoy bed sport as much as Leela did. She'd insisted on learning how to use her mouth to please him in the same way he pleasured her. Hunt was not gentleman enough to refuse her request.

"We can try again if you'd like," she offered. "I think I am getting the hang of it."

"Oh, I would like." He took her hands and helped her up. "But I might just die of pleasure if you take me into your mouth again this soon. A man needs some recovery time."

Together, they collapsed onto the crumpled bed linens with their bare limbs intertwined. These past few weeks, he'd taken to visiting Leela at Peckham House almost nightly, arriving after the servants retired for the evening. He'd slip in an unlocked side door at midnight and depart at five in the morning before the servants stirred. Leela consumed his thoughts, especially when they were apart. He spent his days impatiently waiting for evening to fall so he could visit her.

They lay on Leela's comfortable feather bed, Hunt on his back with Leela cuddled up to his side. "How is the sale of the mill proceeding?" he inquired.

"Very well. It should all be settled in the next month or so. Mr. Avery, the mill manager, has already viewed a prepared copy of volume three and is ready to begin printing as soon as I direct him to do so."

"And you are intent on retaining Foster to comanage the property."

"I was, but he turned down my offer."

"He did? Why? I thought he was desperate for a situation."

"Mr. Foster is determined not to accept what he perceives as charity from his wife's family. He believes he can succeed on his own."

"Foolish young man. He should have taken your offer. He won't find another that is half as generous. Not after the way he betrayed me."

"He told me how much he sincerely regrets any inconvenience he had caused you."

Hunt grunted. "Inconvenience. That's one way to refer to making me a laughingstock of the Season."

"I know you cannot forgive what he did, but I do believe Mr. Foster fell deeply in love with Tori and could not help himself. Surely you can understand that."

"Hmm." He ran a hand down her back and over her hips. "I can certainly understand what it is like to come under the spell of an enchanting woman. But to throw everything away? To risk penury? To readily embrace certain ruin is another matter entirely."

She playfully bit his chest. "No one will ever mistake you for a romantic, Mr. The-Rules-Must-Always-Come-First."

"Ouch." He slapped her rump. "Be careful with your rough play. You might awaken the beast in me."

"I should be so lucky." She shifted up to press her lips against his. Their tongues entwined in a long, leisurely kiss. Interest stirred between Hunt's legs. She noticed. "Mmm. It feels like the beast is definitely awakening."

"What can I say?" He grinned. "You make me as randy as a fifteen-year-old boy." He leaped out of bed. "I'm thirsty. I'll need some water if I am expected to perform to your satisfaction."

She sat up and plumped the pillows behind her before reclining back against their softness. "Satisfaction has never been a problem between us."

He poured some water. "Truer words were never spoken." He held out the glass. "Would you like some?"

"No, thank you."

He gulped the water down, taking in the delightful view of her bare body lounging against the pillows. Shifting his weight, he almost tripped over an old faded tapestry valise on the floor. "What's this?"

"One of my travel bags." She yawned, extending her arms high up in the air. "It has some of the practical items I like to carry with me when I travel."

"What is it doing here?"

"I am going through it to see what I'll need when I leave for Morocco."

He almost choked on the water. "You're leaving?"

She smiled. "Not right at this minute, no." She opened her arms wide, beckoning him. "Come back to bed. You've had your water."

"When are you leaving?" he asked tersely.

"I'm not certain."

The muscles in his neck tensed. "Surely you have an idea."

"I'd like to stay until the second volume of *Travels in Arabia* is released. I was traveling when the first volume came out and I am rather curious to witness the reception it receives."

He set the glass down with a thunk. "That's in three weeks. Volume two will be published in three weeks, and after that you intend to leave for Morocco? For how long?"

"I imagine I shall be gone several months. I'll sail to Gibraltar and then on to Tangier."

He tried to lighten his voice even though all of the air had left his lungs. "You're leaving me so soon?"

"You could always come with me."

"To Morocco?" He scoffed. "You comprehend full

well that I cannot be away from the duchy for months at a time. I have responsibilities."

"And yet you expect me to put my life on hold while your life continues as before."

He stiffened. "I wasn't aware that you consider these past few weeks together to be wasted time." He'd characterize this glorious interlude with Leela as the best period of his life.

"You know I didn't mean it like that." She kept her watchful gaze on him. "Do not ask me to stay here until you tire of me."

"Is that what this is about?" He stepped toward her, kicking the worn valise out of his way, his foot coming into contact with something hard inside the bag. Pain shot through his big toe. "I will never tire of you. Never."

"Even if our intimate association does continue for the next decade, you will eventually have to take a wife and produce an heir."

"But that's many years away. We don't need to think of it now."

"Yet the day will eventually come."

"Is that what is happening here? You seek to punish me for wanting to do my duty? Surely you know I would stay with you forever if I could."

"But you cannot. And so I must look to my future, to a time when you will be occupied with the dukedom, a wife and your children."

"But why must you travel now?" He tried to hide his devastation. "We were supposed to have years together. You agreed to a long liaison. What has changed?"

"Me, I suppose," she said softly. "Being with you has changed me."

"In what way?" What had he done to drive her away? "How have I offended you?"

"You have done nothing wrong. You have been lovely."

"Then why are you leaving?"

"Since I was young, I've dreamed of traveling the world and documenting my experiences. I am finally in a position to do so. I have the means to fund my travels and a way to get my books out in the world. It's not as though it's forever. I'll be back within the year."

"It might as well be an eternity," he said sharply. "Tell me the truth. Why do you feel you must go so soon?"

"Because I cannot bear to stay. I think of you constantly. I miss you when we are apart, which is rather ridiculous because we're together every evening. You're like a fever that never breaks."

"I feel the same. But, like a rational person, I view those feelings as a reason to stay together for as long as possible."

"I am becoming far too attached to you. You've shown me what it means to have a true romantic partner."

"All the more reason to stay with me."

"I am tempted," she said shakily, "but I cannot build my life around you. It is so enticing to just concentrate on the present and forget about the future, but I cannot. When you marry—"

He cut her off. "I will never care for anyone as I care for you. Even if she is my wife."

"But you will find some sort of contentment with her, if you choose wisely. And she will give you children. Your life will be full, even if it isn't exactly the ideal you would have chosen."

"Leela," he pleaded. She already felt so far away. How long had she been planning her escape? "Please don't do this."

"While you have your duties and your family, I, on the other hand, will be a woman of a certain age, without a husband or children and with very few prospects in the world—"

"But you always say that you don't wish to remarry."

"I have said that. And I believed it then. But the time we've spent together has changed my perspective. You've shown me how a loving marriage might look. You've made me want to seek a life companion."

"So you are intent on replacing me"—bitterness burned from his chest into his throat—"before you've even given us a chance."

She smiled softly, sadly. "As if anyone could replace you. But it's possible I might find a loving friend, someone to move through life with. A man who accepts my writing. Who might even travel with me. I must open myself to that possibility. Surely, you would not wish to condemn me to a lonely life once we are done with each other."

"But why must you start now?"

"Because if I stay much longer, I will not have the strength to leave you. I must continue my work. I must get back to traveling, to enjoying the things that delight and inspire me, before I completely lose myself in you and this wonderful dream that I sometimes forget can never be real."

He wanted to shake her. To talk some sense into her. She was throwing everything away. They'd just managed to find their way to each other and here she was already tossing him out like yesterday's spoiled supper. His insides felt like they were shattering into a million sharp pieces. He hadn't known it was possible to feel so much pain. "I see." He blindly reached for his trousers and slipped them on.

She sat up. "Wait. You are leaving? Now?"

"I believe you just ended our affair." He couldn't stay. If he remained with her for another moment, he would fall apart in front of her. "Which makes this an opportune time for me to make my exit."

"But not yet." She rose, reaching for her dressing gown. "We have another month or so to enjoy each other."

He pulled his shirt over his head. Another month with her, knowing it would all soon be over, would be agony. Like waiting for the executioner's ax to fall. No, it was for the best to end their affair once and for all. While he could still manage to walk away. "I think a clean break is for the best, don't you?"

"No, I don't. Don't go. It's too soon."

He registered the panic in her voice as he gathered his things. "Good night, Leela." He barely managed to get the words out due to the smothering ache in his throat. "I wish you the best of luck."

"You're walking out on me yet again after we've made love," she retorted. "You promised never to do so again."

"Don't even try." Anger surged in his blood. He rounded on her. "You are abandoning me and we both know it. Do not try to pretend otherwise. You're the one who's leaving. And I am the one left to pick up the pieces of my life while you run away yet again."

"I am not running away. I am reclaiming my life, my work." Her nostrils flared. "You are angry because I refuse to do your bidding. You want me to wait around like that mistress of yours, another plaything to amuse yourself with whenever the desire strikes. Maybe you should inquire as to whether your old mistress is still available."

If only Leela were a mistress he could casually cast aside. Instead, he felt like he was losing a vital part of himself. He could barely breathe through the pain. She might as well tear his arm off. "Perhaps I shall see if Georgina is available. After all, she does still live in a house that I own."

"How convenient for you," she said bitterly from behind him.

He opened the door and quietly slipped out, treading carefully through the dark corridor, his big toe throbbing with pain, pretending his world had not just fallen apart.

# Chapter Twenty-Eight

*I*t's a good thing you married *ajnabi*," *Citi* told Leela. "An Arab man needs a wife who can cook."

"I didn't marry a foreigner," Leela corrected. "Douglas was an Englishman."

"*Citi* thinks anyone who isn't an Arab is a foreigner," explained Reema, one of Leela's newly discovered cousins.

"Delilah has servants," said Hanna, another cousin Leela had met for the first time a few days ago after coming to Manchester to visit *Citi*. She had so many cousins that it was difficult to keep track of them all. "She is lucky that she does not have to cook."

"It must be nice to just show up at the table and have a meal prepared for you," Reema said wistfully.

They were sitting around Auntie Hajar's round kitchen table rolling grape leaves. At least, Leela was attempting to master the skill. She carefully lined up the rice and minced lamb mixture on the open grape leaf. Tucking in both ends, she proceeded to roll it up.

"*Mish hake*." *Citi* shook her head in a way that made Leela feel like a complete failure. "Not like that," the old woman rattled in a raspy voice seasoned by years of smoking.

A sour expression was permanently etched on *Citi's* lined face. Her mouth seemed frozen into a pucker from decades of hookah smoking. "You filled it too much," she admonished Leela in Arabic. "Now it will burst once the rice expands when you cook it." She took Leela's overstuffed *warak enab*, unrolled it, dumped out half of the stuffing and rerolled the grape leaf in what seemed like record time to Leela.

"Imagine never having to wash dishes." Fiona Kate, Hanna's younger sister, had a wistful expression on her face. "That would be a dream come true."

"Stop dreaming," said Auntie Hagar, Hanna and Fiona Kate's mother. She was Mama's younger sister. "Because you'll be washing dishes soon. Right after we eat."

Good humor sparkled in Fiona Kate's eyes. "It's worth marrying *ajnabi* if it means never washing dishes."

Hanna studied Leela with striking kohl-rimmed eyes that matched her shiny sable hair. "Leela, have you ever scrubbed a pot?"

Leela blushed. "Not exactly."

The other girls around the table burst out laughing. Leela smiled, enjoying their gentle teasing. She felt a genuine sense of warmth and camaraderie in the presence of these young women. She felt like she belonged, which had never really happened before. Of course, she could blend into the aristocracy that she'd been born into, especially when dressed in her finery and using her countess manners. But deep down, she'd always known that she didn't quite belong.

But being here, at Auntie Hager's table, felt different. It was the first time she'd met people who were almost like her. Although her cousins were mostly solidly middle class, a sizable economic difference from Leela's circumstances, she still had much in common with them.

They, too, were a mix of both Arab and English. Of course, she'd felt an affinity for the relatives she'd met in Palestine, but nothing like this. The younger women, although of Arab stock, were born and raised in England—just like Leela. They shared many experiences and points of reference. She felt strangely at home among this loud, laughing and oftentimes bickering group of women.

And they helped take her mind off of Hunt. She missed him so desperately that the loss was a physical pain in her belly. She escaped London almost immediately after their parting. Seeing *Citi* again, and meeting the family she'd never known, helped distract Leela from the mammoth hole in her heart where Hunt used to be.

Hanna reached for another grape leaf to roll. "Delilah must pity us because we also have to wash our own clothes."

"Actually, there is something you have that I envy," Leela said to her.

The arch in her beautiful cousin's dark brows became even more pronounced. "And what is that?"

"How in the world is your hair so straight?"

"I know!" Aliya, another cousin, with large doe eyes and sharp cheekbones, shared a look with Leela. "It is not fair that she has straight hair. It looks like it's ironed."

Hanna shrugged. "What can I say?" She spoke with exaggerated loftiness. "*Min Allah*. It's from God."

"You have your mother's hair," Fiona Kate said to Leela. "Auntie Maryam had curly hair."

Leela stared at her. "You knew my mother?"

"Of course." Hanna stood to arrange her handful of rolled grape leaves in the huge shared pot near the center of the table. "We all did."

"When did you meet her?" Leela asked.

"She used to visit twice a year," Auntie Hager said. "She would come down from London and stay two or three weeks at a time."

"She did?" Aside from *Citi*, who'd visited every summer, Mama's family had been a complete mystery to Leela until now. She believed Mama had abandoned the rest of her relatives in order to fit into Papa's aristocratic world.

Fiona Kate's eyes twinkled. "Auntie Maryam used to tell such funny stories about the aristocrats she'd met."

Hanna registered Leela's surprise. "You didn't know? Where did you think she was going when she'd leave for weeks at a time?"

"I had no idea." It felt as though the floor had dropped beneath Leela's feet. Why had Mama kept her visits a secret? "I know there were times when she and Papa left us in the country while they went to London. I suppose that could be when she came to Manchester for her visits. But why didn't she bring me and Alexander with her?"

Auntie Hager's fingers moved rapidly as she rolled grape leaf after grape leaf. "She thought it was best not to confuse you."

"*Khalas.* Enough." *Citi* rose from her chair. She was heavy-set, carrying most of her weight in her upper body, and waddled over to a low straw stool set up by the omnipresent hookah pipe Fiona Kate prepared for her.

"Why would knowing Mama's family confuse us?" Leela asked.

Everyone stood, following *Citi*'s lead. They were out of grape leaves and the pot of rolled *warak enab* was full. As her aunt and cousins washed up and cleared the table, Leela wandered over to sit with *Citi*.

"Why didn't she let us know everyone?" Leela asked. "Why did Mama think we'd be confused?"

*Citi* sucked on the water pipe, inhaling long and deep. "Your father was *ajnabi.* You are the daughter of a marquess. We are just merchants."

"But you are all my family."

"You and Alexander are *kubar.* Your brother is a marquess. You had to fit in among your father's people."

"Just because we are aristocrats, that doesn't mean I should not know all of you," Leela insisted.

*Citi* shook her head. "Maryam was right. She knew her children were from another world. You can never belong here with us."

"But where then do I belong? The nobility does not

fully accept me. Not really. What you are saying is that I don't have a place in either world."

*Citi* took a long low inhale on the water pipe. "You must carve out your own place."

"What does that mean?" She felt a bit frantic, a bit lost. "I don't understand."

*Citi* patted her hand. "You will one day."

HUNT'S SECRETARY POKED his head through the study door. "Beg pardon, Your Grace?"

"Yes, what is it, Banks?" Hunt strived to maintain a patient tone. His new secretary was capable enough, but the duchy was large and complicated. It would take months to train the young man. Again, he silently cursed Foster for his defection.

On top of everything, his head throbbed and his chest felt like it was in a permanent vise. He'd felt this way since his break with Leela a sennight ago. As much as Hunt tried to bury himself in his work, he couldn't get her out of his mind.

Banks stepped farther inside. "It's the question of the house on Half Moon Street."

His former mistress lived in the property. "What about it? I've directed you to sell it."

Banks cleared his throat. "It appears as if, Mrs. Redding, the current tenant, is reluctant to vacate the house."

"She is?" That didn't sound like Georgina. She of all people understood their liaison was a straight business arrangement. And now it was over. He hadn't called upon her in months, since before visiting Lambert Hall. He just hadn't gotten around to officially ending their agreement until now. "Did you not send Mrs. Redding a parting gift as I directed?"

"Indeed I did, Your Grace. A diamond-and-emerald necklace with matching earrings. You were very generous."

"What then is the matter? Did you not tell her that I've granted her one additional month to continue to reside at the property until she secures another protector?"

"I did, Your Grace, exactly as you directed."

"And?" He wished the damned man would just get to the point.

"It seems that Mrs. Redding desires to speak with you."

"Whatever for? Dammit, Banks, you should be able to handle this matter without involving me." Foster certainly would have.

Banks's ears reddened. "My apologies, Your Grace. I shall go directly and visit Mrs. Redding and close this matter once and for all."

Hunt pushed his chair back with a clatter as he came to his feet. "Do not bother. I'll see to Georgina myself." He might as well. Hunt certainly wasn't getting any work done. Some fresh air and exercise might help clear his head.

"I'll ask Hughes to alert the coachman."

"No need. I'll walk." He shut the study door behind him.

It was a brisk day, with the sun sheltered behind the clouds, but Hunt hardly noticed. Burrowing his hands into the pockets of his greatcoat, he strode to his property on Half Moon Street, a tidy brick-fronted house where Georgina had resided these past four years. She was his first mistress. She would also be his last.

Georgina received him as soon as he arrived. "Your Grace." Her smile was warm and gracious.

"Hello, Georgina." He drew off his hat and coat, handing both to the waiting footman, who quickly vanished.

"It is good of you to call," she said, inviting him to join her on the chintz sofa.

"It is not as though you gave me a choice."

"We both know that is not true. No one can force the Duke of Huntington to do anything he doesn't care to."

He sat. Reluctantly. "Why am I here, Georgina?"

"I could ask you the same question."

"You are the one who asked me to call."

"I understand you are replacing me."

"I am not replacing you. But I am ending our arrangement."

"After four years together."

"Precisely." What was she about? "Did you not receive my parting gift?"

"I did. It was very generous."

"Then what is the problem?"

"Have I been a suitable companion to you?"

"Yes. Very."

"I see."

"I don't." He allowed his frustration to show. "Why am I here?"

"Because it is customary for a protector to end an agreement such as ours in person. Not through a new secretary I've never heard of and have had no previous dealings with."

Hunt finally understood. He'd inadvertently slighted his former mistress. "Forgive me if I have offended you. It was not my intent. This has been a challenging time."

"I understand." Sympathy filled Georgina's eyes, and he knew she thought of the public humiliation brought on by Victoria's defection. But it was Leela's abandonment that gutted him. "I thought you might care to extend our arrangement since you remain unattached."

It was not an unreasonable suggestion. Up until recently, he viewed his understanding with Georgina as a tidy business arrangement, ideal due to the absence of emotion, attachment or any other distasteful complications. But now, the notion of paying for sex struck Hunt not only as unsavory, but empty, somehow, and devoid of satisfaction. With Leela, the sex had been far more than a physical act. He'd never view sexual congress as purely physical again.

"I do not think so," he said gently.

"But you said you don't intend to replace me."

"That is true. I am not taking another mistress."

"You are a man with appetites. After four years together, I am in a position to know this."

"With all due respect, Georgina, how I satisfy my needs going forward is no longer your concern."

She tilted her head to the side. "Perhaps you have another prospective wife in mind?"

His immediate instinct was to deny it. But the image of Leela flashed in his mind. Those knowing dark eyes smiled at him, beckoned him. Of course, he couldn't marry Leela. Yet, it struck Hunt with the force of a sledgehammer that he wanted nothing more than to keep Leela with him forever. The duchy be damned.

He shook his head to dislodge the ridiculous notion. He wasn't thinking clearly. He wasn't sleeping well. He was exhausted; his mind not at its sharpest. And yet, the thought of taking Leela to wife, of making her his duchess, made his heart feel light in his chest. It almost felt like joy.

"Even if I did have a particular lady in mind," he said, "I doubt she would have me."

Georgina responded with an incredulous laugh. "What woman in her right mind wouldn't want to be your duchess? That girl who ran away with your secretary is a fool. Any woman with half a brain would fall at your feet."

He smiled to himself. "Except perhaps an extraordinary woman with a mind of her own."

"Will you let her get away so easily?"

He stood. "No, I don't think I will."

# Chapter Twenty-Nine

$\mathcal{A}$re you searching for a particular Levantine trading house?" asked Mr. Cobb, the man from the Manchester Commercial Society, a group comprised of merchants and manufacturers who traded abroad.

"Are there many of them?" Hunt inquired. He'd arrived in Manchester to search for Leela armed with very little information other than the Peckham House butler's word that Lady Devon was visiting her grandmother.

"There are at least a half dozen Levantine trading houses here." Mr. Cobb arranged the papers on his desk. "The export of clean cotton goods from Lancashire to the Levant is a very profitable enterprise. Lancashire sells its goods to the world through us here in Manchester."

"I was hoping that these Levantine traders you speak of might belong to your organization."

Cobb pursed his lips. "They keep to themselves, you understand. We don't mix with them a great deal."

"I see." Finding Leela might prove more difficult than Hunt expected. It had not occurred to him that there would be numerous Arab merchants in Manchester. "Might it be helpful for you to know that the family surname is Atwan?"

"Ah, yes." Comprehension lit the man's face. "That is very helpful."

Hope stirred in Hunt. "You've heard of them then."

"Indeed. They are among the more prosperous Levantines in Manchester. You will find the Atwan Trade Company on Park Street just down the road from here."

About an hour later, after visiting the Atwan Trade Company, Hunt found himself staring up at a two-story brick-fronted house with large sashed windows facing the street. "You are certain this is the place?"

"Yes, Your Grace," his coachman replied. "The clerk at the Atwan Trade Company says this is where the Levantine cotton merchant family resides."

Although modest by Hunt's standards, the handsome symmetrical house appeared large enough to accommodate five or six bedchambers. Single-story additions on either side of the main house made the structure appear even larger. A black wooden door between the main house and one of the small new wings appeared to lead to a rear garden.

"What is that racket?" Someone was beating a drum somewhere, accompanied by an unfamiliar string instrument that produced a deep mellow sound.

"Perhaps they are entertaining, Your Grace."

Hunt studied the wooden garden door. "Is the music coming from the back of the house?"

"That is what it sounds like, Your Grace. Shall I go in with you?"

"No, I can manage." Hunt fervently hoped to find Leela here. He hadn't traveled all the way to Manchester only to come up empty. He longed to see her. He needed to speak with her, to settle their future. Although he wasn't entirely certain what that meant.

The black door gave way when Hunt tried to knock on it, so he let himself in and followed the racket to a sizable garden behind the house. He came upon a line of dancing men and women holding hands as they moved to the rhythm of the music produced by two men sitting nearby. One musician sat on a square, low-to-the-ground stool playing a small round drum. He had the instrument's long narrow neck braced between his thighs as he pounded a beat with the flats of his hands. Next to him, a man sat cross-legged on the ground, playing a pear-shaped stringed instrument.

The people they played for danced with vigorous enthusiasm, crossing one leg over the other, adding in hops with definite flourish. Their energetic movements and obvious joy were at odds with traditional English dances that Hunt was accustomed to, which were characterized by polite restraint and adherence to neat and precise steps. The man at the lead, perhaps in his late twenties, was particularly skilled and appeared to set the tempo for the others. About half a dozen men were at the head of the line, with a handful of women bringing up the rear.

Hunt's eye caught on the last woman in line. Her face was flushed, her eyes sparkling as she followed the steps, perhaps with less skill, but with no less enthusiasm, than the rest of the revelers. Her long curls had escaped their restraints, cascading down her back. Leela laughed as she missed a step. The young woman next to her, with dark straight hair and striking ebony eyes, spoke in Leela's ear, instructing her as both looked down at their feet. Leela's face was a study in concentration as she attempted to copy her companion's dance steps.

Longing curled inside Hunt's gut. He'd missed Leela terribly. But somehow, seeing her at home among this foreign merchant family made her feel farther away than ever, even though she stood just yards from him. Among the ton, Leela stood out due to her beautiful coloring, the midnight hair and bronzed skin. But here, among her mother's people, she blended in with the merrymakers.

Hunt's skin prickled. He felt a bit self-conscious. For the first time in his life, he was the one who was noticeably out of place. It was an extraordinary sensation. Hunt had never experienced what it was not to belong, to be the sole person in a group who was different.

Losing his brother hadn't been easy, but sliding into his ducal role came naturally. He enjoyed the challenge of running the duchy and quickly became accustomed to the deference society showed him due to his rank. Usually, he commanded a room. But here he was an interloper, the odd one out in the crowd. He stood out, and not necessarily in a positive way. It was a sensation he'd never experienced before.

"May I help you?" A man in his late forties, with silver eyes and abundant matching curly hair, regarded Hunt with a polite inquiring expression.

"Yes, I am sorry to intrude." Hunt cleared his throat. "I am the Duke of Huntington. I am here to call upon Lady Devon."

"Hunt?" He recognized Leela's voice. "What are you doing here?"

He turned to find himself staring into her curious gaze. She was out of breath from dancing. Her hair a gorgeous mess around her shoulders. She looked beautiful.

"Forgive my intrusion." He shifted his weight to the other foot. "I did not mean to interrupt your party."

"It is just family. You are not interrupting."

"Family?" He surveyed the garden, the older men sitting around smoking a hookah water pipe, the dancing men and women, and those who watched them, young and old, sitting in a large ragged circle. A handful of children raced through the garden, sidestepping the adults. There were at least twenty-five people present. "All of these people are your relations?"

"My grandmother, aunts, uncles and cousins. Not all of them of course."

"There are more?" Hunt had seven cousins in total, on both sides of the family, including his cousin Alfred, who stood to inherit the duchy should Hunt fail to produce an heir.

Her eyes twinkled. "So I am told. My mother had six brothers and sisters. It's quite a large family."

*How exhausting.* "How extraordinary." The drumming stopped and the man playing the string instrument played on alone. It produced melodic, echoing sounds and felt aggressive at intervals, with lots of picking. The melody conjured up images of vast spaces and faraway places.

"What is that strange instrument?"

"The *oud*? It's very similar to a lute. It's considered to be one of the oldest musical instruments in the world." She turned to lead him into the house. "Come, let's go somewhere we can speak more privately." He followed her into a room dominated by a long wooden dining table surrounded by assorted mismatched chairs, some with upholstered backs, others with ladder backs. A fire burned in the marble hearth on one side of the chamber. Books lined built-in shelves on the opposite wall.

Hunt looked around. "What is this room?"

"The dining room." She gently teased him, "Come now, it's not as elaborate as the one you have at Weston House, but surely you can recognize a dining chamber when you see one."

"I've never seen anyone set up bookshelves in a dining room."

She smiled, her eyes crinkling. She was happy to see him. "People of limited means must find multiple uses for rooms."

"So I see." The books did lend a certain warmth to the chamber. He could envision Leela sitting before the fire with a book. He paused, taking a moment to soak in the sight of her. The mass of unruly curls, her serious gaze, which stayed level with his. He wanted nothing more than to close the gap between them and take her into his arms.

The color in her cheeks deepened. "Why are you here?"

"I miss you." *I cannot stand to be without you.* "And I fear too many things were left unsaid at our last meeting."

"I miss you, too." The pull between them intensified. As though a hundred men were pushing Hunt toward her. "But I do not see a solution to our dilemma."

"I do. You could marry me."

Her eyes rounded. "Marry you?"

"Yes. Why not?" His heart thrashed against his ribs. He hadn't intended to propose. The words just erupted from his mouth, like a volcano that had to purge itself. But he didn't regret his impulsiveness. Not one bit. "We are both adults. We can do as we please."

"I think we both know that is not true. Society would destroy us."

"It didn't destroy your parents. You've said yourself that they cared deeply for one another."

"Mama also kept me and Alexander away from her family, which is unnatural. Aside from *Citi*, my grandmother, I'd never met any of my aunts and uncles and cousins until this visit."

"What does that have to do with you becoming my duchess?"

"Mama kept us away from the Arab side of our family because she believed we couldn't be completely English if we embraced this part of our identity."

He thought of how happy she'd looked dancing with her cousins. "You are content here among them."

"I feel a definite affinity with my relatives here, a sense of belonging that has eluded me until now."

He found that difficult to grasp. Leela had been born and bred in the highest echelons of society. And yet she somehow felt at home here among the middle-class relations she'd only just met? "Even though they are merchants and you are a countess?"

"When you strip all of that away, they are my family. I see myself in them."

"You are also the daughter and sister of a marquess. That is equally a part of you. You were born to fill the role of a duchess."

She grimaced. "I would make a terrible duchess."

He shook his head. "I saw how you presided over the table at Lambert Hall. You are a masterful hostess, just as your mother taught you to be."

"I can preside over a household, but I cannot do as my mother did and all but abandon my family. Especially not now when I've just found them. I will not pretend this part of my family does not exist."

"I would never ask you to."

"You say that now because you miss me. As I miss you. Terribly."

"I am sincere. You must believe me. You should come and visit your family whenever you like."

"And what about you? Would you come too?"

He paused. He could not imagine himself sitting, dancing and laughing among Leela's extended family.

He didn't even interact with his own family in that manner. Formality dictated every interaction with his late parents and certainly with what few cousins he had. "If it would make you happy."

"But would it make you happy?"

"What difference does it make?" He stepped closer, dying to touch her, to feel the warmth of her skin, but he restrained himself. Just barely. "The point I am trying to make is that I would do anything for you."

"And what about heirs? I am, in all likelihood, barren."

"Your husband was old and suffering from the after-effects of a dissolute lifestyle by the time you wed him. It could have been a problem on his part."

"You and I have lain together several times," she pointed out. "I am not with child."

"If I do not produce an heir, so be it. My cousin Alfred will inherit. He already has two young sons. The succession is assured."

"You should have children of your own."

"I prefer to have you by my side than a bunch of brats nipping at my ankles."

"What about my work, my writing?"

"Must you continue traveling?" He tried to keep the desperation out of his voice. He would hate for her to leave him to his own devices for months at a time. "Could you not find something to write about closer to home?"

She smiled sadly. "It will not work."

"It will. Travel if you must. I will be at home waiting for you, missing your terribly, but I would never keep you from writing your books."

"Oh, Hunt." The restraint between them broke. She rushed into his arms.

He tightened his embrace, enveloping her in his love. "Please stay with me." He inhaled her warmth, the sweet scent of exertion mixed with her floral hair rinse. "We can make it work."

"I want to," she whispered. "More than anything."

His lips found hers. He kissed her hungrily, deeply, imbuing everything he felt for her into the intimacy. She returned his enthusiasm, her tongue mating with his, until they were both out of breath and his blood was hot and the natural course of things would be to make love to her right there on the dining room table.

And yet, as much as he wanted to deny it, he felt her slipping away. "But you won't, will you," he whispered into her ear. "You won't stay with me."

"How can I? This is about more than my writing. You will come to resent me for not being the ideal duchess you've always imagined for yourself."

"You are my ideal woman, which is far more important," he said urgently. "I'm a grown man. I know what I want."

"I couldn't bear it if you came to despise me. You will feel the censure of society for wedding me, the loss of not having children. And you will secretly blame me."

"You don't know that. You cannot pretend to know my mind better than I do."

"Still, I won't risk it."

"How can you make a decision this important on

the assumption I might come to regret my decision? That isn't fair to either of us."

"It is not just that. In the end, we are too different," she said. "And you know it."

He wanted to howl at the injustice of it, to rage against a world that contrived to keep them apart. "We aren't so different, you and I."

"We know that," she said, "but the world does not."

# Chapter Thirty

*O*ne week later, Hunt strode down St. James toward White's gentleman's club, hurrying to keep a late breakfast appointment with Griff.

Anything to take his mind off Leela. He didn't feel like seeing anyone. But he couldn't stay holed up in the old mausoleum he called home and wallow in his misery for another minute.

Up ahead at a corner print shop, several people crowded the footpath, staring at something in the bow window where the day's newspapers were on display. The gawkers forced Hunt to step into the street in order to continue on his way. One woman peering into the window shook her head and said, "That sort ain't look like no Quality to me," to general murmurs of agreement.

When he reached White's, Hunt went straight to the eating room, where he found his friend ensconced in a studded brown leather armchair with curved saber legs. Griff put aside his newspaper once he spotted Hunt. "From that scowl on your face, I gather you've seen today's *Times*?"

"No, I haven't read the papers yet." He'd overslept after another fitful, Leela-less night. "And what the devil do you mean by that?"

"It's all anyone's talking about today." The viscount regarded Hunt with an amused expression on his face. "Did you know the truth?"

"About what?" Hunt settled in a matching chair across the round table from his friend. "Don't tell me I've somehow caused another scandal."

"Not you. But it is quite the scandal."

"Stop talking in riddles." Hunt snatched up the copy of the *Times*. He stared at the headline. "Oh. So she's gone and done it."

"Oh indeed." Griff watched his face. "You don't seem terribly shocked."

"I discovered the truth by accident while we were all at Lambert Hall." Hunt stared at the headline:

### He is a SHE! Shocking Truth About Noble Levantine Lady Who Penned *Travels in Arabia*

"Devon must be beside himself," Griff remarked. "First his sister runs off with a nobody and then his stepmother confesses to being a lady who dares to work. Not to mention the scandal of traveling without a chaperone."

"Shhh." Hunt concentrated on the article. The article quoted Leela extensively. She talked about her travels and of meeting her Levantine relatives. "I'm proud of my work and pleased that my fellow country-men and women seem to enjoy it."

"It is a damn good book." Griff sipped his coffee. "I suppose she finally wants to take credit for it."

"That's not it." Hunt tossed the paper onto the table between them. He motioned for a waiter to bring coffee to accompany the kidney pie, breads and assorted cheeses set out before him. "That's not why she did it."

"Is that so?" Griff's forehead went up. "And you know this how?"

"Because I am . . . was . . . acquainted with the lady."

Interest glimmered in Griff's eyes. "That's a great deal of intriguing information in one sentence. Do kindly spell out exactly what you mean."

"I love Lady Devon and wish to marry her." Relief flowed through Hunt's veins. It felt good to say the words out loud to another person. It was like finally exhaling after holding his breath for a week.

The muscles in Griff's face slackened. "I beg your pardon?"

"The reason Lady Devon revealed her true identity as the author of *Travels in Arabia* is to put herself beyond the pale in my eyes."

"Why?" Griff lifted his chin. "Was she *that* offended by the prospect of being your wife?"

"Stop enjoying this so much. Lady Devon believes that emphasizing her Levantine roots, coupled with the scandal of a noblewoman traveling alone and working for money, will contrive to put me off the idea of wedding her."

"I see." Understanding lit Griff's face. "She thinks you'll run because you are a man who embraces decorum and abhors scandal. Does she have the right of it?"

"I certainly detest scandal." He rubbed his tired eyes. They burned against his lids. "But the devil of it all is that I cannot stop thinking about her."

Griff bit off a chunk of toast. "So go after her."

"If only it were that simple."

"Isn't it?"

"I no longer know. She's got me so turned around that I cannot seem to think rationally. All I know for certain is that I admire her more than anyone I know. She's a brilliant writer. She's unapologetic about who she is and what she wants. I would be fortunate if a woman as formidable as Leela consented to spend her life with me."

"Good god, man, if that's how you feel, then why are you still sitting here with me? You should be on your knees at Peckham House begging her to accept your suit." Griff's face darkened. "None of us ever knows what tomorrow will bring. Nothing is guaranteed."

"You are thinking of your parents," Hunt said.

"There's not a day when I don't think of them, of . . . what was done to them." Griff ran a hand gingerly over his affected shoulder, the injury that would never heal. Not unlike the lasting wound to his soul caused by his parents' deaths. "What I would give to have just one more day with them."

"I am sorry." Hunt didn't know what else to say.

"My mother and father are gone. There's no bringing them back. The same is not true for you and your lady."

"Throw all caution to the wind? Just like my late brother did? We all know how that ended."

"You are nothing like Phillip. Being with a decent woman like Lady Devon isn't at all akin to courting disaster on a daily basis like your brother did."

"I always smugly took great pride in the difference between me and my brother." Hunt stabbed his pie with a fork. "He was reckless and passionate. I saw myself as measured and contained."

"And now?"

"I suspect that I've been fooling myself." Hunt stuffed a bite into his mouth. "Maybe Phillip and I aren't so different after all."

HUNT STARED UP at the cluster of back-to-back houses where Lady Victoria now lived. He'd come directly from his breakfast with Griff.

The odors of smoke and sewage drenched the air. A crying baby and an arguing couple sounded over the clatter of the traffic—carriages, carts and single-rider horses—traversing along the mud-logged street behind him. It was hard to fathom how a young lady born into privilege could willingly fall so far.

Hunt had spent the past fortnight trying to convince himself to heed Leela's warning. Did she have the right of it? Would society's disapproval of their union ultimately prove untenable for a man like him, a traditionalist who championed and embraced decorum? Hunt certainly used society's strictures as a guiding light, as protection against becoming his brother, or any of the other miscreant dukes in the family tree.

But the conversation with Griff stirred things up in him again. So he came to visit the two people he'd vowed to avoid. The couple that gave up everything to be together.

He followed the narrow tunnel between two of the buildings that led to the Fosters' front door. The homes, built about a decade ago, were intended for those of modest means. The narrow, two-story houses shared chimney stacks as well as three walls, leaving only one wall for windows. It had never occurred to Hunt to wonder where his secretary lived. Had he given it any thought, he could never have imagined a place like this.

Laundry lines strung with clothing streamed across the shared courtyard. Hunt paused, staring at Number Six, the address where Lady Victoria now lived with Hunt's former secretary. Again he wondered why he had come. What did he expect to gain by forcing an encounter with the two people who'd betrayed his trust and delivered the biggest humiliation of his life?

He finally willed himself to knock. Two quick raps. Lady Victoria opened her own door, something she'd never do in her previous life as the daughter and sister of the Earls of Devon.

Her eyes widened. Shock stamped her face. "Huntington?"

"Hello, Victoria. May I come in?"

Wariness crossed her refined features. "Yes, of course." She moved aside to allow him entrance into the hovel she now called home.

"Your Grace." She reflexively sank into a deep curtsy. The social graces embedded in her after a lifetime as a lady were all worthless now. Society would never view Victoria as a true lady again. She wore a drab dress made of rough fabric. The short skirt exposed worn ankle boots. But her eyes were clear and her complexion healthy. She did not look in the least bit miserable. "Would you care to sit?"

The chamber was small but neat. He sat on the quality upholstered sofa that dominated the space. It looked new. "Forgive me for intruding."

"It is no intrusion." She lowered herself into one of two matching faded chairs flanking the hearth. She sat, spine straight, at the edge of the seat, as any lady would while in polite company. "I am happy to see you. I must beg for your forgiveness."

"Why?" he asked, genuinely curious. "Do you regret the choice you made?"

"No, but I hate to think of the humiliation and hurt that I caused you. It is the sole thing that mars my happiness now. You were nothing but kind to me. Although I do not deserve your good regard, I still admire you and hold you in great affection."

He surveyed the dark space. The only light came from a bay window by the door. "And yet you prefer to live in squalor than to be wed to me."

"No, that is not true." She looked around. "And I am told these are rather decent accommodations for the middle class. Those who live in true squalor reside in cellars, which can be damp and very poorly ventilated."

"I see you've certainly learned a great deal about the lower classes since your marriage."

"I am one of them now."

"You are a lady and will always be one."

"A lady who now not only serves the tea, but also actually heats her own water."

"Is it difficult?" Hunt imagined that boiling water couldn't be all that challenging. He'd never actually done it himself.

"No," she confessed with a wry smile, "but I did manage to burn myself a time or two before I mastered the skill. May I offer you some tea?"

"No, thank you." Silence ensued. Except for the braying couple on the opposite side of Victoria's back wall.

"If you would get off your arse, you drunken lout!" the woman yelled through the wall.

"Shut your trap, you filthy whore!" the man bellowed back.

Victoria cleared her throat. "Why have you come?"

"To ask you if it was worth it." Looking around, it was obvious that Victoria had literally given up everything to wed Foster. "Was it worth leaving your old life for this?"

She smiled gently. "I do not expect you to forgive me."

"I do forgive you," he said impatiently, "but I am eager to understand your motivation."

"It is difficult to explain." She looked down at her clasped hands in her lap. "When Mr. Foster looks at me, it is as if the sun is shining on me. It is the most glorious feeling. My happiness does not require fripperies and ball gowns. All it needs to flourish is Mr. Foster by my side. The time we spend in each other's company is priceless to me. I do not expect you to understand."

And yet he did. He knew what it was to bask in Leela's sunlight. He took in the petite, slim woman sitting opposite him. She looked fragile, but she obviously possessed the strength of Hercules to be able to defy her family and society in order to follow her heart. It was more than Hunt was capable of. "I find myself facing a similar dilemma as you."

"How do you mean?" Her face brightened. "Are you in love?"

He nodded. "But there are complications."

"Why? Because the lady in question would be an unsuitable duchess?" Her eyes widened. "It is Mrs. Redding?"

"My mistress?" he asked, shocked. "How do you even know of her existence?"

"People gossip. If it is Mrs. Redding, your new scandal will undoubtedly be even greater than the last one."

"It isn't Georgina. It is"—he paused—"Lady Devon."

"Leela?" Shock stamped Victoria's face. "No!"

"I realize this news might prove distressing—"

She looked dumbfounded. "She did mention seeing you from time to time, but I had no idea matters progressed beyond friendship."

"It is not my intention to upset you."

"I am not upset, just surprised." She seemed to turn the idea over in her head. "I believe I would be delighted if you could make Leela happy."

"Unfortunately, she has turned down my offer of marriage."

"But why? Does she not feel the same about you?"

"She believes we would face society's censure and that I would come to resent her for it."

"She's a lady and you're a duke. No one would dare to cut you."

He shrugged. "Certainly not to my face." He studied her. "Do you miss anything about your old life?"

"I must admit I have a newfound appreciation for servants and for Cook's delicious food." She shrugged her shoulders. "However, I do not miss the ton. I never cared for society, but it might be different for you as a man who places a great value on being respectable and setting an example for others to follow."

"Honestly, what I find most rewarding about my position is the challenge of running the duchy in a way that proves both profitable now and sustainable in the future. If I wed Lady Devon, that would remain unchanged."

"Then perhaps you should fight a little harder to keep her by your side."

"Perhaps I should." He'd struggled to avoid being ruled by passion, fearing it would lead him down the same destructive path as his brother. Yet following society's strictures made him miserable. "Following the rules certainly hasn't proven satisfactory. Maybe everything in life cannot be tied up into a neat little package."

"My life at Lambert Hall was certainly orderly. It was only after my situation became untidy"—she blushed—"when I met Mr. Foster, that I felt like I finally understood what life was meant to be about. I know society believes I made a cake of myself for jilting a duke in favor of the distant relation of a baron, but that cake is delicious and satisfies every need in me. It's rather freeing, you know."

"What is? Being poor?"

"Being free of societal restraints. I realize having society take no notice of me is meant to be a punishment, but it certainly doesn't feel like it. I rather like being free to do as I please."

"But you are living in penury."

"Mr. Foster is bright and ambitious. I have hopes that he will secure employment and we will have all that we need." She spread her arms wide. "As you can see, we don't require much to be happy."

The girl was still young and idealistic. Yet Hunt could not help but envy her obvious contentment and complete lack of regard for what the ton thought of her.

He came to his feet. "I shall go and speak with Lady Devon."

"You're going to Morocco?"

"Of course not." He couldn't go to Morocco any more than he could fly to the moon. "I shall go and see Lady Devon at her brother's residence here in town."

She paused. "You don't know then."

"Know what?"

"Leela is gone. She called the day before yesterday to bid us farewell. I thought that's why you'd come."

"That's impossible." His stomach lurched. "Her book isn't even published yet. Lady Devon intended to remain in town until publication."

"She said it was too difficult to stay here for another day. Leela worried that if she remained in town, she might be tempted to do something she ought not. I didn't understand then but I think I do now."

"She cannot be gone."

"I believe she intended to sail for Gibraltar today and then on to Morocco from there."

Hunt started for the door. Maybe it wasn't too late after all. "I need to speak to her before she sails." He was out the door and racing through the courtyard by the time he called back over his shoulder, "I must go!"

HUNT ARRIVED AT Peckham House flushed and out of breath. He banged on the front door. "Open up."

The door gave way to reveal a bronze-skinned man with determined features. He wore a plain brown jacket, trousers and sturdy shoes—the uniform favored by the working class. No doubt another of Leela's Levantine servants.

The man regarded Hunt with dark, cynical eyes. "Where is the fire?"

"What?"

"You were banging on the door. Where is the fire?"

He ignored the servant's insolence. "Pray go and tell Lady Devon that she has a caller." He stepped up to enter the house.

The other man did not budge, leaving Hunt no choice but to remain on the doorstep. "And who are you?"

"I am Huntington."

The man's brows lifted. "As in 'the duke of'?"

"Yes," he said impatiently. "Kindly go and tell Lady Devon that I am here. I have urgent business with her."

"Do you?" The man crossed his arms over his chest and leaned against the doorjamb, not seeming the least bit in a hurry. "What sort of business?"

"Who are you to question me?" Hunt snapped, a moment away from cuffing the arse. "That is none of your concern."

"As Lady Devon's brother, it is indeed my business."

Hunt's mouth fell open. This man in old, worn clothes was Leela's brother, the marquess? "You're Brandon?"

"In the flesh."

Hunt took a good look at the man and realized he had Leela's dark almond eyes. "I wish to ask your sister to marry me. I must see her. May I come in?"

Brandon stepped aside. "Good luck with that."

Hunt brushed by Leela's brother, scanning the front hallway as if he expected to find Leela waiting for him. "Where is she?"

"My sister sailed for Gibraltar late last night."

"Impossible." Hunt swung around to face Brandon. "She's leaving today."

"The ship's captain decided to depart early while the weather was favorable."

Hunt suppressed a curse. "That cannot be."

"Can't it?" Brandon closed the door. "I realize you are a duke, but even you cannot turn back time."

Hunt wanted to pummel that flippant attitude out of Leela's brother. "Are you not listening to me? I want to make your sister a duchess. I wish to elevate her."

"What an honor." The words leaked with sarcasm. "I know how much your sort values titles."

"My sort? You're a marquess. You are my sort."

"Hardly. Tell me, does Leela know you wish to *elevate* her place in life?"

"Yes, of course." Hunt ran a flat hand down over his face. He was too late. Leela was gone. What a fool he'd been to let a life with her slip through his fingers.

"So my sister knows you wish to grant her the honor of wedding her and still chose to travel to another continent." Brandon stretched his closed lips wide in a mirthless smile. "It seems to me that you have Leela's answer to your proposal."

Hunt rounded on the man. "Listen to me, you whoreson—"

Brandon straightened. "Watch your insults, Huntington. Don't give me an excuse to call you out. There's nothing I'd like better."

"Why?" The man's obvious antipathy baffled him. It wasn't as though Hunt wished to dishonor Leela. "You don't even know me."

"Oh, I know your type, which is quite enough." Brandon pulled the door open and, with a sweep of his hand, gestured for Hunt to go through it. "I believe our business is concluded."

Hunt saw he'd get no help from this bastard. Adjusting his cuffs, he strode out without giving Brandon the courtesy of another look or further acknowledging his presence. The door closed hard behind him.

Hunt stood there, taking no notice of the carriage traffic rattling through the square, as the reality sank in. Leela was gone. It would be months before he saw her again. Months during which time she might meet someone else. A man who would know his own mind. Who would not allow a diamond like Leela to slip away. Meanwhile, Hunt would be thousands of miles away. Oblivious. Powerless to stop them.

The strength drained from his legs. He sank onto the top stair, blind to anyone who might question why the Duke of Huntington was perched on the Marquess of Brandon's front steps.

All Hunt could think of was the enormity of his loss. Leela was gone.

It was over.

# Chapter Thirty-One

*L*eela hurried through the city gates just as the sun began to lower beyond the horizon. She knew to return from her Gibraltar explorations before sunset, when the gates would close and remain shut until daybreak.

"You made it," said the soldier who checked her residency permit. She'd secured a ten-day permit to remain on the Rock—as Gibraltar was known—until she could find passage to Tangier.

"Is it really necessary to secure the city gates?" It seemed somewhat medieval to her.

"The Rock can only be taken by treason," the young man returned. He had red hair and a cockneyish accent. "So we must protect her."

She thanked him and went on her way, surrounded by a sea of people going about their business. The island retained a distinct international flavor, even though Spain had ceded Gibraltar to Britain more than a century ago. Around her, many were dressed in their native costume. Turks in turbans and Moors in white robes passed her while speaking in foreign tongues. She'd purchased delicious dates from a hand-

some Black merchant who told her he came from Tim-
buctu on the edge of the Sahara. And proprietors with
foreign names, such as *Manuel Ximenez—Lodgings
and Neat Liquors*, were common.

Leela was at the crossroads of the world. All nations
met in Gibraltar given the Rock's location between Eu-
rope, Africa and Asia. It was a place valuable enough
to fight over, which explained the heavy presence of
British soldiers everywhere she went. It was hard to
miss the defensive artillery and rows of sentries stationed at intervals around the island.

Leela hurried to the inn where she had a room, eager to be inside before darkness fell. Homes made of
brick and plaster and woodwork, all tightly woven
together, lined the streets. Hashem and his daughter, Hasna, who'd both made the journey with Leela,
were visiting an old friend who'd made his home on
the Rock. In two days' time, they would set sail for
Tangier, landing in Morocco within three days. She
was almost there.

But no matter how far she traveled from England,
she could not get Hunt out of her mind. In the month
since she'd last seen him, she thought of him every
day, wherever she went. Hunt constantly entered her
thoughts, no matter how mundane they might be.

At the fish market, she wondered what he might think
of the bright-colored, alien sea creatures. She thought
of him while exploring the surface of the Rock, which
was bare in summer and verdant in the spring and autumn, and tried to guess which state he'd prefer. When
she stood on sea-sprayed cliffs taking in the spectacu-

lar view, or on a fragment of a centuries-old Moorish castle, Leela lamented that Hunt was not there to share the experience with her.

In addition, she constantly felt as if she'd forgotten something. And then she would remember that what was missing was Hunt. And she would berate herself and tell herself to get on with it. And she tried. But it wasn't easy.

She entered Miss Duncan's lodging house and proceeded directly to her chamber. Passing the eating room, she heard the Scottish proprietor conversing with a new arrival.

"My apologies, sir. But we have no rooms."

"A salon then," the impatient masculine voice demanded. "Surely you must have a parlor at the very least."

Leela froze. She knew that voice. And then she told herself that she was imagining things.

"You might try Mr. Ben Elia's lodging house," Miss Duncan advised the man. "It is nearby on Bomb House Lane."

"Bomb House Lane? That doesn't sound particularly restful," the traveler remarked. "One shudders to think how it got that name."

Leela's heart lifted. She wasn't imagining things. It was him. She rushed into the eating room.

The traveler had his back to her. He wore an old coat and weathered buckskin breeches tucked into scuffed boots. The fastidious Duke of Huntington would not be caught dead in such an ensemble. But

Elliot Townsend would. He'd worn these same clothes at their very first meeting at the Black Swan Inn near Coventry.

Leela's heart dipped. Maybe this was just wishful thinking. Hunt couldn't possibly be in Gibraltar. The man never left England.

"Hunt?" She held her breath as the man turned to face her. An annoyed face stared back at her. A face that she loved beyond measure. Then Hunt's features shifted into joyous disbelief. "Leela?"

"Do you know this gentleman?" Miss Duncan asked her.

Hunt's gaze held Leela's. "Of course she does. I am her husband."

Leela pressed her lips inward to hide her smile. Laughter bubbled up inside of her. Hunt was here. She couldn't take her eyes off him. She feared he might vanish if she so much as blinked.

"Is that true, Mrs. Chambers?" Miss Duncan wanted to know. "Is this Mr. Chambers?"

"Of course it's true," Hunt snapped, still holding Leela's gaze. They both moved forward to meet each other.

Leela just barely managed to keep from launching herself into Hunt's arms. "I cannot believe you are here."

"As if I could be anywhere else." He took Leela by the elbow. "Come, my dear." To Miss Duncan, he said, "If you do not mind, my wife and I have much to discuss."

Still somewhat dazed, Leela allowed Hunt to direct her toward the steep wooden stairs. "Is this the way to your bedchamber?"

The scent of worn leather and warm skin filled her nostrils. "You are taking the liberty of sharing my bedchamber?"

"It is only fair. The last time one of us was stranded without a bedchamber—that would be you—the other one of us—namely me—generously offered to share the space with you."

"I remember." She grinned. "It was the best night of my life."

"Not for long," Hunt said. "This evening is about to become the best night of your life."

LEELA FELL BACK against the door as soon as they entered her bedchamber and stared at Hunt. "What are you doing here?"

"I should think it would be obvious." He nudged her back against the door. Interlocking his fingers with hers, he pulled her hands up over her head and kissed her heatedly. His demanding tongue pushed into her willing mouth. Urgently. Decisively. Like he couldn't get enough. Leela's knees gave out beneath her.

"God, I missed you." He kissed and nibbled his way down her neck, sucking her tender tissue. His rough unshaven jaw chafed as it rubbed against her. Clutching him to her, Leela relished the burn of their skin-to-skin contact. It was proof that he was here in the flesh and not some figment of her imagination.

Hunt's big warm body pressed up against hers, his

prodigious erection digging into her pelvis. "I need you now." He began to lift her skirts.

Leela had never wanted anything more. She felt like she was on fire. But panic welled up inside of her. "No. Wait. Stop."

Hunt stilled, his erection still pressed into her. "Stop?"

"Yes." She fought for breath to steady her pounding heart. She could barely hear herself think. "Please stop."

"You cannot be serious." But he did as she asked and pulled back so that they were no longer touching. He stared at her in disbelief.

"I need a moment to think."

"Can you think later?"

"What are you doing here?"

"I came all the way to this rocky godforsaken island to find you. Doesn't that tell you everything you need to know?"

"Not quite." She straightened, righting the neckline of her gown. "Why did you make the journey?"

"Isn't is obvious? I came for you."

"I cannot embark on another affair with you only for us to be parted again. I cannot bear it." Emotion roiled in her chest. "I won't survive it."

"I'm not going anywhere. We are going to be married and that's my final word on the matter."

She smiled. "Is that so? And am I to have any say in this?"

"Yes, of course," he said impatiently. "It is inevitable that we will end up together. But if you must talk it through then, by all means, have at it."

"We've already been through this. We are just too different."

"Balderdash. I am fully committed to this course of action. I even secured a special license before I left London."

"You did?" she asked, momentarily distracted. "Is that legal here?"

He shrugged. "I've no idea. It should be. This is a Crown territory. But just in case, I also have a letter signed by the prince regent himself directing the Gibraltar registry office to marry us."

"You sought special permission from the regent?" she asked, incredulous. She fought the warm, giddy hope ballooning inside of her. "And you will accept my being away for months at a time?"

"No. That's where I must draw the line . . ."

Leela's heart sank.

"I insist on coming with you."

Her jaw dropped. "But you hate to travel."

"I never said I hated it. I believe what I said is that I cannot neglect ducal affairs by being gone for months at a time."

"My journeys take several months."

"That is why I have engaged a very capable man to act in my place and manage my business concerns while I am away. Or, I suppose I should say reengaged. Foster is back in my employ."

"He is? I thought you would never forgive your secretary?"

"I would not go so far as to say I *forgive* him. But I do realize that if Foster had not run away with my intended bride, I would not be here with you, my fated bride. In the end, Foster did me a great service."

"He did us both a service," she concurred. "And Mr. Foster has agreed to work for you again?"

"Of course. The man is not a complete fool. Foster will oversee matters in my absence. As part of his compensation package, he and Victoria will reside at a modest home I own on Half Moon Street."

"Half Moon Street?" Why did that address sound familiar? Leela narrowed her eyes at him. "Isn't that where you house your mistress?"

"Where I *used* to house my mistresses. Yes. But now I will have a wife to attend to all required mutual pleasures of the flesh."

"But what about the scandal of it all? You abhor being the subject of gossip and ridicule. There are those who will mock you for taking a wife like me, whose mother was the daughter of a foreign merchant."

"That's the beauty of spending our wedding trip in Morocco. I shan't be there to witness any of it. By the time we return to London, several months from now, another scandal is sure to have supplanted ours."

Leela knew there were many other obstacles to being with Hunt, but at the moment she could not think of a single one. "But all of the things keeping us apart haven't just magically disappeared."

"They have in my mind. I have finally come to my senses." He ticked each point off on his long, masculine fingers. "First, I am not my brother. Wedding a smart, capable, ridiculously talented and incredibly beautiful woman will not suddenly turn me into an out-of-control wastrel. Although"—he winked at her—"I do feel out of control whenever you look at me like you are now, as if you wish to devour me."

"I am not looking at you like that," she protested.

He ticked off another point with his fingers. "Secondly, Foster can run my affairs while I am away, which means the ducal estate is in capable hands in my absence. Thirdly, while it is possible that I might detest traveling, you will be at my side, and I feel certain you'll do everything in your power to ensure I don't regret my decision." He cast a heated look in her direction.

Leela felt the impact of that stare deep into her belly. She licked her lips. "Go on."

"Fourthly, your Levantine relations are a part of you and I adore you so I am certain to find them somewhat tolerable."

"Very generous of you."

"Oh, I intend to be very generous with you," he drawled. His gaze traveled the full length of her body. "In all ways."

She resisted the urge to fan herself. "Is there more?"

He ticked off the last remaining finger. His pinkie. "Fifthly and most importantly, a very wise person once told me that I should marry a woman who looks at me as if I am the moon. I have found her. In fact"—he smiled tenderly—"I am looking at her."

"You seem to have thought of everything."

"All that is left is for you to say yes."

"You are asking me to return to society." A chill

went through her. "To subject myself to that scrutiny again. And to always be found lacking."

"God forbid." He grimaced. "The fewer ton entertainments we attend, the better. We can only accept invitations that interest you. The rest we shall happily toss into the waste bin."

She bit the corner of her lower lip. "You make it sound so easy."

"We are both through with allowing society to dictate our behavior. It's well past time that we make our own rules. As a duke, by design, I am supposed to do as I please. And, as my duchess, so shall you."

She smiled softly. "That would be something, wouldn't it?"

"I was planning on making this a gift to you on our wedding day." He withdrew a small red silk pouch from his pocket. "But perhaps this will encourage you to reach a decision more promptly."

She watched him open the pouch. "What is it?"

"See for yourself." He handed it to her.

She spilled its contents into her open palm, revealing a gold necklace and pendant in the shape of a half moon. "It's beautiful."

He removed his worn, wrinkled cravat, baring the matching necklace around his neck.

Her eyes widened. "You're wearing the other half to my necklace."

"Exactly. Together the moon is complete. As with our necklaces, I can only be whole when you are with me."

"What a lovely sentiment." She laid her hand against his pendant, the mate to her half, and relished the warmth of his body heat.

He put his large hand over hers on his chest. "Lovely enough for you to consent to becoming my wife? I cannot promise an easy path for us. There will be bumps in the road. But I think you are worth it. *We* are worth fighting for."

She gazed up at him. "Yes, *ya umar*, I will marry you. Only a fool would turn you away."

His handsome face lit up. "Thank goodness you're no fool." He grinned. "It's settled. We shall wed tomorrow. Before we sail for Morocco."

"Yes, tomorrow," she assured him. "It cannot come soon enough."

"Excellent." He swooped her up into his arms and walked over to the bed, tossing her onto it.

"Whatever will we do in the meantime?" she asked breathlessly.

"I am certain we can think of something." He crawled onto the bed on his hands and knees, like an animal on the prowl. "Perhaps I should begin by searching you for that strange knife of yours."

# Epilogue

*London*
*One year later*

Leela watched Hunt lift his glass. "To my beautiful and brilliant wife." She could hardly believe they were a family now. It still seemed like a dream.

The friends and relatives who'd gathered at Weston House to celebrate the publication of the third volume of *Travels in Arabia* raised their glasses. "Hear, hear," they called out.

Standing beside her husband, Leela smiled. "Thank you all for being here to celebrate with us. I am full of gratitude. Now please do enjoy yourselves. There is plenty of food and drink."

The guests dispersed, some heading in the direction of the dining room, where a generous spread was laid out. Others gathered around the table to peruse copies of *Travels of Arabia*.

Together, Hunt and Leela mingled with their guests. His large hand, draped lightly around her waist, slipped to her bottom. "Stop that," she admonished him. "We are in public."

"You were hard to resist before," he murmured in her ear, "but now that your hips are lusher than ever—"

"Yes, yes, I know." She cut him off. He could barely keep his hands off her now that her figure was fuller. "There is more of me to love, as you keep saying."

"So true and for such good reason."

Warmth filled Leela. She couldn't disagree. She had so much to be thankful for. The sounds of the *oud* and drums filtered through the room, evidence that her relatives had commandeered one of the smaller public rooms. It hadn't taken Leela and Hunt long to discover that music, dancing and hookah pipes followed Leela's Arab relatives almost everywhere they went.

"There you are." Tori emerged from the crush with a rosy-cheeked babe in her arms. The little boy gnawed at his fist as though it was the most delicious thing he'd ever eaten. Tori smoothed a gentle hand over the boy's pale, downy-haired scalp. "Someone is looking for you."

Mr. Foster appeared behind his wife, carrying a younger infant with a shock of black hair. Hunt stepped forward.

"I'll take my daughter now, if you don't mind." It never ceased to amaze Hunt that this beautiful little angel already had her mother's luxuriant hair. *Many Arab babies are born with hair*, Leela informed him when he'd rhapsodized about Maryam's lovely locks after her birth. Hunt pressed his lips against his daughter's tiny temple, knowing that Leela was wrong. No one's hair was as lovely as his wife's and daughter's.

"Mrs. Foster and I are most eager to read your latest volume," his secretary said to Leela.

"Wait until you read *Travels in Morocco*," Hunt said proudly. "It's her greatest manuscript yet."

"Hunt only says that because he came along on that journey and provided feedback on each chapter."

"Your Grace." Hughes, the butler, appeared, directing his attention toward Leela. "Will you be signing your books? Your guests are wondering."

Leela looked over to see people waiting in line holding copies of her book.

"Go on," Hunt urged her. "I'll go and deliver Maryam to her nurse and return to assist you."

"I don't need assistance signing my books."

"All the same. My plan is to hurry you along."

"Why? The party has just begun."

"I think we should get to work on providing a sibling for Maryam right now. I hope our next child is a girl as well."

"Why is that? You need a boy to carry on the title."

"Exactly." He pressed a kiss against her cheek. "You of all people know how seriously I take my responsibilities. Think of how much fun we shall have while trying to do our duty."

"Oh." Her cheeks flushed. "It is important to secure the succession. We must keep trying until we get it right."

"Precisely. Come to think of it, I'll deliver Maryam to Nurse and meet you upstairs."

"And leave our guests? What will people say? It'll create a scandal."

"I've come to appreciate scandal."

"You have?"

"Every scandal I've been involved in has brought great joy into my life."

"I see your point." Her breath hitched. "I'll sign fast and meet you in our bedchamber."

"That's my girl. See? I had the right of it all along."

"About what?"

Hunt's eyes twinkled. "I told you that you'd make an ideal duchess. And you are definitely my ideal."

# Acknowledgments

$\mathcal{D}$elilah Chambers and her travels were informed and influenced by original sources that I was thrilled to find and fascinated to read, including: *Domestic Life in Palestine* based on Mary Eliza Rogers's observations of Ottoman-era Palestine during an 1855 visit; *A Visit to the Holy Land, Egypt, and Italy* by the Austrian travel writer Ida Pfeiffer, who visited the region in 1842; and the letters that Regency-era traveller Lady Hester Stanhope wrote to her physician, which were published in 1845 under the title, *Memoirs of the Lady Hester Stanhope*. In addition, I was excited to find details about daily life in Gibraltar in *A Handbook for Travellers in Spain* (1847). These sources provided rich details that I hope made these places more vivid to the reader.

I have many people to thank, including my editor Carrie Feron, for taking a chance on characters with backgrounds readers aren't used to encountering in historical romance. And for elevating the original manuscript with her edits and suggestions, aptly described to me by another author as "little nuggets of gold."

Assistant Editor Asanté Simons is always just an email away with a ready answer, no matter what the question. Amy Halperin, Patricia Barrow, and Chris Cocozza gave me as beautiful a cover as any author could hope for. My thanks to everyone at Avon, including Pam Jaffee, Imani Gary, and everyone in the Avon publicity department, who helped bring *Her Night with the Duke* to readers.

This book was truly a family-and-friends affair. My friend Megann Yaqub made sure Leela appreciated both sides of her heritage. My sister Amy Hamad and my friend Margaret Besheer helped keep the Arab characters authentic. My sister-in-law Mais Hasan's expert advice ensured the Arabic words and expressions were on point. My friend Faith Lapidus Weiner made sure I tied up any loose ends.

There are few experiences I relish as much as being part of a generous community of writers. Joanna Shupe and Michele Mannon are my die-hard writerly support system. Thank you for everything, ladies, especially those conference slumber party read-a-longs and pandemic happy hours. I'm so grateful to Sarah MacLean for her early support of my writing and this series, to Sophie Jordan for her generosity and willingness to answer any questions, and to Lenora Bell for her encouragement and advice. And thank you, Evie Dunmore, for doing a thoughtful sensitivity read and gently suggesting some needed changes.

None of this book business would be worth anything without the readers, librarians, and bloggers who read our books and spread the word about them. Interacting with you on social media or via email is always a highlight of my day. Thank you for spending a few hours with me via my books. I hope you've found it worthwhile!